CW00693385

Shadow Sun
Expansion

Book Two of the Shadow Sun Series

Dave Willmarth

Copyright © 2019 by Dave Willmarth

All rights reserved. No part of this publication may be reproduced, distributed, or transmitted in any form or by any means, including photocopying, recording, or other electronic or mechanical methods, without the prior written permission of the publisher, except in the case of brief quotations embodied in critical reviews and certain other non-commercial uses permitted by copyright law.

All characters and events depicted in this novel are entirely fictitious. Any similarity to actual events or persons, living or dead, is purely coincidental.

Chapter 1

Bears Do It In The Woods

Allistor and Helen both sipped coffee from thermoses in the early morning silence. They'd pulled the ranger truck over to the side of the road and let Fuzzy out when he indicated that he needed to go. The bear cub was now more than twice the size he'd been when Allistor first found him trapped at the waterfall. Though he was only several days older and just as cute as ever, the cub had leveled up several times and his body had grown larger. Watching him waddle into the brush alongside the road, Helen chuckled.

"He's like one of those big prize bears you see at the carnival. Just as cute as the little ones, but on steroids."

Allistor smiled as his companion disappeared amid much rustling and shaking of bushes. "He's not exactly stealthy, is he? And at this rate I'm going to have to dedicate a part of each day hunting just for him. He eats like a full-grown bear."

Turning in her seat so that she was facing forward, she looked down the road ahead of them, then consulted the map in her lap. As usual they were taking back roads, exploring the territory and looking for interesting potential Outposts or sources of useful loot. They'd left the Citadel before sunrise, two days later than Allistor had planned. There had been business he needed to take care of at his various properties, like driving up to the Gun Shop to retrieve a second Barrett .50 and other weapons. But now they'd hit the road again and were headed in the general direction of Laramie, about fifty miles west of Cheyenne. Allistor meant to establish a Stronghold there before moving on to Denver. It wasn't safe to travel the roads over long distances anymore, but with the ability to set up a teleportation network that he'd won for constructing the first Citadel on Earth, they could establish a wide network of Strongholds and Citadels and travel instantly between them.

"At our current pace, assuming Fuzzy cooperates, we should be in Laramie by noon." Helen observed. Before the world ended, the trip would have taken about an hour, cruising along on the interstate. But those days were over. Abandoned and destroyed vehicles littered the roads, and creatures both native and alien had claimed their own territories. Earth's predators had begun to grow and mutate under the laws of Earth's new 'game' system as they killed and consumed their prey. Just as Fuzzy had done, the wolves, bears, snakes, birds, and even fish had grown larger, stronger, faster, and hungrier. So travelers needed to keep a constant lookout for threats anytime they were outside a safe zone.

"Good." Allistor followed Helen's gaze down the empty road. He saw nothing but tall trees and brush on either side. "That'll give us some time to poke around a bit before we have to find shelter for the night."

A sudden thrashing in the underbrush nearby had both of them gripping their weapons. Helen held a Winchester .30-06 hunting rifle with a scope, while Allistor produced his shotgun, loaded with slugs for stopping power. Not wanting to shoot past her head, Allistor climbed into the back seat of the ranger's SUV and rolled down the window even as Helen pointed her rifle toward the disturbance.

Speaking just loud enough for Allistor to hear, Helen said, "That's right near where Fuzzy went, so hold your fire until we're sure it's not him." Allistor nodded, then let out the breath he didn't know he'd been holding a moment later when Fuzzy emerged from the brush with a rabbit in his jaws.

Helen snorted. "Maybe you won't have to hunt as much as you think. He seems to be pretty good at feeding himself."

Allistor opened the back door and got out, holding it open like a valet for his furry companion. But before he let Fuzzy hop in, he held out a hand. "Give me the rabbit, Fuzzy. I'll put it in storage for you. You can't be making a mess of it in the back seat. We'll roast it for you later."

Fuzzy glared at him for a moment, obviously not thrilled about giving up his kill. He was, after all, a wild bear until very recently. But becoming Allistor's bonded pet had civilized him quite a bit. Still, rather than politely hand the prize to Allistor, he dropped it at his human's feet. Then with a derisive snort, he climbed up into the truck, spun around twice, and plopped down on the seat.

"Oh, so it's like that? Maybe I should have named you Grumpy instead of Fuzzy." Allistor bent down and retrieved the bunny corpse, storing it in his inventory ring. The extradimensional space inside the ring was a timeless void, where the meat would remain exactly as it was until removed.

Closing the door, he walked around the back of the truck and got back into the driver's seat. Putting the truck in gear, they continued on down the road. Helen held the atlas book a little closer to her face and squinted a bit. "Says there's a small lake and a marshland up ahead just a bit. I don't know this area as well as I know my park, but it might be a good place to stop and get some fish. To feed his majesty back there." She jerked her head toward the back seat, and Fuzzy chuffed in agreement.

Allistor looked at his bear in the rear-view mirror. "Oh, hush. You just want to play in the water." To which Fuzzy replied with what Allistor had come to call his 'innocent' face. With a sigh, Allistor agreed. "Sure. We've got poles in the back. We'll catch some fish for all of us. Maybe you or I will be able to raise our *Cooking* skill tonight."

Allistor was all about developing and improving skills. Not just himself, but all his people as well. Since their homeworld had been taken by the aliens and the near genocide of the human race commenced, the surviving humans had basically become NPCs in some kind of universal game. Allistor was determined that if his people were going to be NPCs, then they would be *elite* NPCs. Not pushovers for the alien invaders when they arrived in less than a year's time.

Another of the rewards that came with the first Citadel was an extensive library filled with knowledge that could help his people grow stronger. He had Ramon leading a team of people investigating the library and its contents. Ramon was to train a few additional people in his *Scribe* skills, which allowed him to make copies of spell scrolls and, Allistor hoped, eventually entire books and manuals. Those copies could then be passed on to his people and the spells learned. He wanted, at a minimum, for every one of his citizens to be able to fight, heal, and craft something.

Thirty minutes down the road they came upon a gravel parking area that sloped down toward the lake Helen had spotted. Already the grass and shrubs were starting to encroach on the cleared area, reclaiming it for the forest. Allistor parked the truck and got out, walking to the back to retrieve the fishing gear as Helen let Fuzzy out. His nose held high in indignation, Fuzzy strolled down to the water's edge and began to sniff.

"Hey, buddy. Don't get into the water just yet, okay? The last lake I visited had a fish big enough to swallow you whole."

The bear cub, who had a foot raised and was about to step into the water, pulled back and sat down on the gravel, now staring suspiciously into the water.

Chuckling, Allistor carried a couple of poles, a bucket, and a tackle box down the slope to where Helen stood looking across the water. Handing her one of the poles, he set the rest down and opened the tackle box. After a quick glance toward Fuzzy, he whispered, "We can use bits of the rabbit for bait. Cast it way out there. If nothing big hits it, we'll know it's safe for him to go in."

Helen just winked, preparing her pole.

"Hang tight Fuzzy. We'll test the waters real quick." Allistor freed the already threaded hook from one of the guide rings on his pole, then reached into his inventory and produced the rabbit. Using Helen as a shield so Fuzzy couldn't see, he used his belt knife to cut a few furry meaty bits from the rabbit's leg before stowing it back in his inventory. He ignored the curious sniffs from his bear as he handed a chunk to Helen before baiting his own hook. Quickly casting the bait far out into the water, he risked a glance at the bear, who was sniffing at the breeze and giving him and Helen both a suspicious look.

Helen managed to keep a straight face as she pretended to ignore the bear cub, casting her own line out a good fifty yards to splash down in the mostly serene water. She immediately began to reel it back in very slowly, a few inches at a time in jerky motions, hoping to attract the attention of any aquatic predators. As Allistor did the same, Fuzzy got up and paced back and forth along the water's edge. He sniffed at the ripples caused by their lines as they reached the gravel shore, but remained out of the water.

They each had to cast three more times before Allistor got a bite. Whatever it was, it hit his bait like a pit bull grabbing a hot dog and immediately tried to swim away with it. Allistor's reel screamed as the fishing line unwound at a rapid pace. He increased the drag a bit, hoping to slow the thing down before he set the hook, worried about snapping the filament line. Eventually it slowed enough that he felt confident that the line would hold, and he jerked back on the pole as he leaned backward to put his body weight into it.

A violent thrashing began, far out into the water, where his fish reacted to the jerk of the hook. Allistor immediately began pulling on the rod to create slack then quickly reeling it in. Every few seconds he gained ground on the fish, pulling it toward him then taking up the slack.

The pole bent nearly double each time he yanked on it, and he began to fear it would break.

While he fought his catch, Helen got a hit on her line as well and began to reel it in. Fuzzy, excited now, hopped up and down with his front feet, grunting as if encouraging them to hurry up. Allistor gave another heave on his pole, and his catch shot out of the shallow water near his feet.

It was a lake trout, maybe six feet long. When Helen saw the size of it, she nearly dropped her pole. "Damn. That's... a big one." She gave her pole another tug, and it too bent nearly double. "If they're growing this fast, we're gonna need a bigger pole."

Allistor snorted. "If I had a dime for every time a woman said that to me..." He saw her roll her eyes before he returned his attention to the fish flopping around on the gravel. It was as long as he was tall, and fat. He thought it might be heavier than him. Just the one fish could provide meat for several people, or one bear cub, for days. He was just bending down to take hold of its tail to drag it farther from the water, when Fuzzy took over. Grabbing the tail in his jaws, he clamped down and began to walk backward, pulling the fish up the slope. It continued to thrash a bit, but was quickly suffocating. Allistor looked at the five-gallon bucket he'd brought along to store their catch in, and just laughed. "We're gonna need a bigger bucket, too."

Using a pair of pliers from the tackle box, he carefully and quickly pried the hook free of the lake trout's jaw and stepped away. Fuzzy was sniffing and licking the fish, but didn't seem inclined to take a bite. Allistor left

9

him to it. He stepped back to the water's edge, cut himself another bit of bunny bait, and got his line back in the water just as Helen landed her catch. It was another lake trout, this one maybe fifty pounds. She took a minute to catch her breath and admire the thing before calling Fuzzy to help her. He quickly obliged, dragging the second fish back to sit next to the first after she freed her hook.

"Um, I think maybe one or two more each, and we'll have plenty of fish for a week." she observed, as Allistor paused to grab her a new chunk of bait.

"When I catch the next one, I'll see if they stack in my inventory. If they do, we might as well grab a bunch of them and take some back to our friends. Maybe... a dozen?"

Helen nodded. "That'd be enough to feed everyone we've got now, at all three locations."

They continued fishing for a solid hour, chatting occasionally but mostly silently as they cast and reeled. Fuzzy got his feet wet, sniffing at the water, but didn't go in. Allistor thought maybe the sheer size of the fish they were landing intimidated him. He helped them drag each catch back from the water's edge until they had a full dozen of the big fish. Allistor tried a couple of them and found that they did indeed stack in a single inventory slot in his ring, which was awesome.

As they packed up the gear and headed back to the truck, Helen said, "Best estimate, we have about seven hundred pounds of fish there. Meaning about four hundred pounds of usable meat, and three hundred in heads, tails, and other parts Fuzzy will probably eat."

As if in agreement, the bear licked his lips and bobbed his head several times. Helen laughed. "Glutton! It's not even lunchtime!"

Allistor produced the rabbit from his ring and tossed it to the bear. "We need to wait a few while you dry out, so you might as well eat." He then deposited the rest of the fish into his ring.

Fuzzy sniffed at the rabbit, then nosed it over so that the carved-up leg Allistor had stolen bait chunks from was visible to the humans. He gave an annoyed snort and shake of his head, obviously accusing his master of stealing. Allistor laughed. "Sorry buddy, but those chunks were the bait that helped us catch all those tasty fish."

Somewhat mollified, Fuzzy plopped down on his belly and began to pull apart the bunny. Allistor opened the back end of the truck and was stowing away the gear when Helen screamed, followed immediately by a roar from Fuzzy. Allistor hit his head on the door frame as he straightened up to see what happened. Pain lanced through his brain as his vision went spotty for a moment. Rubbing the sore spot, he stepped back from the truck and stood upright Looking toward Helen even as he was reaching for his shotgun, what he saw initially had him thinking his vision was still off.

Hovering just above Helen was a dragonfly the size of a golf cart. Its four wings buzzed angrily as it swooped down and tried to take hold of her with its six clawed legs. Helen ducked and swerved, running toward the truck and screaming again. Allistor didn't blame her one bit. The thing was nightmare fuel. Its dead black eyes focused on its prey, revealing no anger, offering no mercy, or showing feeling of any kind.

> ***Dragonwing Hunter***
> ***Level 12***
> ***Health: 9,000/9,000***

Allistor pumped a slug into the chamber and took aim. At the same time, he shouted, "Helen! Get down!" The moment she dropped to the ground, he fired at the massive flying insect. The slug tore through one of its wings near where it joined with the bug's torso, causing it to falter midair. He pumped another round and fired again, this time hitting its midsection. The exoskeleton cracked, but the slug didn't penetrate.

Now distracted by Allistor's attacks and abandoning its pursuit of Helen, the dragonfly recovered some semblance of control and shot forward into Allistor's face. He couldn't help but scream as the multi-eyed, chitin-covered face pressed in close, mandibles snapping hungrily at him. He managed to avoid having his face eaten by dropping to the ground, but was too slow to escape the grasping legs. Its barbed appendages latched on to his left arm and shoulder, and the wings beat furiously.

Allistor yelled, "Help!" as the thing began to drag him away from the truck. With its damaged wing, it wasn't strong enough to lift him into the air. Still, being dragged away by a giant insect was more than enough to send his lizard brain into a panic. He screamed like a ten-year-old girl and began to beat at the legs holding him. Remembering his shotgun, he aimed it upward and pulled the trigger without even thinking.

The slug blasted into the creature's abdomen, punching through the exoskeleton and into the nasty-smelling guts inside. Allistor gagged as the fluid gushed out onto his face, covering him from head to toe. The wingbeats gradually slowed, then stopped, and the insect's corpse dropped directly on top of him. He felt suffocated, trying not to inhale the nasty ichor that still leaked from the corpse, while pushing to lift it off of him. A moment later he felt some fresh air on his face as Helen helped to drag the thing off him. Rolling onto his stomach, he propped himself up on his hands and knees and puked out his breakfast onto the gravel.

When he was done vomiting and spitting, Helen handed him a canteen. He swished some of the water around before spitting it out. Getting to his feet, he saw the disgusted look on her face. "You've got bug juice all over you. I recommend a dip in the lake. You're certainly not getting in the truck like that."

Anxious to get the smell off of himself, Allistor didn't hesitate. He walked to the water's edge, got down on his knees, then plunged his head into the water. Scrubbing at his face and hair, then his neck, chest, and arms, he managed to get all the nasty goo off. When he straightened back up, he was soaked from the waist up. Fuzzy was sitting there, a grin on his cubby face. He took a few tentative sniffs of Allistor and shook his head. Reaching into the water with one paw, he splashed some water on his human.

"Ha! I think he's saying you missed a spot or two." Helen laughed.

Allistor sniffed at himself, but his nose was already so polluted by the stench he couldn't tell if he still stunk or not. So he stripped down to his boxers and just walked into the water. When he was waist deep, he sank down and began to scrub himself in earnest using sand from the lakebed. Helen took hold of his abandoned clothes and started using the gravel and sand in the shallow water to scrub them clean. Fuzzy thought it was some kind of game, and kept pouncing on the laundry as she laid it out flat to dry in the sun.

Allistor called to her from the water. "It's actually quite refreshing in here. You should join me! And yes, you can swim too, Fuzzy."

The bear cub didn't hesitate, charging into the shallow water then leaping toward Allistor as Helen quickly finished scrubbing and laying out his clothes. Then she stripped to her bra and underwear and hopped in to join the fun. The water was cold, but not terribly so. The sun-warmed shallows were invigorating. They swam around and dunked each other, Fuzzy being very careful not to scratch anyone with his claws.

After fifteen minutes or so, the two humans walked back up onto the beach. Both of them looted the dragonwing's corpse, getting some pieces of chitin, two hundred klax each, and a translucent wing each. The wings were highlighted in their inventory, likely making them some kind of rare crafting material. Allistor looked around and found a log to sit on while they dried off. There was evidence of a fire pit right in front of the log, but neither of them was cold enough to feel the need for it. They sat in companionable silence, basking in the sun and watching

Fuzzy chase small fish in the shallows, or just roll around in the water, using the gravel to scratch his back.

When the sun and breeze had dried them enough, Allistor and Helen got dressed. She put her same clothes back on, he pulled dry ones from his inventory. They called Fuzzy out of the water so he could dry off too, and the bear complied, hesitantly. He was still a cub after all, and bear cubs love to play. To mollify him a bit, Allistor engaged him in a game of tag. The two of them chased each other around the cleared area, occasionally tackling and wrestling each other. When the bear was reasonably dry, Allistor gathered up his still damp clothes and they all piled back into the truck.

Even with the fishing side quest distraction, they reached the outskirts of Laramie just after noon. The city was in much the same condition as Cheyenne, with only a few areas heavily damaged. One large area, about two square city blocks, had burned to the ground, and there was evidence of a few other isolated fires. Most of the homes and retail buildings had smashed windows, and there were old, dried blood splatters in many places.

"Somebody put these fires out. Kept them from spreading." Allistor observed as the truck crawled down a main street. It was relatively clear of vehicles, which was another sign of survivors.

Five minutes later as they approached the heart of the city's downtown district, a man stepped out and pointed a rifle at them. "Hold!" he shouted.

Allistor slowed to a stop and put the truck in park, turning the engine off. He opened his door and stuck both hands out, like he'd seen so many bad guys do on TV.

"We mean no harm!" he shouted. Helen copied his movements on her side, and the two of them exited the truck. "My name is Allistor! I lead a group of survivors not so far from here. I was hoping to find more here in Laramie, and here you are!" He gave the man his friendliest smile.

The man's rifle barrel lowered slightly as he straightened up. "Allistor? We got a system message about you. Something about a Citadel?"

"Yep! That's me. I built a Citadel in Cheyenne. You know about Strongholds and safe zones?"

The man nodded his head. "I read about 'em. We tried to build one, but the message thing said we didn't have enough resources."

Allistor grimaced. He'd managed to build the Warren with less than a dozen people and just the food they'd gathered from the convenience store, plus whatever resources were in the city hall cellars. If these people didn't have enough resources to create a Stronghold, then they weren't doing well. Rather than sharing that thought aloud, he called out.

"Hey, we've got a bunch of food with us. Just caught some fresh fish. We could share, if you're hungry. How many of you are there?"

The man lowered his rifle. "There are eighty of us here. Other groups spread out around the city, too. But it's hard to get supplies. The biggest group in town is run by an asshole named Barden. He and his boys steal from us and the other groups if they catch us foraging, and only let us keep just enough to stay alive. Took some of the women, too. They're better armed than we are, and mean as hell."

Helen shook her head. "Seems like we find a few assholes everywhere we go. Always somebody choosing to prey on others instead of working to keep each other alive." She dropped her hands and added, "My name's Helen."

The man blushed slightly. "Sorry. Bad manners. Have to be suspicious of strangers these days. My name's Daniel. Welcome to Laramie, such as it is." He stepped forward, offering a hand to Allistor and Helen. As he did so, five other men and two women emerged from various points of cover all around them.

Helen elbowed Allistor. "Smooth move. Drove us right into an ambush."

He shook his head, feeling embarrassed. "I didn't hear any warnings from you, miss lookout."

Daniel chuckled. "Don't sweat it. We've had a lot of practice defending ourselves lately. A few of us have military training. When we heard your engine approaching, we figured it was Barden's guys. Thought maybe we'd take a few of them out."

Allistor nodded, shaking the man's hand. "Sounds like a good idea to me. We had to do the same for another group of survivors not so long ago. Some assholes up there attacked and trapped them in their Stronghold, nearly starving them out. Then, after we helped them get free, and moved them to my Stronghold, the same group attacked us there as well. We've killed maybe twenty of them now. And a trio of tweakers that tried to kill us in Cheyenne."

One of the men who'd walked up from behind said, "Damn, son. Sounds like you've been busy."

Allistor turned, nodding his head. "We've also killed a sixty-foot void titan that stomped my home town flat, three dragons, a massive level 22 turtle monster thing, and a bunch of other critters. Cleared a couple dungeons, too."

"Dungeons? No shit! What were the bosses like?" Daniel asked, suddenly grinning and rubbing his beard.

"Ah, a brother gamer!" Allistor held out a fist for Daniel to bump. Two of the other men, and one of the ladies, held out fists as well. Allistor looked surprised. "All of you?" As they all nodded, he grinned. "I guess that makes sense. With the new system, us gamers were bound to recognize it early and do better than some of the other folks."

One of the ladies said, "I'm Virginia. That's my husband, Bob." She nodded toward the man next to her. Neither of them had been among the gamers, but her next question let Allistor know they'd made an effort to learn the new system, at least. "So, you're the guy who built the Citadel? Is it true that the monsters won't spawn there?"

Helen answered first. "It's true. Allistor has built a Stronghold in his hometown, another in Cheyenne, along with the Citadel, which is the old shopping mall. And a couple small Outposts scattered around. That's how I met him. Each one is a safe place, where the monsters don't spawn. They can still attack from outside, which is how we ended up fighting that last dragon."

"That would be *epic*!!" One of the younger gamers pumped a fist in the air. "Real life dragon battle! How'd you kill it?"

Virginia rolled her eyes. "Forgive my grandson. Austin gets excited about fighting. Still thinks it's a game. Even after seeing some of his friends and family die." Austin lowered his eyes for a moment and mumbled an apology, but when he lifted his gaze again, Allistor could still see the familiar gamer lust in him.

"Nothing to forgive. If I hadn't been focused on trying to save my own ass at the time, I might have thought it was epic, too." He winked at the young man.

Another man cleared his throat. One of the gamers. "My name's Richard. And I hate to break up the party, but it's not safe out here in the open. We should head back."

Allistor nodded along with the others. He turned to get back in his truck, when he remembered Fuzzy. "Uhh... guys? I've got somebody else to introduce you to first. I sorta accidentally bonded with a grizzly bear cub..."

"No way!" Austin practically shouted. "You got a pet already? Are you some kind of hunter class?"

Allistor grinned at the kid's excitement as Austin and the others watched him open a back door of the truck and let Fuzzy out. The bear jumped down, and stood next to him, facing the crowd, sniffing. Allistor scratched his head, "It's okay buddy. They are friendly. Fuzzy, say hello to Daniel and the gang."

Fuzzy chuffed in a friendly manner at the group, and Austin dashed forward. Startled, Fuzzy growled and took a step back, causing the kid to pause. "I'm… sorry. I didn't mean to. Can I…" His voice drifted off.

"Sure, he likes to have his ears scratched. Just move slowly."

Austin slowly approached the rest of the way, one hand held forward as if he were allowing a strange dog to get his scent. Fuzzy obliged, sniffing carefully for a moment before licking the hand. Austin crouched down and began to scratch both the cub's ears at once, which Fuzzy didn't mind at all.

Richard said, "We'll lead you back. It's only a few blocks. We've sort of walled off a section using cars and trucks."

Austin got back to his feet as Fuzzy hopped back into the truck. Allistor looked to Helen. "If you wouldn't mind driving? I'll walk with these guys." She nodded and got in the driver's seat, and they all set off at a brisk pace toward the center of town.

Chapter 2

Doggone Good Seats

The walk back only took a few minutes, and Allistor noted with approval that each of the party walking around him kept their heads on a swivel, constantly looking out for danger. He decided to break the ice.

"So, besides the asshole humans, how bad has it been here? A lot of monsters spawning?"

Daniel shook his head. "I'm not sure what you'd consider a lot. The first few days were rough, because most folks didn't know what to expect. Those canid things, and the octopoids, they spawned inside houses and businesses without warning. So a lot of folks died in those first couple days."

Allistor sympathized. It was much the same in his home town. People making the mistake of going outside after dark, or leaving windows and doors open. A lot of his neighbors were already dead by the time the void titan showed up.

"How many survivors do you think there are here in Laramie?" he asked as they circled around a burned-out truck.

Daniel thought about it for a while, then said, "Best guess, a thousand? There are groups scattered all over. I met a group the other day that had actually fled Cheyenne, and only made it this far. Barden and his people attacked them, killed several, and took their vehicles." He paused, looking ashamed. "I would have taken them in, but we don't have enough food as it is..."

Allistor stopped walking, causing the rest of them to pause as well. The brakes squeaked slightly as Helen brought the truck to a halt.

"Listen. I can provide you with food, and shelter. And this other group as well. I'll go into the details later. Do you know where they are now?"

Richard nodded, saying, "I just saw a couple of them foraging yesterday, over that way." He pointed roughly southwest.

Daniel nodded. "Smart. They put us between Barden and themselves."

Allistor said, "Let's get you guys and your people a good meal, then you can show me where they are. I'll talk to you about Strongholds. I came here to Laramie with the intent to set one up."

They resumed the trek to their base, which was literally a city block with a four-story apartment building that was surrounded by a makeshift wall of cars, trucks, and buses lined up bumper to bumper. Daniel raised his rifle in the air, and three guards on the roof returned his salute. One of the cars rolled aside, and the group passed through the barrier. Helen parked the truck, and she and Fuzzy joined the others inside. The first floor of the building sported a wide open lobby with a reception desk and an elevator bank in the back. Allistor immediately noticed there were lights on inside. Virginia caught him noticing, and said, "Yeah, we picked this building because it had solar panels on the roof. Before the water stopped running, we actually had hot showers."

Daniel led them out a side door from the lobby into a courtyard that was completely enclosed by wings of the building on three sides, and a brick wall with a gate on the fourth. There were several grills set up, along with long tables and benches. "We stole these from the school down the street. The gym was a shelter for a little while in the first few days, until a pack of those canids spawned in there. It… wasn't pretty." Bob explained.

Helen coughed to get Allistor's attention, holding up three fingers and looking significantly toward the grill.

"Oh! Uh, here." Allistor walked over to the nearest table and produced three of the giant lake trout, setting them on the table. "Anybody got a good trout recipe?"

There were gasps of surprise from the gathering crowd, and runners were sent to bring someone that Daniel said would be able to cook the fish. Heads popped out of the windows above, looking to see what the excitement was about. Soon more than half of the residents were crowding into the courtyard.

Helen added to the excitement, pulling some supplies from her own inventory. She brought out some potatoes and carrots from Nancy's garden at the Warren. When she saw some wide-eyed and hungry looking kids staring at her, she also produced a big bag of chocolate kisses, handing out one to everyone. Allistor grinned at her, saying, "You raided the goodies at the mall, huh?"

Shrugging, she just gave him a small smile. "Hey, I didn't know how long we'd be gone, and a girl needs her chocolate."

The fish were quickly removed to a prep area to be cleaned, with Fuzzy following behind, his nose in the air. Allistor warned the folks that Fuzzy would want the guts and unused parts, and nobody objected. Taking a seat on one of the benches, he waited for the group that had greeted him to sit down as well.

"Before we get started, is there anyone else here that needs to hear this?" Allistor looked around. Daniel shook his head. "Fine, then I'll give you the background, and you can decide whether I should make the offer to all your people."

Allistor told them his whole story, from day one of the new era they found themselves in. He gave them the short version, as the detailed story up to that point could fill a whole book. When he was through, he added, "I plan to create a Stronghold here. I'd prefer to do it with a group of good people like yourselves, but I'll do it regardless. You've heard some of the benefits of becoming my citizens, and there are more I haven't shared because I don't know you that well yet." He paused and looked around at each of the faces. A few still seemed skeptical. "I can help get rid of Barden. In fact, I'll kill him myself if one of you will show me where he is and point him out. It's in my own best interests, since I plan to have a Stronghold here, one way or the other. And ideally, I'd like to bring all the groups together, all thousand of you, and build a Stronghold big enough for all of us. Or move some folks back to the Citadel at Cheyenne, or the Warren. Plenty of room there."

Bob spoke up first. "But we'd have to swear an oath to you? Accept you as some kind of king?"

Allistor nodded. "An oath of loyalty. Basically, it keeps you from betraying or harming our people. I'm not some tyrant ordering people to kiss my feet or send me their daughters. What I want is for all of us, humans in general, to get as strong as humanly possible before our year is up. So that we can take and hold as much of the Earth as possible, then take the fight to the asshat aliens that brought us here."

"Right on!" Austin pumped his fist in the air, but when he saw that he was the only one, he lowered it again, looking sheepish.

Daniel had been looking thoughtful through the whole conversation. After throwing Austin a look, he asked, "What's stopping us from creating a Stronghold of our own. Why do we need you?"

Allistor shrugged. "You tell me. Why don't you have a Stronghold by now?" He looked around, finding a few angry faces staring back. "I'm not trying to be a dick, it's a serious question. If I had been in your shoes, I'd have found a way to consolidate the other groups and eliminate Barden by now. I'd be damn tired of going to sleep wondering if an octopoid was going to spawn in my bed every night." That got some heads nodding.

"What I can offer in the short term is food, resources, and a safe place. And the willingness to take on Barden. Between us, I think Helen and I have enough resources in our inventories to qualify for a Stronghold right now. If you agree to join us and swear the oath, we can pick a good spot and create a Stronghold before dark.

You and your people can sleep in safety. Then in the morning, if one of you is willing to guide me, I'll assassinate Barden. Sometimes cutting off the head of the snake is good enough. If that doesn't work, we'll kill some more of his people. But you told me they took innocent prisoners, so I'd like to make things as surgical as possible."

Bob looked around the group, getting nods or shakes from each of them. "Looks like we need to discuss this a while. Can you wait until morning?"

Allistor thought about it. He didn't like the idea of sleeping in an unsecured location. There were no respawns in this world, and one stupid mistake could end everything.

He shook his head. "I'm going to create a Stronghold this evening, if for no other reason than to have a safe place to sleep. You guys can take until morning to decide if you like. I'll leave the invitation open." He looked around at the group. "Some of you gamers have probably put some thought into this already. Where would you put a Stronghold around here?"

"The stadium." three of them stated together as others offered up places like "the hospital" and "city hall."

Richard was one of the three that had voted for the stadium. He clarified, "War Memorial Stadium. It's not far from here, close to the interstate and the railroad tracks. If you can put walls around it, it's tall enough to see the whole surrounding area. Room inside to grow crops. Lots of covered space under the stands for housing, et cetera. Even more if you include a couple of the adjacent buildings."

Allistor nodded. "Good enough for me. And yes, we can build walls around the whole thing." He thought about it for a moment. He was pretty sure, despite his claims a few minutes earlier, that he needed more people to create a Stronghold. So he tried something.

"I'll tell you what. You and your people come with me to the stadium after lunch. I'll create the Stronghold, and you can all stay one night as my guests without taking the oath. Get a good night's sleep, and have time to think without having to watch your backs. In the morning, you can choose to join me, or come back here and try to continue as you have been." After a brief pause, he added. "I'm going to kill Barden either way."

"What about the other groups? There are some good people out there." Bob asked.

"One step at a time." Allistor answered. "Again, not to sound like a dick, but I'm confident that Helen, Fuzzy, and I could hold our own against your people if it came to that. So I'm comfortable having you in my home, so to speak, for a night without you swearing loyalty. But I'm not foolish enough to invite several hundred people I don't know inside the gates without having an oath in place. I'd be asking to have my throat slit. And I have people depending on me. If, in the morning, you all decided to join me and swear the oath, then we'll bring in the other groups one or two at a time, and expand as needed."

Bob nodded his head. "Good answer."

"I'll swear the oath right now." Austin said in a surprisingly calm and sincere voice. Several others nodded their heads.

Allistor smiled at him. "Thank you, Austin, I appreciate the support. But I'm guessing your family has something to say about that.

Virginia shook her head. "No... I think he's right." She looked at Bob, who nodded. "An hour ago, I thought you were just some kid on a power trip. But you obviously know what you're doing, and you care about your people. You're feeding eighty strangers their best meal in weeks on the off chance that we wouldn't kill you outright. My family will swear your oath and join you at the stadium." Austin beamed at her as she spoke.

"Thank you, Virginia. I accept." Allistor reached out a hand and patted hers. He gave Bob a smile and Austin another wink.

A few others opened their mouths, but Daniel held up a hand to interrupt. "Before any more of us go making promises, let's talk to our people. We'll eat lunch, and put it to a vote after."

The smell of grilled fish was already filling the air, and nobody objected to a lunch break. Allistor regretted not taking the opportunity to help with the cooking and potentially raise his skill, but he'd needed to have the talk with these folks.

As it turned out, Virginia's family was larger than just the three Allistor had met. Austin's parents appeared when the bell was rung to call everyone together for the meal. He introduced them, and explained that they'd been on guard duty all night, and had been asleep since. Allistor wasn't sure, but he thought he could create a Stronghold with just that family, himself, and Helen.

28

They all sat for the meal, during which, several of the survivors approached Allistor and Helen to thank them for the food. Fuzzy snored contentedly over by the grills, having eaten a gluttonous amount of fish parts. He lay on his back, paws in the air, one of them occasionally twitching as he dreamed his bear cub dreams.

When the meal was done, Daniel gave the entire group a quick rundown of Allistor's offer. He opened up the floor for questions, and Allistor and Helen answered them honestly. When it was done, Daniel surprised Allistor by adding, "I believe we should join Allistor and his people. Today. Now. I've never been so tired in my life as I am right now. A safe place to lay down my head tonight sounds pretty damn good to me. But I won't ask any of you to join me. You all need to decide for yourselves."

He sat down, and Virginia stood up. "My family and I are joining Allistor and Daniel." As she looked around, every single one of the gamers stood, almost in unison. They gave each other and Allistor a round of fist-bumps with grins on their faces. The others began to stand in ones and twos, then small groups. Eventually, all but about twenty were on their feet.

Daniel looked at those still sitting. He picked out one of them, a middle-aged man with graying hair and a white beard. "Ray, you have a concern? Speak up, and maybe Allistor can address it."

Ray nodded, standing as the others all took their seats. "Seems to me this kid is in over his head. How old are you, boy? Are you even old enough to drink?"

Allistor stood to answer. "You're absolutely right, Ray. I am in over my head. So are you, and Daniel, and every single human here. There are freakin' *dragons* flying around eating people, and alien monsters hiding under our beds. I didn't ask to become a leader, it just sort of happened because I knew a little bit more than my neighbors about how to stay alive in our new world. And I certainly didn't ask to become a lord. You can blame Helen for that." He turned and winked at his companion, who blushed. "But the fact is, I have become a leader for my people, because somebody had to. And while yes, I am young – only twenty – I have more experience with fighting and living in this world than anyone I've encountered so far. I've made mostly good decisions so far. But most importantly, there isn't anyone more motivated than me, or willing to do more than me, to make sure you, your family, and the rest of us all thrive. I want us to become a nation of badass humans ready to take on whatever the universe throws at us. And I have risked my own neck nearly every day to make that happen."

Ray looked at him for a good long while. His face was difficult to read, though he was clearly weighing Allistor's words. Allistor decided to add a little more to his argument.

"Ray, I'll tell you this right now. If you want to take my place, to be the leader of hundreds, maybe thousands of survivors, I'm all for it. Prove to me that you have the skills needed, and that I can trust you, and I'll promote you to big boss right then and there, and go spend a few days fishin' with Helen and Fuzzy."

This earned a few laughs from the folks gathered around. Even Ray cracked a small grin. Sitting back down, he said, "Fair enough. I'll follow you."

Since everyone had retaken their seats, Daniel called out. "Is there anyone else who has questions? Or that doesn't want to join us at the stadium? Now's the time to speak up."

A woman near the back of the crowd stood up. "How do we know that you won't order us to go on some suicide mission or do something else against our own best interests? If we refuse such an order, will the oath kill us?"

Allistor took a deep breath. These people weren't going to like his answer, but he needed to be straight with them.

"I can't promise that I won't get any of you killed. There are going to be times where fighting is necessary. In your case, we may need to fight against Barden's group. People may die. I am not a one-man army, or all-powerful. If we're going to thrive, we're going to have to do it together. We'll all have to make sacrifices, and some of us likely will give our lives. Including me. I can't and won't promise you otherwise." He took a breath as his voice started to crack.

"But what I can promise is that I won't intentionally throw lives away. The most valuable thing on Earth right now is a human life. I want to preserve as many as I can. As for the oath... to be honest, I'm not positive. The notice I got when Helen first took the oath was that the penalties were variable depending on the seriousness of the oath and the consequences from breaking it. Like, if your breaking

31

the oath results in someone getting hurt, the penalty could include death."

Daniel nodded. "Yeah, the system so far seems very 'eye for an eye'. I killed one of Barden's guys a week or so ago, and when I did, I got rewarded all kinds of Fame Points and stuff. He looked to Allistor, who was fervently hoping that Daniel didn't mention that one got xp and loot from killing other humans. The fewer folks who learned this, the better. Daniel seemed to share this point of view and didn't mention either.

Helen spoke up next. "As Allistor mentioned, I was the first to take the oath with him. It was one I made up myself, and was a simple pledge of loyalty. It doesn't keep me from telling him he's being an ass when he's wrong, or even from disagreeing with him." She gave him a light smack on the back of the head, smiling at him as she did so. "The oath isn't meant to control any of you in any way other than to keep you from betraying or harming him, and each other." As she looked around at the mostly blank faces, she added. "And I'll add that I only swore my loyalty to Lord Allistor here *after* he swore an oath to protect his lands and the people on them with his own life. An oath that the system registered, and will hold him to. Plus, he saved my life. Oath or no, I'd lay down my life for him."

"What do you mean 'the system registered'?" Austin asked.

Helen shrugged. "When he swore to me, there was a blue flashy light that surrounded him, then sort of seeped into him. I can show you, if you're still willing to swear?"

Austin nodded his head, and Helen had him repeat the simple words. When he did, the same blue glow surrounded him, fading into his body.

"That's it." She looked around the room. "That's all there is to it. No legalese or clauses offering up your firstborn." She winked at Austin, who was examining the bare skin on his arms, looking for any physical change. After a moment, his eyes unfocused, and he said, "Hey, there's a little icon on my interface now that says I'm oathbound. Cool!"

Daniel raised his hand and addressed the woman who'd asked the question. "Does that answer satisfy you?" When she nodded and sat down, he asked again, "Anyone else have questions?"

No one spoke up. In a corner near the grills, Fuzzy broke the silence with a loud fart.

Shaking his head and grinning, Daniel asked, "Alright then, if you are not willing to swear loyalty to Allistor and, by extension, the rest of us… please stand." Daniel waited for half a minute for people to think it over, and when everyone was still seated, he said, "Great, seems like we're all in agreement. Let's get this oath thing over with, and get packed."

Helen stood in front of the group. "Is this everyone? Anyone still asleep or out somewhere?"

Virginia did a head count. "There are two children not here."

The same woman that had asked about the oath spoke up. "My kids have colds. They're sleeping." Helen nodded, and administered the oath. Each person repeated the words back to her, and the blue glow penetrated all of them.

"Thank you, all of you. And welcome! Our first order of business is to get all of you safe for the night. As Daniel mentioned, load up all you can carry in, or on, your vehicles. Helen and I, and Fuzzy if I can wake him up..." He paused while a few people chuckled. "Will go ahead to the stadium and scout it out. As soon as you arrive, we'll establish the Stronghold and figure out the details of housing and feeding everyone."

As the gathered survivors dispersed, Allistor asked Richard, who was standing nearby. "Anything I should know about the stadium? Any groups to get through between here and there? Anybody currently calling it home?"

Richard shook his head, rubbing his chin at the same time. "It's not like we have formal territory boundaries established, so you might run into some foragers out there. If they're not Barden's folks, or they don't confuse *you* with Barden's folks, they should be friendly enough. As for the stadium, I haven't been there in a couple weeks. Don't think anyone else has, either. We pretty well cleaned it out of food and stuff in the first week. We saw evidence of those canid things running around in there." Richard pulled up his interface and shared his map with Allistor and Helen.

"Great. Thanks for that. We'll head over there and scout the place. Secure it if we can. If we find something we can't handle, we'll pull back and wait for you guys. How many fighters do you have?"

Richard grinned. "You met us all out on the street, pretty much. Austin can shoot, but his family keeps him here. He's a little… enthusiastic when it comes to fighting. Some of the others can defend themselves well enough, but I wouldn't call them trained fighters."

"Good enough. We'll see you at the stadium." Allistor shook the man's hand, then Daniel's as well. Waving to the others, he went to retrieve a softly snoring Fuzzy.

Back in the truck, they made their way down one city block, then another, weaving through abandoned cars in areas that hadn't been cleared. It was only about a mile from the group's base camp to the stadium.

Helen spotted movement when they were within sight of the building. Pointing off to her right down a side street, she said, "Just saw two people walking. They saw us, and ducked around a corner."

Allistor considered stopping, but his priority was to reach the stadium and clear it. They could make more friends, or enemies, after. "Keep an eye out. And try to note the location on your map. We'll come back and look for them later, maybe."

Continuing on, they reached the stadium and found the wide chain-link gate standing open. Allistor was able to drive the truck right in under the concrete stands that stretched up and out above like a giant bowl. Rather than park the truck and walk the whole circumference, he drove through the wide walkways that had once been filled with people on game days. The truck easily fit between the massive concrete columns that held up the structure.

They passed empty concession stands that had clearly been ransacked, though it was hard to tell whether the culprits had been human or animal. They passed locker room entrances, maintenance shop doors, elevators, and open walkways leading in to the field. When they'd made a complete circuit without finding any people or monsters, Allistor stopped the truck. He got out and went to the gate, closing and latching it. He didn't engage the simple padlock that hung there, as he wanted his new friends to be able to get in. He just wanted to make sure that canids or other non-humanoid monsters wouldn't be walking right in at his back while he and Helen tried to secure the place.

Helen offered up a suggestion. "I know you want to wait until the others are here before you claim this place as a Stronghold. But you could start with an Outpost, then upgrade it. And claiming it as an Outpost will tell us whether anyone or anything else is here."

"You're a genius!" Allistor grinned at her. He'd been planning just that, but didn't figure it hurt to give her credit for the idea. He opened up his interface and clicked through to the appropriate tab. When he clicked *YES* next to the *Outpost* prompt, he received a familiar message.

> ***This structure is currently occupied by a life form that has a prior claim to your own. To claim the structure, you must kill the prior occupant, convince it to relinquish its claim or banish it from the vicinity for twelve hours.***

Allistor shared the news with Helen, who sighed deeply. "Well, damn. It's gonna take a while to clear this place. Hey, Fuzzy? Do you smell any people, or monsters?" She looked down at the bear cub sitting by their feet. He snorted once, then lowered his nose to the ground. They followed him as he wove his way around the area, sometimes sniffing the ground, other times raising his nose and seeming to scent the light breeze that drifted through the concrete passages.

They'd gone maybe a quarter of the way around the outside of the stadium when he huffed, then began to growl. Turning toward one of the walkways that sloped upward toward the field and into the stands, he looked from the tunnel to Allistor and back.

Allistor stepped forward and laid a hand on the bear's head, scratching his ears. "Good job, buddy. This makes up for that ass-blast you embarrassed me with earlier." Helen laughed behind him.

"Right. So somewhere in there is a person, or people, or monster, or whatever." He drew his shotgun from inventory, and Helen equipped her rifle. "I'll go first. Let's take this slow. If it's people in there, they might be friendly."

Taking the extra precaution of casting *Barrier* to place a magic shield in front of himself, he moved upward into the short stadium tunnel. When he neared the other end, he crouched low and hugged the wall on one side. A view of the stadium opened up before him, the wide open expanse of the field, the hundreds of rows of color coded and numbered seats. As he paused to scan the area, no movement caught his eye.

When Helen poked him with her rifle barrel, he turned and whispered, "This sucks. I don't see anything, but there are a dozen tunnels like this one on each side.

Could be something or someone hiding in any one of them."

Helen whispered back as she peered around him at the field. "What do you want to do? Go back for the others? Maybe split up into groups and clear this place?"

Allistor thought about it, but shook his head. "No, I don't want to put them in danger unless absolutely necessary." Leaning his back against the cool concrete wall, he took a minute to think.

"Only one way to get this done quickly. You and Fuzzy wait here. I'm gonna walk out there and make some noise. If something comes out and tries to eat my face, please shoot it."

Helen snorted. "Maybe. But you're gonna owe me some more chocolate for saving your scrawny ass if I do."

Allistor adopted a mock offended face. "Amanda says my butt is cute."

"She probably also told you you're the best she's ever had. We do that. It's good for your egos. You pout a lot less and get more stuff done that way." Her grin told him she was teasing, but he made a mental note to check with Amanda anyway.

"Right. Thanks for that confidence boost right before I go out to play bait." He smirked at her. One last quick scratch of Fuzzy's ears and a 'Wait here with Helen, bud.' and he straightened up to his full height before walking casually out of the tunnel exit and down the stairs toward the field. When he was several steps down, he began to whistle a little tune. The sound warbled a little from nerves as he descended the stairs. He felt very alone and exposed out in the open.

As he reached the bottom of the stairs he stood there, just above field level with a knee wall between him and the sidelines. Spinning slowly, he paused to look at each tunnel on both sides of the stadium. Most were dark in the early afternoon light with the sun nearly straight above. Changing his tactic, he hopped over the wall onto the field and coughed loudly. Once, then again. When that didn't elicit any reaction, he called out. "Rover! Here boy! C'mon Rover! Stupid dog, always running off..."

His voice trailed off as a rumbling growl echoed out from across the field. A moment later, a creature emerged from the shade. Walking on four thick, muscular legs, Allistor could only describe the thing as a cross between a bulldog and a rhinoceros. Except it was bigger than any rhino he'd ever seen. Its head stood easily six feet high, and Allistor could only see its front half, but from that he estimated its body was ten feet long or more. Instead of hooves, its front legs ended in paws with claws much like Fuzzy's, only several times larger.

Canis Lacerta
Level 12
Health: 9,000/9,000

As it stepped farther out into the sunlight, Allistor could see it was covered in midnight black fur. There was a long serpentine tail that ended in a wickedly sharp, barbed point that looked like it might be hardened bone. At the other end of the monster, dead black eyes were spaced widely on a massive bulldog-ish head. Its shoulders and neck were so thickly muscled that Allistor couldn't help picturing it charging headfirst into a bulldozer, and winning. In its abnormally elongated jaws, still dripping blood, was what looked like the hind leg of a canid.

"Uhh… nice doggy-lizard?" Allistor's voice cracked as he spoke. Now fully revealed, he guessed the thing was closer to twelve feet long, without the tail. It had to easily weigh a ton, maybe two. Its gaze centered in his general direction, though it didn't seem to focus on Allistor directly. Dropping the canid bits onto the turf, it took a few steps forward and raised its head, sniffing the air.

Allistor held very still, hoping the monster was nearsighted, or like he'd heard T-Rex was, only focusing on movement. He suddenly wasn't sure he wanted to fight this monster. It wasn't the highest level mob he'd fought to date, but with the others he'd either had a group behind him or howitzers to shoot it with.

As it turned out, the monster didn't need him to move. Its gaze followed its nose and zeroed in on his location. Though he still didn't think it was focused on him personally. There wasn't that connection you get when you see someone or something looking directly at you.

Still, it took several steps in his direction. Its nose leading it closer as saliva began to drip in long, bloody strands from its jaws. Allistor knew he didn't have long before Helen fired on the approaching beast. He didn't want it going after her and Fuzzy, so he did the only thing he could. He cast *Mind Spike* on it, causing it to wail and shake its head. The spell did some damage, but he didn't pause to see how much. Instead, focusing on the ground directly in front of the ponderous beast, he cast *Erupt* and caused a stone spike to shoot up from the earth, directly into the lizard-dog's gut.

The spike penetrated its belly, causing the disoriented monster to rear up on its hind legs. Allistor got a glimpse of what looked like scaled skin, very similar to an alligator's belly, with a gaping hole. Even as it rolled over backward, its innards began to push out of the opening. Taking advantage of its vulnerability, he cast *Flame Shot* in the form of a column of fire descending directly onto the wound. The beast howled in pain and rolled back to its feet, the last bit of flame scorching the hairs on its back.

A shot rang out from above, and Allistor saw the thing flinch at the impact of a round from Helen's .30-06 rifle.

> **Canis Lacerta**
> **Level 12**
> **Health: 5,100/9,000**

Allistor was elated. They were doing serious ranged damage to the beast. It was still nearly thirty yards away from him, and it was almost half dead. Focusing on its face, he tried out his other new spell, *Vortex*. It took three seconds to cast, and in that time the mob had regained its senses. Staring balefully at Allistor now, eye to enraged eye, it let out a howl that nearly caused Allistor to lose track of his cast. At the last instant he managed to retain control and finish the spell. A small whirlwind of compressed air sprang to life right in front of the lizard-dog's muzzle. It quickly picked up dust, sand, turf, and even some of the creature's dripped blood, spinning them in a tight cone that expanded slightly to engulf the monster's head.

Allistor was preparing another *Flame Shot* when the monster burst forward through the vortex. It had used some kind of charge or speed boost ability, and covered the ground between them in less than three seconds. It smashed through his magical shield with seemingly no effort, and all two tons of it smashed into him. The snout slammed into his chest, knocking him backward to smash into the wall. He felt his neck pop at the same time that several of his ribs broke, and there was searing pain both inside and out. His health bar dropped below half as his vision flashed red.

Nearly unconscious, he managed to cast *Restore* on himself, raising his health bar slightly. The monster was three feet from his face, growling and pawing at the ground. Allistor managed to fire a round from his shotgun directly into its face, taking an eye and half its cheek in a spray of blood and bone.

The massive lizard-dog yelped and rolled away from him, pawing at its ruined face, disoriented by the sudden lack of sight on one side. Allistor took advantage and cast another heal on himself, hoping to live long enough to get back over the wall and breathe for a moment. But when he looked up, the wall he was still leaning against looked impossibly high, at least seven feet if it was an inch. The pain of his ribs healing themselves nearly caused him to pass out as he tried to stand.

Turning back to the monster, he cast *Mind Spike* again. The lizard dog went insane, growling and thrashing its head. Allistor managed to get to his feet and, leaning against the wall for support, back away several steps. He cast another *Erupt* directly at the ground under the monster's head. This time the spike shot up and into its neck. Blood fountained, and the thing whined in pain. It sounded so much like an injured dog that for a moment Allistor felt pity for the thing.

He took a step forward, his hand already raising and his mind preparing to cast a heal on it. Something in the back of his head was saying *'maybe you can tame it'*. But the monster sealed its own fate. Seeing his movement toward him, it lunged forward trying to eat his face. It managed to clamp down on his wrist before he could pull back, but at the same time it drove the stone spike farther into its flesh.

Allistor screamed at the same time the lizard-dog did. But it didn't let go of his wrist, even as it died. The weight of the collapsing corpse dragged him down to the ground, his wrist bones snapping and his skin tearing. Blood began to pump from the wound, and Allistor felt light-headed. The impact with the ground caused a flare of pain in his half-healed ribs. He lay there on the ground, looking at his arm where it disappeared into the monster's jaws as blood began to pool under it.

A moment later he felt the twin tingles of leveling up and being hit by a heal spell at the same time, then the pain of his wrist bones knitting themselves back together. "Damn." he gasped between labored breaths. "That hurts." He waved away the notifications that popped up, one of which told him he'd reached level thirteen.

Helen was there next to him a moment later, with Fuzzy right there sticking his nose into Allistor's face and licking, as if that would somehow help.

"Gah! Please, Fuzzy. Your breath is worse than that lizard-dog thing's!" He tried to push his bear cub away, but lacked the strength. His health bar was refilled but he was short quite a bit of blood. Helen handed him a health potion, which both improved his condition and restored some of his lost fluids.

Leaning against the wall, he pulled a water bottle from his inventory and gulped it down. Following it up with some dragon jerky that Andrea had handed him before he left the Citadel, he chewed and swallowed the tough meat. It almost instantly made him feel better, and gave a buff of +4 *Stamina*. Holding it up to show Helen, he said, "Should have thought to eat some of this *before* I pissed off the big gator-doggy-thing."

Helen looked nervously around the field and up at the stands above. "Don't get too relaxed. These things might run in packs."

Allistor stopped mid-chew, resisting the urge to gulp down the chunk of dragon jerky he'd just bitten off. He too started looking around, his ribs hurting as he turned his body. "Shit. I didn't even think of that." Fuzzy chuffed at him, licking his face again, causing Allistor to wince and cover his nose.

"Park ranger, remember? Animal behavior is kinda my thing. Especially wolves. Which this thing sort of resembles. Kind of."

Not pausing to loot the dead monster, Allistor quickly opened up his interface as he chided his bear cub. "Fuzzy, seriously. We need to find you some mint leaves or something." When he got to the proper tab, he mentally clicked on the *Outpost* button. This time there was no rejection notification. Apparently, the lizardy-dog-gator thing was the last living resident in the stadium.

"It's clear now. Says I can claim this as an Outpost. But I don't want to waste resources. Let's head back toward the gate and wait for the others."

"No need!" Daniel's voice came from the tunnel above. "We're here. And what the hell is that thing?" The others were filing in behind him, all of them going wide-eyed at the site of the dead mob.

"That's the former landlord here. We couldn't agree on the rent, and things got a little ugly." Allistor grinned weakly up at him. Then with a wink, he added, "You know how I said I'd help feed you?"

He watched a few of them turn pale at the idea of eating the gruesome dog monster, but Richard spoke up. "Hell, I've had gator meat. It ain't so bad." He opened his mouth to add more, but Virginia stopped him.

"If you say it tastes like chicken, I'll smack you." The others chuckled, and the mood was broken. Allistor walked slowly over to the corpse and gingerly bent to loot it. His ribs and wrist were healing, but weren't all the way there yet. And the muscle around them wasn't fully healed either. Helen looted it as well, while Fuzzy sniffed at the corpse, then growled. Each of them got twenty pieces of meat, some teeth and claws, three hundred klax, and Helen got the tail spike. She called Austin and a few of the

45

others down, and they skinned the corpse and harvested the remaining meat. Fuzzy helped himself to the internal organs, much to the disgust of nearly everyone present.

*****

Half an hour after the monster fight, Allistor was standing mid-field with the entire group of survivors. He had his system interface up, and was about to make the stadium into a Stronghold. He'd given them warning about what would happen, but when he pushed the button to confirm, there were still gasps of surprise as the bright light surrounded them and the area immediately around them became a translucent grid. A few people grabbed onto others to keep from losing their balance. Someone made retching noises.

Allistor quickly made his selections, having had a little practice with the features. He chose solar power, water, walls, security system, and greenhouse. He tripled the size of the greenhouse, having it occupy most of the field area in the center of the stadium. His expectation was that many more of Laramie's survivors would be joining this first group.

On the advice of Daniel and a few others, he also incorporated the nearby facilities like the indoor practice field and the round auditorium building, and extended the walls out to encompass some of the parking area outside. The land could be broken up and used as farmland, or space to construct more housing. And when it came to living spaces, well, the stands became wide terraces, each about twelve feet high and forty feet deep, upon which sat row after row of housing units. Allistor left the wide stairways that had run up and down between the seats, cutting them in half vertically. The left half remained stairs, while the right half was smoothed out into ramps. They were steeper than he would have liked but, with handrails to hold on to, items could be rolled up and down. He also added two more banks of elevators large enough to drive a car into.

There were oohs and ahs as he completed his selection and the structures modified themselves, the stadium reshaping its basic form, walls rising up around them, the components seemingly appearing out of nowhere.

The net result was a sort of stepped apartment complex on either side of the field, with structures on both ends that could be used for any number of things. The residential units pushed back through the bleachers into the walkways behind, so that each home had at least two bedrooms and a thousand square feet. Some of them he designated as three and four bedroom in case there were large families still living, or new families that would expand. These were much larger, and also featured two or three bathrooms. The Stronghold, the largest he'd constructed so far - not counting the Citadel - now had housing for up to twelve hundred people. There was a thirty-foot high stone wall that encircled the entire Stronghold, with a single large gate sporting massive twin metal doors. The walls had the usual staircases and ramparts, with four guardhouses at the compass points. There were also protected guard posts along the tops of the stadium itself.

He reserved the skyboxes for himself and his officers, breaking them into eight large residential units, four on either side, that looked down over the rest of the Stronghold. He also created larger units in the top floor of both the end zone buildings. He reserved the southwestern corner unit for himself, and let Daniel and the others choose who would get the remaining 'executive units', warning them to leave some for leaders of the other groups.

"Please, take a few minutes to look around and claim a living space. We'll work out spaces for crafting and shops later. Daniel, I'd like to speak with you and your fellow leaders. Let's say... thirty minutes. I built a large meeting room in that building at the south end zone, right behind the greenhouse." He pointed at the four-story building that had filled in one of the open ends of the stadium. The others nodded and everyone moved off to explore.

When they'd gathered back together, Daniel had brought Richard, Virginia and Bob, Ray, and the woman who'd asked about the oath, whose name he learned was Angela. Allistor got them all seated at a long conference table with simple wooden chairs.

"I don't know how many other groups there are, but we should talk about which ones you've met, where they are, and how best to reach out to them. And the sooner the better." Allistor told them right off. "This place isn't exactly inconspicuous, and its creation may trigger rash action by Barden, or one of the other groups. And, speaking of Barden, we'll need to make a plan to draw him out and deal with him."

The planning session took about two hours, then everyone headed out to get dinner and a good night's sleep. For most of them, their first in a very long time.

Chapter 3

Shot Through the Heart

As it turned out, they didn't need a plan to draw out Barden.

Shortly after breakfast the next morning, the lookout that had been stationed atop the Stadium roof shouted down that there were vehicles incoming. He pointed down toward the former parking area to the east. Allistor and most of the Stadium's new residents ran to the eastern wall, weapons in hand.

When he reached the top of the wall, he saw that the scout had given plenty of warning. The vehicles were moving slowly and were still a quarter mile out. Richard, standing next to Allistor, said, "That third vehicle back, that's Barden's truck." He sounded very sure of himself.

Looking to his left and right at his fellow survivors, Allistor said, "Uhh… guys. You're about to hear a voice. Don't freak out, it's just Nigel. He's the AI that runs all of our facilities. Nigel, please say hello."

"Good morning Lord Allistor, and to the rest of you. It is my pleasure to meet you all."

Several of the group just stared at Allistor, while others mumbled greetings. Austin held his stomach, laughing quite hard for some reason.

"Nigel, how far out does your sensor grid extend?"

"Two hundred yards in every direction, Lord Allistor."

Allistor estimated that the line of vehicles would shortly cross into Nigel's range. "All of you pull up your maps. In a moment you'll start seeing red dots. One for each bad guy. Nigel, I'm designating the approaching force as hostile. Please mark and track them accordingly."

"Of course, Lord Allistor. They are entering my perimeter now. Shall I secure the gates?"

"Yes, please lock them down. Thank you, Nigel." Allistor looked around. Anybody got anything like a bullhorn? Something that'll make it so Barden can hear me down there?"

One of the ladies on the wall raised a hand. "Um... I was poking around this morning, and I found the press box and the broadcast booth. It looks like all the equipment is still there. So the loudspeaker they used to announce the games might still work."

Allistor laughed out loud. He bowed his head to the woman. "Thank you. I should have thought of that. It's a damned stadium after all. Let's make some noise! Nigel, can you access the stadium's loudspeaker system and broadcast my voice through it?"

"Of course, Lord Allistor. One moment." They all waited while Nigel did whatever it was he needed to do. After about twenty seconds, the AI prompted, *"You are now connected. Let me know when you would like me to activate the loudspeaker feature."*

Allistor didn't speak right away. Instead, he reached into his inventory and pulled out two metallic cases. One long and sleek, the other shorter and thicker. After Dean had used the Barrett .50 so effectively against

50

the dragon at the Citadel, Allistor had left the weapon in his care. He'd taken the time to retrieve a second one from the gun shop Outpost before he and Helen set off on their current trip. He'd also nearly emptied the shop of firearms, distributing them between the Warren and the Citadel.

Opening the rifle case, he produced the long gun amid appreciative whistles. He opened the weapon's bipod legs and set it atop the wall. Taking his time, he opened the other case and removed the scope, carefully securing it to the sniper rifle. When it was all assembled and loaded, he took a knee. Sighting through the scope of the rifle, he adjusted slightly to get it comfortable against his shoulder. The recoil from this weapon was no joke, and improper placement could become painful.

It only took a moment to discover that down on one knee he couldn't get a good angle on the approaching vehicles. So he stood up again, and leaned over to sight through the rifle. It wasn't an ideal posture, but he could now see his target.

Sighting in on the third truck, he asked, "What does Barden look like?" There were men in both front seats of the truck, and he thought at least two more in the back seat.

"Pudgy guy, maybe fifty. Grey hair at his temples." Daniel answered. Allistor checked both the men in the front seat carefully, but neither matched the description.

"He must be sitting in the back. Which means I'll probably have to wait until he gets out." He turned to look at Daniel. "Swear to me this is a bad guy, and not just a rival."

Daniel raised his right hand. "I swear to you that Barden is a sick, murdering asshat who has killed several of our people, captured and taken our women, and should die a slow death."

A green swirl of light surrounded Daniel, and Helen chuckled. "Seems like the system or whatever agrees with you."

"Nigel, loudspeaker please. Full volume." Allistor waited a moment, then called out.

"Barden! Stop where you are. If you approach any closer you will be destroyed." his voice boomed throughout the Stadium, startling many of his people, and even Allistor himself a little. The lead vehicle slowed to a stop, as did the others behind it. Except the third vehicle, Barden's truck, which pulled out of line and continued forward until it was even with the lead vehicle. The doors opened as Allistor began counting. There were six vehicles in all, and at least four people emerged from each. A quick check of his interface showed there were actually thirty-two people down there.

Helen called out loud enough for their people to hear. "Everybody with a rifle, pick a body and get ready to shoot. But do not fire unless Allistor says so."

Allistor was laser focused on the truck in his scope's field of vision. The doors had opened, but only the two men from the front seats had emerged. After a good half minute, the driver opened the back door behind him and a man stepped out that fit the description of Barden.

The man stepped a few paces forward, standing just in front of his truck. "Who is that up there? And who do

52

you think you are? Laramie is *my city!*" Barden yelled up at the wall.

Allistor's voice boomed back. "I am Viscount Allistor, and this is my Stronghold. Your time of killing and stealing is over! I'll give you one chance to leave Laramie, right now, and keep your miserable life. Any of your people who have killed or hurt other humans get the same offer. You leave, or you die." Allistor took aim through the rifle's scope even as he spoke. He didn't expect Barden to give in, and to be honest, he didn't want him to. Letting him leave would only mean he'd have to deal with the man later, when he might be stronger. But he had to at least give the appearance of trying to work with the man, rather than just outright murdering him.

Barden played right into his hand. "Ha! Screw you, mister fancy *Viscount* man! I'm gonna kill you slowly, as a lesson to the others! You-"

Allistor squeezed the trigger, ending Barden's boasting by putting a large hole all the way through the center of his chest. Blood, bits of spine, rib, and heart tissue exploded out his back and liberally coated the two men behind him, as well as his fancy truck. The others on the wall took that as a sign and opened fire. Within two seconds more than half the men and women that had emerged from the vehicle caravan were dead or wounded. The rest had mostly fled, but a few had taken cover and were returning fire.

Allistor chambered another round and was about to put down another bad guy when a cry of pain next to him caused him to look over. A woman he hadn't spoken to yet was holding her hand over one eye, blood pumping

53

between her fingers as she fell backward. Bullets pinged off the wall nearby as the enemy fire zeroed in.

Allistor quickly cast *Restore* on the woman, hoping it would keep her alive. He couldn't see the wound, but he hoped it was just a bit of shrapnel or something, not a bullet in her brain. A moment later Virginia was there, grabbing the woman's hand and pulling it aside to pour a health potion directly into the wound. Allistor left her to it.

Angry now, he turned back to the fight. There were still seven red dots within range of Nigel's sensors. A quick look over the wall showed several people firing semi-automatic rifles in his general direction. A few more had fallen, and were either lying dead on the street, or writhing in pain as they bled. He selected one man whose burst of fire corresponded with a scream up on the wall. That guy was way too accurate to live. The man crouched behind a sedan with its windows already blown out. But he'd made the mistake of not hiding behind the engine block, or even a tire.

Allistor took aim, the target within easy range of the sniper scope's sights. He placed the red dot where he estimated the man's torso would be behind the trunk of the car, and fired. What happened next surprised even him.

The .50 caliber round smashed through the trunk of the car, and must have struck its gas tank on the way through. There was a ping of impact, followed by a loud thump as the tank exploded. The car lifted up into the air slightly, and the shock wave shattered any glass in a thirty-foot radius. There was no sign of the man's corpse, but Allistor hoped he'd died screaming. Anyone who'd waste precious human life at this point deserved no less.

The explosion had the bonus effect of knocking two more of the shooters out from behind their cover. A volley of shots from the wall put several rounds into each of them. There was a lull as everyone either reloaded or reassessed their situation. On his right, Helen let out a breath and fired, taking the top off the skull of a woman hiding behind a newspaper stand.

Allistor checked his interface. There were no more red dots. Those who had been injured in the first few volleys had either bled out, been finished off by the explosion, or picked off by additional shots from his people. He quickly counted twenty-four grey dots, indicating dead enemies. That meant eight of them had gotten away.

Unfortunately, he immediately noticed a couple grey dots on his side of the wall as well. The woman that Virginia had tried to help lay dead where she'd fallen. Another citizen had fallen backward off the parapet, the bullet wound in their shoulder not fatal, but the landing had snapped their neck.

Another regrettable result of the fight was that several of his people had leveled up. They'd received experience points both for defense of the Stronghold, and for their kills. There were quiet murmurs along the wall as people checked in with each other, comparing the experience they got and talking about their newly available points, as well as Fame Points. While leveling in itself was good, the fact that they'd done it by killing other humans, not so much. Plus the award of Fame Points... And they were discussing this while two of their companions lay dead nearby. He was going to need to address this. The last thing he wanted was for his people to start thinking murder was a good way to level up.

Austin and another young man Allistor didn't know came rushing up. "We need to go after them! If they get back and tell the others, they'll come back with a hundred guys!" He was pumped up on adrenaline and yelling without realizing it.

Allistor put a hand on his shoulder. Breathing deeply to calm his own adrenaline-fueled heart, he shook his head. "We're not going after them. They could be setting up an ambush already. We'll stay safe behind these walls for now."

Both youngsters looked disappointed, and Austin looked as if he might argue, until Virginia called his name. "Austin! Come over here and help me." She was directing another man to take hold of the dead woman's legs and prepare to move her off the wall.

As Austin moved toward his grandmother, his friend's face brightened. "That first shot, the way you took out Barden, that was *awesome*! You were all like 'pow!' and his back exploded like 'bwah!'.

"Stop." Allistor growled. The boy, who was maybe fifteen or sixteen years old, clamped his mouth shut and looked confused.

"Taking another human life is never a good thing, do you hear me? There are too few of us left already. Barden and his people chose to kill others for profit, or greed, or just for the fun of it, I don't really know. So they had to be put down. You heard me offer him a way out, and he refused it. Killing him was the best possible outcome of a horrible situation, and it cost twenty-six human lives, including two people I just last night swore to protect!" He felt Helen's hand on his back and realized he was yelling at the kid. And that everyone else was watching.

Taking a deep breath, he said, "I'm sorry. This isn't your fault. But don't ever let me catch you celebrating the death of another human. Any of you. This had to be done, but that doesn't make it any less horrible." The kid nodded, tears forming in his eyes. He dropped his gaze to his feet and retreated.

As Allistor looked around, several of the adults nodded at him, or gave him a thumbs up. Helen rubbed his back a bit more before giving him a comforting pat on the shoulder. Fuzzy, who had remained on the ground level with a small group of children, chuffed at him in an inquiring tone. Allistor climbed down the nearest stair and went to his bear companion. As he approached, several of the children backed away in fear, their eyes wide.

Allistor spoke softly. "I'm sorry, kids. I didn't mean to scare anyone. The bad guys are gone, and I'm just upset that some of our people got hurt. Please, it's okay." he scratched Fuzzy's ears as he spoke, and the bear leaned against him. A few of the kids stepped closer, and Allistor tried to smile even as he realized Fuzzy's vouching for him did more to put the kids at ease than his reassuring words or soft tone.

A few adults came and claimed the kids, herding them away somewhere, offering Allistor a few words of encouragement as they did. Every survivor had experienced death and the emotional roller coaster that came with it over recent weeks.

Allistor picked a spot on one of the stairs and sat for a while. As he calmed himself, he mechanically cleaned his rifle. Something his father had drilled into him as a kid. "You fire your weapon, you clean it as soon as you're done. Don't wait for later, because you never know what might happen between now and later." Fuzzy sat next to him, sniffing at the gun oil then sneezing and shaking his head. Helen sat above and behind him on the steps, observing him and nodding as he cleaned.

When he was nearly done, she spoke quietly to him. "We should open the gates and go loot the dead. If for no other reason than to claim their weapons and keep them out of the hands of those who might use them against us."

Allistor smiled as she used his words from their conversation about the nukes at the Silo. "Good point. Smart thinkin', right there." He flashed her a small smile as he got to his feet. "Nigel, can I have loudspeaker again, please. About half volume this time?"

"Certainly, Lord Allistor. It is now active."

"Attention people. Anyone who was up on the wall and fired a weapon, please report to the gate. Armed and ready." Allistor followed word with deed and began to walk toward the gate himself. It wasn't far, and in just over five minutes all the fighters had joined him.

"We're going out to loot the bodies. All of you know about loot, yes? Anyone who doesn't, please raise your hand." He waited, and no hands went up. "Okay good. When we go out there, find the bodies you hit.

58

There should be a sort of… glow that you'll be able to see. It tells you that you participated in the kill, and are eligible to loot. There will be several bodies that more than one of you hit. Loot every body that you can. When you're not looting, watch each other's backs. There were eight more of them, and we don't know for sure they ran all the way home." He paused to let that sink in.

"Another thing. I know you all got experience and probably Fame Points for killing these men and women. And you're about to get loot. Some of it might be exceptionally *good* loot. I know a few of you were already aware, and the rest of you are just learning this now. We need you all to keep this to yourselves. I can't have you encouraging others to kill humans for the xp and loot. That's murder, and will be dealt with quickly, and brutally. You all saw how Barden died. I will not hesitate to do the same to any murderer. Am I clear?"

"Aren't we already murderers, then?" a young man near the back spoke up. He had a smirk on his face, and was looking around accusingly at the others.

Allistor began walking toward him, and the crowd parted. He stopped two feet from the man, who was puffing out his chest and still smirking.

"Do you *feel* like a murderer?" he growled at the man. He was taller than Allistor by a good four inches, but with a much less muscular physique.

"No. But then, I didn't hit anything. I just fired my gun in the air. I don't believe in murder." There was a grumbling from the crowd behind Allistor.

"If you know you didn't hit anything, why are you standing here?" Allistor was quickly losing patience. The man was still smirking, and challenging him with his eyes.

"You *said* everyone who fired a weapon. I fired my weapon. So here I am. Not my fault you're unclear in your directions. Maybe you shouldn't be the leader after all. You don't seem to be very good at it. You got two of us killed the first day."

Allistor had been holding his shotgun in one hand. He raised that hand and holstered the weapon on his back. Clenching his fists, he turned his back on the man to gaze at the rest of the crowd. He saw a lot of hard faces, but couldn't tell if they were for him, or the idiot behind him.

"What's your name?" Allistor asked without turning.

"Me? My name is Justin. Shouldn't you know that?" the man practically spat the words out.

"Justin, how many attackers were there?"

"There were, uhm… thirty." Justin hesitated before answering.

"There were thirty-two. How many died in the first volley?"

"How the hell should I know?" the retort came quickly. Allistor still hadn't turned, as he was watching the faces of the others. Each time Justin spoke, more and more of them looked disgusted.

"More than half of them went down in the first volley. There might have been one more, if you'd actually aimed at the enemy instead of firing into the air. That *one*

60

enemy that you let live could have been the one that killed the lady standing near me. Or the man that fell to his death." his voice was very quiet, and dead cold. He watched as the others gripped their weapons more tightly, and there was some grumbling in the group.

Justin took notice of it. "You can't put that on me. I'm not killing someone over a house in a stadium. It's not worth it! You're a bunch of murderers, no better than them!"

Allistor finally turned toward him, seeing what he'd needed to see in the crowd. "That's good to hear. I'm glad you don't think a safe place to sleep is worth killing for. What about the children inside these walls? The other men and women. The ones who've already been taken away by Barden's people. Are any of them worth killing for?"

Justin's eyes began to dart around, looking for a friendly face and not finding any. "What? N-no!"

"So, despite the fact that the people lying dead outside this wall were here to kill you, or steal your food so that you starve, you accuse all of us of murder for defending ourselves?"

"Yes!" Justin raised his weapon and pointed it at Allistor. "You're a murdering piece of shit, and I'd be doing the world a favor if I shot you!" Justin's face had gone scarlet and spittle sprayed as he spoke.

Helen raised her rifle, and within two seconds so had everyone else in the crowd. Every barrel but his own was pointed at Justin.

Allistor continued. "Daniel, did Justin here come to your group late?"

Daniel answered with one word. "Yes."

"Justin, you've been working for Barden since before you joined the group, haven't you?"

"What? No! Of course not!" Justin began to panic. He pulled his rifle tighter against his shoulder and raised it so that it pointed at Allistor's face. Helen's rifle fired, and Justin's body was knocked backward even as the back of his skull exploded.

Allistor turned to the others. "Anybody have a problem with that?"

"Hell no." Bob's voice was first to answer. "He was about to shoot you."

The others all lowered their weapons, muttering words like 'traitor' and 'coward'. Helen bent down and looted the body, taking Justin's weapon when it didn't transfer as loot.

Allistor spent a little time looking each one of them in the eye, searching for any sign of resentment or malice, or doubt. Not finding any obvious indicators, he said, "Nigel, please open the gate. Just enough for a person to pass through. Be prepared to close it on my command."

The massive bolts that held the gate shut disengaged, and the twenty-foot tall metal doors parted slightly, leaving an opening about three feet wide. Allistor stepped out first, shotgun back in his hands. He led the procession of fighters around to the east side of the wall and the collection of corpses. As they spread out to loot their kills, Allistor walked directly to Barden's corpse and looted it. He received several thousand klax, as well as a key ring, three handguns, two grenades, and a pair of fancy snakeskin boots. Looking around, he found what was left of the man who'd died in the explosion, and looted him as well.

Apparently, the explosion also counted as an attack, because he was able to loot four others that had been killed after the explosion impacted them. When he was done, he looked around. The others were either standing guard over fellow looters, or walking back toward him.

"No point in exposing ourselves by walking back. Get in the cars that have keys." He held up the key ring he'd looted, which had Barden's truck key on it. "Or some of you may have looted keys. Let's load up as many as we can into the vehicles and we'll take them inside."

He tossed the truck keys to Helen, who climbed into the driver's seat. The group piled into the other vehicles, all of which were now running, until they were full. It left a dozen or so to walk. Allistor walked with them. Helen and the other drivers formed a sort of rolling guard around them, keeping the cars' speed at the walkers' pace and surrounding them all the way back across the parking area and around to the gate.

Nigel opened the gates farther at Allistor's command, and the convoy rolled through. Allistor was the last to enter, and the gates clanged shut behind him.

*****

Allistor let everyone calm down for an hour or so. Lots of the citizens had seen Justin's execution, and had concerns. Daniel, Virginia, Bob, and the others quickly circulated the truth of the situation, and things calmed down. Apparently, Justin didn't have friends within the group looking to avenge his death.

Just before noon, Allistor called the leaders together again. "Barden's group should be in disarray for a day or so, but I expect they'll be back. I'd like to bring in a few of the other groups before then, if possible. But I'll need to stay here, in case they come earlier than expected. So, I'm looking for volunteers to go out and approach groups you know. Folks you've run across that you think might be good additions to our little community. We've got extra vehicles, and lots of extra weapons now." He winked at Bob, who grinned back.

"I'll go!" Austin instantly volunteered before his grandmother smacked the back of his head.

In all, seven men and women stepped forward to volunteer. They were given food and water, extra weapons and ammo, and one of the captured vehicles. Not Barden's, as Richard reminded everyone that it would be recognized as his, and likely fired upon. An hour later, the vehicles exited the gate with invitations for the other leaders to come and speak with Allistor.

While they waited, Allistor went into the Stronghold interface and pulled up the building menu again. He constructed a market kiosk, and called Helen and Virginia over to him. "The fact that Justin was able to take the oath and still be working for Barden troubles me. I'm hoping you two can help me find something to deal with that. Ideally it would be a spell to detect lies, or something similar. It could also be an item. I'm not sure what the market might have." He looked from Virginia to Helen. "Helen, if you wouldn't mind giving Virginia a quick introduction to the market and how it works? Then the two of you can try and find something that will help us? If I'm about to bring a thousand people in here, I need a way to make sure one of them isn't going to murder us in our sleep."

Leaving them to their search, he walked up to the quarters he'd claimed for himself. Fuzzy followed at his side, having recovered his Fibble doll from somewhere and once again drooling all over it.

Secure in his quarters, he spoke to the ceiling. "Nigel, please ask Andrea, Dean, Sam, Meg, Amanda, Nancy, George, Michael, and Ramon to get someplace where they can speak privately, preferably together in one place, for a call in thirty minutes."

"Of course, Lord Allistor."

While he waited, he took some time to survey his quarters. The system had provided basic furniture; a sofa, some chairs, a dining table, and a bedroom set. Nothing fancy, like in the Citadel, but comfortable enough. He moved one of the chairs over so that it sat right in front of the floor to ceiling skybox window, and sat for a while enjoying the view of the city.

Fuzzy poked around for a while, then moved to the bathroom and plopped down with his belly on the cool floor tiles. Allistor laughed aloud as the bear uttered a contented sigh and closed his eyes.

Allistor let his own eyes drift shut, and was nearly asleep when Nigel notified him that the others had gathered.

"You are connected, my Lord."

"Hey everyone. Sorry for the short notice. I wanted to update you all on what's going on…"

He spent the better part of thirty minutes telling them about Laramie and the happenings there. They asked a few questions, and he answered to the best of his ability. Then he got to the main reason for the call. "Ramon, I'd like you and your people to check around the library for information about the teleport hubs. Specifically, I need to know whether they are movable once they've been set up." He paused, then continued as if thinking aloud, "I'd rather not waste a teleporter on a Stronghold that's only fifty miles from the Citadel and Silo. The only reason those two both have one is the dangerous nature of the weapons in the Silo. But I may need to quickly evacuate these people here in Laramie, or bring you guys in as reinforcements. So, I'm wondering…"

Ramon finished it for him. "If you can set up the teleporter, then move it to another Stronghold when the immediate danger there has passed. Got it. We'll check into it."

"Great, thank you Ramon. Also, if you find anything about truth spells, that would be extremely helpful as well." He paused, then changed the subject.

"I should have asked this first, but how are things in your respective communities? Anything you need me to know or help deal with?"

He spent another hour speaking with his inner circle about the various goings-on at his properties. He laughed along with the others when Nancy admitted one of the bunnies had been born with a mutation. Nothing all that sinister, just a third eye. She insisted that it wasn't a result

66

of her rapid aging of the critters, just a natural occurrence. When Allistor told her about the massive greenhouse at the Stadium, she immediately volunteered herself and George to help get it up and running. Allistor asked her to wait until things were more secure.

Sam mentioned that he'd created a few new recipes, and that both his and Meg's *Cooking* skill was leveling through Journeyman toward Expert. Michael was now enchanting items with enhancements as high as +5 to a single attribute. Ramon and his people had copied the *Restore* spell and passed it on to more than half the residents of the Warren, Silo, and Citadel.

Allistor found that talking with his friends helped him unwind quite a bit. When they'd covered all they needed to, he thanked them and congratulated them on jobs well done before ending the call. With nothing else needing his immediate attention, he decided to go back down and help Helen and Virginia search the market for useful items.

*****

By dinnertime, all of his ambassadors had returned. Only one came back alone, unable to convince the leader of the group he'd visited to accept Allistor's invitation. Allistor had purchased several long tables from the market, and had them set up on the field not far from the dining hall. With potentially a thousand people, he was going to need to either expand the hall and the kitchen, or add at least one more.

As the other leaders arrived, he had them escorted to one of the long tables where he and Helen sat with Daniel and Richard. He greeted each of them with a smile and a handshake, asking them to sit and offering food and drink. He'd pulled some freshly grilled dragon steaks from his inventory for the occasion, giving the potential allies a tasty meal that gave +5 to *Stamina* for four hours.

They made small talk until all had arrived, sharing stories about the first days and the troubles they'd had. Each of them thanked him for killing Barden, but most were also concerned about the fallout to come.

After the last of them arrived and had taken a few minutes to eat, Allistor thumped the table a few times to get their attention.

"Thank you all for coming here today. I appreciate your open mindedness and the faith in humanity that you've shown by accepting our invitation. I hope you'll leave here thinking it was worth it."

He spent a good hour telling them about his experiences since the apocalypse, sharing what he'd learned, minus a few important details like selling rare items for big moolah. He wanted to encourage these people to join him, not give them the tools to go out on their own and potentially become rivals. And he didn't mention the teleport pads.

He saw many of them nodding their heads and smiling at him as he continued, so he decided to bring things to a close and ask them to join him.

"I've been lucky enough to claim a large territory, and successfully build several facilities like this one. I already own more land than we would need in the next hundred years, but I need people like you and yours to make it all work. People to live on the land, to produce crops and crafts, and to help secure it from people like Barden, or the aliens when they come." He stopped talking to look at each of them for a moment, then sat down and lowered his voice, adopting a less formal attitude.

"Look. I can offer safety. Ask the folks around you how good it felt to sleep safely through the night last night." Richard, Daniel, and all the ambassadors nodded and spoke in agreement. "I can offer food, both from hunting and from the greenhouses, which we can set up to grow fruit and vegetables at more than double the normal rate. I can offer access to the market, where we can buy what we can't grow or kill. Running water and electricity mean hot showers. We have healing spells as well as offensive magic."

Pausing again after offering the carrot, he switched to the stick. "Our world as we knew it is gone. There's no more government here, no more organized military that we've been able to find, at least not on a large scale. We've got less than a year to prepare ourselves for an alien invasion. I'm trying to form a new nation here. A small nation, I grant you, but a nation of humans. I don't care what race, religion, nationality you are, just that you're human. And willing to help me build. I don't just want to survive here. I want us to thrive, and to grow stronger, and eventually reclaim our whole world. And more than that, I want to take the fight to *their worlds* and repay them for the billions of us, our family and friends, that they've slaughtered."

Allistor stopped talking when he noticed a few of them looking nervously at him. He realized he may have gone too far.

"I know that might make me sound like a madman. And I admit, I *am* angry after watching my sister and parents killed in those first days. And too many friends since then. My plans might seem a little lofty and far-fetched right now. And maybe I can't pull it off. But what I *know* I can do... *what we can do...* is work together to ensure that you, and you, and your children, and their children, live decent lives." He pointed at those who seemed most unsure as he spoke.

He let the silence reign for a while, simply sitting there looking at his visitors one by one. He was pretty sure of three of them, as they had been nodding and smiling even while he ranted about fighting on alien planets. Another seemed on the fence, but he thought she might be swayed when the first three agreed. The other two he had doubts about.

Something his father had taught him years earlier, when they'd been discussing politics, was that in a situation where you want something from someone, you make your pitch then shut up. From that point on, the first one who speaks loses. They'll either accept your proposal, or ask a question that gives you another chance to convince them. But if you speak first, you're admitting that you failed to get your point across, or that you aren't confident enough to wait for their response.

So, he sat, and he looked. His people began to shuffle a bit, tapping their feet or drumming fingers on the table. He tried to calm each of them with a look, but he didn't have telepathy. Yet. He smiled to himself, thinking about finding a *Telepathy* scroll on the market and building a nation of telepaths.

Oddly enough, that unintended smile seemed to sway one of the two doubters. He smiled back at Allistor and stuck out his hand. "I can't commit my people without talking to them. But I want to join you. And I think they will too. There are eighty of us, including the kids. Do you have room?"

Allistor saw the others all lean forward at this question. "Absolutely. I built this place to handle twelve hundred residents. And there's room to expand." Their eyes widened at the number, and several of them turned to take a closer look at their surroundings.

Two minutes later the three he had expected to join him had done so, along with the woman he'd labeled as 'on the fence'. That left just one of the visiting leaders as a hold-out. Allistor looked at the man expectantly, and waited.

Finally, the man stood. "I'm just not sure. My group has taken heavy losses from raids by Barden and his people. I'm sure you can understand we have... trust issues. When he first arrived at our camp, he made a lot of promises of safety and cooperation. We believed him. He came back the next day with thirty guys and killed my dad and ten of our people. Stole most of our food, and four women. Two of them had kids that he left behind as orphans. Another had a seven-year-old son that Barden killed when he cried too loudly for his mother."

The grief in the man's voice brought tears to Allistor's eyes. He tried to be a strong leader, but in truth

71

he was still a twenty-year-old man who'd lived a relatively sheltered life. True, he'd been hardened by events and losses since the end of the world. But his heart still hurt for this man and his people. And his anger burned over the dead Barden's actions."

Allistor took a deep breath, wiping the tears that formed in his eyes without caring who saw them. "I'm sorry. I'm sorry that asshole found you before I did. For your losses, and for the loss of your ability to trust most of all. I think that'll be among the hardest things for all of us to regain."

The man nodded. "I will speak to my group. And… if you're willing, you can come and speak to them as well. That's the best I can do."

"It'd be my pleasure." Allistor held out a hand, and the man shook it. Turning to take in the others, he said, "You're all welcome to spend the night here. It'll be dark very soon, and we all know that more of the monsters come out after dark."

The man who was still gripping his hand shook his head. "I'd like to return now, if that's alright?"

"Of course. I'll drive you myself." Allistor looked at Helen, who nodded. Fuzzy, who had been lying nearby hoping for scraps, simply got up and started walking toward their truck.

When she saw the alarmed look on the man's face, she smiled and patted his shoulder. "Don't worry, I'll sit in back with the smelly beast. But be ready to roll your window down. When he farts, it qualifies as a chemical attack."

The others all elected for a safe night's sleep, so Daniel volunteered to show them to some empty exec quarters. Allistor led the man and Helen toward the truck. "I'm sorry, tell me your name again? I'm afraid I'm terrible at names."

"I'm Lang. My daughter and I, we're originally from Cheyenne. We left there after the monsters started coming out. Thought it might be safer to be out of the city. A whole bunch of us felt that way, and we gathered together. Laramie is as far as we got."

They got into the truck, and Allistor drove them out the gate, which opened and closed for him automatically. Lang pointed to the right. "Head west. Camp's about a mile and a half."

Helen prodded him a little from the back seat, where she was scratching Fuzzy's head. "Why'd you stop in Laramie?"

"Barden." Lang answered bitterly. "We stopped and made camp here, planning to siphon gas from some cars, do a little foraging. Planned to just stay a day or two, then continue on. There's a reservoir about forty miles west of here, with a big park. We figured we could hunt and fish, build ourselves a little fort like our ancestors did. We heard reports that cities attracted larger numbers of the monsters."

Neither Helen nor Allistor had heard anything similar, but Helen replied, "I suppose that makes a sort of sense. Predators naturally go where there's abundant prey."

Lang nodded. "Anyway, Barden showed up our first night. He must have had scouts watching the roads or something. He came to us with his promises of protection, and we told him we'd think about it and take a vote. He left us for the night, and we talked about it. Some of us wanted to stay, but most of us wanted to keep going. Laramie's a smaller city than Cheyenne, but it's still a city."

He paused and took a deep breath. "They attacked us the next morning before half of my people were even awake. Killed anyone who picked up a weapon, took most of our vehicles and food, and a few of our people. He threatened to kill anyone who tried to leave, because we worked for him now. We had to forage and provide a quota of food every week."

"That night, a family of four decided to sneak away under the cover of darkness. I don't know if they made it, but when Barden came back, he saw they were missing and claimed to have killed them."

They traveled on in silence after that, except when Lang instructed Allistor to turn. It wasn't long before they reached his camp. Allistor started to slow when he heard a shrill whistle, but Lang whistled back with some kind of bird call and told him to keep going. They drove into a courtyard of an office building that rose ten stories above ground. Lang explained; "There's a parking garage below, and it has solar panels on the roof. So we can have working lights underground without the monsters seeing. And we can collect rainwater from the roof for washing and flushing."

Allistor parked the car and got out. As the people gathered around, he saw that it was a larger group than expected. Something close to two hundred people were standing around him when Lang introduced him. He also introduced Helen and Fuzzy, who caused a bit of a stir. When everyone was calmed, Lang vouched for Allistor, then gave him the floor.

Allistor took a deep breath… and began his sales pitch again.

Chapter 4

Kill Or Be Killed

The following morning, Helen administered the oath to the entire group, then took the truck filled with Fuzzy and six orphaned children back to the Stronghold right after breakfast. She was to deliver the children, and return with every working vehicle their people could get together.

Lang and his group had unanimously agreed to join Allistor. There were two hundred and thirty-one of them, including the orphans, who got a vote as well. Allistor and Helen had been amazed that they'd been able to feed themselves for so long. Lang said it wasn't easy, and that they wouldn't have been able to do so for much longer. His people were good foragers, but Barden had taken more than half of everything they'd gathered.

The group had witnessed the bright lights of the transformation of the Stadium from afar, and some had wanted to go investigate before Allistor's ambassador had shown up. A few were so anxious to get to safe shelter that they didn't wait for a vehicle, they simply packed their belongings on their backs and began walking. Though they were armed, Allistor tried to talk them out of it. Lang reassured him that his people had been foraging in the area, and knew the risks.

The rest of the group packed up their belongings and piled up everything of value they'd foraged. When a convoy of nearly thirty vehicles arrived there were cheers, and more than a few tears. They quickly loaded up the supplies, and as many people as possible piled into the vehicles. The rest walked alongside for the mile and a half trip.

When they arrived and the gates opened, every single one of Allistor's Laramie people were there at the gate to welcome the newcomers and help get them situated. There were more cheers, lots of handshakes, crying, and hugs. Allistor beamed with pride.

Through the day, the other groups showed up. One by one, they gathered outside the gate and took the oath, then were welcomed inside. Another two groups had arrived as well, recruited by friends in the first six groups.

All told, by the time sun set, Allistor had more than seven hundred new citizens.

There were two other notable arrivals that afternoon. The first was a small convoy led by Nancy and George that included a panel truck full of fresh fruit, vegetables, and meat, and a flatbed covered with saplings and seedlings for the greenhouse. They instantly became the most popular people in the Stadium.

Meg and Sam were there too, Sam insisting that they organize the kitchen. When Meg saw the size of the crowd, and the size of the kitchen, she went after Allistor with a frying pan, threatening to put a lump on his head if he didn't add two more kitchens immediately. Laughing, he did as she asked, saying he'd meant to get to it, but had been a little busy.

Ramon had accompanied the others, bringing along bags of scrolls for the basic spells; *Light, Restore,* and *Ignite.* He also brought a supply of skill scrolls which he entrusted to Helen for distribution to folks who wished to begin crafting, or to further crafts that they'd already begun to pursue.

That night there was a celebratory feast. Canid and turtle steaks, chicken soup and rabbit stew, along with freshly steamed vegetables and sweetened fruit preserves for dessert. For the first time in a long time, the survivors laughed and joked, sang and danced without fear of monsters rushing in from the dark. Their bellies full, the aura of joy and contentedness was heartwarming.

Allistor was considering heading to bed when Nigel alerted him to the other notable arrival. Unfortunately, about half of those gathered heard the alert as well.

"Lord Allistor, a humanoid approaches the gate."

Allistor and many of the others jogged to the south wall and climbed to the top. Looking down, they saw a woman in dark clothing stumbling toward the gate. Allistor scanned the horizon as best he could in the dark, but saw no other movement. And Nigel wasn't detecting anyone else within two hundred yards.

"Hold it there, miss." he called down when she was within about a hundred feet. The woman stopped walking and wobbled slightly on her feet. Then she simply gave up and plopped herself down on the ground.

Her faint voice drifted up to them. "Please… help."

One of the children, upon hearing the voice, screamed, "Mommy!" and tried to jump over the wall. The nearby adults restrained her, but she kept trying to break free. "That's my momma! Momma!"

Allistor picked up the girl and jumped off the back of the parapet, his enhanced *Strength* more than enough to absorb the impact. "Nigel, open the gate."

As the gate opened, he carried the child out and dashed across to the woman, who was struggling to her feet after hearing her child's calls. "Lacey? Is it really you, baby girl?"

The child struggled even harder, and Allistor let her go, setting her on her feet whereupon she promptly sprinted toward her mother. "Mammaaaa!"

Allistor walked slowly, allowing the two of them to embrace, the mother sobbing in joy as she wrapped her little girl in her arms. "It's me, baby. I'm here. It's gonna be okay. Everything's gonna be okay."

When he reached them, Allistor introduced himself. "I'm Allistor. And you are…?"

"Her name's Moira." Lang's voice came from right behind him. "She was one of the ones taken on that first morning."

Allistor was instantly suspicious. "So, you've come from Barden's camp?"

Moira nodded, tears still streaming down her face as she gripped her daughter tightly. "I escaped. The camp is tearing itself apart. Some of the fighters came back yesterday saying Barden was dead, along with most of his men. The ones that are left have been fighting over what to do and who's in charge."

"And you just walked out of the camp?" Allistor's tone was suspicious, and Lang noticed.

"Hey, she's one of mine. They *took her at gunpoint*, she didn't volunteer."

Allistor looked at the man, then stepped closer to him and whispered, "I need to do this. For all of us. Just be patient."

Lang glared at him for a moment, thinking. With a nod, he stepped back. Allistor turned back to Moira. "I need you to let go of Lacey for a minute. We're going to take you inside, but we need to search you first."

Moira began shaking her head, holding tight to the little girl. "What? Search me for what? I don't have any weapons."

Helen stepped forward, her rifle slung over her shoulder and both hands up. "That's great. We just need to check that to be sure. Then we'll take you both inside where we can talk. We need to do this quickly, as you may have been followed."

Moira was still shaking her head. "I ran. Ran the whole way here. They were chasing the others. No way they followed me."

Now it was Helen's turn to shake her head. Her tone hardened. "If you believed that, you wouldn't have run yourself into the ground. Which means you've just lied to us. Now, let me explain this clearly. You *are* going to let go of your daughter and be searched. The only question is whether that happens with you alive, or dead."

Moira glanced over her shoulder into the darkness. Her eyes wide, she nodded once and let go of Lacey. Lang stepped forward and scooped up the crying girl who immediately began to scream and reach for her mom. Lang hugged her to his chest, mumbling into her ear to try and calm her. Moira held out her arms to the sides. "Fine. Get it over with. Just hurry." Her gaze darted to her crying daughter, then back to Helen.

"Are you carrying any storage devices? A ring, maybe?" Allistor asked as Helen stepped forward and began to search the woman, quickly and efficiently.

Moira shook her head. "No. Nothing. I ran with just a canteen, and I dropped that along the way. And-" she stopped mid-sentence, then cursed. "Shit, I do have a weapon. A knife in my boot."

Allistor raised his shotgun and pointed it directly at Moira's face, the end of the barrel less than a foot from her nose. "You said you had no weapons."

Lang put a hand on his shoulder. "Easy, Allistor. She's scared. She just forgot."

"Or she realized Helen was about to find it." Allistor kept his weapon leveled.

Helen had just bent down to retrieve the knife from Moira's ankle when a shot rang out. Moira grunted, falling backward as the others all ducked instinctively. Allistor heard sounds of a struggle behind him, then a scream that cut off quickly with a thud.

Helen called out, "Moira's hit." She and Allistor both cast a heal on the woman, as did at least one other unseen person. The round had struck her shoulder, blasting away a large chunk of meat. Allistor didn't spend time watching the wound close, turning instead back toward the wall.

He heard Austin's shaky voice up on the wall saying, "I didn't push him. He jumped. I…I tried to stop him."

Leaving Moira with Helen, Allistor jogged back to the wall. Laying on the ground not far from the base was one of the men he'd just taken an oath from earlier in the day. The man was dead, his neck snapped. A rifle lay next to him. Looking up at the faces on the wall above, he asked, "What happened?"

Virginia's voice answered. "That man took a shot at you. Austin and a few others grabbed him, but he broke loose and tried to jump off the wall. Austin got ahold of his foot, and it tripped him up so that he fell face first…"

Allistor looked again at the man, who had clearly landed face first. He skull was partially caved in, and his head rested at an impossible angle. Looking back up at the wall, he said, "Austin, come down here and loot this man. A couple others come down here with him. Drag the body a hundred yards away from the wall and leave it."

Walking back to Helen, he saw that Moira was fully healed. The skin visible through her torn shirt sleeve not even showing a scar. Helen held up a sheathed knife and said, "I didn't find anything else. No ring, or any jewelry at all."

Moira mumbled, "Assholes stole everything I had before they…" She just hung her head and didn't finish. Allistor nodded to Lang, who put down the little girl. Lacey ran back into her mother's arms, still crying. He felt sorry for the girl and the woman, but he needed to be sure.

"Before we walk inside, tell me how you managed to get away."

Lang and Helen both opened their mouths to object. Allistor held up a hand. "I'm sick of being betrayed by people I've put my trust in. We've found two of Barden's spies in two different groups in two days."

Both Helen and Lang quieted, and Moira swallowed hard. "A few of the guards that were left had been talking about killing us all and moving on. Saying we were too many to control, and feed. A bunch of us decided to run. All at the same time. One of the men said it would be best if we went different directions. We all saw the lights here yesterday, and I decided to run this direction. I waited a few seconds after the others took off. One of them got spotted, and the guards surged in that direction, shooting like crazy. That's when I ran."

Allistor watched her face as she spoke. He didn't pick up any kind of deceptive vibe. Then again, who the hell was he? He didn't have any training in interrogation or spy craft. He looked up at Helen, who nodded once. She even handed Moira back her knife, which was enough for Allistor.

"Right. Everyone back inside. Moira, I'm sorry, but we needed to be sure." He held out a hand, indicating she should walk through the gate. Once she and the others were inside, he waited for the body detail to return. Clapping Austin on the shoulder as he passed through the gate, he said, "Well done, kid. You did what you had to do."

Back inside, he looked around. Hundreds of sets of eyes were focused on him, Moira, and Lacey. He put his shotgun away in his inventory and put a hand on Moira's shoulder. The woman flinched slightly, but didn't move away.

"It's okay folks. Sorry about the excitement. Go on back to your dinners now, and let's finish this celebration!" he tried to sound as upbeat as possible, but he didn't think anyone bought it. To his surprise, people turned and headed back toward the tables. The folks on the wall filed down the stairs and joined them. He kept Moira with him as the crowd passed by. Lang and Helen remained with him, as did Meg, who squatted down in front of Lacey and held out her arms.

"How 'bout we get you some of that yummy chicken soup? I made it myself." When Lacey continued to cling to her mother's leg, Meg added, "It's okay sweetie. Your mom's safe now. She just has to have some grown-up talk with Allistor and Lang. She'll be joining you for some soup soon enough."

Moira crouched down and hugged Lacey again, then kissed her forehead. "It's okay, baby. Go with this nice lady, and I'll catch up real soon. Go ahead." She gave Lacey a gentle shove, and the little girl nodded once before stepping into Meg's arms. Meg lifted her up with a groan and carried her away.

Looking at Lang, Moira got back to her feet. "Thank you. For keeping her alive all this time. I wasn't sure..." she broke down and began to cry. Lang reached out and pulled her into a hug, patting her on the back and just letting her cry. Allistor and the others waited patiently. Eventually she got herself composed, and Lang escorted her as they followed Allistor to the nearby first floor conference room. As they walked, Sam, Ramon, Richard, Daniel, Virginia, and Bob joined them. Austin tried to as well, but Allistor gave him a mission.

"You know who the leaders of the other groups are? You'd recognize their faces? Can you gather them up and bring them to the conference room?"

Austin nodded. "I think so. If not, I can ask around. I'll find them and bring 'em here." He took off at a dead run.

Once inside the conference room, Allistor pulled some jerky and a bottle of water from inventory. Handing them to Moira, he said, "Again, I'm sorry about the welcome. This place isn't exactly utopia, yet. Barden has seriously screwed with people's heads, including mine, apparently." He waited as she took a long drink, emptying the bottle, then handed her another one. "Take it easy. Eat and drink slowly. We've got a little time before the others arrive. When you've answered our questions, we'll take you to find Lacey and some better food."

It was only about five minutes before the others arrived, Austin proudly leading them. Allistor took in the boy's grin and said, "That was fast. Well done."

Austin beamed at him. "I decided not to waste time chasing them down."

One of the men walking in behind him laughed. "Yeah, he just stood up on a table and shouted that we should come and follow him." Virginia snorted, and Bob chuckled.

Austin's smile faded a bit, and he walked over to Moira. Handing her a bowl of something, he mumbled,

"I'm sorry you got shot. I tried to stop him." Turning to Allistor he said, "I thought he was aiming for you. I bumped him as I reached for his gun. I… think it might be my fault she got hit."

Moira put a hand on Austin's arm. "No, he was aiming for me. He was one of Barden's guys. Probably wanted to shut me up before I said anything about the camp. You saved my life. Thank you." She patted his arm as he blushed and backed away. Bob caught his attention and pointed to the door, giving him an approving grandfatherly smile.

When the door closed, Allistor said, "Please, eat up. When you feel up to it, tell us all you can about Barden's people and the camp."

Austin had forgotten to bring any silverware, so Moira used her knife to stab a piece of meat from the rabbit stew. When she'd chewed and swallowed, she began her report.

"There are about thirty of his guards left. Men and women. Another twenty or so are people who support him. Cooks, scouts, people he uses as spies like the one you just killed. There were more than a hundred of us prisoners. They used us for labor, foraging parties, and… other things." Her eyes dropped to her hands, which she placed in her lap. Virginia rubbed her back in sympathy.

After a moment, Moira continued. "About thirty of us ran when it got dark. I don't know how many got away. Or how many others might have run after I was gone. I didn't look back."

For the next ten minutes, the members of the group asked their questions as gently as possible while Moira answered the best she could. When they thought they had a good idea of the location and disposition of Barden's camp, Allistor called an end to the meeting. Before Virginia escorted Moira out, Allistor looked directly at her. "I'm going to need you to take the oath. I'm sorry, but I can't let you stay without it. Not that it seems to make a big difference." he added bitterly.

Helen spoke the words for Moira to repeat, which she did without hesitation. And a moment later Moira was off to be reunited with her daughter.

Sam shook his head. "We really need to find that truth spell or whatever. I mean, what's the point of swearing an oath that's bound by the system if there are no consequences when you break it?"

"I wouldn't be so sure about that." Bob mused aloud. Seeing everyone looking his way, he said, "I saw the man fire the shot, and his attempt to jump off the wall. Austin did touch his foot, but I doubt it was enough to flip him the way he did. I think maybe the system stepped in somehow and made sure his fall was fatal."

Every jaw in the room dropped open as they considered Bob's words. Sam was the first to speak. "Well, damn. If that's true… that changes things a bit."

*****

The next morning was spent getting the large number of newcomers settled. Nancy, George, Ramon, Meg, Sam, Helen, and Allistor all set themselves up on one side of a long table. One by one the new folks were brought to sit in front of one of them. They talked briefly about the person's skills, stats, what they'd done before the apocalypse, and what they wanted to do in the new world. Lists were made, with notes next to each name.

There was a wide array of professions among them. Teachers, cops, accountants, construction workers, even a professor of mechanical engineering. To Allistor's surprise and amusement, there was a group of three friends who'd been exotic dancers. They'd asked for space to open a club and continue their professions. Allistor had told them they'd have to wait and see. As a red-blooded young man, he wasn't opposed to the idea, but he wasn't sure the others would approve.

It took most of the day to get through all the interviews, each of Allistor's advisors and himself having to speak with more than a hundred people. There were no breaks for lunch or dinner, they simply had food brought to them as they worked. When it was all done, they had a massive list of skills and desires to sort through.

Worn out from the long day, Allistor decided to stop for the evening, and pick it up again in the morning. They packed up and were about to retire when Nigel sent out an alert.

"Lord Allistor. Several unknown non-human creatures have crossed into my sensor range. They are moving in a seemingly random pattern toward the gate."

With a tired sigh, Allistor ran toward the same wall they'd climbed the night before when Moira appeared. Right behind him were about fifty people with rifles already in hand. As he climbed the stairs, he checked his interface map. There were maybe twenty red dots in a loose cluster moving up toward the gate from the south. While he watched, the nearest dot stopped about a hundred yards out and remained still. There was a howling noise, and the other dots began to close in on the first.

"Canids. Or regular wolves." Allistor said, remembering that he'd told Austin to leave a corpse out there. "Feeding on that ass who shot Moira."

Reaching the top of the wall, he looked in the direction of the dots. The suns had set, but there was enough light from the stars to see a cluster of bodies low to the ground gathered around what he assumed was the body.

Others joined him along the wall, and a few aimed their rifles. Allistor called out. "Hold on, let's do this the smart way. Give me a second." He pulled out his rifle and looked through the scope at the predators. He used *Examine* on several of the beasts.

> **Canid Scavenger**
> **Level 7**
> **Health: 1,900/1,900**

Most of them were between level five and seven. Killing them himself would gain him no experience, and probably only low level loot. Turning to his people, he said, "Listen up. These things are level seven and lower. They're just sitting ducks out there. So, here's what we're going to do. If you're level five or lower, and can hit these things at a hundred yards, raise your hand."

About thirty of the people on the wall with him put hands up. "Okay, the rest of you, I want you to step back from the wall. You with your hands up, step up and take aim." He waited for them to comply, then said, "Alright, you higher level folks, spread out at either end of this group. Let them shoot first. In fact, let them shoot twice. If any of the mobs start to get away, you help take them out. I want our lowest level folks to get a chance to level up. Everybody clear?"

When they all agreed and had arranged themselves properly, he said, "First group, left side fire at the dogs on the left, center on the center, right on the right, got me? I don't want thirty rounds hitting the closest mob. First round on three, then fire as fast as you can. One... two... three!"

The thirty or so people in the first group fired a nearly simultaneous salvo that mowed down about half the canids as Allistor watched through his scope. He heard the sound of more rounds being chambered, and the second burst of shots was more staggered, but not by a lot. These days, everyone was getting used to firing in a hurry.

Almost immediately after the second volley, more shots rang out as the backup group picked off fleeing or wounded canids. All of the red dots had turned to grey, the whole thing lasting maybe twenty seconds. Most of the folks on the wall leveled up, as did several of the survivors throughout the compound. Everyone apparently received experience for a successful defense of the Stronghold.

"All right. You know the drill. Go loot the corpses. Take knives with you, and after they're looted, harvest their hides and their meat. We've got seven hundred plus people to feed here. Between what the system gives you, and what you can harvest manually, we should get at least a few days' worth of meals for everyone."

A few of them looked squeamish, but the regular hunters in the group took charge and led them out. Allistor remained on the wall to watch for any additional threats.

While he waited, he pulled up his own stats sheet to take a look. He hadn't assigned his attribute points since level nine, which seemed like a long time but had only been a few days ago. He now had ten attribute points available to use. His new class selection of *Battlemage* was now displayed, as well as his title as Viscount. Checking over his stats and considering the happenings of the last week or so, he assigned two points each to *Intelligence* and *Will Power*, bringing both up to ten and giving him a decent boost to his mana pool. He dropped two points into *Charisma* as well, figuring he'd need them if he was going to continue to recruit. Because he kept taking damage in fights like the one with the lizard-dog, he added a point each to *Constitution, Strength,* and *Stamina*. He considered adding his final point to *Luck*, but decided to save it for an emergency. He was overall pretty pleased with the updated numbers.

Designation: Viscount Allistor, Giant Killer	Level: 13	Experience: 19,500/210,000
Planet of Origin: UCP 382	Health: 3,100/3,100	Class: Battlemage
Attribute Pts Available: 1	Mana: 1,800	
Intelligence: 10	Strength: 5	Charisma: 5
Adaptability: 6	Stamina: 5	Luck: 3
Constitution: 8	Agility: 3	Health Regen: 230/m
Will Power: 10	Dexterity: 3	Mana Regen: 100/m

Chapter 5

Liberation Through Termination

The morning found Allistor and the leadership back at the conference table. The discussion centered around the information they'd gotten from Moira, who was also in attendance. Allistor started things off.

"We need to deal with Barden's camp today. I was hoping they'd send another wave of fighters here and we could take them from the safety of our walls. But that doesn't seem to be happening, so we need to go after them."

There were murmurs of both support and disagreement among the group leaders. One of them raised a hand. A woman who'd brought in about fifty survivors. Her name, if Allistor remembered correctly, was Julia. "We'll lose a lot of people trying to take them down."

Allistor nodded. "Maybe. Though with the information we have, I think we can devise a strategy that'll minimize our losses. Still, we will probably lose people." He watched her grimace, and saw a few similar looks on other faces. "What's the alternative? We can take them out at a time of our choosing, when we're all together and we outgun them. Or we leave them be, and risk our foraging parties being ambushed when *they have the numbers* and at a time and place *they* choose."

Julia considered for a moment, then nodded her head. Allistor moved on. "Moira says they are set up in a warehouse district about five miles from here. They occupy two large buildings. One is a distribution hub with several semi-trailers parked around it. The other is a building supply warehouse." He motioned for Moira to continue.

She stood up, using a marker to draw on the glass conference room window. "Most of us prisoners were forced to sleep in the truck trailers, where it was easy to keep an eye on us. Twelve or fifteen per trailer. They used some of the lumber to build crude bunk beds inside." she drew as she spoke, making one long box with little 'trailers' sticking out, then another big square box next to it. "Barden lived in a set of offices inside the supply warehouse. The place has solar power and air conditioning. It also has a well for water. About half the guards slept in there as well, and the prisoners that they've been... using."

She paused, and the group let her gather her composure. It was clear from her demeanor that she'd suffered at the hands of the guards. After a few deep breaths, she continued. "The rest of the guards slept in the hub. Mostly in little cubicles they built by standing mattresses upright or stacking boxes. But since you killed Barden and so many of his guards, I'm not sure who sleeps where anymore. There are only about thirty of them left. And I don't know how many prisoners."

Allistor thanked her as she sat down. Taking up the marker, he stood by the window. "Are there any tall buildings nearby?" He drew a big circle around her sketch. "Like within a hundred yards or so?"

Moira nodded. "The water tower is within that range. And there's a nasty old boarded-up building. Used to be a hospital, I think. Barden wanted to use it, but it was so filthy and moldy inside he decided to pass."

A thought struck Allistor. "Moira, why didn't he make his camp a Stronghold? He had enough people, and it sounds like lots of resources."

She shook her head. "Barden was stupid. I mean, he was sneaky and cunning, like he knew how to manipulate people with fear and blackmail. And he was a good judge of character as far as who could be manipulated most easily. But I'm not sure he could even read. I'm positive he never took the time to go through all the tabs and figure out things like Strongholds. I heard one of the guards bitching about him being the leader, saying he was just a dumb cattle-herder from the sticks. The other guard told him to shut up and looked nervous. The next day, both of them disappeared. I don't know if they ran, or somebody reported them and Barden killed them."

Allistor took it all in. He had to be careful what he said next, because none of the other leaders in the room had created Strongholds either, despite having larger groups than he'd started with. He didn't want to offend them or make them feel incompetent.

"Right, well that's good for us. We can put people in the hospital building on the upper floors, assuming they can get up there safely. And we can have a few climb the water tower. From there our people can snipe at the remaining guards in relative safety. I'll go in and 'attack' them, drawing out the guards. Our people are to shoot anyone holding a weapon. And shoot to kill. Any issues with that?"

Every head at the table shook left and right.

"We'll form a ring around the place, let's say three hundred yards out. Our people will be behind cars, trees, buildings, whatever. Anyone who tries to escape that is carrying a weapon, they take down. Those not carrying weapons will be captured and secured. Moira here will then tell us who was working for Barden, and who were just prisoners."

He waited for objections, but there were none. Most of these people had suffered at the hands of Barden's fighters. There were no qualms about repaying them in kind.

"I'll take a force of ten higher level fighters with me. We'll set up an ambush point a hundred yards out or so. I'll go in and draw out the guards, and my team will mow them down. Between the ambush, the overwatch, and the perimeter ring, we should get all of them."

That plan established, he continued on to other business. "I'm not sure how many more people we'll end up with here at this Stronghold, but the crowd is already so large that it'll be hard to manage at this early stage. After Barden's camp is dealt with, I'll be asking for volunteers who want to transfer to either the Warren or the Citadel. There's room at both places, and the smaller groups will be easier to feed and manage. I'll make an announcement at some point, but I thought I'd give you all a heads-up in advance so you can think it over."

Lang raised a hand briefly. "I already talked it over with my people. We want to go back to Cheyenne."

"Great! That's a good start right there. We'll set it up after we get things straight here in Laramie." Allistor gave the man a sincere and thankful smile. He'd been worried that his harsh treatment of Moira the night before might alienate the man and his group.

Allistor pulled out a leather satchel that Ramon had given him. It wasn't a bag of holding, just a simple, large, leather bag filled with scrolls. He began to read the tags attached to the string that bound each one and pass them out.

"Everybody gets one of these healing spells. It's called *Restore* and it'll heal a thousand points of health. I want you to be able to keep your friends and neighbors alive." He made the rounds of the table, handing out the scrolls with the green string. Next, he pulled out a few with a brown string. The label said *Erupt*. "I've got a few spells here that do damage, but they require at least a six in *Intelligence*. Anybody here been working on a caster build?"

Moira raised her hand, as did Virginia, and two of the newcomers. As he handed them *Erupt* and then *Vortex* scrolls, Virginia said, "I'll take these, in case I'm needed. But I'd prefer to be a healer."

"We can never have too many healers." Allistor smiled at her, patting her shoulder as he walked behind her. "I'll introduce you to Amanda as soon as possible. She's got some interesting discoveries to share with you. And any other healers, for that matter."

He passed out a few *Flame Shot* and *Restraint* scrolls as well. Not surprisingly, many of the leaders had invested mainly in *Strength, Stamina, Constitution,* or *Charisma.* Not all of them had the *Intelligence* to cast more than the basic first level spells.

For the next half minute, the room was lit with flash after flash as the folks unrolled and read the scrolls. Allistor watched as they absorbed the information needed to cast the various spells. Some of them made very entertaining faces, including Bob who stuck his tongue out one side of his mouth and furrowed his brows in concentration.

When it was all over, he sent them to round up any of their people who wanted to fight. He was hoping for a hundred shooters – ten to go with him for the ambush, ten more to take up overwatch in the hospital and water tower, and eighty to form the perimeter.

As the new leaders left, Allistor's original gang remained with him in the room. He started with Ramon first. "Anything on the teleport pads?"

Ramon shook his head. "We haven't found any books on teleportation magic yet. But the library is huge, and we still don't know how the information is organized. It doesn't follow any system that we've been able to detect. We did find a mention of the teleport pads in a book about City management." He paused to clear his throat, obviously trying not to smile as he continued. "It… suggests that the one in charge of the city has extensive information available to them via their interface?"

Allistor stopped pacing and looked at his friend. "Are you telling me… to read the directions?" His mouth went slack as Ramon nodded and several of the others chuckled. Allistor opened his interface and went to the Citadel tab, then found a sub-tab for the Teleport Hub. Mentally selecting it, he found pages and pages of stats and information. Closing it again, he said, "Huh. Seems you are correct, sir. I'll get to reading ASAP." Meg snorted, saying, "Typical man. Never reads the instructions."

Nancy changed the subject. "George and I have begun setting up the greenhouse, but it'll take several more days. We've planted a lot of fruit and veggies, and we're coaxing them to grow. In a week or so, we should have enough mature plants going that they can help feed this group on a daily basis. Also, since I increased my skill level to Expert, I can teach the *Grow* spell to people directly, without them having to use a scroll. So I'll share it with a few folks here. This greenhouse is going to be a full-time job for at least three people, maybe more."

George added, "We've had several volunteers. I don't think that will be a problem." He thumped the table a few times, then added, "I don't mean to be pushy, but we've got something else we need to talk about if we're going to feed this many people."

Allistor nodded. "Meat."

"That's right. We can bring some chicks and bunnies here and establish them, but we're getting to the point where we need to talk about herding cattle and sheep."

Helen said, "I have the *Animal Husbandry* skill, and so do at least two of the others we interviewed yesterday. And I talked to one cowboy that I remember."

George nodded. "I talked to two. Then I checked the list. It looks like we have eight here in Laramie that have experience with running cattle. And two who lived on a sheep farm." When he saw Allistor nodding, he kept going. "There are thousands... hell, hundreds of thousands of cattle roaming around out there. At least, there should be. The critters may have got to some of them. We should round them up and make a safe place for them, maybe up on the plateau at the Citadel. And keep at least a few at every Stronghold to breed or to slaughter in case of a siege." George hadn't forgotten being trapped in his own Stronghold by Evan and his men.

"I agree one hundred percent." Allistor was thrilled they'd already put so much thought into it. "We'll make that a priority."

The group spoke for another half hour before Austin showed up to tell them the others had gathered. Allistor led the way outside, and his heart skipped a beat when he saw the gathered fighters. He'd hoped for a hundred. There were easily twice that many. Some were smiling at him, others had grim faces that promised painful retribution to Barden's fighters.

He stepped forward, Helen standing at his right and Fuzzy on his left. "I'm… wow! I want to thank you all for volunteering! I'll leave it to your group leaders to tell you the plan if they haven't already. But I need a team of ten to come with me as a strike force. You need to be at least level 8, and know how to shoot."

Several clusters of men and women along the front row stepped forward. There were two dozen of them. Allistor picked six that had semi-automatic rifles with magazines rather than single shot bolt action rifles. "Since we have so many of you, I'm going to ask that you five…" He pointed to a cluster to his left, "take overwatch at the hospital. And you over here…" he pointed to a group of six, "take the water tower. The rest of you will be a second level of the ambush, let's say twenty yards back from the first group. They'll lay down rapid fire, and you'll take your time to pick off anyone who sticks their heads out to fire back. Any questions?"

When nobody raised a hand, he said, "Excellent. They won't know what hit them!" A mental picture formed in his mind, and he grimaced. "Uhm, speaking of hitting things. For all of you out on the perimeter, please choose your targets carefully. If something goes wrong and the ambush group has to retreat, I don't want them shot by our own people. In fact, can someone please grab some white sheets and start cutting them into strips. We're all going to wear white bands on both arms, so there's no question who's friendly."

Several people ran off to retrieve sheets. While they waited, Allistor added. "This is going to be a tough day. Not so much the fighting, though I'm sure that will be a challenge. But you're going to have to shoot other people today. And do it without mercy or hesitation. Today it's kill or be killed." He paused to let that sink in. "I know from experience, it's not easy to kill other human beings. And I'd prefer not to, especially now. But these are killers, rapists, thieves, and maybe worse. They can't be allowed to live. They can't be allowed to escape, to regroup and return to kill off any more friends or neighbors. Period." He waited again, but nobody voiced an objection.

"If you see someone who's not one of us with a weapon, shoot them. Don't wait to see if they raise the weapon at you. Shoot. Those are my orders. Anyone have any questions?"

"If they're not armed?" a voice from the crowd asked.

"Then you capture them. Nobody passes the perimeter for any reason. I don't care if it's a pathetic looking kid or a kindly old grandma. Nobody passes you. We'll interview those captured, and determine whether they cooperated with Barden, and to what extent."

By the grim looks on their faces, at least some of them had been told what would happen to collaborators. And they were ready to do what was necessary.

Trucks were rounded up, along with every car, bus, and minivan available to them. They even hitched a horse trailer to the back of one of the trucks, and a dozen people packed themselves in there. They rejected a few of the vehicles for having engines that were too loud, but eventually they got everyone situated, and set off. Moira rode up front in the ranger truck with Allistor and several others. They put Fuzzy in the very back end, where he promptly fell asleep.

As requested, Moira took them to within about a mile of the camp. There, they parked the vehicles and began to walk. When they got within a quarter mile of the camp, Allistor halted them again. He whispered to them, walking up and down the line. They didn't know how far out the guards might be stationed, and didn't want to lose the element of surprise. He directed his team to follow him, pointed the overwatch teams toward the targets, and sent the perimeter teams out in wide circles in both directions. Since there were too many of them for a raid, he invited ten of them to his party, so that they could at least see each other on the map. That way he'd have a good idea when everyone was in position. He also gave them a warning that if they were spotted before the attack, to kill as quickly and silently as possible. Knives or arrows, whatever.

With that, he took his group and set off. Helen and Fuzzy remained with him as they moved down an alley to a back road that ran in the general direction of the camp. Moira was there as well, though she remained in the back.

They moved slowly, having plenty of time as they needed to wait for the perimeter teams to move all the way around the other side. Allistor was about to step out into an intersection when Fuzzy gave a low growl. The bear's wet nose was in the air, snuffling away at the breeze. He shook his head, then looked upward.

Leaning against the nearest wall, Allistor slowly peaked around the corner. Looking upward, he spotted a man sitting in a lawn chair on a patio half a block away. He had a rifle sitting across his lap, and he was drinking something from a bottle.

Leaning back behind cover, Allistor stowed his rifle and pulled out the bow he'd used against the octopoid right before meeting Fuzzy. He set the quiver down, pulling two arrows. Handing one to Helen, he nocked the other and took a deep breath. Leaning slowly out beyond the wall, he drew the string back and took aim. When he thought he was dead on the man's chest, he loosed the arrow. He immediately held up his hand and Helen handed him the second arrow even as he watched the first slam into the man's chest. It wasn't a fatal shot, and the impact knocked him backward out of his chair. Allistor couldn't see him for a moment, but he drew the second arrow and took aim.

He heard the man groaning, the sound seeming like a shout to Allistor's ears, and he began to panic.

A second later the man's movements pushed the lawn chair aside, and Allistor had a clear view. He aimed and loosed, the arrow flying below the rail and straight into the side of the man's chest below his arm. It sunk deep, all but the fletching disappearing. Allistor watched him go limp and fall face first onto the patio concrete.

Helen patted him on the back as she stepped past him and moved across the open space toward the house. She found an open door and went inside as the others followed her across. They waited outside, hugging the side of the house and scanning the area. A minute or so later, Helen whispered, "He's dead. Heads up." right before she rolled the corpse off the edge. It landed with a thud, and Allistor saw his second arrow had gone all the way through the man's chest, puncturing both lungs at least, and possibly his heart.

He bent down and looted the man, then pulled the arrows free. No point in wasting them. Helen hopped down to join them, and they moved on. Allistor kept a careful eye out, but also one eye on Fuzzy as the bear sniffed the air.

It was Moira who spotted the second guard a couple minutes later. He was two blocks away and downwind, so Fuzzy hadn't caught his scent. She only noticed him because he coughed as she passed by an alley, the last in line. By the time she managed to get Allistor's attention, they were another half block away. He doubled back, leaving the others behind cover, and she pointed the man out. He had his back to them, standing outside a retail office with a broken storefront. There was a pair of binoculars around his neck, and he kept raising them to look at something, then dropping them again.

Allistor left Moira there and crept forward. The suns were high in the sky, and there weren't a lot of shadows, so he tried to move quickly while the man was looking through the glasses, then hold still or move very slowly when he put them down.

It took him a solid three minutes to creep close enough that he was sure he could hit the man. He didn't want to risk needing two shots again, so he'd moved to within fifty feet. Raising the bow, he nocked and pulled, then released. The arrow sped true, slamming into the back of the man's head and embedding itself deeply. The guard fell forward, his hands not coming up to break his fall, which Allistor considered a good sign. He dropped the bow and ran forward, equipping a hunting knife as he went. The man didn't even twitch as he approached, but Allistor still rammed the knife into his back and through his heart to be sure.

Skill Level Up! Your Archery skill has increased by +1

He looted the man, getting a few hundred klax, the binoculars, and a deck of playing cards. He picked up the man's weapon, and unhooked a holster with a 9mm from his belt. Then he lifted the body and tossed it inside the storefront where it wouldn't easily be seen.

He walked quickly but quietly back to rejoin Moira, then the others. They continued until she put a hand on his arm and pointed. Leaning very close, she whispered, "That's the hub."

He followed her finger and saw the long building about a block away. There were several trailers docked at various loading bays just as she'd described. He saw a few people with weapons milling around in ones and twos, as well as several people cooking or working at various menial jobs.

Looking left and right, he backed up several steps. Whispering to his group, he said, "This is as good as any place. Spread out and find cover. Make sure you've got a route to retreat if necessary. When the time comes, I'm going to bring them straight down this alley."

He watched as his people spread out. A couple went into the buildings on either side of them and disappeared. Three more took up positions behind vehicles. The secondary group moved back a block and disappeared behind cover as well. Helen took Fuzzy and went behind a dumpster. After a minute or so, Allistor caught a wave from one of the ones that had gone inside. She was up on the second floor, her rifle barrel pushing out an open window.

He studied his map, watching as the green dots of his party leaders moved around ahead of him. The one assigned to the water tower was in place and not moving. The group he sent to the hospital were in the right general area, but still moving. He figured they were in the building, trying to get upstairs. The perimeter groups were nearly in place, only three of the dots still moving, and they were already well past the camp, closing the circle.

He waited another five long minutes until all the dots were in place and had stopped moving. Taking a deep breath, he stood upright and walked forward. He almost felt the shooters behind him tense up as he moved closer to the camp. Targeting the nearest of the guards, a man holding a shotgun, he cast *Restraint,* causing the man to seize up. A second later he cast *Mind Spike* on a second guard. That man screamed and fell to the floor, causing several others to gather around him, asking what was wrong. Allistor stopped and crouched down in the shade of an office awning, raising his bow and putting an arrow into the chest of the man still frozen by *Restraint.* Then he began casting *Flame Shot,* holding the spell in his hand as it grew into a larger and larger ball. Five seconds later he hurled it at the group of guards watching their comrade squirm and scream on the floor.

The fireball struck, blasting three of them off their feet and doing burn damage to all five of them. The screaming intensified, and Allistor fired another arrow into the crowd. When that didn't reveal his position, he put away the bow and took out his shotgun. Running forward, he raised it to his shoulder and put a round into the gut of one of the guards on the ground. He quickly pumped another round into the chamber and fired again. This time a man's head exploded.

Finally, somebody pointed in his direction and shouted. Allistor turned and bolted back the way he'd come, running right past his people as shots began to ring out and impacts blasted away bits of brick and glass around him. He crouched down as best he could as he ran, going another half block before ducking around the corner.

Breathing hard and feeling a massive adrenaline rush, he laughed to himself. "I just LoS'd a bunch of humans. Let's see if it works."

Another couple deep breaths and he poked his head around the corner. There were half a dozen guards running after him, and two more of the ones he'd injured firing at him from one of the loading bays. He stepped out and fired again, hitting the arm of one of the runners before ducking back. He was about to shout for his people to fire, but they beat him to it. Shots echoed down the alley at him, followed by screams. He looked around the corner to find all six of the men down. His people had already shifted fire, and Allistor watched as the other two guards went down.

Running back up to their position, he could now hear shots from near and far. It sounded like a TV gun battle. Concerned, he checked his map and saw that all ten of his dots were still green. There was shouting and screaming from inside the building ahead, and visions of the guards killing prisoners invaded his thoughts.

"I'm going in. It sounds like they're killing people. You guys hold here."

"No way." Helen answered, getting to her feet and moving forward ahead of him. Two of the others got up and followed as well. Allistor motioned for the rest to stay in place, and they obeyed. He dashed across the open space with Helen and the others, hugging the wall next to the open dock where they'd just killed the guards. When nobody emerged after a few seconds, he dashed up the metal stairs and into the building.

Instantly regretting the move, he was temporarily blind in the dark space. He crouched down and waited for his eyes to adjust, searching for any movement or signs of guns. As his pupils widened and he was able to see better, he found a score or more people lying on the ground, staring in fear at him and his people.

"Where are the guards?" he called out to nobody in particular, scanning the floor area. It was a huge open space with twenty-foot high ceilings and piles of goods stacked here and there. Allistor felt extremely exposed, and moved to crouch next to a stack of wooden crates. Helen and the others all moved to different areas of cover, their weapons ready.

A man sat up, holding both hands in the air in the classic 'surrender' pose. "I... I think you killed them all." He pointed to the dead guards on the floor by the bay opening.

Allistor shouted, "Get back down! Stay there till we tell you to move." He noted that the sound of gunfire was fading rapidly. Only an occasional shot was heard. A single woman screamed somewhere on the other side of the building, and Allistor got up to move. He looked at Helen and said, "Get Moira in here. I need to know who's who." She nodded and stepped back outside, shouting for Moira.

Allistor left his people there and moved across the floor. He cast *Barrier* in front of himself, hoping to catch any bullets flying his way. As he moved around mattress walls and stacks of boxes, he found more people laying on the floor. Some were simply scared, but others were bleeding, or dead. One woman frantically pointed toward an office at the back, saying, "He took her. The little girl. He took her!"

Allistor ran toward the office, no longer caring whether he was exposed. The office door was open, and he could see that the room was empty. Another door at the back was also open, so he moved through the office to stand next to it. A quick look through the door nearly earned him a bullet to the head. He heard the round whiz past him and strike the door. A rough male voice shouted, "I'll scramble this girl's brains! I mean it!"

Allistor dropped to a sitting position and took a couple deep breaths. His heart was racing, and he could hear his own pulse in his ears. His hands were actually shaking with adrenaline, or fear, or both.

One more breath, and he mumbled, "Screw it." before leaning out into the doorway just above floor level. He saw a man walking backward holding a pistol that was pointed at the doorway even as he gripped a little girl by her hair with his other hand.

The man saw Allistor and began to adjust his aim, but he was too slow. *Mind Spike* blasted into his brain, and he let go of both the gun and the girl as he gripped his skull with both hands and screamed. Allistor waited a few seconds for the girl to crawl free, then put a slug through the man's chest. When he hit the ground, Allistor got to his feet and put another slug in the man to be sure.

He walked out the door and went over to the girl, who was curled into a ball and crying. He was just bending down to pick her up when he felt a tug at his back, followed by blinding pain. Falling down, he turned to look behind him. The woman who'd pointed him toward the man he'd just killed was standing in the doorway with a pistol in hand. A smug look on her face, she shouted, "Fool!" and pulled the trigger again. This time the round hit Allistor's arm, dropping his health bar down below twenty percent. He desperately cast *Mind Spike* on the woman, then *Erupt* on the ground in front of her. A stone spike burst up from the ground and impaled the woman through the gut. She screamed briefly, then stopped as she went limp and her body slid down the spike.

Allistor cast *Restore* on himself as he fished a healing potion out of his inventory. He gulped the potion down, then cast another heal on himself a second later. The combination brought his health back up to full. There was a grinding in his back, and he thought he felt his shoulder blade shift. He just lay on the ground for a moment, next to the crying child, and dealt with the pain.

Helen and Fuzzy came out the door a minute or so later, Fuzzy dashing forward to sniff at Allistor's back and lick it. The appearance of the bear that seemed, from her angle, to be eating Allistor caused the girl to scream even louder, which in turn scared Fuzzy. The bear retreated as Allistor and Helen tried to calm and comfort the girl.

More gunshots rang out in the direction of the other warehouse. Allistor got to his feet and lifted his shotgun. His mana was still over fifty percent, and his health was full. He took a moment to load a few more shells into his weapon, then turned to Helen. "Can you take her back to the others?" Helen nodded reluctantly, taking the girl back through the door. Fuzzy elected to follow Allistor.

They stepped through an open door, and the first thing Allistor saw were four bodies on the floor about twenty feet away. One held a shotgun in a dead hand, a long kitchen knife protruding from his neck. The other three had gunshot wounds. Two were clearly dead, but the third was still breathing. Allistor cast a heal on her, then another. She groaned and rolled over. "Did I get him?"

she asked, looking toward the dead guard. When she saw him staring blankly at the ceiling, she smiled. "Bastard."

Allistor crouched down, helping her to sit up. Fuzzy licked her bloody face, causing her to jerk back and scream. Allistor calmed her, as best he could. "It's okay, that's Fuzzy. He's friendly. It's okay." The woman eventually calmed, and Allistor asked, "How many more guards in here?"

She shook her head. "Not many. There were only five or six when we heard the shots. I saw at least two of them run outside before we attacked this one." She looked at her two dead comrades, and tears filled her eyes. "That was maybe not the smartest move."

"You're alive. Focus on that for now. Which way did the other guards go?"

"Upstairs." She pointed to a metal staircase that ran upward then doubled back and reached all the way to the ceiling. "They went up on the roof."

Allistor sighed. "Okay. I want you to round up the other prisoners and take them out that door." He pointed to the door he'd just entered. "I want you to call out for Helen as you do, so that my people don't shoot you. Can you do that?"

The woman nodded, and he helped her to her feet. She reached down and pulled the knife from the dead guard's throat, then looked at him oddly. A moment later she bent down and looted him, and Allistor realized she'd seen the 'lootable' glow on his body. "Cool." was all she said.

He left her to it, climbing the stairs with his faithful bear cub at his heels. Fuzzy snorted a few times and gave a small growl, as if he thought this was some kind of game. Allistor just shook his head and kept climbing. With his increased strength and stamina, the climb was no trouble, and he wasn't even breathing hard when he reached the top.

There was a landing with a metal security door. The door was closed, and Allistor really, really didn't want to open it. A quick look at his interface told him his mana was up to two thirds, so he could cast several spells if needed.

Putting his back to the wall next to the door, he reached out slowly and turned the knob. The moment he did, two rounds impacted the door from the other side. He flung the door open, and two more shots rang out. Fuzzy squealed and fell over on the stairs where he'd been standing. Allistor realized too late that the bear had been in full view of the open door. He cast a heal on Fuzzy, then jerked his head around so he could see outside.

He cast *Mind Spike* on the first person he saw before jerking his head back. A single shot was fired this time, and it pinged against the door. Leaning out again, he cast *Restraint* on the other guard. The man froze, and Allistor stepped into the doorway. He quickly put a slug into the gut of the frozen guard, then a second. The remaining guard was writhing around on the ground, his gun tossed aside.

Allistor turned and cast another heal on Fuzzy. It didn't seem necessary, as his little buddy was already on his feet and walking out the door. The bear growled as he walked up to the living guard. He turned to look at

Allistor, who said, "Do your thing, buddy. One of these two bastards shot you."

Fuzzy gave his best bear cub roar and bit down on the man's throat. The screaming ceased when he jerked his head and ripped away flesh and vocal cord. The guard choked to death on his own blood even as Fuzzy chewed on his flesh. Allistor left his bear to his meal and walked over to the edge of the roof.

He didn't hear any more gunshots, so he looked up toward the hospital building across the street. He waved a hand, and received waves in return. A voice called out, "All clear as far as we can see!"

Another voice from the water tower shouted, "Clear here too. We count thirteen dead guards! Counting those two you just took out!"

Allistor did some math in his head. Thirteen dead out here. Two scouts, six in the ambush, three more in the dock. The man and woman by the little girl, the one with the knife in his throat. Twenty seven total. Moira had thought there were maybe thirty left. He shouted as loudly as he could so that both overwatch positions could hear him. "I get twenty-seven total, then! Keep an eye out, there may be a few more!"

Allistor paced around the edge of the roof, scanning the streets and alley below for any movement. He briefly considered going back down and searching the warehouse, but an idea struck him.

He opened his interface, found the Outpost tab, and tried to claim the warehouse. The message he received made him smile.

You have conquered an enemy camp by eliminating one hundred percent of enemy forces. Do you wish to claim this structure as an Outpost? Yes/No

Allistor clicked *Yes* and the usual golden light surrounded him. He didn't add any frills, as he was in a hurry. Instead he let the system do its thing, then called out, "Nigel! Can you hear me?"

"Of course, Lord Allistor. Congratulations on your victory, and the new Outpost."

"Thank you, Nigel. Please give me loudspeaker. Full volume."

"Ready when you are, Lord Allistor."

Allistor shouted to add to the volume. "Attention, perimeter team! The warehouse buildings are secure! Work your way to me. Check every building, every car, every bush! Do not let anyone past you! Each of you give me one shot if you can hear me."

All around him single shots rang out. He smiled and took a seat on an air duct that ran across the roof. The sun-heated metal burned his butt some, but he didn't care.

He tried to avoid looking at Fuzzy as the bear mauled his victim's face. Helen arrived, along with the other two who had followed him into the building. One of the men saw what Fuzzy was up to and lost his lunch. The other chuckled, and said, "Right on, Fuzzy bear."

Allistor looted the two bodies, leaving their weapons for the others to pick up. Calling Fuzzy away from his meal, they all walked back down the long stairway. His primary ambush team were standing around a group of about twenty survivors sitting on the floor. As Allistor approached, another group of twelve walked in, escorted by the backup ambush team. They joined the first group sitting on the floor, and Moira pointed to one of them, saying something to the fighter next to her.

Allistor moved up to her other side. "Something specific about that man?"

Moira jumped slightly, not having heard him approach. "Yes. I never saw him with a gun, but he worked for Barden. And he took full advantage of the... spoils." Moira pointed to a dead woman on the floor across the room. "He raped that woman, and at least one other that I don't see here."

Allistor motioned for the man to get to his feet. "Is this true?"

The man stammered, wringing his hands together as he spoke. "I... I didn't want to work for him! He made me! Said I could do what he said, or die. I didn't have a choice!"

Allistor's growl was nearly as low as Fuzzy's. "You didn't have a choice not to rape women?"

"No! I mean, he made me. I..." The man dropped his hands, hanging his head in resignation. "I had a choice. I just... I thought that's how things were going to be from now on. The strong make the rules. I wanted to be one of the strong, not one of the victims."

Allistor pointed to a spot away from the others. "Go stand there." As the man complied, with two rifles pointed at him, Allistor turned to Moira. "Any others?"

115

She shook her head. "As far as I know, all of these people were prisoners. Some of them were on work crews with me. A few others I saw out foraging at gunpoint."

Allistor surveyed the group. "How about you? Any of you see anyone in this crowd that worked for Barden in some way? Other than at gunpoint?"

A man near the back stood up. He pointed down at a woman in a sun dress near the center of the group. "She shared Barden's bed. I saw her going in and out of his quarters willingly enough. There were no guards escorting her."

All eyes went to the woman, who began to cry. Allistor motioned her forward. She reluctantly got to her feet and stepped around the others until she stood in front of him. "Is what he claims the truth?"

She nodded her head, but when she spoke she said, "He took my little boy. Said as long as I did what he wanted, Jeremy wouldn't be hurt. Barden let me see him every three days for an hour." she whimpered, tears rolling down her face.

Allistor looked around, not seeing any small boys. "And where is your son now?"

She shook her head, sobbing now. "I don't knowww…"

"Sit back down. We'll see if we can find him." The woman dropped to the floor where she stood, hugging herself and rocking back and forth as she cried. Allistor took a step back, uncomfortable with her proximity.

"Anybody else?" He looked at the group. All the heads were shaking 'no' or not moving at all. "Alright. Let's deal with this quickly. You survivors need to know that we think we've killed every one of Barden's people now. You're all free to leave, or to join us. I'll talk to you about that a bit later. We have these two people here who cooperated in one way or another with Barden."

He moved over to the man and motioned for him to get up. "What should be his penalty for multiple rapes?"

There were multiple responses that ranged from "Shoot him!" to "Death!" to one woman's vehement "Cut his nuts off and feed them to him!"

Allistor waited for the demands to die down, then asked everyone in the room, prisoners and his people alike. "Any one of you object to executing this man?"

No one spoke up.

The man began to try and negotiate, saying he'd leave and never come back. As Allistor took hold of his arm and began to march him toward the door, he switched to begging. "Please! I can do better. I'm sorry! I didn't mean to… I mean, I didn't want to…" As they reached the door, Allistor pushed the man ahead of him with his left hand, drawing a 9mm with his right. Without ceremony, he raised the weapon and shot the man in the back of the head. The body fell to the pavement outside, and Allistor looted him before stepping back in.

You have completed a hidden quest: Punish the Wicked!

For eliminating the murderer Barden and those who committed crimes in his name, and for the

117

unflinching execution of Justice, you have been awarded the title "Vindicator". Reward: 100,000 klax. Vindicator's Seal. Experience points awarded: 85,000

At the same time the message popped up on his interface, he also saw a large number of Fame Points awarded, and a lesser number of Infamy Points, he assumed from a different faction. Not for the first time he wished he knew how the Fame Points system worked and who was awarding them. He had a lot to learn before the year was through.

Taking out the Vindicator's Seal, which had been deposited in his inventory, he *Examined* it.

Vindicator's Seal
This item is awarded only to those who show a willingness to serve Justice. Like all Seals, it is bound to the bearer upon receipt and cannot be stolen or removed, even in death. Attributes: The Seal grants +2 to Will Power, +2 to Charisma, and +1 to Luck. In addition, the Seal may be used to verify the veracity of statements made by any accused you have detained.

Allistor saw there was a new slot on the avatar in his interface. It glowed with a pulsing purple light. He put the Seal back into his inventory, then mentally moved it up to place it in the new slot. As soon as he did, his stat sheet updated with the attribute increases. "Sweet!" he mumbled to himself. Nothing like an epic reward just for doing what he considered to be the right thing.

Half an hour later the perimeter group had pushed all the way in to the warehouse, bringing with them another fifty or so prisoners they had rounded up outside. Among them was Jeremy, the little boy Barden had been holding hostage, who instantly ran to his mother's arms. The group leaders he'd invited to his party all gathered around to report. The fighting he'd heard outside the building had involved some casualties. In all, they reported seventeen prisoners had been killed, all by Barden's men. Two of Allistor's people had been killed in the battle, and six others injured. Helen immediately went to help heal the injured, stopping Allistor as he tried to join her. "You have things to deal with here." was all she said.

Allistor turned to the newcomers and went through the same process as before, but neither Moira nor anyone in the crowd identified any more collaborators. Helen returned after just a few minutes, nodding her head. Newly healed survivors filed in behind her.

A quick head count showed Allistor there were eighty-five prisoners total, including Moira. He asked his people to share food and water with all of them, handing out all of the jerky he and Helen had left in their inventories. Then, he spent ten minutes while they ate giving them 'the speech' about the workings of the new game-like world, his experiences, and the establishing of the Citadel and Strongholds. He described to them the world he wanted to rebuild, then asked them to join up.

"If you'd like to join us, to help us build our community, you are welcome. You'll have the choice to stay here in Laramie, or move to the Citadel, or choose one of the other Strongholds. If you join us, you *must* take the oath of loyalty. Breaking that oath might result in your death."

Allistor scanned the faces sitting in front of him, looking for any open hostility or fear. Based on recent events, he was pretty sure at least one of the people here was loyal to Barden, or since he and his men were dead, at least hostile to Allistor. He continued to watch as he asked, "Any questions?"

"Will you be paying us to work?" a woman with a small child in her lap asked.

Allistor considered that for a moment. "No, at least not initially. During this first year I'll be providing food and housing, and a safe place to sleep. I think you'll all agree those things have some value?" The woman and most of the others nodded. "You'll be given the chance to pursue a trade, whether that's crafting or foraging, fighting, farming or cattle herding, teaching, healing, babysitting, whatever. To start with, we'll be on a barter system. But you'll also have the opportunity to be earning klax, either from kills and dungeons, or by selling your crafting items. And for those that take up support professions for the community, like teaching the children, cooking, or cleaning, we'll work out some kind of payment."

His face darkened slightly. "I will not tolerate any slackers. If you've lived this long, you're not weak, and hopefully not stupid. You're survivors. You likely have skills we can make use of, or can learn some new ones. I'll provide some limited training to start with. We're on the knife's edge right now, surviving but not yet thriving. There is no welfare system, no free ride. You work, you contribute, or you get put out. Understood?"

Allistor thought every head in the group was nodding. He looked to Helen and motioned to the group.

She stepped forward and said, "If you wish to join us, take a knee and repeat after me. If you don't wish to join us, go stand over there." She pointed to one side of the big open space. Everyone got up off their butts and took a knee. A short time later the usual light swirled around and into them. But Allistor noticed two individuals around whom no light appeared.

Pointing, he said, "You! And You! Stand up."

The man and woman he'd pointed to got to their feet, and Allistor raised his shotgun. The moment he did, every one of his people raised theirs as well. The man spit on the floor, smirking at Allistor. The woman just looked terrified.

"You two didn't take the oath. Did you think we just wouldn't notice?"

The woman shook her head frantically, holding both hands up in a patting motion. Then she began to sign rapidly with her hands. When she was done, she pointed to her mouth and shook her head.

Allistor lowered his weapon, aware that the other couple hundred guns in the room were more than enough safety. Motioning for the woman to approach, he called out, "Any of you know sign language?"

Richard, who was standing close by, offered, "I don't, but I'm pretty sure she just said she can't speak. So she wasn't able to take the oath."

Allistor and everyone else in the room just stared at him. He blushed slightly as Helen said, "Thank you for that, captain obvious." earning a few chuckles.

Nobody in the building knew sign language, but Allistor thought he remembered seeing it on the list of skills from their interviews. He looked at the woman, now standing in front of him. When he spoke, he enunciated clearly. "Can you read lips?"

The woman shook her head, then pointed to her ears and gave him a thumbs-up. Surprised, he asked, "You can hear, but you can't speak?"

She nodded once, and smiled at him. She had a lovely smile.

"You heard the oath Helen recited. Do you remember it all?"

Again, she nodded, and flashed him that smile. He couldn't help but return one of his own. Helen chuckled behind him.

"If you agree to the terms of the oath, please nod your head for me."

She nodded, and gave him a double thumbs-up, which she then converted into a double-guns gesture accompanied by a wink. The light binding her to the oath appeared and was absorbed into her.

Allistor said, "I'd say that was a pretty emphatic yes. Welcome." He and several others chuckled as he held out a hand and she shook it. "When we have some time, we'll find you a translator or some paper and a pencil, and we can have a little talk. Starting with your name."

She nodded, then went to sit down with the others. Allistor turned to the man who was still standing. "You have issues with your voice as well?"

The man spit on the floor, narrowly missing another man who cursed at him. "Nope. I speak just fine." The man was maybe twenty years old, and the smug look on his face made Allistor want to punch him.

"Then would you like to share with us the reason you didn't take the oath?"

The man shrugged, and his punchability factor rose even higher. "I'm not gonna swear my life to you or anyone else. I thought I'd just blend in with the crowd, get some food and a good night's sleep, then see where things went from there."

"At least he's honest." Richard said. "He's a dick, and I have the urge to whup his ass, but he's honest."

"Maybe, maybe not." Helen observed. "I believe he doesn't want to swear. But I think he would have stayed and mooched off of us as long as he could. Maybe let us waste a few scrolls on him, give him a weapon, eat our food until he was ready to screw us somehow."

Allistor looked to the man. "What's your name?"

"Kyle." the man practically spat the word out. Allistor waited a moment for a last name, then shrugged.

"Okay Kyle. I don't like you. Everything about you screams 'asshole'." There were grunts of agreement from both groups of people. Apparently, he hadn't made a good impression among the prisoners either. "But as I have said, every human life is precious to me. So, I'll give you a rare second chance. Swear the oath, and hold to it, and you'll be welcomed among us."

Somehow the smirk on Kyle's face intensified. Allistor had to restrain himself from punching it. "And if I don't?"

"Then my statement from earlier was probably wrong, and you're too stupid to live. The oath the others swore is simple, and basically only keeps you from screwing over your fellow humans. Your refusal to do that says a lot about you. So I rescind my offer. You no longer have the option to join us. Leave. Now."

Allistor pointed to the door.

"Leave? And go where?" Kyle's voice became whiny, making him even more annoying. Allistor found himself wondering if the guy somehow had a negative *Charisma* number.

"Don't know, don't care." Allistor answered. "This Outpost belongs to us. You have chosen not to be one of us. You may not remain here. And as the day is quickly passing, I suggest you go find shelter somewhere. Preferably far away." Several people clapped, and somebody in the crowd whistled.

"You can't do that! I lived here before you. I claim this place!"

Allistor just laughed, pointing at the door again. "You have ten seconds to leave, or I will declare you an enemy of the state, and let Fuzzy eat your face."

One of the two men who had been up on the roof with him, the one who had puked, called out. "Trust me, you don't want that. Damn that was nasty." His buddy elbowed him in the gut, gently.

124

Cursing under his breath, Kyle started toward the door. As he passed a crate with several looted guns sitting on it, he reached down to take one. Allistor cast *Restraint* on him, and he froze with his hand just inches from a rifle.

"Those are our guns. I didn't say you could take one. Did you just try to steal from me?" He turned to Fuzzy, who was already looking up at him with a cubby grin on his furry face. "Fuzzy, escort this man out of here, please." He watched as his grizzly cub walked up and thoroughly sniffed the still frozen man, then growled.

"Kyle, Fuzzy will not hurt you as long as you keep walking." Allistor warned.

A few seconds later when the stun wore off, instead of walking away, Kyle made a grab for the weapon. He took hold of the rifle and thrust it at Fuzzy, clubbing him in the head with the rifle butt. The cub's health bar dropped a small amount. Fuzzy yelped in pain, then roared. He lunged forward even as Kyle was turning the weapon to aim it at him. Clamping his jaws down on one wrist, he shook his head back and forth. Even as a juvenile, a grizzly has impressive neck musculature. The action snapped the man's wrist, causing him to scream. He dropped the rifle and began to try and run, pulling at his injured arm with his other hand, attempting to get free. "Stop! Stop! I'll go! Call him off!"

Fuzzy pulled back, and blood began to spray from the man's wounds. When Kyle uttered a wordless scream and tugged even harder, Fuzzy let go. The man stumbled backward, falling on his butt and crying as he tried to stop the bleeding by clamping his hand over the wound. Fuzzy

125

stepped forward and placed a paw on his chest, turning to look at Allistor.

Before giving the bear permission to eat Kyle's face, Allistor turned to the crowd. "You all witnessed what happened here. I can let Fuzzy finish him, or heal him and send him away. I'll let all of you decide." He paused as Kyle shouted something angry and unintelligible.

"Raise your hand if you think I should let him go." Allistor looked around, and a good number of hands went up. He thought it was probably a majority.

"Looks like it's your lucky day, asshole." Allistor turned back to the prone and crying man. He cast *Restore* on the man, and watched his bleeding slow as Fuzzy stepped back.

When the wound had healed, and the man stopped weeping, Allistor said, "Get on your feet."

Kyle sullenly stood, glaring at Allistor with open hatred now. But for once he kept his mouth shut. Allistor pointed to the door again. "Not only are you a complete dick, but you attacked my bear when you had the option to just walk away in peace. For that, I declare you an enemy." There were murmurs among his people as a red dot appeared on their interfaces. From the zoned-out gaze, he guessed that Kyle was suddenly seeing a few hundred red dots in front of him as well. "You will leave here right now. You will walk as far away as you can. Or run. Ride a bike. I don't care. If I or any of my people come across you again, you will be shot on sight, and if you survive the gunshot you will be fed to Fuzzy. In gamer terms, you are now KoS to my people. That includes all of my people, everywhere. So I wouldn't head toward Cheyenne if I were you. Or Denver, because I'm headed there next. In fact, any Stronghold you see within a couple hundred miles of here is likely to be mine, so you should avoid them all. Go find a cave to hide in, and think about how you got yourself in this position. Or, not."

Allistor turned his back on the man, and Fuzzy growled menacingly. There was the sound of rapid footsteps, then the word, "Asshole!" drifted in from somewhere outside, nearly drowned out by the applause inside.

Moira stepped up and said, "That guy was a total ass-hat from day one. Good riddance."

Allistor shook his head, still angry but also sad. "I hate doing that. But that asshole practically demanded it. I tried to give him a chance, more than once. Waste of a human life." He suspected Kyle would ignore his warnings and try to get into one of his properties at some point. If he survived that long. But Allistor couldn't have that kind of toxicity among his people.

The rest of the day was spent rounding up as many vehicles as possible to transport everyone back to the Stadium. While folks went out foraging for vehicles and supplies, Allistor took a little time to beef up the Outpost. At first, he considered abandoning it, since it had served its purpose. But with all the useful materials and supplies gathered there, he couldn't resist keeping it. So he put a wall around both warehouses, added in water, electricity, and the remote gate access.

As he was taking an informal inventory of all the materials, Bob approached him. "Got a minute?"

"Of course. What's up?"

"I'm looking at all this building material, and I can't help but think of things we could build with it. I have the *Carpentry* skill, and *Builder* as well. I did some puttering around when this all started, finished building a shed I'd started in the back yard. I've always loved building things, especially out of wood."

Allistor opened his interface and gave Bob full access to the Outpost, then designated him as one of his Advisors, giving him access to all the facilities. Bob smiled as he saw the notifications pop up on his interface.

"You are officially my Superintendent of Building Stuff." Allistor patted the man on the shoulder. "We'll come up with a fancy title later."

Bob chuckled. "I like that one. Superintendent of Building Stuff. Virginia will be so proud." He looked around. "If you don't mind, I'd like to spend the night here. Maybe leave me a few volunteers to secure the place? That way I can go through everything and make an inventory-"

He paused as Nigel's voice came to them from out of nowhere. *"Pardon me, Lord Allistor, Superintendent Bob. But I have compiled a complete inventory of every item in this facility, as well as all the others. I can provide a verbal accounting, or display a list directly to your interfaces. If you create a Pedestal at this facility, I can also offer a three-dimensional holo-display of the grounds and the inventory items in their current location."*

"Ha! I like this Nigel fella!" Bob grinned at Allistor. "That would have taken me days to accomplish. Just the list, I mean. A map would take a week."

Allistor quickly led Bob to one of the offices in a corner of the building. He used his interface to raise a pedestal, then showed Bob how it worked, asking Nigel to display both the inventory list and the 3D map. Bob played with it for few minutes, shaking his head. "Maybe this new world's not all bad. Can I access this same display back home?"

Allistor smiled at his use of the word, 'home'. Having this man that he already trusted claiming the Stadium as his home gave Allistor a surge of hope. "I'll raise a pedestal in the conference room so you can access it. There will be one at every facility."

"Then I don't need to stay here tonight." He clapped his hands together. "Wait till I tell Virginia about all this!" He paused, then added, "It might still be a good idea to leave some guards here. Like, all the time. So this stuff doesn't get stolen."

Allistor agreed. An hour later when nearly everyone was gathered together near a whole fleet of vehicles outside, he asked for volunteers. Surprisingly, several dozen of the prisoners offered to stay. As did some of the fighters he'd brought with him.

Jeremy's mother, whose name Allistor had forgotten to ask, approached him shyly. "Thank you, for sparing me and for finding Jeremy." She stepped forward and gave him a brief and awkward hug. "We'd like to stay here for a little while, if it's safe." She looked out through the nearby loading dock door at the new wall outside. "It is safe, right? Even outside the building?" She looked at Allistor, her eyes questioning. "Like, even the trailers?"

Allistor was intrigued by the odd question. "Nothing will spawn inside the walls, if that's what you're asking... I'm sorry, I forgot to ask your name before." Several of the semi trailers were now within that perimeter.

She nodded, her face relaxing considerably. "I'm Cindy. It's just that... you know they had most of us sleeping in the trailers?" She waited for him to nod. "Well the other day one of those octopoid things spawned inside a trailer. There were a dozen people asleep in there. The screaming..." She gulped visibly. "By the time the guards unlocked the doors and let them out, there were only four still alive."

Allistor reached out and set a hand on her shoulder. "You sure you wouldn't feel safer at the Stadium?"

She shook her head. "When Barden first captured us, it was Jeremy, my husband, and me. We had actually been camped here with a few others when he decided he wanted this place. My husband was killed in the fight. We... we buried him in a small yard not too far from here. I'd like to stay close to him a little longer, if that's okay. Visit him once in a while."

"Of course. You're welcome to stay here as long as this place remains. I can't guarantee that'll be forever."

She nodded. "That's fine. Thank you." She hugged him again, more warmly this time, then took hold of Jeremy and walked away."

They worked out who would be staying, made sure to leave enough food and other supplies to last at least a week, as well as a healthy supply of weapons and ammunition, then rounded up everyone and everything and hit the road.

The return trip was much faster, as they could drive the whole distance and not worry about stealth. Someone had found a working Mack semi truck and they'd been able to hook up one of the trailers and fill it with both supplies and people. Still, darkness was falling as the Stadium gates opened to receive them. As before, everyone inside showed up to help welcome the newcomers and get them situated. Meg and Sam had supervised the cooking of a delicious meal with plenty for everyone. The rest of the evening was spent in quiet enjoyment of the food, the company, and the security of the safe zone.

Chapter 6

Steak Does A Body Good

Over the next week, Allistor focused on organizing and strengthening his people. More ambassadors were sent out from the Stadium and from the Citadel in search of survivors to bring into the fold. The former prisoners were interviewed, and everyone began receiving assignments based on their skills or preferences. Allistor purchased a few more scrolls to help, but the majority of the training boosts they gave people came from Ramon and his fellow scribes. They were working around the clock creating copies of spells and skill scrolls to pass out.

Through the week, several more groups in Laramie joined up, and by the tenth day after Allistor shot Barden, he had just over fifteen hundred citizens. The population at the Warren was now close to three hundred, there were five hundred plus at the Citadel, fifty at the Silo, a hundred more at the Warehouse Outpost, and five hundred at the Stadium.

Allistor had decided against placing a teleport pad at the Stadium. There were enough residents there to defend the place, and his people were clearing the road between Cheyenne and Laramie. Hunting parties of five or six were working their way along the route and gaining both experience and meat by hunting the various monsters living nearby.

Bob had convinced Allistor not to waste system points or klax on construction within the walls, and had recruited a group of twenty-five men and women to become his crew. He had carpenters, plumbers, and electricians, as well as three stone masons who were newly trained in *Masonry* via scrolls that Allistor purchased on the market.

After making use of Nigel's ability to inventory everything in all the facilities, some interesting discoveries were made. Sam and Meg took a truck and drove back to the Warren, stopping at the Gun Shop Outpost on the way. Allistor authorized Sam to access the warehouse area in the back, where he picked up two more of the uber-expensive Barrett .50s as well as some shoulder rocket launchers, grenade launchers, three belt-fed 5.56 LMG's, crates of grenades of multiple kinds, and even some Claymores.

But the thing he'd been sent for, the thing that had made them sit up and take notice when they saw Nigel's inventory, was a pair of belt-fed, tripod mounted HMGs. Specifically, the Grandfather, the Centurion, Ma Deuce, the ever-reliable Browning M2 .50 caliber heavy machine gun. Sam and Allistor were calling it the BFG.

The gold standard since WWI, the simple, durable, reliable design of the weapon made it unnecessary to alter it in any significant way. Thus, the ones Sam found in the back room of the Gun Shop were very nearly identical to the first one manufactured more than a century before. The only real change being that it had modified replaceable barrels, which Sam found a dozen of in a crate nearby. The barrel replacements were necessary because the rate of fire heated the barrels after a period of continual usage. There were also ten thousand rounds of various types, including armor piercing, incendiary, and tracer rounds.

These guns could be mounted atop a wall and used to take down monsters like the giant tortoise, the void titan, or attacking dragons. Unlike the one-shot sniper rifles, the belt-fed M2's could lay down a maximum of five hundred rounds per minute with an experienced two-man crew. In normal use though, one would fire in short bursts and no more than fifty to a hundred rounds per minute. Because the rounds were meant to penetrate. And what they hit, died. These were guns that were used against trucks, planes, armored vehicles, and buildings.

Sam actually did a little dance when he located the two guns. Meg shook her head as he hugged one of them, and spoke to it. "Hello there darlin'. Daddy's 'bout to take you home. He's gonna oil you up and take real good care of you."

"You old pervert." Meg chuckled, prompting him to turn toward her with his most innocent face. "Don't stand there trying to seduce it. We've got places to be. Load them on the truck and let's go."

They weren't the only ones traveling the roads. George and Nancy returned to Cheyenne, then teleported to the Warren. From there they loaded up one of the RVs and a panel truck with supplies and took a group of twenty up to Luther's Stronghold near Denver. They found it still locked, though there was evidence someone had been inside and searched the place.

They unloaded and got comfortable for a day, with George claiming the Stronghold in Allistor's name since Luther had been killed, then making some minor modifications using the system. He added a large greenhouse, an underground level, and the sensor system.

The following day they returned to the RV lot and brought back five of them. One for selling on the market, and the other four for traveling between Strongholds. They also took the panel truck and a couple of the Humvees up to the train wreck where they did a more thorough search of the box cars. George agreed with Sam about not risking the unstable pile of Howitzer rounds, but they discovered crates of fully automatic assault rifles, forty in total. There were six more of the belt-fed LMGs along with crates of both 5.56 and .50 cal ammunition, and oil-filled barrels with spare parts. They found uniforms of all sizes, more than a hundred of them. Crates of MREs, pallets of empty canteens, two dozen heavy canvas tents large enough to sleep six each, and an entire car filled with pre-packed parachutes. George grabbed a couple dozen of those just for kicks, thinking they'd make nice hammocks, or the silk-like material and cords could be used for something. But, by far, George's favorite find was a straw-packed crate filled with bottles of brandy.

As they approached the gates with their loot, they met up with a second wave of folks coming from the Warren. A total of a hundred people took up residence in the Stronghold, which they named Luther's Landing. Allistor had asked that they reopen the Stronghold, and planned to put a teleport pad there, at least temporarily, as it was a two-day trip from the Warren, a full day from Cheyenne, and a good staging area for their venture into Denver. George opted to remain there for a while, with most of the original inhabitants and a few new faces. He wanted to get the greenhouse set up, and spend some time with the folks there.

After spending another day assisting George with the setup of the greenhouse, Nancy returned to the Warren with the convoy of RVs. She'd been away from Chloe for most of a week, and was anxious to get back to her rambunctious little girl. They stopped at Cheyenne on the way to drop off three of the RVs, taking the last one the rest of the way to the Warren.

The folks with the *Animal Husbandry* skill, along with the cowboys and sheep herders from Laramie were sent to the Citadel where Dean took over supervision of the group. They used the few horses that Dean's group already had to locate and capture more, until they had a mount and a replacement for each of them. Then they proceeded out to round up cattle.

Allistor had expected a few hundred head, which they could use for both breeding and for a food supply to supplement their hunting and farming. When the cowboys came back with over five hundred head of cattle, some milk cows, goats, a dozen pigs, and sixty sheep, there was no way they could stay inside the walls of the Citadel. So Allistor had to improvise.

Returning to Cheyenne with Helen and Fuzzy, he rode the elevator up to the top and climbed to the roof of the tower. Surveying the grounds around the Citadel, he saw what George had mentioned – there was not a lot of space on the plateau outside the walls. Such a large herd of livestock needed significant grazing land, as well as shelter from storms and the cold in the winter.

He'd created a large barn inside the walls at the Stadium before he left, and Bob and his crew were building a corral. The space would be large enough for fifty or so cattle and other critters. An emergency food supply in case of siege.

That wasn't going to work at the Citadel. And Allistor couldn't think of a structure large enough to hold that many beasts. His solution came as he was thinking about where to construct a barn at the Warren. He remembered the large underground area they'd started with, and he had his answer!

The Citadel sat upon a raised plateau that the system had created when he'd upgraded the shopping mall. The front of the plateau, the part facing the main gate, featured a switchback road that sloped from the level of the rest of the city up to the gates. Allistor turned toward the back wall and the land beyond to the north.

Just outside the walls was a Lowe's, the massive building supply store, with a couple of other large department stores next to it. In between the stores and the plateau walls was a large parking area, sufficient for several hundred cars. And farther north, behind the big box stores, was a wide, open field, followed by a neighborhood of single family homes on large lots. Plenty of green space for the livestock to graze. There were even a few shallow creeks for them to drink from.

Opening his Citadel interface, the first thing he did was check his System Points. With more than a hundred thousand available, he could afford to do some upgrades. The first thing he did was create a massive open cavern underneath the Citadel. He constructed two exits – one with a ramp leading up to an opening inside the walls at one of the grassy areas that used to be the mall parking lot.

For the second exit he made a wide tunnel that led directly north to the Lowe's parking lot.

Calling together Helen, Fuzzy, and a small force of guards to accompany him, he descended the ramp into the cavern. Using his interface as they walked, he added some scattered lights to the ceilings, and a water source that fed into a long trough, which Fuzzy immediately slurped some water from. Walking out the northern exit at ground level, he stopped to add a massive metal gate, three feet thick with one-foot reinforced steel lock bolts. The high walls and massive gates up top would do him no good if an enemy could just sneak in through this new tunnel.

Proceeding across the parking area, Allistor and his group entered the open doors of the Lowe's. Weapons ready, they surveyed the massive space with its rows of twenty-foot high shelves. Rather than potentially waste time clearing it, he immediately tried to claim it. A broad grin appeared on his face when a message popped up.

Do you wish to annex this facility into the adjacent Citadel? Yes/No

He immediately selected *Yes* and waited as the familiar golden glow surrounded them all. When the blank template appeared, he made no changes to the place other than to remove all the shelving and inventory, transferring them to the Citadel's existing storage. He did add power, and extended the sensor system outward far enough to include the green area to the north. Lastly, he added a half dozen bunkhouse rooms toward the back, as well as some horse stalls and a tack room, two bathrooms, and a kitchen.

They proceeded out the back of the store, which had massive roll-up loading dock doors plenty wide enough for

138

the cattle to pass through. Walking out into the field, he claimed that as well. His best guess when he'd been looking down at it from the tower was that it was about a square mile, or close to 650 acres.

Pulling up his interface again, he searched for a way to enclose the space. It was bordered on all sides by roads, except where it butted up against the plateau. His first choice was a fence, but the system didn't have an option for barbed wire. And no way was he going to have enough points or klax to extend a wall a full three miles plus to encompass the whole area. Looking to Helen, he said, "I guess Bob and his guys could help the cowboys fence this in, eventually. Until then, they'll have to herd the cows into our new barn at night, and watch them during the day."

One of the guards with them, a man Allistor thought was named James, replied. "We'll help. There's plenty of hands to do the work. Having the meat is important to all of us."

Another said, "You probably just put a mile of barbed wire into inventory from the store behind us. We can make a run to the farm supply place and get more. Or if we have to, we'll steal some from other fields. We'll figure it out."

Allistor was encouraged by everyone's willingness to help. Even if it was based on mutual love of steak, and not purely on charitable thoughts. Turning to Helen, he asked, "Is this enough grass for the herd we have?"

She shook her head, looking thoughtful. "I'm not sure? Probably? But, if necessary, we can always move them to other spots. The airport is just across the street, and there's plenty of open space with grass there. The cowboys will know better." She looked around for a minute. "I do suggest we plant some shade trees here and there. It won't hurt the grass much, but cows appreciate shade, and if they're tall enough and scattered well enough, they might discourage dragons from swooping in to steal a meal."

James smacked a hand on his leg. "We could make the whole thing a dragon trap. Set up some poles and run razor wire across the open spaces. Dragon comes down, it'll slice off a wing or maybe their head if we're lucky."

Allistor liked that idea immensely. "James, you are now officially in charge of dragon traps!" He clapped the grinning man on the back. "Let me know if you need something we don't have." He turned and led the group back through the tunnel and up the ramp to where the cowboys were managing the herd. Helen waved one of them over, and they updated him.

"Hell yes! That'll work out real well, Allistor. Er, Lord?" the man asked.

"Just Allistor, please. And you're... Jason, right? Austin's dad?"

"Yep! That's me. I suppose we haven't been formally introduced. Austin has talked about you plenty. I want to thank you for all you've done for him. And for all of us." He reached down from atop his horse and offered his hand, which Allistor shook.

"My pleasure. Do you think you guys can handle the fencing?"

"Ha! This is the big country out here. Three miles of fence is nothin'! We'll have it done soon enough. I'll head the herd down there now, if you'll excuse me?"

Allistor held up a hand. "Are any of the cowboys here more experienced than you?"

Jason thought for a moment. "Old Jerry. Not what you'd call a cowboy, but he had a corn and soybean farm for something like forty years, and I think his neighbors had cattle, which is where he picked up the *Animal Husbandry* skill. He took over wrangling them when the neighbors got killed by the canid things in the early days."

"Alright, I'll leave it up to you. I need a... boss. What do you call them? Ramrod? Foreman? Head honcho?"

Jason laughed, "Foreman is fine. I'll ask Jerry if he wants the job, but I don't think he will. He retired once, and I think he just likes being able to poke around with us a bit."

"Great. I'm going to add both of you to my advisory council. Bob and Virginia are already there, so we might as well keep it in the family. And Jerry can advise us on farming operations when we start cultivating fields outside the walls. If he's willing, of course."

"I'm sure he will be. I'll let him know." Jason gave a half-salute and turned his horse back toward the herd. Minutes later the mass of beef, pork, and lambchops on legs was flowing down into the wide tunnel.

With that major component of their ability to feed themselves resolved, Allistor decided to take a little personal time. He'd been running and fighting nonstop since the apocalypse, and he felt a little worn down.

"Helen, I'm gonna go spend a few days at the Warren, catch up with Amanda for a bit. You could probably use some down time, too."

She slung her rifle over her shoulder. "Actually, I was thinking I wanted to take some time and learn a few more skills. Maybe level them all up a little bit."

"Great. Ramon will give you whatever you want. How 'bout we meet back here, in three days?" She nodded, and he set off toward the teleport pad with Fuzzy following. He verbally activated the teleport, and a few seconds later was looking around the main area of the Warren.

*****

Back at the Warren, Amanda was using her *Internal Analysis* on a hunter who'd just come back after a fight with a Lanx, during which he'd been badly injured. His companions had healed him, but Amanda wanted to check whether his broken bones and torn skin had healed back stronger than they were originally.

Since discovering that Allistor's bones had become stronger from his multiple battle injuries, she'd been making a study of any injured people she could find. She'd even secretly experimented on a bunny, making sure Chloe was thoroughly distracted at the time. Slowly but surely, she was developing a theory that she hoped she could use to preemptively strengthen everyone's bones and skin, rather than waiting for them to be injured.

142

It was a little like inventing a new drug, or inventing some new procedure. She was, in effect, trying to create a new spell. But that was still a ways down the road.

When she heard the knock on the door frame behind her, she was focusing on the man's forearm where the big cat's bite had crushed bone. She could see the faint marks from where it had shattered, then been pulled back together by healing magic. By comparison, the broken areas were much denser than nearby unbroken bone.

"If you're not bleeding to death, have a seat. Be with you in a minute." She didn't even bother to look who it was.

"I'm gone a few days and you've already found a new guinea pig." Allistor's amused voice replied.

The hunter suddenly looked nervous, his eyes darting from Allistor to Amanda and back. Allistor held up a hand letting him know he was joking, and there wasn't about to be a throwdown over Amanda's affections. Relieved, the man slumped a bit, saying, "This guinea pig stuff ain't exactly fun. She's kinda… bossy."

Allistor snorted. "It's part of what I love about her." Amanda just ignored them both and finished her scan of the man's injuries.

"Right. We're all done. You can flee now, you big brave hunter." She pushed him toward the door. The man gratefully hopped up and exited the room, giving Allistor a respectful nod on the way out.

"So…I've had a few injuries since I saw you last… if you like I could get nekkid and let you…"

She snorted, interrupting his offer. "No need to traumatize anyone who might wander in. The scan works perfectly well through your clothes. Sit." She pointed to the exam table and he obligingly hopped up.

"I missed youuuuu…" He leaned toward her with an exaggerated puckerface and proceeded to make kissy noises. She slapped his face lightly, then rewarded him with a quick smooch.

"I missed you too. Now hold still. This will only hurt a little." She began to poke and prod at him, bending and twisting his limbs as she used the scanning spell. "You really did take some proper wounds out there." she observed.

"There was this big dog-lizard thing that tried to eat me. I killed it. There was a woman who shot me in the back. Killed her too." He grinned at her, puffing out his chest in a heroic posture.

"It's your winning personality." She paused for a second to look into his eyes. "Everyone and everything that meets you just naturally wants to eat your face. Or shoot it off." She softened her words with another kiss, this one longer and softer.

He reached out and tried to pull her closer, but she smacked his hands away and retreated. Picking up a pad and pencil, she began making notes. "At this rate, by the end of the year you'll have broken everything at least once. You'll be stronger, like the six hundred dollar man."

"Million. It was six million dollars." he corrected absently while examining his arm himself. He remembered the wound, but couldn't see what she could see.

"I said hundred and I meant it." She grinned at him. "You're nowhere near as sexy as he was."

"But could he do magic?" Allistor cast *Levitate* and lifted her a foot off the ground. She kicked her feet a few times, but was unable to get any purchase as he pulled her into his lap. He canceled the spell as he gathered her into his arms.

"Talk to me when you can leap tall buildings in a single bound." She kissed his cheek, but didn't try to get up.

"No, that was... ya know what, never mind." He squeezed her and leaned in for a real kiss that lasted for half a minute. When he came up for air, he said, "I've come to spend a few days with you. Taking a little vacation. A little "Amanda Time." He gave his sweetest smile.

"Oh, really?" She leaned back a bit. "And what if I'm busy?"

"I... I'm sorry. I should have checked with you first." His face fell, and she instantly regretted her words.

"Hush, silly man. As it happens, I'm not busy. A lady just likes to be valued. I don't just sit around waiting for you to bless me with your presence, ya know?"

He nodded his head, the smile returning slowly as he tried to decide whether he was in trouble or not. "There is literally no one on Earth I value more than you."

"Not even Fuzzy?" she asked.

"Well, okay, maybe Fuzzy." He winked. "And Helen's probably right behind you. And Chloe, cuz I mean how cute is she? And-"

145

He quit when she kissed him again. "Hush, stupid."

They spent the night in her small original quarters, getting reacquainted. In the morning they had breakfast with the gang from the Warren, then teleported back to the Citadel to spend the next two days shut in his opulent lord's quarters on the upper level. Amanda had Nigel keep track of anyone who was wounded so that she could examine them later. Allistor informed Nigel that they were not to be disturbed unless someone was dying, or something was on fire. Except for room service.

*****

Helen left Allistor and headed to find Ramon, who was back in the Citadel's library. She found Nancy there with him, the two of them sitting quite close together and examining something on the table in front of them.

She cleared her throat, and they both looked up and smiled. A tiny voice from behind her said, "Don't mind them. They cuddle like that *all the time* now. Gross."

Helen turned to find Chloe standing behind her, holding a baby bunny in the crook of one arm and scratching its head. She seemed a good bit taller than Helen remembered. "Well, hello miss Chloe. I think you've grown since I saw you!"

Chloe nodded enthusiastically, a conspiratorial grin on her face. "I learned the *Grow* spell and tried it on myself. Mom got *reeeeeally* mad. I'm grounded. Till I'm twenty." She grimaced. Helen tried not to laugh.

146

"Well, sweetling, your mom is right. You can't just go casting spells on yourself like that. You'll grow up soon enough. And believe me, you should enjoy being a kid while you can."

Chloe rolled her eyes. "That's what Ramon said." She looked at Helen for a moment, then added. "Being grounded is boring. I have to stay with momma wherever she goes, including this dumb place. Almost none of these books have any pictures." Her face changed from sad to hopeful as she asked, "Did you see any cool monsters 'n' stuff while you were out with Allistor?"

"Sure did!" Helen led her to a table and lifted her up to sit on it while she took a chair, placing them nearly eye to eye. "There was this *huge* lizard-dog thing hiding in a stadium that we wanted to turn into a Stronghold..."

She spent the next half hour entertaining Chloe with their adventures as Nancy and Ramon canoodled over whatever they had on their table. When she got to the part about the giant dog injuring Allistor, Chloe giggled.

"He's really not good at fighting, is he? I keep telling him not to let stuff bite him, but he never listens."

Helen couldn't help but laugh with the adorable little girl. "I'll be sure and remind him for you when I see him!"

Eventually Nancy reclaimed her daughter, giving Helen a hug and making small talk for a few minutes before taking Chloe away. Helen took a seat at Ramon's table, though not nearly as close as Nancy had been. "Hey there, pal!" She grinned at him. When he looked up, she made smoochy faces at him. "Got a few minutes for me? Or should I wait while you grab a cold shower?"

Totally unphased, Ramon just returned her smile. "I always have time for you. Thank you for… distracting the munchkin. When she's bored, she can be quite a handful."

"You two looked like you were studying something serious." Helen observed.

"Well, not serious, exactly. More like interesting. I've been helping Michael with his enchanting. It's not easy to get the materials he needs, so we've got all the foragers on the lookout for usable stuff. One of them brought back some geodes the other day – she just thought they were pretty." When he saw a blank look on her face, he added, "The rocks with the crystals inside."

When she nodded in recognition, he continued. "Michael used a tiny chisel to break one of them free, then tried to enchant it. The results were surprising. The crystal held a much stronger spell than he'd ever managed before." He pointed at a diagram of a geode on the table in front of him. "I was telling Nancy about it, and about how Michael was thinking if he could get his hands on larger crystals, he could create some truly powerful items."

Helen followed along, making a leap of intuition. "And Nancy thinks she might be able to find bigger crystals? Or… no! She thinks she can *grow* the crystals you already have!"

Ramon nodded, pulling over a book and showing it to her. "We were researching how they grow, and what minerals or materials they need."

"That's very cool!" Helen thumped him on the shoulder. "I hope you guys can pull it off. Speaking of research, Allistor said you might help me with learning or improving some skills?"

"Absolutely!" Ramon gave her a double-thumbs up. "We depend on you to keep him alive when he does something stupid like make himself giant turtle bait. Whatever you need."

"Well, we were in a fight the other day where I wasn't much help. Needed silence, and all I had was guns and my knife. I sort of know how to shoot a bow, from when I was a kid. But I haven't tried it since the world ended. Will I pick up the skill if I just go shoot for a bit?"

Ramon nodded. "Yup. You will. And I suggest you do that. We're finding that skills you earn naturally level up faster than skills learned from books or scrolls. And if you learn it naturally *then* use the skill scroll, it boosts you to a higher level than normal."

The two of them spoke for another hour, Helen considering skills she'd like to learn, Ramon either coaching her or providing scrolls.

For the next couple days, she was in and out of the library, practicing skills like *Archery, Horseback Riding,* and *Skinning* between sessions of studying books or scrolls. She discovered *Navigation* and combined it with *Cartography,* enabling her to create detailed maps as she traveled with Allistor. She spent a little time with cowboys, helping to care for the livestock and raising her *Animal Husbandry* skill to Level 4.

In fact, she spent a good part of her time off with the horses and cattle. It didn't hurt that one of the cowboys had rugged good looks and a singing voice that made her tingle a little.

*****

The morning that Allistor was supposed to meet up with Helen and set off on their trip to Denver, he woke well before dawn. He gently kissed Amanda's forehead, careful not to wake her as he slid out of bed and grabbed a quick shower. After writing her a note and leaving it on his pillow, he slipped out of his ridiculously large bedchamber and made for the elevator that would take him down to the main floor, and breakfast.

But as he descended, the elevator stopped after only one floor. When the doors opened, he found a surprised Helen staring at him. As she began to mumble some kind of flustered greeting, the cowboy standing behind her tucking in his shirt did the same.

"Ha! Good morning, both of you." He grinned widely at Helen, who was now blushing. "I'm guessing you both slept well?"

The cowboy, now over his initial surprise, chuckled and gave Allistor a wink that Helen didn't see. They both got on the elevator and continued downward. Allistor couldn't resist teasing Helen a bit as they walked toward the dining hall. "So, Amanda told me she thought she heard someone fighting below us last evening. Something about thumping and screaming. I asked Nigel, but he said no one was injured. You guys hear any of that?"

Helen snorted. "Shut it, *Viscount* Allistor. You and her ladyship weren't exactly quiet yourselves."

"Heh. Well, I don't know about you, but I'm simply *starving.* I hope they have pancakes. And bacon and eggs. Maybe one of those dragon steaks? Think they have any of those left?"

Chapter 7

Grass, Gas, and Snack Cakes

Over breakfast they discussed their plans for the trip to Denver. Amanda had decided, much to Allistor's chagrin, that he was the most likely among their people to be injured on a regular basis, so she was going to accompany him. Helen welcomed her happily, and when they both turned and stared at Allistor, the cowboy, whose name was Nathan, laughed heartily.

"Yer outnumbered and surrounded, partner." he said, earning a pat on the leg from Helen as she continued to stare at her boss.

"Clearly." Allistor pretended to complain. He had no qualms about bringing Amanda along, she had handled herself well at the hospital. And it never hurt to have a healer around. With a grin for Nathan, he added, "So I guess you'll have to come along to even things out."

The cowboy looked surprised. So did Helen. "Really? What about my duties on the ranch?" he asked. "I don't want to leave the fellas a man short."

"They can recruit someone to take your place for a week or two." Allistor countered, even as he noticed Helen trying to shut him up. She was frowning at him, and very subtly shaking her head *no,* at least until Nathan turned to look at her. At which point she adopted a smile and started nodding.

"Yeah, that'd be great!" she said in a tone that probably sounded happy to Nathan, but Allistor could tell was fake.

"Cool! I'll grab my gear and meet you back here in ten?" Nathan didn't wait for a reply, hopping up from the table after grabbing a last piece of bacon and jogging away with it.

As soon as his back was turned, Helen kicked Allistor under the table. "What the hell, man?"

Allistor gave her his most innocent face as Amanda poked him in the ribs. "What?"

"Just cuz I hooked up with a cowboy doesn't mean we're a friggin' couple. I'm not trying to have his babies or anything."

"Babies? I mean, isn't that kind of sudden? You just met him a few days-"

He didn't get to finish the sentence as Helen kicked him again, harder this time, as Amanda simultaneously elbowed him in the ribs. Both women were giving him dirty looks.

He held up his hands in surrender. "Okay, okay. I'll make it better. Let's bring somebody else. We'll use one of the RVs, that way were not all crowded into the truck with Fuzzy. Who should we bring?

"Another woman." both women said at the same time. Allistor looked confused for a moment, then rolled his eyes. "Seriously? You're gonna throw her at the cowboy? That's... diabolical. Are you that afraid of a relationship?"

153

Helen shook her head. "Just keeping my options open. He's not a bad guy, as far as I can tell so far. But I didn't exactly choose him for his deep thoughts." She smirked at them, and Amanda laughed.

"Me either." She shoulder-bumped Allistor gently, taking his hand at the same time. "I just thought he was semi-pretty. Turns out he has a brain. Don't write the cowboy off too quickly."

Allistor decided to take her words as a compliment, beaming at Helen. "I'm pretty. You heard her."

Both women snorted and got up. Amanda said, "I need to go gear up. Helen, help pretty boy here pick another party member?"

"Yup." Helen gave her a thumbs-up. "I think I know who we should bring." As Amanda walked away, Helen scanned the people sitting at various tables in the former food court area. Spotting her preferred party member, she shouted, "Dawn!" and waved the woman over. Looking at Allistor, who was still sitting, she said, "I saw Dawn practicing at the archery range when I was there. She's really good. And she's already level 8. Mostly from hunting parties. So she should know how to behave out there."

When the woman arrived at the table, she smiled openly at them both. "Hey Helen, Lord Allistor, good morning." She was of medium height with long brown hair and a trim, muscular build. Her posture was rigid, almost military. A woman who was used to hard work.

"Just Allistor, please. And good morning to you, too. I hope we didn't interrupt your breakfast?"

"Nah. I was just shootin' the shit with some of the fellas. Talking about the last hunting trip. What can I do for you?"

"How'd you like to take a little road trip? To Denver." Helen asked.

"Really? With you guys?" She scratched Fuzzy's ears as he sniffed curiously at her leg.

"With us, and a few others. It'll be close company, even in the RV. And we might be gone a few weeks. Also, we don't know what we'll find there, so it could be dangerous. In fact, assume it *will be* dangerous." Allistor let her think about that for a few seconds. "No hard feelings if you pass. Absolutely none at all."

"Ha! Don't threaten me with a good time!" Dawn grinned at him. "I get myself on every hunting party I can, so I can be out there killing those things. They took my parents and the rest of my family. I owe them some payback."

Helen looked at Allistor, who nodded. He liked this woman, and kind of felt bad knowing that Helen might sacrifice her as an offering to the cowboy at some point. He decided it was none of his business.

"Good! I'll go gear up, meet back here in ten?" Dawn smiled.

"We'll be taking the RV, so meet there."

"Great! Lots of space for gear." Dawn was already moving.

Allistor was confused by the statement until he looked at the woman's hand and didn't see a storage ring. As she hustled away, he mumbled.

"Shit. We don't have storage rings for everyone, do we?"

Helen shook her head. "Some folks have bought their own, and you gave out a bunch to the original crew. But no, lots of folks don't have them yet. The folks with the *Leatherworking* and *Tailoring* skill have been making some solid backpacks for people."

Allistor dashed over to the market kiosk, which wasn't far away. He did a quick search for the hundred-slot storage rings, and found thirty of them available. The price was two hundred klax each, but he didn't hesitate. Having his people able to carry the gear they needed, and store the loot they found, was invaluable. There was a reason the VR games gave players inventory bags to start with. Carrying everything you need without them was cumbersome, noisy, and in this world, could get them killed. He purchased all thirty of them, and made a mental note to ask Michael what he needed to start enchanting rings for storage.

Looking around, he spotted Ramon having breakfast. Keeping two of the rings for Dawn and Nathan, he handed the rest to Ramon. "Hey man, could you take charge of these? Make sure the people going out on hunting parties have one? For now, they'll just be loans. They can return them when they come back. I'll work on getting one for everyone to keep.

"Sure thing, Allistor. I was actually going to ask you about this at our next meeting. I'd like them to start

156

grabbing stuff like technical manuals while they're out. Anything that might help us level up skills. Especially mechanical and trade skills. I don't know if they'll help, but if they do, it's a cheap way to skill up."

"Do it." Allistor put a hand on his friend's shoulder. "I'm taking a party to Denver in a few. I'll set up an Outpost as soon as we're there so we can talk. Let Nigel know if you need me."

Fist-bumping Ramon, he walked back over to Helen, who was trying to get Fuzzy to do tricks for bacon. The bear was resisting, preferring to rely on his cuteness factor to mooch treats. He knew his audience well, as Helen eventually just gave up and handed him the bacon.

"Sucker." Allistor teased as he sat down. "He's got you wrapped around his little... claw."

"Helen shrugged. "Not my fault. I think he has a really high *Charisma* stat."

Amanda joined them then, rifle over her shoulder. Allistor saw Nathan approaching not far behind her. When he took a seat next to Helen, Allistor caught them up. "A woman named Dawn is joining us as well. She's got some archery skills, and you never know when you need to kill something quietly." He looked at Nathan, feeling a little sorry for the guy. Tossing him one of the storage rings, he said, "Stow all your stuff in here."

Nathan thanked him for the ring, and took a moment to move all his items into the storage slots. "This is great! Thank you."

"You're welcome. Just be sure and leave at least half the slots for loot." He paused, then asked, "You mind

157

grabbing one of the RVs, make sure it's got a full tank? Meet us at the gate."

The Citadel was only about a hundred miles from Denver, straight down the interstate. But they wouldn't be getting highway mileage having to weave around abandoned vehicles. Plus, Allistor preferred to take the back roads when possible, where they might find likely spots for foraging or to create another Outpost. And they didn't know for sure that they'd be able to gas up anywhere in Denver. For all they knew, the whole city could be a smoking ruin. Each of the RVs was equipped with a pump and tubes that could be used at gas stations without power, or to siphon gas from other vehicles. Still, it was better to be sure they had enough fuel to get back, just in case.

Nathan nodded and set off toward the exit and the motor pool.

Dawn returned a few minutes later, and they all piled into the RV. Fuzzy tried to claim the shotgun seat, but Helen shooed him away, saying, "Unless you can read a map, that's my seat, buddy." Fuzzy tried his best cute face, but to no avail. He settled for curling up on the floor behind Helen. The others settled onto the bench seats that lined both walls behind the two front chairs.

Allistor handed Dawn her storage ring, and had a repeat of his convo with Nathan. Amanda had decided to drive to start off with, so she fired up the engine and they were off. Nigel operated the gates for them, and they were on their way.

Fuzzy was snoring before they were even outside the Cheyenne city limits. Dawn was enchanted by the cuteness, and Allistor began to wonder if the bear did

158

indeed have some kind of *Charisma* boost. Bear cubs were naturally cute, but Fuzzy seemed to take it a step further.

He chatted with Dawn and Nathan as they wound their way down back roads that Helen located as she worked to level up her *Navigator* skill. They stayed roughly parallel to the interstate as they moved south, occasionally crossing under it and back again. It turned out Dawn had worked at a large nursery where they grew flowers that supplied a lot of the flower shops in the area. When Nathan asked her what life at the nursery was like, she snorted. "I hauled a lot of shit. Fertilizer. Horse shit, pig shit, cow shit. Half my day was spent shoveling shit and spreading it around."

Nathan had worked on various local ranches in three states, beginning with his own family's ranch as a kid. When he got older, he had an itch to see some new sights and joined a rodeo for a while. But he lacked the skill to be a professional bull rider, so he went back to what he knew best – wrangling cattle.

They stopped a few times along the way. The first time was when Helen spotted a house with a very nice boat on the trailer parked next to it. "We should hook the boat to the back." When she turned and saw Allistor looking at her with one eyebrow raised, she added, "I mean, we might have to cross a river where a bridge is out, or something."

Allistor didn't mind, and it was a nice boat, so he just nodded. "Let's check out the house. Might be some canned food or weapons or something."

They spent an hour looting the house, which yielded up a surprising amount of goodies. Besides the boat, there was a fully stocked pantry that held enough food to feed the group for weeks. Amanda found a stack of clean sheets and blankets, as well as a decent first aid kit. There were twenty-four bottles of wine in a wine fridge in the kitchen, which Dawn slid into her storage ring. They also snagged a few pots and pans, as the RV hadn't been stocked with utensils yet. The small kitchen operated off a propane tank, so they could cook decent meals if they needed to.

Allistor found a couple shotguns and a hunting rifle in a gun rack in the basement, and a Colt .45 in a nightstand drawer. There was ammo for all three on a shelf in the rack. The house had an office with several full bookshelves, so Allistor took a few minutes to search for anything Ramon could use. The closest thing he found to training manuals were a half dozen gardening books on a bottom shelf, along with a couple cookbooks.

Nathan had the boat hooked up by the time they exited the house. They unloaded most of the canned goods and food items into the boat to free up their inventory space, and they were off again.

As they rode along, Allistor opened one of the cookbooks. He'd earned the basic *Cooking* skill, and was curious about whether Ramon's theory was correct. His mother had taught him some basic cooking skills as a kid. He could boil pasta, and bake cookies, and cook a pot roast in a crock pot. But he was by no means a skilled chef.

So, starting with the first recipe, he read through carefully, thinking about what the various ingredients would do, whether they were meant to add to consistency, or flavor, and how they might interact with each other. It happened to be a chili recipe with a wide variety of ingredients. When he was through reading it, he got the notification he was hoping for.

Skill Level Up! Your Cooking skill has increased by +1

He handed Dawn and Nathan a cookbook each, and explained what he'd just done. They both began to read just as earnestly as he had. By the time they stopped again, Allistor had gained two more points and each of them had learned the skill and gained a point.

Helen had called the stop as they approached the outskirts of Denver. She'd spotted a gas station food mart that still had all its windows intact. That was a rare enough sight that it had caught her attention. Amanda pulled into the lot and right up next to the glass doors. They piled out, weapons at the ready, and peered through the dusty glass to look inside.

The interior appeared to be intact. The shelves were still upright and stocked, though the normal selection was greatly reduced. Allistor motioned for the group to split up and circle the building. He, Amanda, and Fuzzy went left while Helen took the other two around to the right. A minute later they met up at the back door. A quick check of the dumpsters revealed no critters lurking, though something had clearly pulled some of the trash out and ransacked it. Nathan tried the back door and found it locked, so they made their way back around to the front.

The glass doors opened with just a bit of squealing, the hinges having not been used for a while. Helen started inside, then stopped and backed out. "Man, let's leave the doors open for a minute. It smells pretty ripe in there."

Fuzzy, not seeming to mind the odor of rotted burritos, ham sandwiches, and ice cream strolled right in with his nose in the air. Allistor watched him carefully as the rest of them waited outside with the doors propped open. Eventually, Nathan volunteered to go through and open the back door for a little cross-ventilation. He held his breath as he walked through, grabbing a six-pack of soda on his way to prop the door open with.

Eventually, when the place had had a few minutes to air out, they all braved the smell and stepped inside. A quick check of the entire building told them what Fuzzy had already indicated – that there was nothing living inside. Stepping back out after grabbing some lukewarm drinks from the shelves, Helen tapped Allistor on the shoulder.

"This would make a great Outpost. It's close to Denver, but obviously nobody has been here in a while. It has gas, and if you turn on the electricity we can use it as a refueling station. There's enough non-perishable food in there to feed a small group for a week or more. And you could put some bunks in the office or stock room."

Everyone was nodding in agreement before she was even through talking. Allistor pulled up his interface and chose the Outpost option. As the familiar light surrounded them, he added a wall around the place, and the usual electric, water, and sensor system. When the light faded, the glass storefront had been altered to stone walls with smaller windows. The interior hadn't changed much, except the lights were on and the coolers were now humming.

The group spent an hour hauling spoiled food and drinks out to one of the dumpsters, which they then wheeled outside the wall and onto the road. There was a slight grade to the road, and they gave the bin a good shove in the downhill direction, watching as it wobbled its way a few hundred yards, picking up speed until it eventually went off onto the shoulder and tipped over.

"We probably should have burned all that." Allistor observed afterward.

Amanda shook her head. "Better not to send up smoke signals until we know whether the locals are friendly."

By the time the cleanup was done, Allistor's favorite drink was chilled enough that he grabbed one and popped it open. The Monster Irish coffee still tasted good after all that time, and he missed the taste. He quickly grabbed a handful of them to put in the RV fridge. The others all did the same, and as the ladies gathered up snacks to stock the cabinets, Nathan turned on the pumps and gassed up the RV.

Allistor took the time to ask Nigel to put him in touch with Ramon.

"Go ahead, Lord Allistor."

"Hey, Ramon. Just thought I'd let you know we claimed a gas station food mart as an Outpost. It's on the north side of Denver…" he gave the location and a brief description of what was in the place. After being assured that things were going well at the Citadel and the other locations, he said goodbye.

Back in the RV, he found Dawn face-deep in a pink snowball snack thing, with the sugary pinkness smeared all over her face. When he paused to stare, she looked up at

163

him. "What? I looove these things! And they stay good for, like, a hundred years." She stuck her tongue out as far as it would go and tried to lick up all the sticky goodness, then held one up for him.

Allistor declined. "Thanks, but I just had a blast of caffeine that'll keep me awake all night already. Don't need the sugar. Knock yourself out."

Dawn shrugged and, after opening the package, made a show of smushing the entire thing against her face, shoving it all into her mouth at once. In the background Allistor heard Nathan chuckling. "Right on, sister. Get it!"

"Iz Guuuud." she mumbled around her full mouth, causing pink coconut shavings to fly.

Amanda shook her head. "You know how much of that is just sugar?"

Dawn pretended to look thoughtful for a moment, raising her eyes to the ceiling and tapping a sticky pink finger to her chin. "Umm… all of it?" She grinned at Amanda, revealing gooey pinkness stuck to her teeth.

Amanda couldn't help but laugh. "I suppose it's fine. It isn't like you'll be eating those every day.

"Only every day that I can find them. I've got like ten more in my inventory ringy thingy." Dawn waved her hand proudly, getting a laugh from everyone. Which only got louder when Fuzzy took a good lick of her hand, grabbing hold of her forearm with both paws to hold it still while he lapped up the sugary goodness. "Hey! I was gonna do that!" she grumped at the bear, who was already eyeing her other hand and her face. Noticing this, she retreated to the back of the RV shouting, "Noooo! Bad Fuzzy!"

Amanda got back in the driver's seat, and they exited the gates, Nigel obligingly closing them behind the RV as it turned southward. Helen called out from the passenger's seat. "We've got a few hours of daylight left. I've divided the city into sixteen sectors. We can probably cruise a couple of the northern ones, and still make it back here before dark."

Chapter 8

Skeleton Keys

Hel watched the display as Baldur zoomed in on the new Outpost created by the human they'd been monitoring. "He chooses wisely. Fuel to keep his vehicles moving, a location with easy access to several avenues of retreat should he need it. And now he ventures close to the other humans. This should be interesting. He has killed many humans who have opposed him. Will he kill these as well?"

Baldur shook his head. "I think not. So far, this Allistor has only shown violence toward those who have attacked him directly, or committed violent acts against other humans. If the humans of Denver do not provoke him, I expect they will become allies."

"You wish him to succeed." Hel observed, the tone of her statement half accusing as it floated through the mist toward Baldur.

Her uncle waved two of his tentacles in their species' equivalent of a shrug. "We helped to evolve man from the primordial slime of their planet. They have shown great promise, though they are one of the more violent species we've raised. The ones who survive shall become members of the Collective, and shall be a reflection upon us as our creation. Of course I wish them to be looked upon favorably by the others."

The mist swirled as Loki entered the chamber. "Ah, but are they smart enough to thrive? Or will they become pets, coveted for their rarity? Perhaps slaves used as attack dogs for their aggressive tendencies?"

Hel waved one tentacle in a slashing motion, a negative indicator. "They breed too slowly for slaves. Only one or two per year, and those are useless for many cycles. More likely they will become a delicacy. Maybe we should consider preserving more of them. One could earn significant reputation creating a market for the more succulent bits…"

Baldur spat his reply, causing the mist to push almost violently against the other two. "Enough! I have warned you both already. We will not tolerate interference. Neither for amusement, nor profit! I tire of your disregard for the rules we all agreed upon. You will not be warned again."

Baldur's bulky, tentacled form rose from its resting place and exited the chamber, the mist trailing behind in angry, volatile patterns. When the door slid shut behind him, Loki looked to his daughter.

"When he learns Xar' Dakra stalks his pet human, he will not be pleased."

Hel remained motionless, her reply drifting almost serenely across the chamber. "He will not know who loosed the beast unless *you* reveal it to him, father."

The two ancient beings stared at one another, both of them considering betrayal, the odds of success, and the consequences.

"Like father, like daughter." Loki breathed at her before turning and exiting the room himself.

*****

As it turned out, it took much longer to cover each sector than Helen had expected. They were still cruising the first sector when the sun began to set the first day and they had to return to the Outpost. For the next three days they rolled up and down street after street, stopping at likely-looking homes to forage, or where they saw signs of movement. There were monsters to fight – a pack of canids here, a roaming octopoid that followed them into a house and cornered Dawn. One basement had half a dozen of the oversized rats munching on a recently deceased human. The poor guy must have been asleep when they spawned right on top of him.

By mid-afternoon of the third day, they were working their way toward the center of town, having covered most of the north. As they rounded a corner and emerged from behind a four-story building, Nathan stopped the RV and called out, "Uhhh, guys? You need to see this."

They all crowded toward the front of the vehicle where the large windows gave them a good view of the road ahead. Or the lack of road. A block and a half down, the road ended in a familiar-looking gate connected to twenty-foot tall walls.

"Somebody built a Stronghold!" Dawn gave a little clap of joy. "This is cool! I wonder how many of them are in there?"

Allistor added, "And whether or not they're friendly. I'll go approach them. I'll leave Fuzzy here so they don't mistake him for a monster. And most of you should stay here and guard the RV, in case there's an ambush set up around us. One of you ladies want to come with me? Keep in mind it could mean being shot on sight."

Amanda volunteered, kissing his cheek and taking hold of his arm. "If you get shot, I just couldn't live without you!" she rolled her eyes with the sarcastic statement. Allistor just snorted.

Nathan shut off the engine and moved back from the large windshield, making himself less of a target. Allistor stepped out of the side door and made a show of putting his rifle over his shoulder. Amanda followed suit, and both of them began to walk toward the wall, hands out to their sides and open.

When they got within about fifty yards, a voice called out from atop the wall. "That's close enough. Who are you, and why are you here?"

"My name is Allistor! This is Amanda! We're here looking for other survivors! I have a few Strongholds myself, and I'm hoping we can be friends!"

"Friends are overrated! Go away!" another voice called out, this one off to their left, down at ground level. Allistor thought it came from behind a pickup parked at his ten o'clock.

"Okay… not looking for friends. I can understand that. Can you at least tell me your name? And whether there are other Strongholds? Maybe I can make friends with them?"

The first voice called down. "If you plan to make friends with Paul and his murdering filth, I'll just shoot you down right here and now, save myself the trouble of doing it later!"

Allistor raised his hands high. "Hold on! I don't know Paul, any more than I know you. If you two have problems, that's none of my business." He paused, trying to think. "Look! My people and I are just trying to make sure we all survive the year, and make ourselves strong enough to deal with the aliens when they come! There is strength in numbers. Right now, we're about fifteen hundred, and growing. If we can be allies, help each other out, that makes all of us stronger!"

"You just want our food and weapons!" the second voice called out again.

Amanda stepped in. "We have four Strongholds like this one, a Citadel, and several Outposts. We have plenty of food and a whole arsenal of weapons! What we're interested in is YOU. You and the rest of our fellow humans. We really do just want to be friends."

Allistor wasn't sure if it was the tone of her voice, or the fact that she was female, but her words caused a man atop the wall to stand. He lowered his weapon, which had been aimed at Allistor, and called out again.

"My name is Lars! I've heard your name. That announcement a while back, about the Citadel, that was you. It called you a Duke or something."

Allistor nodded his head. "Yeah, that was unfortunate. I didn't realize the system would do that. But yes, I'm that guy. Please just call me Allistor. I'm not big on the whole 'lord' thing.

"How do we know you're not with Paul? Here to worm your way into our Stronghold and kill us all?" The voice behind the truck rang out again. Whoever it was, they were really starting to annoy Allistor.

"We came from the north. From Cheyenne. We've been here three days, searching the city, block by block. You are the first living people we've come across. I don't know Paul. I take it you guys don't get along?"

"He's a lying, thieving murderer!" The man behind the truck finally revealed himself, standing upright with an assault rifle aimed at Allistor, finger on the trigger.

"Well I'm not him! Could you maybe take your finger off that trigger? I don't want you to sneeze and shoot me by accident."

The man pulled the rifle tighter against his shoulder and leaned forward. "Screw you! Let's just waste them, Lars!"

"Hold it!" Lars shouted from atop the wall. "Let's hear them out."

"Lars, I really am sincere about wanting to be friends. I've asked nicely, but if your friend here doesn't take his finger off that trigger and point that thing somewhere other than at my face, I'm going to have to kill him. Then we probably can't be friends. And I'll bring all fifteen hundred of my people down here in an unfriendly mood." as he spoke, Allistor cast *Barrier* in front of himself, motioning discreetly for Amanda to move behind him.

Allistor felt the guy by the truck itching to pull the trigger. He held his breath as Lars considered his words. Behind him, Amanda whispered, "Maybe not the best time to play tough-guy there, pretty boy." Allistor winced. She

171

was right. He'd let his anger, or his hormones, or his fear, dictate his words. It was probably a stupid thing to do.

"Put your rifle down, Chris!" Lars shouted from above. The man didn't move a muscle.

"Dammit, Chris! Point your weapon at the ground or I'll shoot you myself!" Lars' voice got angry. Chris looked up for a moment, then lowered his weapon.

"Thank you, Lars. And you too, Chris." Allistor gave a little bow toward Lars on the wall. "Lars, how 'bout we have a little talk? I won't ask you to let us inside your walls, so how 'bout you and a few of your people come talk to us? We can pick a building and chat, or you can join us in our luxurious recreational vehicle!" he said the last part with a smile, and earned a chuckle from Lars.

"I'll be down in a minute. We can talk right where you are. Chris, don't shoot anybody."

The gates opened half a minute later, and Lars came walking out with two other people behind him. One was a giant of a man, nearly seven feet tall and all muscle. He looked as if he could lift the RV if someone made him angry. The other was a woman in a plaid shirt and jeans with her dark hair pulled into a ponytail. She was maybe forty and had a no-nonsense look about her.

Lars himself was an older man, maybe sixty, but built like a lumberjack. Wide shoulders, thick arms and legs, and a square face framed by shaggy blond hair. He looked like he'd stepped out of the forests of 1850s Norway.

The trio stopped a few yards from Allistor, and Lars raised a hand in greeting. "Sorry about Chris. He's a good man, just a little short-tempered." He gave the man a sidelong glance where he remained behind the truck.

"I understand. We've had our share of betrayal and assholishness from other humans too. Had to kill a few, unfortunately."

The large man behind Lars bristled at that. Allistor gave him a friendly smile. "I don't think we'll have that issue here. You folks seem friendly enough, for the most part."

Lars was about to speak when a howl rang out, echoing between the buildings. Instantly Chris and the others had their weapons back up. Chris shouted, "You brought friggin' wolves with you!"

Allistor shook his head. Pointing down the street to his right, he shouted, "No! The howl came from down there. We came from that way!" He pointed left at the corner they'd come around in the RV.

"He's right!" the big man shouted, his rifle pointing down the street. "We need to get back inside!"

"Not them!" Chris had his weapon pointed at Allistor again. He was walking sideways now, retreating from behind the truck toward the open gate. Allistor watched him for a moment, then looked down the road where a small pack of canids was emerging from a building.

"I'm sorry." Lars said, as he too backed toward the gate. "I just can't let you in. Not yet."

"No worries, Lars. Get your people inside where it's safe. We'll take care of the canids. Also, I have a pet bear in the RV. I'm going to bring him out. Don't let your people shoot him, okay?"

Lars nodded briefly, then turned with his people and jogged through the gates. As they closed, Allistor called out, "Nathan! Dawn! Helen! We've got a pack to deal with!"

The three other party members, along with Fuzzy, emerged from the RV and joined Allistor and Amanda. The canid pack, seven of them that Allistor could see, were now loping down the street toward them.

Allistor and friends all raised their weapons. Their fights over the previous days had helped them coordinate as a group. Fuzzy roared a challenge at the six-legged wolves as all five rifles fired. Three of the canids dropped to the ground, and a fourth staggered but didn't fall. It continued forward, limping and slowed significantly.

The remaining canids had to leap over or dodge their fallen pack members, but once they were clear they merged into a rough line, one in the lead and the others behind. No more taking out several at once with a single volley.

Allistor shouted. "One at a time, in line. Me first!" He fired another round, knocking down the lead canid but not killing it. Amanda fired next, but the canid she was aiming at leapt up over the one Allistor had hit, causing her to miss. Dawn hit it as it landed, and Nathan hit the one behind it. Helen's shot slammed into the shoulder of another. None of them were kill shots, but that was okay. They just needed to slow the pack's advance enough to give them time to finish off the wounded.

Only two were still on their feet, and only one of those was moving at full speed. The other was the one wounded in the first volley, and it was still limping along.

Allistor cast *Restraint* on the last fast-mover and told Amanda to kill it even as he started casting *Flame Shot.* He built up the spell in his hand while he waited for the limper to get closer to the second group of injured canids. When he let it loose, the ball of flame flew toward the monster, impacting it directly in the chest and splashing flame onto two of the other wounded. Howls of pain echoed down the block.

Amanda had taken careful aim and put a round through the head of the stunned canid. It lay dead at the front of the pack. Nathan began to walk forward, firing at the prone or slow-moving wounded mobs as he got closer. Dawn and the others followed his lead, getting closer and taking time to make sure they hit the monsters in vital spots. Fifteen seconds later, the entire pack was dead. Dawn and Amanda leveled up, both of them smiling as the glow surrounded them.   Dawn said, "One more level and I get to pick a class!"

They took a moment to loot the monsters, then Nate, Helen, and Dawn took out knives and began harvesting the skins and additional meat. This was standard practice by this point, and nobody even stopped to think about it. Fuzzy helped himself to some leftover bits they discarded. Allistor turned toward the wall and shouted, "Hey, you guys like canid meat?"

Lars and the others had already emerged from the gates, having seen how one-sided the fight was. As they approached, they watched Nathan and Dawn working.

"It... never occurred to us that we could get more from the monsters than what we looted."

"Yep! We've learned a lot of things like that. For example, if you have the points for it, you can set up a sensor system that would have alerted you when the canids got that close."

Even Chris looked impressed at this point. Still, Allistor hadn't forgotten that the man pointed his gun at him again when the monsters showed up.

"Lars, I hope we can continue our conversation. But not with him here." He jerked a thumb toward Chris. "I warned him that if he pointed his gun at me again, I'd kill him. His first reaction when the canids howled was to aim at me, instead of them."

He paused while the others looked at him nervously, except for Chris, who was instantly angry and started to raise his weapon. "You son of a-"

He didn't finish the sentence, as Allistor cast *Restraint* on him. The man froze with the barrel of his gun at about waist height, a snarl on his face.

"I won't kill him, for your sake, and in the hopes that we can still be friends. But get him out of my sight. I won't forgive him again."

The big man carefully removed the weapon from Chris' frozen grip. Two seconds later, Chris unfroze. "Bitch!" he finished his sentence. He tried to step toward Allistor, but the big fella backhanded him, knocking him on his butt. Not saying a word, he just pointed back toward the gate. Cursing under his breath, Chris got to his feet and walked back inside.

"I apologize, again." Lars stuck out a hand, which Allistor shook. "He managed to keep his wife alive through the early days, only to have her die at the hands of Paul. He has nothing but hate in him lately."

Allistor sighed. "I won't antagonize him, but if he comes at me again, I'm going to have to deal with him."

"Understood." Lars said, and both his people nodded their agreement as well. "That was some cool magic you got there. We've found a few basic spells from the market, but nothing like that."

"Yeah, I've been scouring the market, too. Not a lot of spell scrolls for us low level noobs. I got lucky early on, and found these. And I've used them quite a bit since, so they're leveling up, getting more effective. This new world is all about using your skills as often as you can."

"Well, I'd say you've earned an invite. You're welcome to come inside. You mentioned something about canid meat?"

Allistor grinned. "We have this really good recipe…"

*****

They spent the evening with Lars and his people, sharing a meal and talking about their experiences since the apocalypse. It turned out Lars was a gamer too, currently level eleven, and had established his Stronghold about the same time Allistor had created the Warren. He had more than three hundred people living inside, and he told Allistor he and his people had come across five other Strongholds in Denver. Two that he knew of were larger and much more heavily populated than his, with thousands of people each. He'd heard of a few others, but not seen them.

"Are you allied or affiliated with any of the others?" Allistor asked.

Lars shook his head. "As far as I know, each Stronghold is a stand-alone community. We don't interact much, except when we bump into each other while foraging or hunting. The other groups are friendly enough so far. The only one who actively seeks contact is Paul, when he attacks one of us."

"He attacks Strongholds?" Dawn asked, eyes wide.

The woman who had accompanied Lars outside finally spoke. They'd learned her name was Eden. "No, he's not stupid. He attacks foraging parties. Usually with a large group. The coward doesn't believe in fair fights."

Allistor grimaced. "Where is his Stronghold?"

Lars laughed. "The asshat set himself up in the federal depository. You know, the one where they store all the gold? But the joke's on him. The upper levels are a good place to hole up, it was like a fortress before the world ended. But the lower levels, where all the loot is, are full of mobs. It's a damned dungeon, or might as well be. He has manpower, but his people apparently don't have the levels or the skills to clear it. We've heard he sent several parties of poor slobs down there, and they never came back."

"So... if there's mobs in the basement, he hasn't actually claimed it as a Stronghold?" Allistor asked.

178

"Nope. The fool loses people every once in a while when something spawns in their rooms. But he refuses to move and risk losing all that gold. And it is well defended, even if it doesn't have walls. He's got plenty of guns."

Allistor shook his head. "Just how much gold is in there? Is it worth dying for?"

Lars answered, "We looked it up before the internet died. There should be about fourteen hundred *tons* of gold down there. At least, that's what the government tells the public. Could be more, could be less."

Allistor's jaw actually dropped open. He started doing the math in his head. Lars saw him calculating, and said, "I'll save you some time. Current pricing for an ounce of gold is twelve hundred klax. Which makes a pound of gold worth just over nineteen thousand klax." Lars' face split into a wide a grin. "If you sold all fourteen hundred tons of gold in that building on the market, it would be worth about *fifty-three billion klax*! That's billion with a B."

Allistor's mind blanched for a moment, before it spun up and began to list all the things he could buy with that much currency. His own private tropical island was high on the list. Alien weapons. Vehicles that didn't need gas. Hell, he thought he could probably buy his own spaceship. Maybe a fleet of them.

Lars misread the look on his face. "Yeah, if Paul got his hands on that kind of dough, it would be very bad for the rest of us."

"Then we'll make sure that doesn't happen." Allistor looked at the man and his people, his face becoming stern. "I'll tell you here and now, I'm going to take that building. If you have a problem with that, we can part company now as friends. You're free to try and beat me to it, I won't try to hinder you. If you make it inside before we do, we'll wait for you to clear it, or…" He didn't finish the thought, as everyone present knew failure to clear probably meant death. And there were no respawns.

Lars shook his head. "Nope. We thought about it. But fighting Paul in his own Stronghold would cost us too many people. We wouldn't have the strength to take the lower levels afterward. As much as I'd like to claim the place, it's not worth the cost."

Allistor nodded. "I'm glad you think that way. Human life is precious now, and it's good to meet another leader who keeps that in mind. My people and I have a little experience clearing our new world's equivalent of 'dungeons'. Had to beat a nasty one with a dragon boss to claim my Stronghold in Cheyenne. We'll clear this one too."

The giant, who had earlier introduced himself as Logan, cleared his throat, giving Lars a look. Lars nodded once, and Logan turned to Allistor. "I'd like to go with you, help you take out Paul. I've been in the building, back when I worked security. And I have a personal score to settle with that man. I'll help you clear the dungeon too, if you like."

"Personal score?" Dawn asked. "Did you lose somebody?"

Lars answered for Logan when the big man just nodded. "Logan's little sister Suzy was killed in an attack on one of our foraging groups. She was also Chris' wife. He was actually a decent guy before that. Her death has... changed him."

Logan added, "I know you don't like him, but if you give him a shot at Paul, I'm sure he'd agree to obey your orders. I'll vouch for him, and keep him away from you as much as possible. He's a vet, and knows his way around a firefight."

Lars agreed. "It's why we had him out there in the ambush position. He was with the foragers when they were attacked. Killed four of Paul's guys before they retreated. It eats him up that he wasn't able to save Suzy. He's been on a mission ever since, hunting Paul's hunters."

Allistor was happy to include Logan in his group, but had mixed feelings about allowing Chris. On the one hand, he could totally understand the man's pain. He was angry a lot of the time himself, over losing his family, his friends, and the general injustice of what had been inflicted on his world. On the other hand, he seriously wanted to shoot the man in the head for being such a dick.

Helen decided for him. "If he wants to come, he's welcome. But know that Allistor wasn't kidding – if Chris goes at him again, that's the end of him. You and he both need to know that before you sign up."

Logan offered a hand, and Allistor shook it. Lars said, "I'd go along too, but if I get myself killed..."

Allistor raised a hand. "I know exactly what you mean. I've been in the same situation. You need to be here for your people, but at the same time you need to be out getting stronger. It's a hard choice to make. You are, of course, welcome to join us and level up a bit. And I'll pledge to do all I can to keep you alive, but you know I can't guarantee anything."

When he saw Lars actually thinking about it, he added, "If it helps any, all of my people know healing spells, and Amanda here is our best healer. We also have some potions that our alchemist Nancy created. Before we attack Paul at the depository, I'll establish a Stronghold here. I'll bring down some of my people to help clear the place, and they'll bring scrolls with them. If you want to join us, I'll gift you a healing spell, and a few offensive spells if you have the stats for them. But you'll have to take an oath never to use them against me or my people."

"It doesn't sound like you need my help. You'd do all that to help make us stronger, even though we're potential rivals?" Lars asked.

"I don't see it that way. You're human, and the way I look at things, it's humans against the aliens that brought us here, and maybe all the aliens who are about to colonize our world. I have already claimed enough land to keep hundreds of thousands of people fed and comfortable. And I'll claim more before the year is through. But I don't need to claim it all. There's more than enough for the few of us that are left. At this point, I'm playing a prevent defense. Taking as much territory and resources as I can to prevent them from claiming it. And our most valuable resource is ourselves. So, if I can help make you and my fellow humans stronger, and I have assurances that you won't try to use that strength against me, then it's a win for both of us. And if I can either recruit you as citizens of my lands, or form solid allegiances with you and the other

Strongholds, we can help each other defend what we have when the time comes."

They talked well into the night, sharing their experiences, knowledge, and pain. Allistor held back some vital information, like the fact that he could set up teleports, and that he had control of nuclear weapons at the Silo. He trusted Lars, but some things just had to remain secret for the time being.

In the morning they met again for an early breakfast as the sun was rising. Logan offered some suggestions for Allistor as they ate.

"We've scouted most of this area. How big of a Stronghold are you looking to build? The pro stadium is already taken." His mouth twitched in a slight smile. They'd told Lars and his people about the Stadium in Laramie the night before.

"Not too large. When we take the depository, it'll be our main location here in Denver. So maybe location is more important than size. Something with some height to it, so we have a view? Like an airport with a tower? Maybe something with gas pumps? Or underground levels?"

Helen added, "Something with some space, too. Need to be able to graze some livestock."

Lars chuckled. "Why not just take the capitol building?"

Logan's eyes widened. "Hey, that's... not bad. It's like four blocks from the depository, it's tall enough you can see for quite a ways, there's parkland around it that'll work if you don't have too many cattle. And more parks nearby."

"Sounds perfect. Is it really big?" Allistor asked.

"Smaller than a stadium." Lars winked at him. "There are tons of rooms inside that could be converted to living spaces. I kind of wish I'd thought of it before I made this place."

"Alright! Let's go check it out. If it's that close to Paul and his people, I'm guessing there will be guards, or scouts. We'll take the RV as close as you guys think is safe, then walk the rest of the way." Allistor got to his feet.

Logan cleared his throat again. "Um, about Chris?"

"Bring him along. But if he points a weapon at me, he's dead. I won't wait for you to talk him down."

The big man looked solemn, putting a hand to his chest. "If he points his gun at you, I'll shoot him myself."

"And if he doesn't, I will." Lars stepped forward. "I've decided to join you. I can't pass up the chance to level up. And I believe you have what it takes to succeed."

"Awesome!" Dawn pumped a fist in the air. "Team Lars and Team Allistor, kickin' ass and takin' names!"

All geared up, the group loaded themselves into the RV. Lars, Logan, and Chris joined Allistor, Amanda, Dawn, Helen, and Nathan as well as Fuzzy. Logan took over as driver, being the one who knew the area best. He kept the pace slow, averaging about fifteen miles per hour as they weaved through Denver's side roads. They passed the occasional burned out building, even a few entire neighborhoods. Buildings with broken doors and windows, cars abandoned in the middle of the streets or crashed into buildings as their drivers panicked or died.

The city looked like every post-apocalyptic movie ever, except for one thing. There were no bodies. Anyone killed by the monsters unleashed upon the world was also eaten. The only trace of their existence being dried bloodstains.

In less than an hour, Logan pulled the RV into a parking lot and turned off the engine. "We're about a half mile from the capitol building. I've never seen Paul's people patrol farther than a quarter mile out, but better safe than sorry, right?"

"Right on. We'll walk from here." Allistor and the others piled out. They had to wake up Fuzzy, who'd decided to take a nap under one of the bunks in the back. The oversized cub complained about being disturbed as he followed them out. The group spread out, and Logan led the way. Allistor was right behind him, with Helen and Lars bringing up the rear. Chris kept Amanda and Dawn between himself and Allistor. As a group, they hugged one side of the street, sticking close to the walls of the buildings they passed. Logan kept a sharp eye out for both monsters and other humans. The way he moved and kept his eyes moving reminded Allistor of soldiers he'd seen in movies.

It was only a few minutes before they reached the edge of the capitol building's grounds. The once manicured park grounds hadn't been tended in quite some time, but it was still lovely. Logan spent some time surveying the area before he motioned with one hand for them to move forward. Nobody needed to be told to keep quiet. They were approaching the building from the north, down Sherman Street. Logan paused one last time before crossing the last street and moving up a wide stone stairway to a side entrance. The granite building rose several stories

185

above them, with the central tower extending up to the dome that topped out at nearly twenty stories high.

"I'm not so sure this place is smaller than a stadium." Helen whispered as she looked sideways at Logan and Lars. "But I like it!"

They found the doors unlocked, and made their way inside, pulling the doors closed behind them. Lars took a moment to lock them using the bolts that sunk into the floor, in case anyone or anything tried to follow.

Allistor immediately tried to claim the building as a Stronghold. Unsurprisingly, the system wouldn't allow him to do so.

You cannot claim this structure as a Stronghold at this time. This structure is currently occupied by a life form that has a prior claim to your own. To claim the structure, you must kill the prior occupant, convince it to relinquish its claim, or banish it from the vicinity for twelve hours.

"Yep, knew that was coming." Allistor mumbled to himself. Turning to the others, he said, "We're not alone in here. Someone or something is keeping me from claiming this place. I say we start with this floor, clear every room as we work our way up. If we don't find anything going up, we'll come back down and hit the basement. But first, hang on. I promised you something, and now seems like a good time to deliver."

Pulling some scrolls from his inventory, he handed each of the three men a *Restore* scroll. All three of them eagerly opened the rolled parchment and learned the spell.

186

Allistor noticed Amanda using her *Internal Analysis* spell to watch them as they absorbed the information. Next, he held up an *Erupt* scroll. "Any of you have a six or higher *Intelligence* stat?"

Logan and Lars both raised their hands. Chris looked sullen but said nothing. Allistor resisted the urge to comment on his lack of surprise. Instead, he handed both of the other men scrolls for *Erupt, Vortex,* and *Flame Shot.* Chris likely could have used the latter, but Allistor was not going the give the man a spell that could be used to ambush him at an opportune moment. And though he trusted Lars and Logan, he held back the *Restraint* spell as well. If they decided to betray him, that spell could keep him from defending himself or his people.

Spells all absorbed, the group proceeded to search the floor. Room by room they made their way down the main corridor, closing each door behind them. Locked doors were kicked in, creating more noise than any of them would have liked. But nothing came charging at them in response to the racket.

When the first wing was cleared, they found themselves in a wide and beautiful rotunda, columns around the perimeter leading up to graceful arches. A look upward revealed the space was open all the way up to the dome that capped the building. Allistor stood there, gazing upward with his mouth open, taking in the view until Amanda bumped him with her hip. "Gawk later. We've got work to do."

They moved on and cleared the balance of the first floor. As they passed the exterior doors, they secured them from the inside, either with the floor bolts, or by tying the handles together.   Allistor was starting to rethink his earlier plan.

Speaking in a normal voice, since they'd blown any chance of surprise long ago, he said, "Hey, guys. This would be a lot faster and quieter if we had keys. We don't have time to search every desk in every office, but if we could find a security office or a superintendent's office, we might find keys. Since we didn't find either on this level, my guess is that one or both are downstairs. What do you think?"

The others all made generally agreeable noises, and they proceeded down the nearest stairwell, Amanda casting *Light* to create a globe to illuminate their path. One floor down they exited and began again. The room at the end of the hall turned out to be the maintenance office, and after making sure there were no monsters, they split up and began to search. Dawn was the one to discover a box on one wall with dozens of keys attached to numbered tags. The keys were hefty and metal, made to look like the original keys used in the late 1800s when the building was constructed. There was a diagram on the inside door that showed each of the floors and the numbered offices that corresponded to the key tags.

"That's helpful, but I don't really want to carry around a hundred keys. Let's keep looking for a master." Allistor opened a desk draw and began to rifle through. A few minutes later, Lars held up a ring with six keys.

"The tag on this says *Skeleton Keys*. I'm guessing this is what we need."

"Right on!" Allistor gave him a thumbs-up. "Let's go. We'll clear this level, then head down. Might as well clear the rest of the way down.

The balance of the first basement level was cleared without incident, other than a rat that scared Dawn nearly as much as she scared it. The rodent disappeared around a corner, and Fuzzy took off in pursuit, his nose to the floor. A moment later a growl and a squeak spelled the end of the rat.

The next level down was a completely different story.

The moment Logan opened the stairwell exit door on the lower level, he was attacked. Tentacles shot through the half-open doorway and latched onto his arm, tiny hooks biting into his skin and pulling at him. Dropping his shotgun, he used his other arm and one leg to brace against the door frame and push, trying to free himself. Allistor blindly cast *Flame Shot* through the opening, where it burst against a pair of octopoids, illuminating them for a few seconds.

They were larger than any octopoids Allistor had previously faced. Easily eight feet tall, their heads nearly reached the ceiling of the corridor. Allistor *Examined* one.

Octopoid
Level 14
Health: 23,220/24,200

Taking hold of Logan's waist, he added his strength to the tug of war. The two men together were able to out-muscle the creatures, and free Logan's arm. A good bit of flesh was removed, and several heals hit Logan all at once.

The lead octopoid, enraged by the flame damage, which the amphibious creature was especially susceptible to, pushed through and forced the door farther open. Lars and Chris both fired shotguns directly into its face from just a few feet away. At the same time, now on his back after he and Logan fell free, Allistor cast *Erupt* into the monster, stopping it cold partway through the door and blocking the one behind.

Allistor saw an experience notification float across his interface as the front octopoid expired. Logan quickly surged back to his feet and kicked at the corpse, pushing it off the stone spike and knocking back the monster behind it. He then slammed the door shut and put his back to it, sliding down to sit on the floor. There was some thumping, but the metal door easily held.

Dawn snorted, sitting on one of the stairs. "We're good. Those things are tough, but they're dumb. They don't know how to turn a doorknob."

The others looked at her in stunned silence. That thought had not occurred to any of them. After a few seconds, Lars said, "That makes a lot of sense, actually. It's why we haven't found any of them upstairs. They spawned down here and have been trapped on this level."

Amanda added, "And they must be feeding on each other. Unless they're spawning at higher levels now. That thing was level 14. I dinged when it died."

Dawn nodded her head. "Me too."

They took a moment to catch their breath and recharge, those who cast spells regaining their full mana. Logan was fully restored and though he'd lost some skin in

190

the fight, he hadn't lost much blood due to the prompt attention of the others with their heals. Amanda had observed the multiple spells dropping on him, and addressed the group. "Hey guys, it's great that everybody dropped a heal to support Logan. But we can't all do that all the time, or we'll be out of juice in the first five minutes. I'm dedicating myself to healing, at least as far as spells go. I'll do damage with my gun when I'm not healing. If I start to get low, or can't keep up, I'll call for help. Helen, Allistor, and… Lars? You guys can alternate backup heals. I'll shout your name and a target. Good?"

Everyone nodded their agreement, even Chris. Good group mechanics were important, and this was a life and death situation. Octopoids had a habit from the very first day of spawning inside homes and places where people were sheltering, often catching their prey asleep or otherwise unaware. They were responsible for a huge percentage of the losses the human race had suffered. Helen stood next to Lars at the door, where the pounding had ceased. "They've backed off. Must have learned that pounding on the doors was useless during their time down here. If these things can learn, they might become a problem."

Back on his feet, Logan raised his shotgun and aimed it at the door. "One of you want to open it for me? I'll blast whatever's closest, try to give us some breathing room. Don't know how many are in there, but I saw several bodies moving when they tried to pull me in. We need to push into the corridor. Whatever you do, don't let them into this stairwell."

Chris stepped forward and took hold of the door knob. After a quick look around to make sure everyone was set, he nodded at Logan and yanked the door open. Before it was even halfway open, Logan had his barrel thrust forward and was firing, pumping, and firing again. Behind him, the others were aiming to either side of him and added their rounds to his. Three octopoids that were clustered in front of the door took slugs and buckshot to their heads and torsos, but none went down.

Octopoid
Level 16
Health: 22,400/29,500

Allistor cast *Restraint* on the nearest, which was to his left. He hit the center mob with *Erupt*, stopping it cold before he chambered another round in his own shotgun and blasted it in the face from less than ten feet. He saw the slug punch into its bulbous head, then exit out the back with a spray of spongy flesh and blood, and it dropped dead. Allistor and the others had learned that regardless of a creature's remaining health pool, destroying its brain, decapitating it, or taking out its heart would kill it.

He didn't see who cast the spell, but someone hit the third octopoid with a fireball. He thought it was probably Lars or Logan, as the spell was relatively weak.

He was about to fire again when Logan called out, "Moving in!" He waited a heartbeat for the others to hear and hold fire, then stepped forward through the doorway, blasting the burning octopoid as he went. From just three feet away, the impact from the blast knocked the eight-foot tall monster onto its back, still burning and waving its six tentacles wildly.

Allistor and Chris were the next two through the door. Chris naturally moved to help Logan with the burning monster while Allistor went for the one on the left, just recovering from his earlier stun. He cast *Erupt* on the ground in front of it, but his aim was off. The spike that shot up from the floor pierced its upper thigh rather than its gut or chest. Still, it did serious damage, pushing through the stumpy limb and nearly severing it. Gouts of blood poured from the wound, but the creature shrugged it off and reached for Allistor. Unable to step forward, it bent at the waist and leaned toward him, all six of its tentacles bleeding from gunshot wounds.

Allistor tried to halt his own forward progress and lean backward to avoid them, but was too slow. Three of the appendages reached him, wrapping around his left arm and leg. Another got hold of his shotgun and ripped it from his grasp. He could feel the hooks on the underside of the tentacles digging into his skin as he set his feet and began a tug of war with the octopoid.

It was at least as strong as he was, and higher leveled. The thing made a bubbling screeching sound as the contest of strength caused the stone spike to do even more damage to its leg. But the spike also helped the monster, giving it an anchor from which to pull at Allistor.

Helen stepped up next to him and shoved her shotgun directly into the octopoid's face. When she pulled the trigger, the head exploded, showering them both in gore. Behind them, Dawn complained, "Hey, dammit! What's with the goo-splosion?" She sniffed at her arm, adding, "I smell like swampy ass covered in spoiled egg-salad."

Despite the pain from the hooks pulling at his skin, Allistor couldn't help but chuckle. Her description was pretty accurate. He carefully untangled the tentacles from his arm, then his leg, and Amanda waited until he was through before casting a heal on him. His leather gear now had several small blood-stained tears in it, and he'd have to get it mended soon.

The corridor was clear as far as they could see. Allistor launched a second light globe and pushed it down the corridor ahead of them. They worked the floor the same as the others, opening each door and clearing the room, then closing the door behind them. It helped to have the keys with them, as they could quickly open the locked doors without having to kick them in.

Three more of the rooms had octopoids in them, but these must have been trapped in the rooms and unable to feed, because they were all low level and easily dispatched. At the end of the corridor was another stairwell leading down. This one was much older than the others, and was carved right into the bedrock beneath the building. As they descended, the temperature dropped, and there was trickling moisture in places along the rough walls on either side.

"This can't be good. Those things love wet places. They wouldn't have stayed upstairs unless there was something down here they didn't want to mess with." Lars observed.

The stair curved around one hundred eighty degrees so that they were moving back underneath the main corridor above. When they reached the bottom, an old iron gate was sitting open. Past that was a wide corridor with rough stone floors and walls, lined on either side by what could only be jail cells. Framed in iron bars, each was about six feet square with a drain hole in the stone floor. A familiar stench emanated from somewhere in the back, where a heavy looking iron door stood open.

Dawn grumbled under her breath. "Great, whatever it is, it's even smellier than the others."

They didn't have to wait long to find out what it was. A massive version of the mobs upstairs stomped past the door at the back. The bedrock below them vibrated slightly with each step. Even with the seven-foot tall door open, all they could see of the monster was from its waist down.

> *Octopoid Alpha*
> *Elite*
> *Level 20*
> *Health: 43,900/43,900*

"Well, shit." Allistor sighed, resigned to having to fight yet another over-leveled monster. At least this time he had help. And an idea.

"This might be easy!" his tone changed as he began to formulate a plan. "I don't think it can fit through the door." He looked at Helen. "We'll kill this just like the dragon inside the Silo. Pound at it from out here, trap it in the doorway if it tries to come through."

Lars nodded. "I like it! We can stand well back from the door and work the hell out of its legs till it falls. Then work the body till it's dead."

They moved forward, carefully checking the empty cells as they went. When they were ten feet from the next door, they paused and spread out slightly. Allistor, Logan, and Chris took a knee while the others stood behind them, making the group look like a revolutionary war firing line. From this position they could see more of the creature, which looked to be at least fifteen feet tall. They still couldn't see its head as it shuffled back and forth. The area of the room visible beyond the door showed it to be a large cavern, at least fifty yards wide, that looked like it had been carved from the stone with hammer and chisel. They couldn't see the ceiling, but it must have been much higher than the room they were in, because the creature didn't appear to be stooping over at all.

Logan whispered, "Alright, as it walks by, we all focus fire on its nearest leg. Aim low, try to hit its ankle. If you aim too low, your shots will ricochet back up and still do damage, so don't sweat it. Let's see if we can cripple it."

They waited as the thing stomped closer. The moment it appeared in front of the door, all of them fired. The impact and sheer blasting power of eight shotguns' worth of buck shot and slugs all striking roughly the same spot was devastating. Most of the monster's lower leg disappeared in a cloud of blood and bits of flesh. It staggered, letting out a roar that hurt everyone's ears. Before any of them could fire again, the beast dropped to its belly and shot through the doorway head first, using all six of its tentacle arms to first grip the door frame and pull it through, then to grab hold of Logan and Allistor.

Both men cried out in pain as the monstrously long and strong appendages wrapped around their bodies. The

196

hooks dug in deep even as the coils tightened, ripping armor, clothes, and flesh like they'd been dumped in a shredder. Allistor's health dropped by thirty percent in seconds, and Logan was faring only slightly better because he'd put more points into *Constitution*. Somehow, the alpha managed to grip him with two different tentacles in opposite directions, so that when they coiled tighter, Allistor's body was twisted painfully at the waist even as his flesh was torn off in chunks.

Amanda shouted, "Helen! Heal Allistor! Lars, you get Logan! I'll help with both. Everybody shoot!"

Allistor felt first one heal, then a second, trying to focus through the pain enough to cast a spell. His health bar quit dropping near the halfway mark, and held there. Finally, he managed a *Restraint* spell that froze the creature and its mercilessly rending limbs. He felt another heal and closed his eyes for just a second. Opening them again, he nearly puked as he took in the state of Logan's body. Much like his own, it was badly shredded, bleeding from dozens of places where half-dollar sized chunks of flesh had been torn away.

He took a moment to cast *Restore* on himself, then on Logan, to help the healers. Then he shouted, "Everybody use Erupt while it's on the ground!" Not waiting for the others, he cast the spell right in front of its bulbous, malformed head. A spike shot up from the stone floor directly into its face, but didn't kill it.

> *Octopoid Alpha*
> *Elite*
> *Level 20*
> *Health: 15,100/43,900*

His spike had missed the monster's brain, but its health continued to drop as Helen, Amanda, Lars, and Logan all sent stone spikes up into its body. The attacks freed it from Allistor's stun, and it began thrashing wildly. The rending and tearing of the tightening coils ceased, but instead both men were smashed against the floor, ceiling, and iron bars.

Allistor tried to cast *Restraint* again, but an impact with the floor interrupted and stunned him. Logan's body was flapping about limply in the creature's grip, either unconscious or dead.

Another round of shotgun blasts went off, and Allistor caught a glimpse of Chris running forward. The man stopped a foot from the prone monster's head and fired a slug from point-blank range, even as he ducked to avoid a flailing tentacle. The slug blasted a deep hole, and blood welled out, but still the thing wouldn't die. Allistor, still partly dazed and with his head ringing, couldn't help but focus on the hole left by Chris' slug. He called out in a weak voice. "Everyone back. Ten steps, get back!"

When he saw the others complying, he returned his focus to the hole in the elite mob's head. A moment later he brought to mind the *Vortex* spell, but before casting he, focused on compressing it, making the whirlwind as small yet violent as possible. When he thought he had what he wanted, he let the spell loose.

A second later the whirlwind sprang to life, just as he'd imagined it. A tiny tornado of air and blood and dirt that spun impossibly fast in a tight cone inside the shotgun wound. A mental push from Allistor sent it deeper, effectively drilling into the monster's melon. The effect was mesmerizing. Everyone in the group stood gaping as the wind drilled its way into the screeching monster, sending a spray of blood that coated everything in the room.

Seconds later, the alpha stopped thrashing. Allistor was slammed into the floor again, but with only the force of gravity this time as the dead limbs fell. Everybody leveled up, and when the lights around Allistor faded, he saw Amanda was already running toward Logan, casting heals and pulling out a potion. Helen went with her, ignoring Allistor. He had to admit that it caused a bit of a twinge inside to see his two favorite women running to help his injured friend instead of him. He told himself it was a triage situation, that Logan needed them more than he did just then. It only made him feel a little bit better.

Surprisingly, Chris stepped over and reached a hand toward the tentacle wrapped around Allistor's chest, then paused and looked at him with a brow raised, a question in his eyes, but no sound coming from his lips. He'd taken Logan's warning seriously. Allistor nodded to him, and Chris began to carefully peel away the end of the appendage, doing his best with a belt knife to free the hooks from Allistor's flesh as gently as possible.

"I've been snagged by these things more than once. Though never one even half this size." Chris looked down along the monster's fifteen-foot length. "The secret is to treat them like fishhooks. Push them through, snap off the barb, then pull them out." He calmly matched deed to word as Allistor watched.

"Thank you, Chris. You did well in the fight. How 'bout we put our past behind us?"

The man paused in his work and nodded his hand. "I'd like that. I'd shake your hand, but…" He nodded toward his occupied hands.

Allistor tried not to laugh. Any movement at all hurt at this point. "Yeah, please just keep doin' what you're doin'."

Dawn came over to help as well, and over the next several minutes Allistor cast heals on himself while the two of them worked to free him. His leather gear was so badly shredded that it was beyond redemption. A pool of blood had formed under him by the time he was free. Logan was conscious but still looking dazed as he sat with his back against one of the cells. Lars had helped the ladies free and heal him, and they were trying to feed him some jerky.

Allistor followed their lead and pulled out some water and dragon jerky. After five minutes spent restoring himself, he felt nearly as good as new. Logan was alert enough to reach over and loot the mini-boss level monster when he saw Allistor do it. The others all paused to take their turns, and all seemed pleased with their haul. Fuzzy happily strolled over, set his Fibble doll gently on the floor, and began munching on the softer bits of the monster.

Allistor checked his notifications. First, his loot list showed a thousand klax, ten of the nasty hooks that had impaled him, a stack of twenty octopoid meat, which glowed green for some reason. His eyes widened when he saw there was also a scroll that glowed bright purple!

Disregarding everything else, he focused on the scroll, pulling it from his inventory. It actually glowed with a faint purple hue in real life, and caught Dawn's attention. "Cool! What is that? In the games I play... I *used to* play, purple meant super rare."

Allistor mumbled, "Yeah, I think it's the same here now." to her as he read the description.

> ***Spell Scroll: Dimensional Step***
> ***Item Quality: Epic***
> *This scroll teaches the user the Dimensional Step spell. When cast, Dimensional Step allows the user to move instantly from the position they occupy, to a position they designate within one hundred feet. User slides into a pocket dimension, emerging at the target location, bypassing any solid obstacles in between.* ***Spell cost****: 300 mana. Requires minimum Intelligence attribute of 10.* ***Cooldown****: One minute. Can only be cast on self. Target location must be within user's sight, or well-known enough for user to picture the location in detail. Failure to adequately recall details of target location increases risk of permanent entrapment in pocket dimension.*

Chapter 9

Get Off My Lawn!

"Holy shit, that's one helluva cheat!" Lars declared after Allistor gave them a brief description of the purple scroll's spell. "That would make you pretty much unbeatable in PVP." He grinned, giving Allistor the double finger-guns. "Remind me never to piss you off."

Dawn looked jealous. "Are you... gonna give that to Ramon to copy for us?"

Allistor shook his head. "I'm not sure. This is a rare item, and even though Ramon has been working hard, I doubt he has leveled his skills enough to copy this. But I won't use it until I have a chance to talk to him. Speaking of which..."

Allistor pulled up his interface and tried to claim the building as a Stronghold. A wide grin spread across his face as the option appeared.

Would you like to claim this structure as a Stronghold? Yes/No

"Yes!" he shouted aloud as he mentally clicked the button. The expected light surrounded them all, and he quickly chose his usual options. He constructed a wall around the building and a big chunk of the park area, added power, water, sensors, then finished. He'd worry about designating housing spaces and the rest later. With a new Stronghold popping up just a few blocks from him, Allistor expected a visit from Paul very soon.

Finishing his selection caused one last flare-up of light as the system constructed the new elements or adjusted the existing ones. When it was done, Allistor realized he had a dilemma he hadn't considered. As the group walked back through the jail cells and up the stairs, he missed out on the conversation as his mind worked through the problem.

He had wanted to keep his ability to teleport a secret.

Now that he'd established this Stronghold so close to Paul's, a fight was imminent. He had planned to quickly set up a teleport pad and bring some of his people through to deal with Paul. When Logan and the others had volunteered to come, it hadn't occurred to him that they'd question how his people arrived so quickly.

So, his options were to reveal his secret, maybe make them swear not to tell anyone using one of those binding system oaths. Or mislead them, distract them somehow and lie about how his people got there. Claim he'd called them down the night before. But he'd also have to somehow hide the teleport pad from his new allies.

The decision was harder than it should have been. The moral thing to do was to be honest with Lars and company. But if Chris, for example, were to disregard his oath and blab to a crowd of people about the teleport system, it didn't matter if the system struck him dead on the spot. The secret would be out. And his Strongholds would quickly become prime targets for groups looking to secure the valuable asset for themselves.

In the end, two factors made the decision for him. First, his desire to have faith in his fellow humans was strong. He was no fool, and the risks involved in sharing the secret terrified him. Humans were inherently incapable of keeping secrets in general. But the second and overriding factor was that he didn't want to begin his relationship with Lars and the others by lying to or misleading them.

As they paused in front of the now operable elevator, he said, "Hold on a second guys."

They all turned to look at him. "Lars, Logan, and Chris. I have some information I haven't shared with you before now, because, frankly, I wasn't sure how far I could trust you. Especially you, Chris. No offense." Chris nodded his head in understanding. He knew his behavior had been uncalled for, and didn't blame Allistor for his response.

"But I think if we're going to move forward as friends and allies, we need to be open with each other. And I've come to trust you three. So, I've decided to bring you in on something that, should it get out, could spell disaster for me and all my people. It would make us a target for every group with any strength on this continent." He let that soak in for a moment.

"Like I said, I've come to trust you. But before I share this with you, I'm going to need all three of you swear a binding oath that you will never speak a word of it to anyone without my express permission."

Chris was the first to raise his hand. "I swear on my life I'll never speak of what you reveal here today to anyone without your express permission."

Lars and Logan looked surprised. Neither had witnessed Allistor and Chris' earlier conversation. After exchanging a look, they both raised a hand and repeated Chris' oath. All three were magically bound as the indicative light swirled around and absorbed into them.

As Helen pushed the elevator call button, Allistor explained. "You all saw the notice when I first raised the Citadel?"

All three men nodded. Lars said, "I was a little jealous." To which Allistor chuckled.

"Well, it turns out claiming huge areas of territory and gaining a title, then constructing the planet's first Citadel, comes with some significant bonuses. Kind of like a first clear of a newly discovered dungeon." He watched their faces light up as they identified with that reference. It was every gamer's dream to be the first to clear a dungeon and claim the epic loot.

"Well, one of those bonuses was a teleportation hub, and six pads. The hub is in Cheyenne, and I can set up the pads at my Outposts or Strongholds. They allow me to teleport people and things instantly from one location to the other. I'm going to place one here, and bring my people in to help with the fight against Paul, and maybe with clearing the dungeon."

Logan began to laugh. Quietly at first, then louder. "I'm glad you're not crazy."

Allistor looked confused, and Logan clarified. "I've been wondering how the hell you figured to take out Paul and his people, and then clear the dungeon, with just the eight of us. I was trying to decide if you had some secret weapon up your sleeve, or you were just a delusional nutjob. I gotta say, this isn't what I expected. But I'm damn glad it's option A, not B."

The freight elevator opened with a ding, and they all piled in. Fuzzy sniffed suspiciously at the doors for a moment before stepping in, forcing the others to pack tighter to make room. Fifteen seconds later they stepped out into the main corridor on the ground floor level. Moving out to the rotunda in the center of the building, Allistor once again took some time to stare up at the underside of the dome high above. "This place is beautiful."

After giving him some time to admire his new place, they turned and exited the main doors, which led out to a two-tiered stone stairway wide enough to march a battalion down. Allistor looked around at the thirty-foot high wall that now blocked his view of surrounding buildings and parklands. The gate faced west, as if the system knew that Allistor's true goal, and his main obstacle, lay in that direction.

The area inside the wall was mainly greenspace. There was a road that circled the entire building with some parking spaces scattered around it. The wall had enclosed two full city blocks, and everything beyond the border road was grass, trees, and shaded walkways. The gate stood open, and Allistor could see more parkland to the west, stretching three more blocks until it ended at an official looking building. Lars saw him staring and said, "That's the courthouse. And right behind that is the mint and the depository. Paul's place."

Allistor called out. "Nigel? Are you there, buddy?"

"Of course, Lord Allistor. Congratulations on the new acquisition. It is truly an impressive structure."

"Thank you, Nigel. Can you put me in touch with Ramon, please?"

"Of course, Lord Allistor. One moment please."

Allistor caught Lars staring at him. "Another one of the perks?"

"Yep. He's an AI that runs all my facilities. Came with the Citadel. You have one at your Stronghold too, it just can't interact with you yet."

"That is correct, Lord Allistor. A Stronghold AI cannot verbally interact until it reaches Level 5. Also, Ramon is awaiting your pleasure."

"Hey Ramon! Guess who!" Allistor couldn't help it. He was in a good mood, and quite proud of his new acquisition.

"Uhhm... the Easter bunny?" Ramon sounded impatient, but he played along.

"Everything okay there, man? You sound a little stressed."

"Just real busy, Allistor. So many people needing copies of spells. My team and I are working full time and it's still not enough."

"Well, first... thank you for all your hard work. Your people's, too. And second... how'd you like to take a little break. Do some fighting? Level up a bit?"

"Hell yes!" Ramon's impatience instantly converted to enthusiasm.

"I'm gonna set up a teleport pad here. Got a sort of Stronghold to attack, some humans to defeat, and then a dungeon to clear. I'm thinking for the first fight we could use about a hundred people. For the dungeon, we've already got eight. I'm thinking you, Sam, Meg, Michael, Dean, Andrea, and maybe the awful foursome can join us. Nancy too, if she's willing. And from Laramie, Richard and any of his leaders that want to come. Can you get the other leaders together and arrange that? Volunteers only. Let them know it'll be a deadly fight. Several parties have already died down there. Nobody has to come that doesn't want to. I'll open the teleport in about two hours." He paused, then said, "Tell Sam I want a BFG and a couple of the little sisters too."

Logan grunted at that. "Haven't seen one of those in years. Remember what I said about having a secret weapon up your sleeve? That would qualify." He grinned at Allistor.

"You can fight Sam for who gets to fire it." Allistor shot back.

The group spent some time looking around the grounds, walking the complete circuit around the massive building. Allistor chose a spot within a dense clump of trees to place the teleport pad, and once it was placed, one could easily miss spotting it if one didn't know it was there. There was an opening between the trees wide enough to allow vehicles to move in and out, but the pad and columns were mainly lost in the high grass and trees.

Allistor had just completed the installation when Nigel's voice came to them.

"Lord Allistor, there are three groups of humanoids approaching from the west, northwest, and southwest quadrants. Fifteen in total. Nine in the western group, three each in the other two. They are moving slowly."

"Thank you, Nigel. Please share your sensor readings with everyone here inside the wall." Allistor enlarged the map on his interface, seeing the red dots just as Nigel had described them. They were moving erratically, obviously going from cover to cover as they approached. That was good. It gave Allistor time to prepare a greeting.

"Nigel, please connect this teleport pad to the rest of the network, and allow my advisors to access it. They'll be teleporting in from different locations." he instructed as the group moved toward the wall. "And please close the gates."

As they climbed up the stair leading to the western rampart, the multi-ton metal doors swung shut, connecting with a clang that reverberated through their feet. Up on top, they spread out and looked through the trees trying to spot the intruders. Allistor asked, "Can any of you identify Paul's people on sight?"

Chris spoke first, while Logan and Lars both nodded. "I know most of them. Been watching them, waiting for them to go out alone, or in small groups so I can pick them off." His lips twitched in an almost-grin. "They stopped going out alone or in small groups."

"Okay, it looks like all three of you can recognize them. I want to be sure the people out there belong to him before we hurt any of them. They could be a foraging party, curious about the new Stronghold. Though I doubt it

209

by their formation. Lars, if you wouldn't mind going to check out the group to the south? Take Helen and Nathan with you? Logan, take Dawn to the north? Chris, you stay here with Amanda and me, as the largest group is coming this way. My guess is that if Paul's here, he'll be in that group."

He sent them all party invites, which they accepted. As they left, he added, "Use Nigel to relay messages."

Allistor pulled the .50 cal from his inventory and set it atop the wall. It was more gun than he needed to deal with human targets inside two hundred yards, but the scope would allow them to get a good look at their targets' faces. Once the gun was set up, he motioned for Chris to take a look. The man embraced the rifle almost reverently, appreciating its craftsmanship and sheer badassery. Looking through the scope, he scanned the parkland to the west. "I only see six. I can see the other dots' locations on my map – that's a little weird, by the way – but those three are staying behind cover. And yeah, these are Paul's people."

Chris set the rifle back down and stepped back. Allistor put it away, producing his normal hunting rifle instead. Chris and Amanda did the same, and the three of them leaned into the wall as they sighted on the incoming creepers. "These guys ain't too smart." Chris spat over the wall. "They should have at least waited until dark. Big mistake."

Amanda spoke very quietly. "I want to feel sorry for these guys, offer them the chance to surrender. I want to believe that they're being coerced somehow by Paul, and aren't really bad people. But… here they are coming to attack us…" She shook her head slightly.

Allistor set down his rifle and turned to her. "Hey, listen. You can just kick back and heal us if necessary. If you have a problem taking human lives, I totally understand. You shouldn't have to do this. None of us should."

Amanda took a deep breath. "No, I don't think I can. I mean, maybe if they're shooting at us and it's us or them. But I just…"

He gathered her into a hug, kissing the top of her head. "I get it. I really do. And I promise I won't kill them unless we have to. But I also won't let them continue hurting people."

Amanda nodded and pulled away from his embrace. Taking up her rifle, she continued to scan the area through her scope, but her finger was nowhere near the trigger.

Allistor watched and waited until the nearest of the intruders was just about fifty yards from the wall, with the others close behind. All but the three who'd taken cover and hung back. The northern and southern groups had both continued to move forward as well. "Nigel, please patch me through to the others." He waited a couple heartbeats, then said, "I'm going to try to talk to them. Please don't fire unless I say so, or they fire first."

When he received acknowledgements from both groups, he said, "Nigel, please open the gates."

"Of course, Lord Allistor."

211

The massive doors swung inward, and Allistor watched as a confused look appeared on the face of the intruder he was scoping. Standing upright so he was clearly visible to the people below, he said, "My name is Allistor! If Paul is one of the three people hiding in the back, tell him to step forward! I'll guarantee his safety while we talk!"

This caused some muttering from down below, too faint for Allistor to make out what they were saying. When nothing happened for a full minute, Allistor shouted again. "I'm giving you thirty seconds! Then, one of three things is going to happen. Either Paul steps inside to have a little chat, you folks all leave my territory at a dead run, or we shoot you all and wait for a smarter group to show up!"

When twenty more seconds had passed without a response or any movement, Allistor tried a third time. "Ten seconds! Your leader is obviously a coward! Do you want to die for a man like that? Send Paul up, or haul ass. We start firing in five... four... three..."

He watched as several of the red dots began to retreat. Not all of them, and not very fast. Two remained directly in front of him, and the groups to the north and south hadn't moved.

"Time's up!" he shouted.

Nodding to Chris, he said, "Nigel, tell the others to shoot anyone not retreating."

Taking aim at a man partly concealed behind a tree, he fired. Almost immediately, shots rang out from Chris and the others. The man he'd shot fell backward with a round in his shoulder, screaming in pain. Chris' shot had

212

been a fatal one, a woman with a sniper rifle fell with half the back of her head gone. On Allistor's map, all but two of the red dots to the north and south went grey. Those two began to move quickly away from the wall.

Some of those who were retreating turned and fired as they moved, but the shots went wild and they continued to flee. The three dots that had remained in the rear moved fastest of all, abandoning their comrades. Though he was growling in frustration, Chris followed Allistor's order not to fire on those who were retreating.

"Good shot, Chris. Let's go down and loot, and pick up the one I wounded. He can answer some questions for us."

As they descended the stairs, he took Amanda's hand. "I'm sorry we had to do that. I tried to give them a chance."

She nodded, tears in her eyes. "I know. You did the right thing. I just wish it didn't have to be like this."

"Me too." He noticed the others coming down from the wall as well. They all exited the gate and split up, each going to loot their individual kills. Allistor walked up to the man he'd shot. He was lying on the ground, trying to apply pressure to his wound with his good hand. When he saw Allistor, he tried to reach for his weapon, but Allistor raised his own and said, "I'll put the next round in your face if you try anything."

"You shot me, you asshole!" the man shouted at him.

"I warned you, *three times* and gave you plenty of time to run. Maybe I should just shoot you in the face anyway. You might be too stupid to live."

"Why'd you shoot me? I didn't do anything to you!"

"You're one of Paul's people. How many humans have you ambushed and murdered while they were out searching for food?"

The man just glared at him, silently projecting pure hatred.

Amanda put a hand on Allistor's shoulder. "Can I heal him?"

He turned to face her, shaking his head. "Not yet. I want some answers, and I don't think this asshat is going to cooperate unless he's bleeding to death." Looking back at the man, he added, "And you are, by the way. Bleeding to death, I mean. Your people bailed on you, the ones that aren't dead. The lady with the sniper rifle, was she a friend of yours? Because Chris splattered her brains like a Pollock painting."

"Screw you!" the man's venom hadn't decreased, but his voice was getting weaker. The red stain on the ground underneath him was spreading.

"Answer my questions, and Amanda here will heal you. Good as new. I figure you've got maybe a minute before you bleed out, so I'll talk fast. I suggest you do the same. First, was Paul here with you?"

The man just glared at him.

"Those were pretty small words. I'm sure you understood. Was. Paul. With. You?" He stepped forward and placed the barrel of his rifle six inches in front of the man's face. "If you're not going to be helpful, I have no reason to let you live. You're no good for ransom, since Paul has nothing I need. Except that building you've been living in." He paused and withdrew the barrel a bit so the man could see his face clearly.

"How much does Paul like you? Would he give up the mint to get you back?" He watched the man's eyes. "Does Paul even know who you are?"

There it was. The look of hopelessness mixed in with the fear and anger.

"I'll ask you one more time. You really are losing a lot of blood. Was Paul here with you?"

The man shook his head no.

"Is that a no, he wasn't here? Or no, you're not going to answer and want to bleed to death?"

"No, he wasn't here. He sent us out to scout. He'd never risk his own ass approaching a Stronghold." the man's voice was bitter.

"Thank you." Allistor smiled at the man. "Amanda, please heal him enough to stop the bleeding."

As Amanda cast her heal, Chris came to stand next to him, having looted the sniper. He looked down and spat in the man's face. "Murdering coward. Let him bleed out."

"He has information we need. If he provides that information, I'll let him go. If he doesn't, he's all yours."

215

Allistor looked Chris directly in the eye, making sure the man understood. Chris gave a brief nod, then glared at the man on the ground.

"Alright. So Paul wasn't here. Who were the three that stayed back and watched you get your asses shot off?"

"Lieutenant. And two of his prisoners."

"Prisoners?" Amanda asked.

"They take people, family or friends, from the ones we capture. Use them to make the others work. If they refuse to do what they're told, Paul executes their loved one. Or gives them to us. The lieutenant always keeps a couple of them with him."

Chris spat on the man again. "To use when he feels like it."

A look of horror appeared on Amanda's face. "You... You've used these prisoners yourself?"

The man smirked at her. "There ain't no law against it anymore. Paul says the weak serve the strong. That's how it was in the beginning, and that's how it is again now."

Amanda's fists clenched, and her eyes bored into the man. "You filthy piece of shit. You sit here proud of yourself, bragging about raping women?"

"You asked, I answered. That's the deal here, right sweetness? And thanks for the healing. It felt real nice." He licked his lips slightly as he winked at her.

Amanda turned to Allistor. "I was wrong. This one dies."

When Allistor nodded, the man's eyes widened. "You promised if I talked, you'd let me go!"

"No, I didn't. I promised if you talked, we wouldn't let you bleed out. And we kept that promise. And I told Chris here I'd let you go if you talked… but that was not a promise to you in any way. Unfortunately for you, when you opened your moronic yap, you sentenced yourself to death." Allistor looked at Fuzzy, who was nearby sniffing at a tree.

"Now you have a different choice. You tell me what I want to know, and Chris here will happily put a bullet through your brain. Quick and painless. You don't talk, and I'll let Fuzzy eat you, face first."

Hearing his name, Fuzzy ambled over with the ever-present Fibble doll flapping in his jaws. He set the doll down at Allistor's feet, then leaned forward to sniff at the man on the ground.

"Y-you can't do this! I have rights!"

Amanda turned and bent down, screaming at the man with her face inches from his. "YOU HAVE NO RIGHTS! You said it yourself, didn't you? The strong versus the weak, right? You're the weak one here. The stupid, raping, murdering, cowardly weakling on the ground begging for his worthless life! But you gave up any right to live the first time you killed an innocent forager and abused a helpless prisoner. You're a waste of oxygen, and I hope you don't talk so Fuzzy can kill you slowly!"

The man tried to scramble backward in the face of her wrath, and Allistor and Chris both took a surprised step back. When the man looked to him for help, Allistor shrugged. "Personally, I vote for Fuzzy too." Chris raised a hand to silently add his vote. Fuzzy took another step toward the man.

"Wait! Wait, I'll tell you. What do you want to know?" the men held both hands up between him and the bear cub. Fuzzy licked one of them, causing the man to wet himself.

"How many people does Paul have living there at the mint?"

"'Bout a hundred and fifty. The number changes, people die, more people come."

"Tell me about the lower levels. How many times has he sent people down, how many did he send, and what did they run into?"

"He sent three groups down. I was in the last one. First group was five, second was ten, mine was twenty. There's those creeper things down there, the little pasty ones with the claws that move real fast. Those octopus monsters too. We managed to kill those, but next there was these spiders that spit acid. Melted the skin right off some of our guys. Barely got past them, then ran into a real monster. Only four of us came back out of twenty."

Amanda asked the next question. "The prisoners. How many are there, and where are they kept?"

"Second floor, most of them. There's close to a hundred. They outnumber us, but we got the guns, so they stay quiet, mostly. The ones that act up don't last long." He looked at Allistor. "I'm sorry, okay? You can't kill me. That'd be murder. I'm sorry for all I did wrong. I can change!"

Allistor looked at the man for a long time, saying nothing. His comment about murder had struck a chord. But this man had come to kill him, and had admitted to abusing prisoners at the very least, if not outright murder. As a head of state, of sorts, it was Allistor's job to enforce the rules, and to deal with those who violated them.

"No… I don't think you *can* change. Further, I don't think you'd want to, if there wasn't a hungry grizzly in your face."

He nodded to Chris, who instantly stepped past Fuzzy and fired a round directly into the man's forehead. The kill earned Chris a level, but he had the good taste not to celebrate. He simply bent down and looted the corpse, then nodded at Allistor and walked away.

When he turned to face Amanda, she grabbed hold of him and hugged him tightly, her face pressed into his chest as she sobbed. He wrapped his arms around her and squeezed her tightly, whispering, "I'm sorry." as he held her.

When she'd let it all out, she gave him a final squeeze and stepped back. "I hate this world." Not waiting for a response, she turned and walked back toward the gate. Fuzzy, who had been gnawing on the corpse, abandoned his snack and scooped up his Fibble before trotting after Amanda. When he caught up to her, he butted his head against her hand. She absently began scratching his ears as they walked.

Allistor waited a while, smiling at his cub and mumbling, "Good job, buddy." He took a look at the man and noticed the 'lootable' glow around the corpse. He'd forgotten that he fired the initial shot that took the man down. That meant he got partial credit for the kill. Bending down, he touched the partially chewed corpse. He received five hundred klax, a set of keys, a box of rifle ammo, and a pack of cigarettes. The keys interested him. If they could get him access to the mint...

Lars called his name, holding up a hand as he approached across the park. "What do you want to do with the bodies?"

"Leave them where they are. If something comes to feed on them, a few of our low level people can pick them off, gain some experience points."

An hour later the teleport pad began to light up. Sam came through first, standing in one of the Humvees with his torso sticking out the top, the BFG mounted to the roof. He waved and struck a heroic pose like he was a homecoming king in a parade as the vehicle rolled off the pad, and Allistor couldn't help but laugh. He laughed even harder when Meg, who was in the driver's seat, slammed on the brakes and nearly made Sam bonk his head on the weapon, ruining his hero pose.

The pad lit up again and again, and in short order Allistor had nearly two hundred of his people at the Capitol, which was the natural name for the new Stronghold. There were the hundred fighters, plus a bunch of support people, and some who were just curious to see the new place. The folks from Laramie had made the drive to Cheyenne in record time to join the fight. Allistor greeted Richard, Bob, Virginia, Austin, and a few of the other leaders along with his core group. Austin had brought a couple teenage friends along, and all three were looking to fight.

220

"We're ready, Lord Allistor! Just point us at the bad guys." Austin hefted a rifle, an eager look on his face. Allistor caught a slight shake of the head from Virginia, who was giving him a look.

"I'm sorry Austin, but not this time. I do have a job for you though. You and your friends. I need you up on the wall. We left some corpses out there, and I expect predators and scavengers will be sniffing around. Need you guys to kill them for me."

Disappointed but mollified, the three young men dashed off toward the wall. Allistor asked Chris to show them where to post in order to cover all three kill sites.

Meg got out of the truck and walked over with Sam. She whistled, looking up at the building with its golden dome. "You're getting all fancy on us, Lord Allistor." She poked him in the gut as she teased him. "This place is real purty."

Allistor hugged the woman and shook Sam's hand. "I haven't touched the inside yet. You wanna design the kitchen and dining? I can give you access…"

"Oh hell yes! Do it. How long do we have before it's fightin' time?" Meg rubbed her hands together in anticipation.

"No rush. We had a little encounter just now with Paul's people. Killed… six of them?" Anyway, I don't think he'll be in a rush to attack again. So we can take our time and prepare before we take the fight to him. How 'bout we attack early in the morning? Let his fighters worry about us all night."

Sam put his arm over Meg's shoulder and started to steer her toward the building. "Sounds good to me. And don't let anybody touch my baby girl." He motioned toward the belt-fed .50 caliber atop the Humvee. "She's sensitive."

Logan cleared his throat. "Um, about that..." He stuck out a hand. "I'm Logan." Sam looked the giant man up and down, then shook his hand.

"Sam. Please tell me you were a marine." Logan walked with Sam as they headed for the building and began what Allistor was sure would be one hell of a sales pitch. He was sure Sam would let the man play with the gun, at least a little bit.

Chapter 10

I'll Feed Fuzzy Your Face

The survivors spent the evening exploring the new Stronghold, setting up the various internal amenities like housing units, crafting stations, and the all-important kitchen-slash-dining area. Amanda insisted on creating a big luxurious residence for Allistor on the top floor, facing north toward the Citadel. He didn't argue, figuring she was dealing with her earlier outrage in her own way, and it was best to leave her to it. Meg muttered something about 'nesting' and cackled at him.

Almost as soon as the sun set, Nigel alerted Allistor that non-humanoid intruders had entered the grounds. He tracked a dozen of them for about half a minute, then gunshots rang out from atop the wall. Austin and his friends fired several times, and eventually the red dots all went grey. He heard some muffled cheering, and hoped the kids had leveled up.

"Nigel, would you ask Bjurstrom and his crew to escort the kids outside to loot the dead monsters?"

"Of course, Lord Allistor."

Allistor sought out Ramon, who was already organizing a workshop for himself and his scribes. It was in one of the ground floor offices, one with its own full bathroom. He'd set up several long tables with comfortable chairs, and there was a whole wall of built-in shelves.

He sat down in front of his friend, saying nothing, with a shit-eating grin plastered across his face. He watched the man work for a while, until finally Ramon looked up. "What?"

"Good to see ya, buddy!" Allistor didn't stop grinning.

"Yeahhhh… okay. Good to see you too."

Allistor was practically bouncing in his seat, and Ramon was getting more suspicious by the second. "What is it, Allistor? You want me to help you do something stupid and dangerous, don't you?"

"Stupid, maybe. But not dangerous, I don't think. Okay maybe dangerous, in that it might waste a very valuable resource."

"What valuable resource?"

Allistor whipped out the purple *Dimensional Step* scroll and set it on the table between them. "TA-DAAAAA!" He gave a little game show hostess flourish with his hands.

Ramon looked at the scroll sitting there with its purple glow. He reached out a slightly shaky hand and touched it, his gaze unfocused as he read the description. "Holy shitballs!" He looked at Allistor. "Where did you get this?"

"Dropped off a really big nasty octopoid in the basement of this building. I was hoping…"

Ramon shook his head. "I know what you're hoping. But no. This is beyond my skill. This is beyond the skill of anyone on this planet for the foreseeable future. This is a Master level scroll." He paused, pulling something up on interface. "According to the info my

224

Scribe interface gives me, the average time it takes to reach Master level inscription is about ten years."

Ramon stared at the scroll for a bit longer, shaking his head. "Damn. That's one killer spell." A mischievous look appeared on his face. "I'd be happy to go ahead and learn it now, then make copies for you in about ten years."

"Ha!" Allistor snatched the scroll off the table and hugged it to his chest like it was a teddy bear. In his best supervillain voice, he cried, "It's mine! All mine! Muahahaha!"

He went to open the scroll, and Ramon shouted, "No!" holding out both hands in a stop gesture.

"What?" Allistor looked confused.

"Before you open that, I need to say two things. First, you could sell that on the market for about a billion klax."

Allistor shook his head. "If things go well tomorrow, we'll have about fifty billion klax. Literally. That's what the gold down there is worth."

"Okay, so you don't need the money. But if you're going to use the scroll, don't do it here and now. Using that thing is like… a historic event. Purple scrolls like that come along once or twice in a lifetime. If you're going to open it, do it in front of everyone. Make a show out of it. It'll be good for morale, and an excuse to get drunk."

"Ha! Okay, good point. I'll do it over dinner tonight. Which should be pretty soon, I think. Want to walk with me and help me find something wrong with Meg's new kitchen?"

Ramon got up and joined Allistor, but said, "I wouldn't say anything other than 'nice kitchen' to Meg. She takes that shit seriously. Teasing her about it is like poking Fuzzy while he sleeps.

"Speaking of which, have you seen my bear? I've sort of gotten used to him just being around, and I'm not sure when he left me."

"Nope. Been in that room almost since I got here. I don't get out much anymore. So many things to read and write."

It didn't take long to solve the mystery of Fuzzy's disappearance. They found him in the kitchen doing his best to mooch scraps from Meg and Sam. Allistor wasn't even all the way through the door when Meg scolded. "Curb your damn flea-bitten, overgrown teddy bear!"

The scolding lost a lot of its heat when she tossed a chunk of raw meat to Fuzzy, who didn't seem the least bit offended by the name-calling. "Don't you ever feed this poor fella?"

Allistor shrugged. "He mostly feeds himself. Just a lil while ago he was chewing on some guy's nose."

Meg stared at him, then pointed to the door. "Out! All of you, out of my kitchen! Take that snot-eating monstrosity with you!" She picked up a wicked looking fork and flung it past Allistor to stick in the door.

Sam chuckled in the background as Fuzzy snatched up his Fibble and retreated, confused. Allistor stopped near the door. "Nice kitchen, Meg!" he called out before ducking through the door. Now Ramon was laughing too.

"Real original, hero." Ramon patted Fuzzy's head to reassure the bear, who was still wondering why Meg was feeding him one moment, then chasing him away the next.

"Hey, I was under fire, had to think fast." Allistor shrugged.

The two men and bear cub made their way to the dining hall, which was a former hearing room or something. Meg had moved walls, rearranged things as she liked them, attached the kitchen, and was already producing their first big meal. Taking seats at one of the long tables, Allistor spent some quality time with Ramon and Fuzzy. They talked about the library, and any new skill or spell info that Ramon might have discovered. As they spoke, Allistor scratched the bear cub's ears, under his chin, then had to get on the floor and rub his tummy when the bear rolled onto his back to demand it. That, of course, turned into a wrestling session, which Ramon couldn't resist getting in on.

When folks started drifting into the room for meal time, they found Allistor and Ramon dive-tackling the bear cub, then rolling around tickling and biting him as he fought back. At one point, Allistor seized the Fibble doll and rolled away. Getting to his feet, he waved the slimy, slobbery thing at Fuzzy. "Got your doll! I've kidnapped Fibble, oh no!"

Fuzzy let out a roar, making nearly everyone in the large room jump, and dove after Allistor. Chairs and tables were flung aside as the laughing human used them as obstacles to maintain his lead. Eventually though, the four-legged speed of the bear cub won out, and he managed to extend a paw and trip Allistor. The human fell on his face,

227

and Fuzzy dove atop him, frantically sniffling and snuffling to find his doll, which was buried under his human.

"Gah! Get that wet nose out of my face!" Allistor complained, pushing the bear's massive head away. Here's your smelly old doll!" He rolled away, revealing Fuzzy's prized possession, which the bear snatched up before retreating to a corner, giving Allistor a dirty look the whole time.

When he got to his feet, Allistor immediately noticed two things. The room was half-destroyed, and everyone was staring at him. With a mostly straight face, he said, "Gotta keep him amused or he'll eat somebody." and began picking up fallen chairs and placing them at their tables.

Some of the others laughed, but the newer folks looked nervously at Fuzzy.

Dinner was a delightful combination of canid steaks, fresh vegetables from one of the greenhouses, and warm buttered bread that Sam had baked. When most everyone was done eating, Allistor stood and raised his hand. The room fell quiet, and he said, "Thank you all for coming here, for volunteering to fight. I thought I'd give you a little more information on why we're fighting tomorrow. First, a man named Paul and his followers are holding roughly a hundred prisoners. People they've kidnapped during ambushes of foraging and hunting parties, during which they murdered others. And the man we questioned today confirmed they're blackmailing and abusing some prisoners, executing others. So... we're going to kill Paul and his people." He waited as he measured the reaction of his people.

"Any of you who do not wish to fight and potentially kill other humans may back out with my blessing, and no repercussions of any kind. Killing another person should be hard, and shouldn't be taken lightly. If you want to opt out, see me after this."

Again, he paused to let people absorb what he'd said.

"After Paul and his people are dealt with, there's the little matter of a dungeon in the lower levels of the building. We're going to clear that dungeon and claim the building… along with the *billions* of klax worth of gold down there. Twenty-five or so of us are going down there. For most of you, the mobs are too high level, and I don't want to get you killed. So, I'll ask that you remain above and defend the building from anyone who might get bright ideas about taking it while we're down there."

He saw a wave of nodding heads and determined faces. "The gold down there can secure our future for generations. We already have the land, and with those funds we can buy the gear and supplies we need to farm, mine, and even create some manufacturing facilities. Or buy ourselves a resort island and a private space ship to take us there!"

This earned some applause, and a few whistles, most notably from Meg in the back. "But for tonight, let's relax and enjoy each other's company!"

He sat down, and Ramon slapped the back of his head. "Oh, shit!" He jumped back to his feet. "Hold on! Hold on! I forgot something."

The room got quiet again. "When we cleared this building, I received a very rare loot drop."

Ramon shouted from his seat. "VERY rare!"

Looking sideways at his friend, Allistor continued. "It's a spell called *Dimensional Step* that could come in very handy in a variety of situations, especially combat." He waited for the 'oohs' and 'ahhs' to quiet down, then produced the scroll and held it high. The purple glow had everyone leaning forward with unabashed lust.

"Before you ask, yes. I consulted with Ramon about copying this for everyone, but he tells me it's a Master level scroll, and beyond our current or near future abilities. So, I thought... well, Ramon thought... it'd be a good idea for all of you to get to see me use it. To make you all very jealous and grumpy!"

He waited for the boos to die down, looking at Ramon. "What was that? No? It's supposed to raise morale? Okay then! Here we go!" He opened the scroll. A flood of information invaded his brain, making it feel like it was burning and swelling and freezing and shattering all at the same time. He nearly passed out from the pain. When he opened his eyes again, he was on the floor, and about twenty people were gathered around, looking down at him. He took a moment to breathe, letting the pain pass.

As everyone backed up, Amanda held out a hand to help him up. "I watched you absorb that with my *Internal Analysis*. The amount of those little suckers gathered around you... it was incredible."

As soon as he was on his feet, he jumped up with arms out and shouted, "Ta-da!"

There was dead silence for a moment, then people began to laugh. A few clapped as he took a bow, and he called out, "Ramon was right! Good for morale!"

Just for fun, he picked a clear spot on the other side of the room, and activated the new spell. Almost faster than he could register, he was standing in his targeted spot. He wobbled a bit, his brain confused by the change in location without apparent motion. It was as if his mind demanded some kind of inertia from the rapid crossing of the room.

Austin was the first to spot him after he disappeared without warning. Pointing to Allistor in his new position, he shouted, "Cool!"

The others all turned their heads, and a roar of exclamations erupted. People surrounded Allistor, reaching out to touch him and confirm he wasn't an illusion. Enjoying the fun, Allistor picked a spot right behind where Fuzzy was lounging, and cast the spell again. There were more exclamations as he popped out of existence, and people who'd been leaning in to touch him found nothing but empty air. He appeared behind his bear cub and launched a sneak tickle attack, causing Fuzzy to squeal in surprise and jump up.

The drain from the spell was significant. Casting it twice had drained a full third of his mana. He noticed a sort of lethargic feeling from spending that much that fast, but it wasn't painful. Making a mental note to discuss it with Amanda, another idea struck him. She was still standing where she'd helped him up from the floor, so he cast the spell again. Appearing right behind her, he wrapped both arms around her waist and bent to kiss her neck.

"Cut that out! Allistor is around here somewhere, and he might see!" she teased.

"Oh ho! So it's like that, is it?" He squeezed harder and lifted her off her feet, pretending to bite into her neck Fuzzy-style. She squealed and squirmed, and the crowd whistled and cheered him on.

The rest of the evening was spent talking, laughing, and generally enjoying life. Which was something folks hadn't gotten to do a lot of in recent months. Allistor spent a little time with the veterans in the group discussing a rough strategy for the coming attack, then released them all to enjoy themselves. As his mana recharged, Allistor played his party trick a few more times, most notably sneaking up behind Meg and tickling her, which earned him an elbow to the face and a broken nose. Sam nearly fell over laughing, then grabbed Meg and swept her into a big showy kiss, saying, "That's my girl!"

When Sam stood her back on her feet, Meg gave Allistor her sweetest smile. "Never tickle another man's woman." Allistor cast a heal on himself, and bowed to Meg, one arm behind his back, the other sweeping outward.

"M'lady, my apologies. Tis a lesson I shall not soon forget!"

*****

Morning came early, and for Allistor earlier than most. He'd asked Nigel to wake him two hours before sunrise. Which prompted Nigel to ask him which sunrise. Allistor hadn't put a whole lot of thought into the fact that there were two suns now, the dark and the light. He'd just sort of taken it in stride and accepted it as normal.

As soon as he was awake, he'd ordered Nigel to sound a quiet alarm to wake the others. An annoyingly pitched beeping sound echoed through the entire building, effectively waking everyone. Then Allistor announced through Nigel, "We leave in an hour. Those who are joining the fight, be at the gate. It's only a short walk to our destination, but I want to attack before sunrise."

He and Amanda donned their gear. During the evening festivities, Lilly had appeared and handed him new leather armor. It was a complete set, and as he *Examined* it, he saw she'd greatly improved her crafting skill. The thick, scaly leather was somehow still soft and supple, providing protection with minimal loss of mobility. Lilly had said she crafted it from the skin of the dragon's belly. The dull red color, so dark it was almost black, made him look a little like Vlad the Impaler.

> ***Lord Allistor's Second Skin***
> ***Item Quality: Uncommon***
> ***Attributes: Constitution +3, Will Power +3, Strength +2, Stamina +2, Intelligence +1***
> *This 5-piece set includes chest, bracers, gloves, pants, and boots all made from the hide of a fire dragon. In addition to the attribute increases of the individual pieces, wearing the full set provides an additional +1 to both Will Power and Intelligence. The natural heat resistance of the dragon's skin reduces fire damage by 40%.*

Amanda poked him in the gut, breaking him out of his admiration for Lilly's work. "I know, it's pretty. But you can admire it more later. You've got an attack to lead."

They descended from their quarters to the main floor, where people were grabbing sandwiches from a long table in the dining area. Taking one for himself, Allistor found it was a bacon and egg sandwich that granted a buff of +2 *Constitution* for four hours. He joined the crowd as they walked and ate, making their way to the gate.

When it looked like the entire group was gathered, more than a hundred twenty in all, Allistor called out, "Everybody take a knee! Let's talk for a minute."

When he was the only one standing, he spoke in a normal voice. "Thank you all again for volunteering. This is going to be a hard day. Not just the fight, but dealing with hostile humans and having to take their lives. But the people we're going after today are murderers, and worse. They forfeited their lives long before today. So don't hesitate. If they're holding a weapon, take them down." He took a deep breath. "We've been told there are about fifty bad guys, and twice that many prisoners. So please be careful not to shoot prisoners, but keep an eye out for enemies who may be hiding among them. We'll sort out who's who after the battle."

Looking around at all the faces, he added, "Every single one of you is important to me. My brothers and sisters. I would give my life for any one of you. You are the future of the human race, and I will give my all to make sure that future is secure. I hope you all feel the same." There was a cheer as people raised fists in the air.

234

"Remember to watch out for each other. You all have heal spells, so use them. If you have a choice to save one of ours or shoot one of theirs, drop your weapon and heal. Someone else can do the shooting for a moment. The most important thing here is that we all get through this day alive. Even if it means we don't accomplish our goal. Live to fight another day."

He looked into the eyes of as many faces as he could while he spoke, trying his best to convey the truth of his words.

Attribute Increase! Your Charisma attribute has increased by +1

"Alright folks, be safe, shoot straight, and let's kick some ass! Nigel, open the gates!"

The crowd got to their feet, cheering. Allistor was concerned that their enemy would have heard the noise, but there was nothing they could do about it now. He was sure Paul would have some scouts out watching for any attack. He hoped that all Paul's people had been up all night, sweating each minute in anticipation of an assault.

As they walked through the park toward the courthouse and the mint beyond, Allistor sent out party invites to a dozen of his people, and designated them lieutenants. The airmen had been exploring the party system, and discovered that large raids could be formed using ranks and sub-groups of up to battalion strength. The main requirement was that the leader be a higher level than the sub-leaders, and they be higher level than their underlings, and so on. The lieutenants in turn sent out invites to as many as ten fighters, until everyone was grouped up. Allistor could track his people on the map, and they had radios to send and receive orders and updates courtesy of Bjurstrom and his guys. Each unit of five to ten fighters would move and fight independently, but in coordination with the other groups. Allistor had relied heavily on the experienced fighters to work out the best way to organize the attack.

Rounding the courthouse, they encountered the first of the scouts. A shot rang out, Goodrich cursed as a round struck his flak jacket and knocked him down. Most of the others crouched down in reaction to the shot, except Logan. He'd seen the muzzle flash, and immediately raised his rifle and returned fire. Sam was right behind him, following Logan's gaze and identifying the target. His shot put an end to the scout, signified by the flash of a small amount of experience points on everyone's interface.

The group spread out a little as they continued on, aware that their enemy was now alerted to their presence. Only a block away now, they began to separate and surround the building. Surprisingly, it wasn't the massive edifice Allistor had pictured. The above-ground part of it was an unassuming two-story stone building with a multitude of small windows along both floors. Which was unfortunate, as that meant there were plenty of firing positions for the defenders inside the structure.

Four of Allistor's groups were sniper teams, with three shooters in each, a designated healer, and the balance providing cover. As his people spread out, the teams each took one side of the building, and did what they could to get to high ground. Fire escapes, knotted ropes with hooks, whatever means they could find to get atop nearby buildings. The remaining groups surrounded the building, taking cover behind trees, cars, and some dumpsters they pushed out of alleys. One advantage to being out in big sky country was that a higher than normal percentage of the people learned to shoot growing up. A lot of families hunted for sport, or to put some additional meat on the table. As a result, every single one of Allistor's volunteers were experienced shooters who generally hit what they were aiming at. The downside was that the people who'd be shooting back at them were likely just as good.

Meg brought up the rear with the Humvee, the .50 cal still mounted to the roof. Sam and Logan joined her as she parked it behind a pickup truck across the street from the building's main entrance. The two men had worked out some kind of agreement as to who would get to shoot the big gun. Allistor hadn't asked for details. He'd just informed them of the prisoners being held on the second floor, and asked them not to strafe that floor with the massive penetrating rounds.

Allistor climbed into the bed of the pickup Meg had parked behind, and shouted toward the building.

"Paul! My name is Allistor! I'm here for two reasons. First, I'm here to kill you! Your cowardly attacks and murders stop now! Second, I'm here to free the people you've taken prisoner and abused. And once they're free, I'm going to clear the dungeon you couldn't clear. I guess that's three reasons. I'm here for three reasons!" He grinned, and his people within earshot chuckled or rolled their eyes.

Nobody inside the building laughed.

"Come on out, Paul! You're outnumbered almost three to one, and we have you surrounded. If you release your prisoners and surrender, you'll receive a trial. If we have to come in there and get you… well, it's gonna hurt. I'll make sure of it."

"Go away!" a man's voice shouted from one of the second-floor windows. "This place is mine! You won't take it without losing half your people! And I'll kill every prisoner in here before I let you take it!"

"Show yourself, you coward!" Meg shouted. "They told me you have no balls, seems like they might be right!" Sam blew her a kiss.

"Screw you! You'll just shoot me. You have one minute to leave, or I start killing hostages!"

Allistor growled. "Paul, listen to me carefully. You harm one hostage, and I'll kill you slower than any human has ever died. I'll cut parts off of you, then heal you, then do it again. I'm talking small parts! You'll die an inch at a time. Your people too! If you're listening, don't let that asshole make you suffer! Put down your weapons and come outside, and you'll get a trial. You'll get a chance to speak for yourselves. But if even one prisoner is hurt, or we have to come in and get you, it's gonna end badly for you!"

Allistor waited a moment, and almost immediately there was some shouting inside. It grew louder, then two shots rang out. A moment later a man came crashing through a window. He was shouting as he was pushed out, the sound stopping abruptly as he struck the ground.

Another man stuck his head out the window. "That's Paul! The dick is all yours!"

Allistor saw the man was still moving. "Fuzzy, go fetch!"

The bear bolted forward, loping across the street toward the man who was struggling to get to his feet. Fuzzy let out a roar, freezing the man for a moment before he screamed at the bear bearing down on him. Fuzzy latched onto the man's throat and pinned him down.

"Move again, and he'll rip your throat out!" Allistor yelled. The man froze as Fuzzy growled again. Allistor found himself wondering what that sensation would be like. Feeling a bear growl through the vibrations of its teeth on your neck.

"Fuzzy, bring him back, please."

The cub let go of the man's neck and took hold of one ankle. Walking backward, he dragged the man across the grass, then the sidewalk, then the street. The man shouted and cried, even tried to struggle free until Fuzzy dropped his ankle and stepped back toward his face.

Resuming his chore, Fuzzy dragged the man around behind the truck, leaving him in front of the Humvee. Taking a seat, he licked the man's face, then looked up expectantly at Allistor.

"Great job, buddy. You've earned a treat!"

Looking toward Logan, he asked, "Is this Paul?"

Logan shook his head. "Nope. This is one of his crew, though. One of the ones that ambushes foragers. That piece of shit just tried to sacrifice one of his people."

Allistor jumped down from the pickup bed and grabbed hold of the man. Lifting him like a child, he stepped back up on the truck. "Nice try, Paul! But your little ruse didn't work. All you did was give me someone to use as an example!"

Allistor lifted the struggling man over his head like he was deadlifting a barbell. With his improved *Strength*, the effort was minimal. "This is how you're all gonna die if you don't surrender!" He tossed the man into the street.

"Fuzzy! Eat!"

The bear cub dashed around the truck and pounced on the man, who screamed like a small child. He raised a hand to try to ward Fuzzy off, but the bear just latched onto it and shook his head. The arm snapped, and the man's scream actually rose in pitch. Letting go of the arm, Fuzzy opened his now bloody maw wide and bit down on the man's face. The screaming stopped, but the man continued to twitch as the bear pulled large chunks of flesh free and swallowed it whole.

Allistor grimaced, the display being a little more gruesome than intended. Still, he needed to embrace the moment and use it to his advantage. "Ohhhh! Damn, that had to hurt!" he shouted. "Fuzzy, finish him!"

The bear clamped his jaws on the man's throat and squeezed, holding his grip until the man stopped struggling. Then he ripped away the flesh, exposing the man's esophagus.

"I really hope those shots I heard weren't aimed at any prisoners, or I'll feed you to Fuzzy here one at a time. He's a growing bear, and always hungry, but even he can't eat fifty people in a day. So, some of you will be locked up. Fuzzy's very own pantry! You can sit and talk to each other for a few days about how much it's going to hurt when he eats your face!"

The front door opened, and a rifle with a white shirt tied to it emerged. "We're coming out!"

"Hold your fire!" Allistor ordered. He watched as eight men and women emerged, each one with their hands up, setting their guns down on the sidewalk as they stopped, putting both hands high in the air. One of the women stepped forward. "We surrender! We want a trial!"

Sam took charge of them, using his best drill sergeant voice. "All of you walk forward! Keep your hands high! Head into that alley, and sit against the wall!" He pointed, and they obeyed. Two of Allistor's people took over, pointing weapons at them as they sat, hands in their laps. "Anybody moves, shoot 'em."

Allistor's radio keyed in his earpiece. "Allistor, we got people tryin' to surrender back here on the south side." Campbell's voice reported.

"Let them surrender. Put them somewhere out of the line of fire, and secure them. How many?"

"We've got six." Campbell answered.

"Four more on the east side." McCoy added.

"Great, thanks guys. Keep an eye out for snipers." Allistor did the math in his head.

"Paul! Apparently, you're such an asshole that your people can't wait to abandon you! We're holding eighteen of your people already! That's... what? Like a third of your fighters? You suck as a leader."

"Leave! The gold is mine! I'll destroy this place rather than let you have it!" The same man as before stuck his head out. "Leave now or I'll start shooting people in here!"

From a different second floor window, a shot rang out. The pickup's back window, right next to Allistor's leg, shattered. A second later, shots erupted from a dozen ground floor windows and a few on the second floor.

Allistor's people returned fire as he dropped down onto his stomach, the side of the pickup taking several rounds. He cast *Barrier* above himself and held still, waiting for the barrage to cease so he could take better cover. Two rounds struck his barrier and it held, but a third round broke through and struck the bed not far from his arm. He immediately cast the spell again as he tried to squeeze closer to the bed wall. Another round penetrated his cover and ripped into his calf.

His cry of pain was drowned out as Sam opened up with the BFG. He strafed across the first-floor windows, the rounds blasting into the stone and shattering glass. When he reached the front doors, he paused long enough to completely destroy them, which took about ten seconds, then continued on until he had exhausted a full belt of ammo. When he paused, there was silence. Allistor took the opportunity to scramble from the pickup bed and get behind the cab, where he crouched down. Checking his map, he saw that three of his green dots had gone grey. Three fatalities already. The impact of that made his stomach lurch, and he very nearly lost his breakfast.

He felt a heal and looked up to see Amanda smiling at him. "Standing up there playing target wasn't the best idea, huh?"

He shook his head sadly. "I never claimed to be the smart one."

Sam and Logan finished reloading the next belt, and this time Logan took over. He fired in short bursts at random windows, making it impossible for the defenders to predict where he'd fire in time to hide.

Meanwhile the sniper teams were busy. While their support troops fired at the ground floor windows, the snipers calmly watched for defenders to expose themselves on the second floor. Bjurstrom put a round through the neck of one that had leaned out to fire down at attackers on the street. A minute later he put a hole in the head of another.

Helen was on the roof of a building above Allistor. She had nearly gotten a shot off at Paul the second time he'd shown himself, but he'd retreated too quickly. The room he was in was too dark for her to be sure of her target, so she scanned the windows along the front, looking for a target of opportunity. She'd picked off two others when she heard Allistor shout.

On the ground, Allistor saw another green dot fade to grey. His anger at Paul, and at himself for bringing these people here, grew until it overrode his good sense.

"Screw this! We're going in! Shotguns!" He shot out from behind the truck and ran as fast as he could, Fuzzy right behind him. The gunfire from his side intensified as his people tried to provide suppressing fire. He didn't look behind to see if any others followed, just focusing on the ruined doors in front of him. Lowering a shoulder, he went crashing through with little resistance. So little, in fact, that he fell on his face. Managing to turn the fall into a roll, he was quickly back on his feet, scanning the entry for targets. What he saw shocked him.

There was not a single intact thing in sight. Living or dead. Several bodies were scattered around, parts of them just blown off, other parts with large holes in them. Walls, furniture, even the chandelier, were all shattered or full of holes. The entire place looked like swiss cheese. "Holy shit." He hadn't realized just how much damage the BFG did. Even the stone walls had some holes where sunlight shone through.

Movement to his right snapped him out of the shock and he spun, shotgun pointed. He fired at a man who'd just rounded a doorway and was raising a semi-automatic rifle. The man's face caved in even as he pulled his trigger, firing past Allistor.

Another movement got Allistor turning again, but this time it was Sam, Amanda, Lars, Nathan, and Dawn coming through the front doors. He grinned at them briefly, then moved in the direction of the man he'd shot. He cast *Barrier* in front of himself, then spoke into his radio. "Logan, we're in the front entry, moving to the right. Hold your fire on that side."

He waited to be sure the .50 cal rounds had shifted to the corridor behind him, then moved forward. He took the lead, with Sam right behind him. The old man said, "You idiot. Logan's getting to have all the fun cuz you charged in here and Meg made me come cover your happy ass."

Allistor looked behind him, seeing Sam was grinning. "You love it and you know it. Just don't get overexcited and shoot me in the ass, old man."

Sam tapped Allistor's ass with the barrel of his shotgun. "Ya never know…"

They moved on, clearing rooms along the front of the building until they got to the end of the corridor. Then they circled back and cleared the back side rooms. Twice they encountered defenders who tried to ambush them. Both times Allistor's barrier either stopped or deflected the initial shot from the defender. And one was all they got.

Contrary to Allistor's promise of a slow death, they decided to finish off the defenders rather than risk having them find a way to attack again, even wounded. So each one was killed and looted while Fuzzy took a bite or two. He'd left his Fibble out by the truck, and Allistor saw him glance that direction more than once.

Back in the main entry, Sam called Logan to cease fire, saying they were moving into the other wing. The big gun stopped immediately. Allistor moved forward, and shook his head. This wing had gotten even more attention from the BFG, and he was frankly surprised that the building hadn't collapsed. They cleared the first room, finding three dead bodies, and were moving to the second when there was a crash behind them. Lars spun, his shotgun aimed back toward the entry, then lowered it when he saw Logan waving at them.

"Couldn't let you guys have all the fun." he explained.

Allistor motioned at the demolished walls, doors, and furniture around him. "Looks like you've had your share already."

Logan took in the scene, and blushed slightly. "I might have overdone it a little. Dude pissed me off."

They continued on, clearing the ground floor. In the third office they checked, they found a man with his left shoulder blown to bits. He was bleeding profusely, sitting against the outer wall below one of those holes that let the sunlight in. Barely conscious, he tried to raise his weapon, but didn't have the strength.

"Fuzzy." Allistor sent in his bear. They waited in the hall as the man screamed for ten long seconds. "Hope that terrifies the shit out of anyone left alive in here." He got a notification that Fuzzy had leveled up with that last kill, and the bear returned a moment later, licking the blood off his muzzle.

Several offices later, they found a man and woman barricaded behind two stacked filing cabinets, which, in turn, were behind an overturned desk. Several rounds had penetrated the desk, but not the cabinets. The moment Allistor opened the door, they fired. One round hit his barrier and shattered it, the second hit him in the gut, knocking him back. He tripped over Fuzzy and fell backward, cracking his head against the marble floor hard enough to see stars.

While a flurry of shots flew back and forth, he felt a heal from Amanda that brought him back to his senses enough to roll to one side out of the line of fire. Eventually Sam tossed a grenade behind the filing cabinets, and the two people disappeared in a cloud of flame and blood. Amanda volunteered to go in and loot them, and nobody argued. The smell of destroyed bowel and other assorted human bits was offensive. Fuzzy still followed her in to poke around, though. Both of them left a trail of bloody footprints as they exited.

After clearing that corridor and looting the bodies that had been ripped apart by the BFG or smaller arms fire, they made a U-turn and headed back toward the main entry. When they were nearly there, the radios keyed again. "This is Bjurstrom. We're inside on the south, approaching the main entry."

Allistor didn't bother with the radio, as he saw the group appear ahead of him. "Hey guys! Just in time to head upstairs with us." He waved, and got a thumbs-up in return. The two groups merged, and Allistor led the way upstairs. Once again, he cast *Barrier,* and this time a notification popped up.

> ***Spell level up! Your Barrier spell level has increased by +1***

With the barrier in front of him, and the combined group following behind, he pushed up the stairway, gun aimed at the level above in case anyone was waiting in ambush.

They were.

As he reached the first landing, a blast from above echoed through the stairway and a piece of the baluster next to him shattered. He felt some shrapnel and possibly some buckshot tear into his leg, but ignored it. Moving quickly, he crossed the landing, turning to aim up the next flight. There was a woman standing there, pumping another round into her shotgun. Allistor didn't wait for her to finish. He fired directly into her gut, the buckshot shredding both of her forearms in the process. She dropped her weapon and screamed, her legs going weak. She fell to the floor above, temporarily out of sight.

Allistor and Logan rushed up the stair as he chambered another round. The stairwell door was closed, and the woman was the only one there. Logan removed a 9mm from a holster on his hip and put her out of her misery with a shot to the head, then they both looted the body.

Standing in front of the stairwell door, Allistor paused. "There's another stairwell at the other end. If we charge in here, he can just run out there, leaving his people to die to buy him time. And maybe he executes some prisoners, if he hasn't already."

Bjurstrom replied, "I got this." He got on his radio. "Groups three, five, and six, get in here. I need complete coverage of all the exits and stairwells. Group three, meet me in the south stairwell. Do not advance upstairs, there is likely an ambush." He gave Allistor a thumbs-up and headed back down, Campbell right behind him. McCoy and Goodrich stayed put.

"While we're waiting, how many dead did you guys see on your way in?" Allistor asked McCoy. The two airmen looked at each other, both counting on their fingers quietly. Then they looked at him and said in unison, "Eleven."

Amanda said, "We counted seventeen in the two front wings, eighteen if you count her." She pointed to the corpse on the floor.

"The guy we questioned said fifty. We've got eighteen outside, plus the dead in here, that's forty-seven. Can't be that many left up here with him."

Chris, who had come in with the airmen, added, "I didn't see the lieutenant or the women he usually keeps with him. Chances are good he's up there with Paul."

Goodrich grinned. "It's like the boss and the mini-boss in the same room. This is gonna be fun!"

Allistor was about to admonish him when the radio transmitted Bjurstrom's voice. "No ambush on this end. In position, good to go."

Logan keyed his radio. "Hold position, we'll go in. Don't want to create a potential friendly fire situation. Anybody comes through your door, waste 'em. We'll call if we need you to breach."

"Roger that. Shoot 'em where it hurts."

Logan looked at Allistor. "That shield thing. Can you only cast it in front of yourself? Can you cast it in the doorway instead?"

"I can block the doorway with it. But it won't last more than two or three rounds."

"Let's hope that's enough. Everybody, move to this side and I'll pull the door. I'll stay behind it when it's open. They'll fire a first blast, 'cause they're scared. Put your barrier up after that, and it'll take the next rounds. Then we go through."

249

The next ten seconds went exactly as Logan had predicted. The door wasn't even all the way open when several rounds slammed into the metal. Allistor cast *Barrier,* and Logan stuck his head out, then crossed in front of the door, prompting another volley, the first few rounds of which were stopped by the barrier. He made it across to Allistor just long enough to take a deep breath and shout, "Go!" before he dove through the doorway. Allistor followed, recasting *Barrier* in front of Logan, who was lying on his side firing at something.

Allistor went left, searching for a target. He saw three men crouched behind overturned furniture firing at Logan. He quickly cast *Restraint* on one, causing him to freeze with his head exposed. The people filing through behind him put several rounds into the stunned man, and he went down. Allistor hit another with *Mind Spike*, causing him to scream and drop his weapon, running right into the line of fire and taking hits from in front and behind.

The third man, shocked by the fact that he'd just shot one of his own, hesitated a moment. That moment cost him his life. A round from a rifle tore into his arm, causing him to drop his shotgun. Then another round punctured his chest. He fell back and rocked a few times, then went still.

Chris didn't wait to be asked. "Nope. None of them are Paul or the LT."

They cleared the furniture blocking the way and proceeded down the corridor. This time, as they entered the first few rooms. they found people huddled on the floor or behind furniture, hands held high or on their heads, begging not to be shot.

This created a dilemma. They had no real way to know if any of these prisoners were actually Paul's men unless Chris, Logan, or Lars recognized them. Amanda solved it by walking into the first room and saying, "You're all going to be okay. We've killed all but the last few of these assholes. But we need to know if anyone in here is one of them. If so, speak up. They can't hurt you now. They try anything, they'll be dead in 2 seconds. So... any of Paul's people in here?"

As one, the frightened people on the floor shook their heads. "Thank you. Stay in here. Do not go outside, or we'll assume you're an enemy and fire. We'll come back for you shortly."

They repeated this process through eight other rooms, someone asking the questions while others covered them. Every room denied any of Paul's people hiding in there.

As they reached the end and a big corner office, the door erupted with shots from inside. Amanda and Goodrich were both hit as rounds stitched their way across the corridor. Everyone fired back into the quickly dissolving door, the shots ceased, and they were rewarded with an experience gain.

Lars kicked in the scrap of a door that was remaining, and was the first through. Logan was right behind him, followed by Allistor.

"Paul. You cowardly son of a bitch." Chris growled, stepping through right behind Allistor. The man stood in the back corner of the room, two women in front of him, effectively shielding him. He had a pistol in each

251

hand, one pointed at each of the women's heads. Allistor assumed the dead man on the floor was the lieutenant.

"If you shoot me, they're dead!"

"Shoot!" one of the women screamed. "Shoot! Kill him!"

Logan and Lars both had weapons raised, but they didn't fire. Both turned to look at Allistor, then at Chris.

Allistor nodded to Chris, who stepped forward. He held a Sig M4 semi-auto in his hands, and his face was dead blank. "You worthless piece of shit. You killed my wife. I vowed to end you, and I'm gonna do just that. You are not getting out of here alive. But you let the women go, I'll give you a quick death. Harm them in any way, and I'll feed you to the bear myself. After I shoot you in the arms, legs, and the gut."

While Chris was talking, Allistor keyed his radio. "Lars, Logan. I don't want to risk *Restraint,* in case it fails. Are you good enough to shoot his hands?"

"Oh, hell yes. At this range?" Lars replied. Logan just nodded slightly. Each man was only six or seven feet from Paul.

"I'll let you guys pick the time. Do it."

The two of them started whispering as Chris finished his threat. Paul looked at Chris, then at the rest of the group behind him. Chris stepped to the side to give his friends a clear shot, having heard Allistor on his earpiece.

Paul shouted, "I swear to God, I'll take them with me. You are gonna let me outta here! I'll take them with me for ins-"

Lars and Logan fired simultaneously. Both of Paul's hands jerked, the guns flying from them. One of the women screamed as some shrapnel cut into her scalp, but it was drowned out by Paul's outraged scream.

The two women had the presence of mind to run forward away from Paul as he hugged his destroyed hands to his chest. "You assholes! You shot me! You're just like the others! Everyone's out to get me!"

Allistor ignored the rant, watching as Amanda healed the injured woman and escorted her out as Dawn helped the other one. As soon as they were out of the room, Allistor looked at Paul, who was still raving about how the whole world had always been against him.

"SHUT UP!" he roared at the man in the corner. Paul stopped rambling long enough to focus on him. "I gave you a chance to surrender, but you refused. Some of my people, and all of yours, are dead now. That's on your head. I promised I'd kill you an inch at a time, but I'm not feeling that patient."

He turned to look at his friends. "Back up."

When they were all behind him, and it was just him and Paul in the room, he simply said, "Lunchtime, Fuzzy."

The bear roared, shoving aside a desk in his rush to get to Paul. Allistor turned his back and walked out as the man began to scream and beg. It lasted a full minute before he went silent. Another half minute elapsed before they all got experience from Fuzzy's kill. He and the others only returned to loot the mangled body.

Chapter 11

Giant Goblins and Bears, Oh My

Logan called for the teams downstairs to sweep the building again, and fifteen minutes later the all-clear was given. The prisoners were rounded up and given the news that their captors were all dead. Allistor had them walked through the lower level to see the devastation and ruined bodies of the men and women who'd taken and held them.

Once outside in the street, he had them gathered together. There were a total of eighty-five of them. Standing back up in the pickup bed, he spoke to them.

"You now know that your captors are dead. They can't hurt you. And we won't hurt you. But I'm going to ask you one more time. If anyone among you is one of Paul's people, someone who either actively abused you, or supported Paul's actions, point them out now. We'll deal with them quickly, and we can all move on."

The entire group looked around at each other, no one saying anything. But Amanda noticed several of them looked at one man briefly before looking away. She hopped up on the truck next to Allistor.

"You." She pointed at the man. He was in his mid-thirties with a scruffy beard and greasy hair. "Why did so many people just look at you?"

The man shrugged. "I'm handsome?"

Allistor caught on, and cast *Restraint* on the man. Then he cast *Levitate* and floated him up several feet above the heads of the crowd. When the stun wore off, he started struggling and cursing. But his efforts got him nowhere.

"Now, answer the question. Why did so many people look to you when I asked about people working for Paul?"

"He's a snitch!" one woman called out. Several others nodded their heads.

"What do you mean, a snitch?" Amanda asked.

"He would hang around and listen to us talking, then report to Paul's people. A few of us were planning an escape. He informed on them, and they were caught and executed." the man standing next to the woman who'd spoken first explained.

"Is this true?" Allistor asked the floater. "Are you responsible for the deaths of prisoners who tried to escape?"

The man kept struggling, wearing himself out. He didn't say a word.

"Alright, since you all were the ones harmed by his actions, we'll have a trial. Anybody know his name?"

"Simon." half a dozen people called out at once.

"Simon, you are charged with aiding the asshole Paul, and conspiring in the capture and execution of prisoners attempting escape. You will be judged by a jury of your peers, being the recently freed men and women you see before you. How do you respond to these charges?"

The man stopped struggling, now hanging nearly upside down from his contortions. "I'm not guilty! You can't prove I did any of it!"

"So, you deny working with Paul, informing on your fellow prisoners?"

"I deny everything!"

Allistor looked to the crowd. "What evidence do you have to present to prove his guilt?"

A second woman raised her hand. "I saw him go in and out of Paul's office three times. My job was cleaning the guard's quarters, including Paul's. Simon went in there less than an hour before Paul caught Lydia and her family and killed them. Simon stood there smiling as it happened."

A man raised his hand. "The day after, Simon got a double ration of food. And actual bacon for breakfast."

"I earned that food! I... I did some scouting. So what?" Simon's indignation looked silly with his feet kicking above his head.

A kid pushed his way through the taller adults. Maybe ten or eleven years old, he was scrawny and dirty. He shyly raised his hand, and Allistor nodded at him. "Go ahead."

"Simon tried to get me to help him spy on people. He gave me a cupcake, and said if I bring him good secrets, I could have more. My mom told me he was bad, and I shouldn't help him. When I told Simon I wasn't allowed... the next day they took my mom away." The boy had tears streaming down his face. "It was my fault. I shouldn't have told him."

Allistor looked up at Simon, who'd gone quiet. "What do you have to say for yourself?"

"That little bastard's a liar!" Simon shouted. One of the women in the group took hold of the boy and gathered him into a hug. "He tried to blackmail me for a cupcake!"

Allistor looked back at the crowd. "Anybody else have evidence they wish to put forth?"

A young girl, maybe fifteen years old, raised her hand. "He's always perving on me. Told me once he could get me double food rations if I let him... you know."

"Little slut! You came begging for it!" Simon's last words sealed his fate. Of all people, Amanda was the last person Allistor expected to take a life. But she raised her shotgun and put a round through Simon's face, sending him spinning away, spurting blood over the crowd and the street. Allistor canceled the *Levitate* spell once he was clear of everyone, and his dead body dropped to the pavement. The prisoners clapped and cheered.

Amanda hopped off the truck and called out, "Anyone know what happened to this young man's mom?"

The looks she got back from the people in the front row made it clear what her fate had been. Several people looked down at the boy and shook their heads slightly.

The boy himself said, "It's okay. They won't say it, cuz they think I don't know. But Paul hurt her, then killed her. I waited outside his office, and I saw them take her away. It's all my fault."

257

Amanda rushed forward and dropped to her knees, taking the little boy in her arms as he began to cry again. She patted his back and whispered to him. Finally, he nodded, and she let go. "None of this was your fault. You need to believe me on this. Simon and Paul were bad men, and they took advantage of you. It's the truth, I swear. Ask anyone."

The little boy looked back at the prisoners, and every single one of them had a smile and a nod for him. A few muttered, "She's right." or, "It's true." Amanda took his hand and led him back to the truck.

"You're coming with me. We'll get you some food, and have a little talk." Pausing, she turned back to the others. "You all saw the announcement a while back about Allistor building the first Citadel? Well, this is Allistor. He's about to invite you to join us. We'll be clearing the dungeon and turning this place into a proper Stronghold. But that can wait. For today, you are welcome to join us at the Capitol. There's meat, fresh vegetables, and a safe place to sleep where no monsters will spawn. I suggest you take him up on his offer to join us."

Picking up the child, she put him in the back seat of the Humvee. Meg fired it up, and Sam hopped in. Allistor knew they'd rush back to the Stronghold and start cooking. There were nearly a hundred new mouths to feed.

Seeing Lars standing nearby, he motioned for the man to join him up on the truck. He quietly said, "You and your guys were instrumental in our success here. I was about to recruit all these people, but if you'd like to offer them the choice of joining you as well..."

Lars snorted. "Are you kidding? I was about to ask you if you'd accept me and mine. I woke up this morning thinking we'd be allies. But after today… I can make sure my people survive, at least for a while. But you have a plan, resources, and skills that I just don't have. Your people are well fed, leveling quickly, and based on that armor you're wearing, leveling their skills as well. Much faster than any of my people, myself included. If you'll leave me in charge of my Stronghold and my people, I think we'll all swear your oath."

Allistor reached out a hand. "Not just in charge of your Stronghold. I want you to be one of my advisors. Logan too. And maybe a few more of your people." They shook hands, and both turned to the crowd.

"As Amanda said, my name is Allistor…." he began to give them the pitch. He made it the short version, as the people were tired and hungry. As he was talking, Bjurstrom and his guys led a procession of fighters carrying makeshift stretchers, atop which sat the bodies of their people lost in the fight. Each was covered in a blanket, and the sight made Allistor forget his words. The fighters set their burdens down, and Bjurstrom explained in a shaky voice.

"We weren't sure what you wanted us to do with them."

Allistor looked to the prisoners. "I'm sorry, I've been talking your ears off. We need to get you back and get you fed, and take our lost brothers and sisters home. It's a short walk through the park, only a few blocks. If any of you need assistance, just raise a hand."

He motioned for Bjurstrom and the others to lift the bodies and head back, but a man stepped forward. "They died helping to free us?"

Bjurstrom nodded, not trusting himself to speak. The man moved to stand next to one of the stretchers. "I'd like to help carry them, if you don't mind? Least I can do. And if they have families, I'd like to be able to thank them."

One by one, more of the prisoners stepped forward and offered to help carry the load. Allistor nodded to his people, who stepped aside and quietly thanked them for their help. Bjurstrom detailed two groups to remain and secure the building, and soon enough the rest of the survivors were on their way, the bodies being carried by people they'd helped to free, with the rest of them walking alongside, in front, and behind as a sort of informal honor guard. When one of them tired, another took their place. A man near the back began to sing a slow, sad song that sounded vaguely Celtic. His voice was beautiful, and though Allistor couldn't make out the words, the song brought tears to his eyes. He let them fall. There was no shame in mourning the dead. He felt much like the little boy had – these people were dead because he'd brought them here. They could have led long and healthy lives if he'd just left them alone at the Citadel or the Stadium, wherever they came from.

He spent the walk back to the Capitol telling himself that these six died so that dozens or maybe hundreds more would never be victimized by Paul and his people.

*****

Back at the Capitol, they herded all the former prisoners through the gates and directly into the building. Allistor didn't want to risk anyone spotting the teleport pad and asking questions. The newcomers waited as the bodies were gently set to one side in the rotunda. Amanda and several of the support volunteers took charge of them, and the prisoners were led to the dining area. Meg and Sam made sure they were all well fed, making more of the breakfast sandwiches that gave the *Constitution* buff. The meal wasn't fancy, but their guests dug in like they hadn't eaten for days.

When they were all fed, Allistor gave them the longer version of his recruiting speech. Then Lars stood up and introduced himself. A few of the people had met him, or heard of him, and the crowd listened intently as he spoke of his plan to join his people with Allistor's.

Once they were through talking, about half of the prisoners wanted to pledge. The others had family they wanted to get back to at other Strongholds. Allistor offered them escorts to get them safely home, and they accepted gratefully. The ones who wished to take the oath did so, repeating after Helen as she fulfilled what was rapidly becoming her traditional role.

"For those who want to return to your families, I ask that you be patient. Stay here for the night while my people and I make arrangements. I need to secure both this Stronghold and the mint while we clear the lower levels, and I need all my people to do that. In the morning we can break off groups to get you safely home. And hopefully we can form alliances with your respective Strongholds as

261

well. I'll be dropping by each one and asking to meet with their leaders."

The folks who wanted to leave agreed to wait, and all were asked to sit tight while Amanda worked her way through them. She'd called for two nurses from the Citadel to help her examine all the guests and assess their health. Most just needed a few good meals to be back in normal shape. A few had suffered more than the others from lack of regular meals.

When she was satisfied that the nurses had things under control, Amanda joined Allistor and the dungeon group, and they headed back to the mint along with fifty of the volunteer fighters to help defend the building if necessary. The others he left at the Stronghold to watch over their guests.

Back at the mint he waited while Logan and the other vets assigned squads to various firing positions throughout the building. Broken furniture was piled high in the doorways, providing both a cover for their defenders, and a barrier to entry for any attackers. After an hour, they were ready to hit the dungeon. The group of twenty-five fighters were among the best of Allistor's people, along with Lars, Logan, and Chris. Allistor had brought Amanda and Nancy along as his best healers, but also to level them up along with Sam, Meg, Ramon, Michael, Helen, Dawn, Nathan, Andrea and her four guys, Dean, and the leaders from Laramie.

Mimicking the organization used in their fight upstairs, Bjurstrom had broken the raid into five sub-groups of five fighters each that could break off if necessary and fight separate groups or separate mobs. Every member had a radio with an earpiece, and was equipped with healing and mana potions as well as both healing and offensive spells. Not to mention being heavily armed. The BFG was too large and heavy to bring down, but Sam had brought two of the belt-fed 5.56 LMGs – one for him, and one for Logan, who made the large weapon look like a toy when he held it. Meg was carrying a supply of her own chemical grenades that she'd crafted, slightly improved from the originals, as well as a few of the manufactured grenades they'd claimed from the train wreck. Everyone else carried shotguns with various loads, a blade of some kind, at least one handgun, and a few carried bows or crossbows. Logan also carried a wicked looking axe on his back.

Meg made sure they all took a moment to munch on some dragon jerky for the +4 *Stamina* buff it provided to go along with the +2 *Constitution* buff from their sandwiches earlier, which still had about 3 hours remaining.

The main entry stairs included a flight that led downward from ground level, so they began there. The descent was quick, the stairs wide enough for them to walk three at a time, side by side. When they reached the lower floor there was a metal door labeled 'B1'.

Logan volunteered to take the lead, but Allistor refused. He cast *Barrier* in front of himself, and had Logan open the door. Shotgun leveled and holding his breath, Allistor pushed through, only to find an empty corridor that stretched maybe a hundred feet. There was a guard station with a bulletproof window immediately to his left, and a gate made of hardened steel bars directly ahead. The door leading to the guard station was metal with a small window at eye level and a key fob reader to one side.

"Without power, how do we get through?" Lars asked from a few paces behind Allistor.

"There's probably some kind of manual release, or keys. Let's check inside the guard room." Sam suggested.

Unsurprisingly, the door to the guard station was locked as well. Logan kicked it a few times, to no avail. He tried his massive axe, but it only left some deep scratches in the metal. They were all huddled around the door discussing how they might get through, when Dawn called out.

"Umm… guys?" They turned as one to see her standing on the other side of the gate, which stood open. "It wasn't locked." The grin on her face stretched from ear to ear as the others groaned or laughed.

"Nice one!" Nathan gave her a fist-bump, as did several others when they passed through the gate. Allistor hung back, still staring at the guard station door.

"I still think we need to get in here. There are probably going to be more locked doors and gates, and our best option for finding keys is in there." He pointed through the window.

"There's another door on this side." Helen moved to the left and tried the door, which opened easily. "Maybe when the power went off, the locks were disabled?"

Sam shook his head. "That doesn't seem right? They wouldn't have such an easily disabled system securing all this gold. My guess is the last guards who were down here abandoned this place and didn't bother to lock up when they left. Maybe they were being chased by newly spawned monsters."

Amanda added, "Don't forget, Paul sent people down here. They may have found keys or something that let them get beyond this point. If we see any bodies remaining, we should search them."

They took a minute while Helen, Dawn, and Meg searched the guard station. They did find a ring of keys, which Meg put into her inventory. They also found some stun guns, more radios, and the most important find of all, a poster-sized map of the underground levels Helen pulled down off the wall.

Allistor studied the map intently, and watched as his own interface map filled out. He had the others all take a look as well, so none of them would be lost down there. Helen took charge of the map after they were done, saying she might be able to use it to level her *Cartography* skill. The map showed that this first level was mostly offices, storage, and a large room labeled as, 'Printing Floor'

They broke into their five groups, four of them each taking a room to clear, then leapfrogging past the others to clear the next in line while the fifth group remained in the corridor as lookouts, or backup if necessary. The offices, storage rooms, and a conference room were quickly cleared with no evidence of monsters. The desks and cabinets had clearly been rifled through, probably by the previous parties sent down here.

The last and largest room was filled with rows of machines. Meg said, "I took the tour here as a kid. This is where they mint coins." She pointed to a pair of large machines to their right. "Those big suckers stamp the blanks with whatever design they're supposed to have."

Dawn drifted over to one of them, exploring the machine with her eyes. A glint of gold caught her attention, and she stepped closer. Reaching her hand inside an opening at the end of a conveyor, she pulled it back out filled with gold coins. "Wooohoo!" she shouted. "Those guys that came down here before were morons. Lookit all this gold just sittin' here."

Allistor shook his head. "We don't have time for that now. Just leave it there, and we'll make sure everyone gets a hefty bonus when we're done. Remember, each ounce of gold, or each one of those coins, is worth about twelve hundred klax. We'll make sure each of you will be able to buy yourselves something nice on the open market."

Dawn dropped the coins back where she found them, a disappointed look on her face. Allistor didn't blame her – it wasn't easy to drop shiny loot once you had your hands on it.

They split up into their groups and spread out across the massive room, advancing toward the other end as they checked behind each machine, in every closet, and under work tables. Near the end they found a badly shredded body in jeans and a denim shirt. Whatever had killed it hadn't had an opportunity to feed on it.

Sam ventured, "The last party must have run into something here. They killed it, but not before it got one of them." Allistor and the others agreed it was the likely scenario. Amanda, not squeamish about rotting corpses, quickly searched the body for keys or other useful items. Finding nothing, she returned to her group and retraced their steps back to the main corridor.

From there, they took another staircase headed downward. This time, the staircase led to another steel gate, which also stood open. When they stepped through, they found another guard station, with a pair of elevators directly across. The elevator doors stood open, and there was another human corpse inside one of them. Again, Amanda searched the body, while a few others searched the guard station, both finding nothing useful.

This corridor was lined with vault doors. Per the map, they stored both silver and gold coins in these vaults, as well as bullion to be used in making more coins. None of the doors had been opened, and they took the time to try each of the keys Meg had found on each of the doors, but none of them worked. There was a sophisticated looking panel with a large screen, camera, and number pad next to each one, but with the power off there was no way to use them or even tell what was needed to unlock them. So, they moved on. There were signs of a battle here, scuff marks on the floor, bullet holes in the wall at the end of the corridor, and a couple of blast marks that looked like someone had set off dynamite or similar explosives. The end of the corridor ended in a T-intersection with another elevator to the right, and a larger, heavier vault door to the left. The massive door, ten feet high by six feet wide and weighing several tons, stood ajar. Several more bodies lay here, legs or arms removed, huge gash and bite marks in them. One was missing its head altogether.

Very quietly, one group went to check the elevator while Amanda's group helped her search the gruesome corpses. They came up with a chain necklace that had six funky-shaped keys strung on it, as well as a few intact weapons, some ammo, and a bloody laminated card with several sets of numbers printed in columns.

While they did all this, Allistor quietly whispered into his radio, "This must be as far as they got. Nobody looted these corpses, which means the survivors ran from whatever killed these people. The only place it can be is behind that door."

McCoy reported via radio from inside the elevator. "This is an old-school elevator, got the metal cage and everything. Gotta be part of the original construction. It's a simple pulley system, operates off a crank. Looks like we can disengage the motor and crank it by hand."

"Alright, come back here and let's see what kind of monster is in this room." Allistor answered, still in a whisper. He wished he knew what level the dead people were. It would give him an idea of how well his group might fare against whatever it was.

Turning to look toward the elevator and McCoy's approaching group, he saw Fuzzy sniffing at the air, his eyes on the door. He let out a low growl, barely audible to Allistor who was only a few feet away, then carefully set his beloved Fibble doll on the ground. After patting it once with a paw as if to tell it to stay put, he moved to stand next to Allistor, his hackles up and bristling.

They used the same plan as previous doors. Allistor cast *Barrier,* Logan yanked the door open. The room beyond was a large storage area that had probably once had boxes of neatly stacked and packed coins. Now it was nothing but wreckage, coins strewn everywhere, covering the floor in a thin layer in some places, piled into huge mounds in others. The tallest of the mounds stretched

268

nearly to the fifteen-foot high ceiling in the back, left corner of the room.

There was no monster of any kind.

As Allistor stepped into the room, the coins underfoot ground together, the metal on metal contact making a scraping sound that echoed off the walls. When he set his second foot down, the pressure flipped a coin into the air, tiddlywinks style. It landed on a nearby pile, causing a small cascade. The tinkling lasted for several seconds as Allistor and everyone behind him cringed.

Allistor exhaled long and slow, letting loose a breath he'd been holding without realizing it. He took a third step into the room, trying his best not to make more noise than necessary. Logan stepped in behind him, along with Sam, Meg, and Lars. Just as Allistor turned to look back and shrug at the others, the mound of coins in the back corner burst upward in a volcanic eruption of gold. A grating, screeching roar accompanied the sudden explosion, and the upper half of a vaguely humanoid creature was exposed.

Cobalus Magnus
Level 25
Health: 23,000/23,000

The monster was easily twelve feet tall, with a round head on a skinny neck. Its ears extended out two feet on either side of its head, which sported both a protruding forehead and severe underbite, from which sharp, broken teeth jutted upward. Its body was thin, with corded muscle on shoulders and arms, and a grotesquely rounded potbelly.

269

Its skin was a greenish grey with matted hair, and it stared at them with malevolent red eyes.

"It's a goblin, sort of." Logan mused as the thing began to thrash its way free of the pile. Gold coins stuck to its skin in random places, and the flesh seemed to be growing around the coins, absorbing them into itself like a tree growing around a nail.

"Biggest damned goblin I ever heard of." Sam mused, raising his machine gun. "Let's see if it bleeds!"

He opened fire on the thing, stitching a pattern across its chest as it struggled to free its legs from the heavy pile of metal coins. Black blood spurted from the wounds, but the monster barely seemed to notice. Logan joined in, both men moving to the side to allow others into the room. Each of the groups followed suit until they were all spread out along the back wall, firing at the monster. Nearly free of its bed, it plunged its sharply clawed three-fingered hands into the pile and flung great handfuls at the humans with significant force. Coins blasted them, moving maybe sixty feet per second, stinging as they hit but not penetrating skin. Several of the party members stopped firing to protect their faces with their arms or turn their backs to the projectiles.

Cobalus Magnus
Level 25
Health: 20,200/23,000

Their initial volleys hadn't taken much health off the thing. Allistor was used to goblins being small, weak creatures that attacked in large groups. Individual goblins were easily dispatched, but they piled on in numbers and killed with a hundred small bites, scratches, and stabs.

Not this one. This was the granddaddy of goblin tanks.

Finally free of its pile, it reached down and took hold of a spear that none of them had even seen behind yet another pile of coins. Stomping forward, it jabbed the spear at Sam, who barely moved aside quickly enough to avoid being skewered. The spear was easily twelve feet long, the same height as the monster. It had a wicked ebony stone tip with jagged edges and a barb along one side. The tip skittered off the metal wall behind Sam, making a scritching noise that set teeth on edge.

Allistor tried casting *Restraint* on the cobalus, but the spell failed. Its eyes glowed a brighter red, as if aware of the attempt and further angered by it. *Mind Spike* worked though, the pain inside the creature's brain causing it to whirl around, the spear flying sideways and hooking Meg behind her thigh. The creature's strength pulled her off her feet and flung her toward the back of the room, a big chunk of her leg ripped away and arterial blood spraying. Her scream ended when she bounced off a wall and landed behind a pile.

"We can't see her!" Amanda screamed, already dashing forward with one eye on the creature, trying to get to Meg before she bled out. Dawn and Nathan followed, placing themselves between Amanda and the creature.

Sam screamed, "Meg!" and started to charge forward, but a flailing backhand from the cobalus knocked him down. A moment later one of its oversized feet stomped on his legs, and everyone heard the bones snap.

271

Roaring in pain, Sam fired up into the thing's loincloth, causing it to scream even louder and stumble backward, removing its weight from Sam.

Nancy and several others began casting heals on Sam, who had begun to scream as sweat poured down his face from the pain of the bones knitting themselves back together.

Allistor moved forward to grab Sam and pull him back toward the wall even as he cast *Flame Shot* at the monster's face. It was still thrashing about from the mind spike, and the added pain sent it stumbling into one of the smaller piles of coin. Losing its balance, it fell backward, rending its own face with sharp nails as it tried to claw loose the *Mind Spike*.

With Sam safely pulled back, Allistor focused on the pile the giant goblin was now reclining on. He cast *Erupt,* and saw the pile shift, but the spike wasn't long enough to push all the way through the pile into the beast. Changing his focus, he recast the spell and sent a spike up through one of its feet.

The monster roared, focusing on Allistor as the effect of the *Mind Spike* wore off. Allistor saw it searching for its spear, which it had dropped not far from where Sam had fallen. Allistor raced forward, picking up the weighty weapon using his increased *Strength*. Charging forward holding the long weapon at his hip like a knight's jousting lance, he plunged the tip of the spear into the monster's crotch with all the strength and momentum at his disposal.

This time the monster's scream was more of a high-pitched yelp as the jagged spear tip sunk deep into its reproductive bits. Allistor twisted the shaft with both hands, even as he tried to pull it free. But the barb had apparently hooked into something, and he couldn't remove the weapon. Instead, he raised his shotgun and fired at the monster's face as he backpedaled toward the doorway and his people.

The massive goblin wasn't about to let him retreat. It lurched forward, screaming as the spear point did terrible things to its insides, and shot a hand forward to grab Allistor. It led with its claws, one sinking into his shoulder and another scraping across his ribs, peeling back a huge slice of skin. The third claw sliced his leg as the thing tightened its grip, lifting Allistor toward its mouth. The maw, already wide open and screaming, was lined in the front with twin rows of a dozen sharp teeth both top and bottom, bracketed by jagged, elongated canines and lower incisors each almost a foot long. Its saliva was a sickly green color and as it brought Allistor's head closer to its face, he could smell its fetid breath. There were bits of colored cloth and sinew stuck between its teeth, including what looked like what was left of a Broncos ball cap.

Allistor cast *Mind Spike* again, screaming as the pain caused the creature to squeeze him even harder. The claw through his shoulder penetrated deeper, but Allistor barely noticed as the thing swung its arm downward, violently slamming him into the floor. Both of his legs shattered, and he passed out for a moment. When he woke just a few seconds later, he was flying through the air, his mangled body crashing into a pile of coins.

Allistor's pain-addled mind still registered that his health bar was below ten percent. He could hear gunfire and cursing, and the monster screaming. He knew he should cast a heal on himself, but his brain just wouldn't

273

bring up the spell. All he could think about was that he was going to die, and let his people down.

His health bar ticked down even further, and he could feel the blood pumping from his shoulder. A moment later he felt a heal spell wash over him, then another, and another. His health moved back above ten percent, and the bleeding stopped. Still, all he could do was lay there, panting from the pain.

He heard the twin machine guns begin firing again, and a roar from Fuzzy. Trying to lift his head, he called out for the bear cub to stay back. The monster's claws would shred him with ease. "Fuzzy! No!"

His words came out as barely more than a wheeze, and he saw his cub rush in to grab hold of one of the monster's wrists. He continued to run forward once he had it, stretching the goblin's arm over its head at an angle that eventually dislocated the shoulder. Everyone in the room heard the pop as Fuzzy turned and began to use all four legs to push backward and pull at the arm like a dog playing tug of war with a rope.

Though he was still a cub, his level increase had caused his body to grow to weigh maybe three hundred pounds now. Add in the muscle in his four legs and neck, and the awkward angle at which he held the big goblin's overextended arm up behind its head, Fuzzy's attack effectively pinned the thing's back to the pile while its foot was still held in place by Allistor's spike.

Cobalus Magnus
Level 25
Health: 4,100/23,000

Gunfire continued to ring out as nearly two dozen party members fired at the monster. Nathan and Dawn appeared, carrying a still-breathing but rough looking Meg between them. Amanda was behind, her shotgun up and firing as she covered them.

Richard ran forward, jumping up and grabbing the shaft of the goblin's spear which now angled upward toward the ceiling. He used his body weight to lever it down, further ripping into the goblin's inner pelvic region. Ramon and Michael both dropped their shotguns and ran up to help. Richard yelled, "Twist and pull!"

All three men put their backs into it, pulling even as they twisted the shaft. The creature screamed and kicked out with its free leg, sending Michael flying backward to slam into the wall. But his grip had held long enough that the force of the monster's kick actually helped them rip the barbed spearpoint free. Black ichor sprayed across the room, covering everyone within a twenty-foot wide cone. Several people stopped firing, trying to wipe the nasty fluid from their eyes and spitting it out of their mouths. A few leaned over and retched.

Ramon and Richard ignored the nasty stuff and pushed forward, climbing the small mound of coin and jamming the spear point up under the monster's chin. It promptly stopped struggling, and everyone but Allistor was surrounded by the familiar glow as experience flowed across their interfaces and they leveled up.

Michael moaned as he lay at the bottom of the wall where he'd landed. Several crushed ribs and a broken spine were rebuilding themselves, and his moan turned into a whimper of pain.

Meg was back on her feet, though extremely pale and unsteady. Sam ran to her and produced some jerky for her to munch on, and a can of Monster Irish coffee. Amanda, meanwhile, jogged over to Allistor who still lay on his pile of coins, the edges of which were digging into his back as he felt another heal wash over him. Amanda handed him a health potion, popping the cork before doing so. He tilted it into his mouth with an unsteady hand and swallowed gratefully.

"That looked like it hurt." Amanda was staring at him, her eyes glowing with her *Internal Analysis* spell. "You've got more broken bones than I can count. Your collarbone looks like it was actually sawed in half. And based on the amount of blood under you, if you were still strictly human, you'd be dead right now." She cast yet another *Restore* on him, still studying his body as it knit itself back together. "The good news is your body's going to be a lot stronger after today. A few more fights like this one, and you'll be more remodeled bone and scar tissue than original equipment." The smile on her face looked a little creepy below her glowing eyes.

Allistor pulled some jerky from his ring and took a bite, washing it down when he was done chewing with the last of the health potion in the bottle. He slowly began to feel less weak as he watched the others heal up, trying to wash the nasty goblin blood from themselves, or help others. A quick check of his interface showed all green dots, no grey. They'd gotten through the fight without any fatalities.

Chapter 12

The Bastion

When Allistor and everyone else were back on their feet and had taken a few minutes to clean themselves up, assign attribute points, and eat or drink a bit, they looted the monster. Each of them got nearly a thousand klax, a few of the gold coins that were melded to the creature's skin, and at least one vial of its blood, the description of which said it was a crafting ingredient. Additionally, there were spider parts – meat, claws, mandibles, and bladders of acid, that Allistor explained must have come from the acid-spitting spiders their prisoner had spoken of. The goblin must have been feeding on them. Eight of the group received one of its claws, and four others each received one of the elongated teeth, which turned out to be hollow like a snake's fang. Andrea ended up with a scroll that imparted a spell called *Dissolve,* but didn't quite have the attributes required to learn it. She pocketed it, saying she'd put the points from her next level into *Intelligence* and learn it then.

Allistor and the others were surprised when Fuzzy declined to snack on the monster. In fact, he kept smacking his cubby lips and sticking his tongue out, licking at his paws as if trying to get its taste out of his mouth. Allistor took pity on him and fed him some of the last chunks of his snake meat. When he was done wolfing it down, Fuzzy gave Allistor a grateful lick, then wondered off, sniffing at the pile the giant goblin had emerged from.

Sam was sitting against the back wall, his arm around Meg. She was silently staring at nothing, her knees gathered up to her chest and her arms wrapped around them. He kept trying to coax her to eat more, but she swatted away his offering. Finally, she said, "If that thing was a goblin, why the hell are they so small and weak in our stories?"

Sam shook his head. "Like Allistor said back when we first met up, it seems like a lot of the creatures they're sending at us are straight out of our myths. But they aren't quite right. Wolves with extra legs, et cetera. Maybe these things just grew smaller as the stories were passed down through the generations."

"Or this one was a friggin' thyroid case." Meg spat on the ground. "Goddamned smelly mutant giant goblin bastard nearly ripped my leg off." She suddenly stood and looked around for a moment before spotting Amanda. Walking over, she wrapped the healer in a tight hug. "Thank you, for coming after me. You saved my life."

Amanda blushed slightly, returning the hug. When Meg let her go, she said, "That's m'job! You make with the shooty-splodey stuff, I throw band-aids when you let the bad monsters bite you, as Chloe would say." Both women laughed and hugged again briefly.

A low growl and a cascade of coins caused everyone to look toward Fuzzy in the back corner. He was using his front paws to dig at the pile, apparently having sniffed out something that interested him. Allistor and the others moved forward, slipping occasionally as they walked across the bed of coins.

In the very back corner of the room, Fuzzy unearthed a pile of skulls, severed spider legs, and other bones that had been buried in the gold eruption the goblin had caused. Mixed in among the bones were several weapons, most of which were still in working order. There were blood-soaked clothing items and packs that had been mostly shredded, and a metal ring with a dozen large keys on it. But most importantly, there was another scroll.

This one glowed slightly orange as Allistor lifted it from the rubbish, which, Ramon informed them all, meant it was one step below the purple scroll Allistor had already found that day. When they examined it, the description caused everyone to start chattering excitedly.

> ***Spell Scroll: Storm***
> ***Item Quality: Rare***
> *This scroll teaches the user the Storm spell. This channeled spell calls down lightning from the sky to strike a target or area selected by the caster. Caster and allied party members are immune to spell damage. At higher levels, the summoned storm may include wind and water damage.* Mana cost: *100 mana/second.* Cooldown: *Five minutes.* Requirements: *Minimum Intelligence and Will Power attributes of 12.*

Several folks in the group immediately began offering Allistor bribes for the scroll. As most of them had been gamers, they all wanted to learn the godlike power themselves. Allistor thought a few of them might even be drooling.

"Who here, besides me, has both *Intelligence* and *Will Power* at 12 or higher?" he raised his hands for silence as he spoke. Looking around, he waited for anyone to raise their hand. Eventually, when no one else spoke up, Helen said, "I'm at eleven for both, so one more level and I could use it."

Nancy raised her hand. "I've got them, but I don't want the spell. Give it to a fighter." Amanda echoed Nancy. "Me too." A few of the group members looked at them like they were insane.

Allistor put the scroll in his inventory. "I could use it now, because of the boosts my armor gives me, but I won't. When we clear this place, those of us who have the stats to use it will draw straws or roll a dice or something. Anybody got a twenty-sided die?"

Andrea, Bjurstrom, and his three companions all raised their hands. McCoy already had one in hand that he'd quickly fished out of a pocket in his vest. Looking around at the people staring his way, he said, "What? The man asked for it. You know you all wish you had one right now. That you were as cool as me." There were several chuckles from the group as he grinned proudly.

Smiling at the geek pride, Allistor said, "Okay, put that away for now. We'll use it to roll for the scroll tonight. For that matter, we can use the D20 to roll for other items that several people could use. I'll make that a rule for our parties going forward. We'll operate on a 'need before greed' basis."

The gamers in the group grinned at his use of the nostalgic term from some of their favorite classic games. Seeing a few of the others with blank looks, he explained. "It means the folks who have the builds, the correct attributes to use something, get to roll for it. So, in the case of this scroll, the folks with caster attributes – heavy on *Intelligence* and *Will Power* – would roll. Folks with focus

280

on *Strength* and *Constitution* would not. Unless all the caster builds pass on the item, then the rest of you could roll." Heads nodded in understanding, and they were ready to move on.

*****

Loki looked up from the three-dimensional display that he and Hel had been watching. Suspicion rolled off of him in waves, pushing through the mist in ripples that rebounded off the walls and Hel herself.

"*Two* high level scrolls in one day? The odds of that are... unlikely to say the least. I suspect Baldur or one of the others is tilting the odds in this human's favor when it comes to loot drops! The *Storm* scroll reeks of Thor!"

"Just as Baldur suspects you of tilting the scale in the other direction, father. And you can no more prove your suspicions than he can prove his. You're both masters of the game after... how many millennia?" The mist carried a scent of amusement from her to her father.

His several arms twitching in irritation and stirring up the mist, Loki seethed in silence. Hel almost felt sorry for the human. She knew her father well, and knew that he would take out his irritation with Baldur and the others on the human rather than risk acting against his more powerful brethren. It would be subtle, for not even Loki would dare openly defy Odin. Or Baldur, for that matter. The penalties were severe. As ancient and powerful as they were, they still followed rules set down by even older beings. But Loki was portrayed in the human legends as a master of deception for a reason.

She was his daughter. She'd learned from the very best, and had complete faith that Loki would focus on Baldur and his ilk, never suspecting that the scrolls had been her doing. She was growing to like this human who so often killed his own kind, despite his insistence that every human life was valuable. The contradictions in him appealed to her sense of irony.

*****

Allistor and company left the room, many of them staring wistfully at the piles of gold as they passed by. Proceeding back through the corridor, they squeezed into the old freight elevator. Logan took charge of the mechanical system, quickly figuring out how to disengage the wheel that would normally be powered by the motor. Then he took hold of the manual crank handle with both hands, released a stopper from the lower pulley gear, and began to crank. The muscles on his massive arms rippled as he cranked the long unused wheel and the cab began to descend down the shaft.

They watched through the welded metal cage as the cut stone of the shaft passed by. Allistor imagined the miners who'd dug this shaft with picks, hammers, shovels, and maybe dynamite roughly two centuries ago.

After a minute or so, the squeal of the rusty pulleys ceased, and Logan stood straight, puffing slightly. They had arrived at the next level. "Need to put some oil on those things." he said as he rubbed the rust stains off his hands. Lars pulled open the cage door and stepped out into the corridor. This one was a stark contrast to the rough stone shaft they'd descended through. The floors were poured and polished concrete, as were the walls that rose ten feet before arcing into a rounded ceiling fifteen feet above the floor. It was lined on both sides with massive rounded vault doors that looked like doors to hobbit holes on steroids. The nearest door stood ajar, and they could see that it was easily two feet thick, with four-inch steel locking bolts. Each vault had a security pad next to it, much like the ones upstairs, with a keypad, a slide for cards or fobs, and what was probably a biometric or optic scanner.

Looking to his left, Allistor saw the corridor ended at the dual elevator bank that led back up to the top level, and between them stood another security station with a closed metal gate. Looking to his right, the corridor ended just thirty feet or so away with a large metal door much like the one they'd found the goblin behind. This one was closed.

Logan spoke in a near-whisper into his radio. "I'm sure if there's anything down here, it heard us coming. Let's clear this by the numbers, starting with this door." They quickly cleared the rooms behind any of the smaller doors in the corridor, of which there were only four standing open. Nothing had spawned in any of those rooms, so it didn't take long. For the closed doors, they thumped on each one with Allistor's rebar spear, but no sound came back to them from inside.

The group moved to within ten feet or so of the large door at the end, and paused. Allistor and Logan stepped forward, neither of them needing to speak by this time. Allistor cast *Barrier* and equipped his shotgun, making sure it had a full load of slugs. Logan reached out to tug on the three-foot vertical grab bar that served as the massive door's handle, and Allistor nodded that he was ready.

Logan yanked on the handle… and nothing happened.

"Shit." he muttered. There was a large spoked wheel to the left of the handle, much like one would expect to see on a bank vault, or naval vessel hatch. Setting his own shotgun down, Logan grabbed the wheel with both hands and began to apply pressure. The wheel moved slightly, a loud grinding squeak echoing down the corridor as the seldom-used and partially rusted mechanism protested. He put some more muscle into it, and the wheel turned maybe ninety degrees.

Just as Logan was adjusting his hands for another turn, the door thrummed with an impact accompanied by the squeal of tortured metal. He yanked his hands back with a hiss, stung by the vibration. Allistor winced in sympathy. Anybody who'd ever played baseball and managed to hit a fastball with a bat they weren't gripping tightly knew that feeling.

Two seconds later, there was another clang as something large and powerful struck the other side of the door again. The squeal of metal was disturbing. Allistor doubted that whatever was in there could bend the thick steel rods that held the door closed, so the sound must be from the monster on the other side scratching or possibly puncturing the metal. He really didn't want to meet any creature that could do either of those things.

"Uhhh… anybody wanna call it a day? Maybe grab one of Meg's tasty sandwiches back at the Stronghold? Whatever's in there is clearly feeling grouchy. I'm thinkin' let it take a nap, and we'll come back when it's in a better mood." Allistor looked around at the group behind him. He used his normal voice, as the monster behind the door clearly knew they were coming.

"Yup." Bjurstrom actually turned around and started walking before Goodrich smacked him on the head and he turned back. Which confused Fuzzy, who had started to follow.

Andrea laughed loudly. "Ha! Who'd have ever thought Bjurstrom and the bear would turn out to be the smart ones in this group?"

A few of the others chuckled, then a few more joined in when Bjurstrom patted the cub on the head, saying, "I know, right?" The laughter was quiet, and more a reaction to the fear they felt than a reflection of the quality of the joke.

Logan had slid on some work gloves and was positioned to resume turning the wheel. Allistor prepared himself again, though this time he was more ready to retreat quickly than to charge through the door. Logan gave the wheel three more full turns before it thudded to a stop and the now unlocked door shifted slightly outward. Allistor skipped backward a step, expecting the door to fly open under the force of some tremendous blow. Logan did the same, not wanting to be crushed.

When it didn't open farther, the two men exchanged a look. Behind them, Meg snorted. "Well, that was anticlimactic." Dawn giggled, quickly covering her mouth with her eyes wide.

Fuzzy let out a low growl, his lips pulling back in a snarl as he faced the door and backed away slowly. Catching sight of the bear retreating, it took Allistor a second to make the connection and turn back toward the door. That second almost cost him everything.

The multi-ton metal door exploded outward, only the massive hinges on one side keeping it from crashing down the corridor and flattening the entire group. When it hit the limit of the hinges' flexibility, metal squealed and the door rebounded. But in those two seconds, a nightmare had stuck its head partway through.

> **Emperor Scairp**
> **Level 28**
> **Elite**
> **Health: 31,000/31,000**

All Allistor could see from his position was a mass of huge claws, mandibles, and jet-black chitin. An angry chittering sound filled the corridor as the monster tried to push its bulk through the doorway. But it was too large even for the massive opening, and it retreated, turning slightly as it pushed a limb through and tried to clamp down on Allistor with one massive foreclaw.

The creature was, as far as Allistor and the others could tell, a giant black scorpion the size of a Volkswagen Beetle, if the little cars came with a long, segmented tail and a pair of front claws, each large enough to cut a man in half with ease.

Allistor hopped backward, avoiding the initial grab but getting knocked down by the jaggedly spiked back side of the claw as it passed effortlessly through his protective magic barrier. The hard chitin spikes slashed at his new armor, but didn't penetrate.

Shots exploded from the group behind him the moment he was clear of the beast. The buckshot rounds had little to no effect on it, other than one that peppered its face and managed to damage one of the monster's twelve eyes. The rest of the tiny buckshot pellets bounced off the scairp's chitin shell. Those who were firing slugs did much better. At close range, the larger, heavier projectiles were punching small holes in the chitin, causing a purplish goo to splash from the wounds.

The creature withdrew its forelimb and retreated from the doorway. The shots died off as the group lost sight of their target in the pitch-black room. Allistor and Logan could hear the scratching of its hard-shelled feet against the stone floor.

"You know it's setting up an ambush in there, right?" Logan looked at Allistor. "The moment one of us goes through there, it'll be snip snip yer dead."

Allistor nodded. "It blasted through my *Barrier* spell like it wasn't even there. This is gonna suck."

Logan switched out his shotgun for the LMG, and nodded at Sam who was doing the same. The two men stood next to each other, looking at Allistor.

"Okay, boss." Sam began. "This is where you earn the hero pay. You just scoot on in there and distract that big bug, and we'll be right behind ya. Try to keep off to one side of it so we don't hit ya by mistake. Maybe light it on fire so we can see better?"

Allistor took a deep breath. Even knowing it wouldn't help, he re-cast *Barrier* on himself. While he waited for the small amount of mana to regenerate, he said, "I'm gonna try something. That thing's been living down here in the dark for who knows how long. So I'm gonna send in a light globe right before I go through. Might distract it enough for me to get past the ambush."

The two men raised their weapons and adjusted the feeder belts so that they draped cleanly over an arm without any snags. Allistor cast *Light* and the globe appeared in front of him. He was about to push it through the doorway, when it occurred to him to try something. Staring at the globe, he re-cast *Light* toward it while picturing a larger, brighter globe.   There was a wave of whispers behind him as a stream of light flowed from Allistor's chest to the globe. It only increased in size slightly, but the light globe grew bright enough that several people blinked or held up a hand to shield their eyes.

Allistor mentally shoved the globe through the door, waited one heartbeat, then rushed through behind it. As he reached the doorway he dove forward, anticipated a massive claw sniping at him from one side or the other. That choice nearly proved disastrous as the expected claw came from an unexpected angle, shooting down from above the door even as the monster squealed in pain from the light.

Which was all that saved Allistor from having his horizontally angled body snipped in half as he dove past. Instead the monster's aim was disrupted, and the claw slammed down onto his back after having already snapped shut. He was driven to the floor, his breath knocked out of him and his jaw slamming against the stone hard enough to crack bone.

Momentarily disoriented, he scrambled forward on his belly, losing hold of his shotgun as he frantically worked his elbows and knees to push himself along, scrabbling with his fingers for some kind of rough spot to latch on to and pull himself forward. He heard the two light machine guns open up behind him, and he rolled onto his back.

The first thing he noticed was that he'd crawled off to one side instead of straight into the room as he'd thought. The giant scorpion boss had dropped off the wall above the doorway and was facing him, both of the deadly foreclaws snapping in his direction. But the damage from the two LMGs quickly forced it to turn and deal with that threat. Sam and Logan stood on either side of the door, backs against the wall. The others were firing through the opening.

Allistor cast *Flame Shot* on it in the form of a column of fire descending directly onto its face. Eyes bubbled and burst as the thing screamed and began to thrash. Its curved, segmented tail shot forward, snaking just past Sam's head to slam into the wall where the tip embedded itself into the stone. Shrapnel from the impact struck Sam's head and neck, drawing tiny blooms of blood. And a spatter of venom from the stinger splashed over him. When it penetrated his skin via the small wounds, Sam's face turned a sickly green and he began to wobble. Leaning his back against the wall for support, he continued to fire. He paused for a moment to projectile vomit, then spit, before resuming fire even as his health bar ticked downward.

"Healers! Get in here!" Allistor cast a heal on Sam but it didn't stop the venom, and the creature was quickly moving his direction. "Sam's been poisoned. Nancy!"

He cast *Restraint* on the monster, and it actually paused for about two seconds. Logan stopped firing and reached across the doorway to grab Sam and shove him ahead of himself through the door. Seconds later the half-blind beast crashed into the wall, only one claw shooting through the door to try and snag some prey. It shuddered under the impacts of a concentrated volley of shotgun blasts from outside.

Allistor realized he was now alone in the room with the scorpion.

Emperor Scairp
Level 28
Elite
Health: 19,700/31,000

His first instinct as a gamer was to try and tank the thing, get its attention and draw it away from the doorway so that the others could join him inside and blast the thing. But good sense overrode instinct. He was in no immediate danger himself, and the monster couldn't get through the door to his people. They could blast away at it for a little while, whittle it down while he healed up and regained his mana.

With that thought in mind, he cast *Restore* on himself and moved a bit farther away from the chittering, squealing boss. Its head was still afire, and most of its eyes were either scorched or punctured by gunfire. Its right forearm was extended through the door, trying to catch a human in its razor-sharp claws.

Allistor took a moment to survey the rest of the room. He hadn't noticed before, but the light from the bright globe hovering several feet inside the door was being reflected back to him in muted hues by thousands of bricks of gold. They were stacked on pallet after pallet, as far back as the light extended. A few had been knocked loose onto the floor, presumably by a hungry and annoyed giant scorpion.

Allistor looked at the nearest pile, then at the monster, and a plan began to form. Pulling a mana potion from his inventory ring, he held it in his left hand, cork popped. Stepping behind the pile for a little bit of cover, he lifted a brick in his right hand. His best guess, it weighed about twenty-five pounds. Too heavy to throw at the boss monster from his position, even with his improved strength. But he *could* toss it in the air a short ways.

He did just that, tossing the brick up and casting *Levitate* on it. The brick froze in midair, and he made a flinging motion toward the scorpion. The heavy hunk of metal took off like a shot, speeding toward the target, but passing right over its back and smashing into the wall.

Frowning, Allistor contemplated the failure while his people continued to pump rounds into the aggravated creature from a safe distance, slowly whittling away at its health. Lifting another brick, he tossed it up and caught it with the spell again. This time, when he made the swift hand motion, he focused his eyes on a spot on the creature's torso. The gold bar shot forward, light glinting off of it as it sped toward the monster and slammed into its

291

side precisely where Allistor had planned. There was a loud crack as what was effectively a twenty-five pound golden cannonball smashed into the chitin exoskeleton, cracks spiderwebbing out from the point of impact.

"Yes!" He pumped a fist in the air. Quickly checking his interface, he saw that the spell had cost him thirty mana each time. He had some attribute points to assign, but with his current mana pool of eighteen hundred, minus what he'd already used in this fight and not yet regenerated, he could throw about fifty gold missiles at the bug boss. As an experiment, he tried simply casting *Levitate* on a stationary bar atop the pile. The bar lifted, and he flung it at the boss mob, striking its torso very close to the previous hit. The network of cracks in its armor expanded. A quick check showed that lifting the bar with magic rather than catching it mid-air cost an extra ten mana.

Allistor got to work. One after another, he tossed gold brick after gold brick up into the air, using *Levitate* to grab and hurl it toward the boss' left side. Each impact sent a web of cracks spidering outward, and shaved a decent bit of health off the scorpion.

After the tenth or twelfth bar, the creature turned toward him unexpectedly, indicating he'd drawn aggro with the damage he was doing. It spun just in time to catch a brick to the face, snapping one of its two mandibles and crushing one of the few remaining eyes.

As the creature rushed toward him, Allistor moved farther behind the stack of gold bullion and flung one more brick. It followed right behind the first, smashing into the giant arachnid's face and stunning it for a moment.

292

The others took advantage of its absence from the door and poured through. With Allistor crouched behind the gold, they fired round after round at the beast's left flank. The weakened chitin offered little resistance, and soon both Allistor and the pile of gold bars were showered in blood splatter.

Emperor Scairp
Level 28
Elite
Health: 9,300/31,000

The elite scorpion recovered its senses and continued its charge toward Allistor. He ducked farther behind the gold stack as one of the massive claws swung across at his head. It knocked several of the heavy bars off the top couple layers as if they were as light as spongecake, trying to get to Allistor. As the heavy things hit the ground around him, one crushing the toes on his right foot, he got another idea.

Picking up a brick in each hand, he shouted, "Hold fire!" When the gunshots ceased, he picked a spot atop the giant bug's head and activated *Dimensional Step.* In an instant he was standing atop the monster even as it seemed to be searching the spot he'd just vacated. Dropping to his knees, he adjusted his grip so that he held each brick by its end, then slammed them one at a time like sledgehammers striking the top of its skull. As quickly as he could, he alternated left, right, and left again, smashing at the chitin and spreading a wider and wider network of cracks.

He heard Amanda shout "Duck!" but didn't react fast enough. The monster's wickedly sharp barbed tail pierced the back of his shoulder, emerging from the front covered in his blood. It effortlessly lifted him off its back, the segmented tail curving as it pulled itself and him backward. Then it shot forward again, this time slamming him into another pallet of bullion. Bricks shifted, but not enough to save him from being badly broken in several places even as the tail spike pushed farther through him.

With not enough air left in his lungs to scream, he sort of moaned and tried in vain to inhale. A heal spell washed over him, raising his health bar a solid chunk. But it was still below fifty percent, and the heal focused on his bones first, so the pain increased rather than being eased. His increased *Luck* attribute seemed to have kicked in, as he didn't see a poison debuff on his interface despite the stinger tip having pushed all the way through him.

He cast a heal on himself, then a *Mind Spike* on the monster, berating himself for not using it sooner. He'd distracted himself with the gold-flinging and pride at how clever he was.

The scorpion retracted its tail, but Allistor grabbed onto the corner of the pallet and held on. The resulting rending of his flesh as the sharp, barbed point ripped its way out of him somehow gave him the breath to scream.

Now out of sight of the healers, he used some of his dwindling mana to heal himself. When the bleeding stopped and his health bar hovered at just over twenty five percent, he rolled farther behind the gold pile to hide from the scorpion. He registered the continued sound of gunfire, hoping with all his might that his people wouldn't draw aggro.

To make sure, he stuck his head out and cast *Erupt* under the base of the creature's tail, which was the part of

294

the monster that hovered closest to the ground. The stone spike shot upward, smashing through the softer underside of the monster and driving upward into its flesh. The scairp let out a shrill scream as its tail with that nasty diamond-hard stinger went limp.

The spike had the added advantage of holding the monster in place. It could shuffle to one side or the other in a rough arc around the spike, but could not move forward or back. "It's trapped, take it down!" Allistor's shout was hoarse, filled with pain and not enough air. But his people heard through the radio, and charged forward with guns blazing. They spread out along its left side and poured lead slugs into it as fast as they could.

Looking to his left hand, Allistor saw that he'd crushed the mana vial at some point, and the liquid had all leaked to the floor. Grabbing another, and a health potion, from his ring, he gulped down both. Reaching into his inventory one more time, he removed his trusty rebar spear. Climbing on top of the gold stack in front of him, he leapt back atop the monster's head.

He immediately realized he'd forgotten to warn his people this time, and just as he landed a slug hit his left thigh. Off balance, he thrust his weight forward and stabbed down with the spear, penetrating the weak spot he'd created with the gold bars.

The tip of the spear sunk deep into the monster's flesh, then even deeper as Allistor finished falling forward and added his weight to it. The scorpion boss' keening stopped abruptly, and its legs simply gave out. The front part of its body hit the floor, while the rear end was still propped up slightly on the spike. Everyone in the room leveled up as experience points and a significant number of Fame Points drifted across their interfaces, earned both from the kill and from clearing the dungeon.

Allistor just lay there, breathing in the stench of the creature's nasty purple blood. His health bar was full again, but he was still suffering weakness and nausea from the extensive blood loss of internal bleeding due to crush damage, and external bleeding from his shoulder wound and the slug in his leg. Not to mention the pain of his broken bones knitting back together.

Since he was already atop the beast, he laid a hand on it and looted. Another set of notifications flashed across his interface, but he ignored them. Rolling onto his side, he saw Sam collapse near the door. His face was still that sickly green shade, and his health bar was ticking downward in small increments every second. Nancy hovered over him, a worried look on her face.

Groaning in pain, Allistor rolled off the creature's head. He'd intended to land on his feet, but that didn't happen. He face-planted on the stone floor, and a few of his people rushed over to help him up.

"Damn, boss. That was brutal. Cool idea with the gold hammers though!" Dawn's smile was full of mischief. Allistor barely registered the words as he pushed toward Sam, his people holding him up as he staggered forward.

Nancy turned to him, desperation in her eyes. "I can't stop the poison! Whatever it is, it's eating away at his insides. I keep healing him, but the damage is getting to be too much for me to keep up with!"

Instantly, Sam was buried in more than a dozen heal spells. His health bar zoomed up to full, then began declining again. Nancy was right, Allistor saw it was dropping faster. Sam squeezed Meg's hand so hard she grimaced in pain.

Amanda shouted, "Stop that! All of you just wasted mana. Don't do it again! We may need to heal Sam all the way back up out of here and to the Stronghold until we find a way to fix this! We'll tell you when we need you to heal." Her sharp words and severe look had many of their people blushing in shame or staring down at their feet.

She softened a bit. "I'm sorry. I'm just worried about Sam. All of you go loot the boss while Nancy and I try to stabilize him. Nancy, what potions do you have?" She squatted down beside Sam and activated her *Internal Analysis*.

While they worked and the others looted, Allistor took a moment to review his notifications. There were the usual experience and Fame Points notifications, as well as his level going up to fifteen. He brushed those away, getting to the good stuff.

> *You have cleared this structure of all inhabitants. Do you wish to claim this structure?*
>
> *Yes/No*

When Allistor selected *Yes*, another, even more interesting notification appeared.

> *You have sufficient population, resources, and title to enable you to declare this structure as a Bastion. Do you wish to create a Bastion at this time? Yes/No*

297

His pulse quickening, Allistor waved away that message again without choosing, quickly opening the tab he'd used to construct Strongholds and Citadels. Sure enough, right there below Citadel was a new bright shiny green entry labeled *Bastion*. A quick read-through showed it to be an intermediate stage between a Citadel and an actual City. A little bit of further exploration led him to an aerial map that showed the mint glowing a pulsing blue, with a dotted blue line running around an area that encompassed both the mint and the Capitol Stronghold and all the blocks in between.

Experimenting, he lifted a hand and used his fingers to move the line, expanding it a single block north, south, east, and west. When that worked, he tried pushing it farther. The limit was a six by ten block square area. If he claimed all of that, he'd have more space than he'd have people to defend it. So he shrunk it back down to its original size, which included the Capitol, the parklands, the courthouse, and the mint.

Going back to pull up the last notification, he selected *Yes* then confirmed the area within the blue line. Once again, the whole area lit up with a golden glow. Allistor quickly selected a thirty-foot wall around the entire perimeter, with north and south gates that were set in the middle of the park area. He added in the power, water, and sensors, and left the rest for later. When he executed that, and the light had faded away, yet another notification popped up. This one was accompanied by similar fanfare, horns, and fireworks as to when he'd created the Citadel.

Congratulations! You are the first native of UCP 382 to construct a Bastion!

Your efforts in conquering territory and accumulating wealth are unmatched on your world. You have earned the Title of Earl, along with commensurate Fame and Infamy Points from the interested factions. Your Bastion will receive complimentary upgrades to its perimeter defense, communication, and morale bonuses.

In addition, as you have achieved yet another First for your world, you have been awarded your choice of either a yacht-class interstellar vessel to be delivered upon expiration of the Stabilization Period, or the equivalent value in System Tech of your choosing, available immediately upon demand.

His elation at receiving such potentially valuable gifts was quickly deflated when another message appeared. And this one, again just like when he constructed the Citadel, was seen by everyone, everywhere.

World First! Earl Allistor has constructed the first Bastion on UCP 382!

Congratulations, Earl Allistor! May you rule long and wisely!

Shaking his head, he returned his attention to the ladies working on Sam. The man still looked green. Despite knowing that it might annoy Amanda, Allistor cast a heal on his friend. Nobody seemed to notice. Meg, Nancy, and Amanda were deep into a discussion on what to do. Allistor took a knee next to them.

"We need to get Sam out of here. I'll stay with him for a minute, you ladies go loot the boss. We can't pass up a chance at another epic spell or something. Then a few of us can work on transporting him while the rest harvest what they can from the corpse."

Meg looked like she was about to argue, but the other two each took an arm and guided her to her feet. Nancy rubbed her back. "It'll just take a few seconds, Meg. Come on."

Allistor put his hand on Sam's chest as the three walked away. The man's heart was thumping in his chest like he'd just sprinted a quarter mile. "How you feelin' bud?"

Sam groaned, his eyes closed and his face covered in sweat. "Been better, boy. But I ain't dyin' to no oversized bug. No sir." Sam had to grit his teeth and push out the last few words as another wave of pain hit him.

There was a commotion over near the corpse, and Allistor looked over to see Nancy motioning wildly with her hands, pointing at people and obviously giving orders. Folks began moving quickly, producing items Nancy demanded and following her as she raced back to Sam.

"Allistor! Did you check your loot from this thing?"

He shook his head. "Nope. Was a little busy. Why?"

"Its venom sac is missing. From its tail, I mean. I just looked for it. If we can find it, I can use my *Alchemy* skills to maybe create an antivenom. I have everyone checking their loot, but you actually got the kill. My guess is you have it."

Feeling bad for letting Sam suffer because he skipped the notifications, Allistor quickly opened both his inventory and the loot notifications. Immediately, he saw a green blob that looked very much like a venom sac. The description confirmed it.

"Yup! Got it right here." He pulled it out and handed it to Nancy, who was already removing crafting equipment from her own ring. He was about to close his inventory when a pair of words in the notifications caught his attention.

Venom Cure.

"Well, shit." He really felt low as he read the whole notification.

You have received: Vial of Scairp Venom Cure x 10

Pulling one of the vials out, he coughed once, then said, "Ummm...Nancy?"

"Not now, Allistor!" she snapped at him. Amanda, who had escorted Meg back at a slightly slower pace behind Nancy, saw what Allistor was holding.

"Nancy! Look up." Amanda said in her best doctor voice.

Nancy, her attention caught by the strange command, looked up at Allistor. Her eyes focused on the vial filled with purplish liquid, and she read the description. She immediately grabbed it and poured half into Sam's mouth. The other half she sprinkled onto her hand a few drops at a time and rubbed it into the cuts on his head and neck.

Sam immediately began to look better. His skin tone returned to normal after only a minute or so. Nancy cast a final heal on him, and his health bar stayed full. Meg helped him sit up, scooting up behind him so he could lean on her. There was cheering from the rest of the group, and smiles all around.

"Thank you, boy. Though, next time maybe check your loot a little sooner? Every minute of that shit sucked."

Allister felt ashamed. "I'm so sorry, Sam. I didn't mean to-"

"I know, kid." Sam held up a hand and interrupted him. "I was just messin' with ya. You did good, killing that thing. Just proves we were right to put our faith in you back at the start."

Meg gave him a dirty look, but didn't speak. Which for her was huge. Allistor chose to believe it meant she forgave him.

They took some time to harvest the massive bug's corpse, taking every usable bit of it, including the meat. Fuzzy helped himself to his share, though Allistor heard Dawn scolding the bear cub about just sitting around doing nothing during the fight. Fuzzy didn't look the least bit contrite, and simply stepped forward to confiscate a recently butchered scairp steak.

Upon further examination, Allistor found he'd also been awarded the stinger as part of his loot, along with two thousand klax, a stack of emperor scairp chitin, another stack of meat, and a scroll that didn't glow any color at all.

Reassured that Sam was okay, he took a minute to look at his stats. He'd leveled twice since he last assigned points, so he added two points to *Constitution,* bringing it up to ten, then added one point each to *Intelligence* and *Will Power,* now both at eleven. His new title of Earl showed up alongside his *Giant Killer* designation. He hadn't looked at his stats since picking up the Seal or Lilly's new armor, and was surprised to see just how many boosts he had from his gear. Especially his *Will Power,* which was a natural eleven, but with boosts shot up to a whopping eighteen.

Designation: Earl Allistor, Giant Killer	Level: 15	Experience: 17,000/520,000
Planet of Origin: UCP 382	Health: 6,500/6,500	Class: Battlemage
Attribute Pts Available: 1	Mana: 4,400	
Intelligence: 11 (13)	Strength: 5 (7)	Charisma: 6 (8)
Adaptability: 6	Stamina: 5 (7)	Luck: 3 (4)
Constitution: 10 (13)	Agility: 3	Health Regen: 400/m
Will Power: 11 (18)	Dexterity: 3	Mana Regen: 130/m

Chapter 13

Payback

It was nearly suppertime when the dungeon group piled into the two newer elevators, which were operable now that Allistor had turned the power on. Nigel's presence was immediately helpful as he opened the steel gates to let the party through.

Back on the main floor, there were hoots and whistles from the volunteers who'd been guarding the building. After a quick conversation with the squad leaders, Bjurstrom reported that three different scouts had been spotted moving around nearby, checking out the building. One had actually stepped out to the center of a side street and waved at Allistor's troops. The other two had seemed content to observe for a while, then fade away. All three had been outside the perimeter when the wall went up.

With Nigel's sensors already up and working, Allistor led the entire group, minus four sentries who volunteered to walk the wall, back to the capitol building. Sam began working with the other cooks to prepare a simple dinner while Meg experimented a bit with the emperor scairp meat. By the time Sam had prepared burgers for everyone, she had created a thick broth by boiling a small amount of the meat with some spices and ingredients only she knew. Using a turkey baster, she dripped a few drops of the broth on each burger.

Allistor was first to dig in. He found that Meg's addition gave the meat a slightly tangy flavor that he quite enjoyed. And the usual buff of +2 to *Stamina* the burgers usually gave became +2 *Stamina* and +2 *Health Regen,* with the buff now lasting five hours.

He complimented Meg and Sam on the meal the minute they finished up in the kitchen and joined him at his table. "Great job guys, and this is an awesome buff!" The others around the table all mumbled agreement with their mouths full.

When the meal was complete, Allistor was told that some of his people who'd stayed behind had buried their lost comrades in a small glade near the teleport hub. The others had seen to the needs of the freed prisoners. All of them now followed Allistor outside, where he stood near the graves and spoke their names one at a time. When he finished the list, he said, "These six brave souls gave their lives for us today. They knew the danger, and went into battle for the sake of all of us. We shall remember their sacrifice, and honor them always. In the coming days, should any of you have doubts about our purpose, about your commitment to reclaiming what is ours, come here to this quiet place, and remember them."

After a quiet service where a few others stepped forward to speak about their friends, they all retired back to the dining hall, where Sam broke out the alcohol and they held a good old-fashioned Irish wake.

*****

Allistor spent the next week putting the Bastion in order. First thing after breakfast in the morning, he assigned Amanda all the rights and privileges necessary to make modifications to the place. He gathered all the fighters from the dungeon together for their loot rolls. It turned out that he, Helen, Amanda, and Nancy were still the only ones with high enough attributes to use the *Storm* spell scroll. The ladies declined the spell, with Helen saying he could make the best use of it, having a tendency to stick his nose into things. The others chuckled, then applauded when he accepted the scroll. After making a short side trip he, Helen, and Fuzzy escorted Lars, Chris, and Logan back to their Stronghold while she organized sleeping quarters, meeting rooms, crafting shops, a motor pool, and the dozens of other details that needed to be settled quickly.

By the early afternoon, and after some occasionally heated debate, Lars' entire population had sworn the oath and officially become Allistor's people. They'd been reassured that they didn't need to leave their homes at the Stronghold, and were welcome at the Bastion if they chose. But the final straw was when Allistor produced and stacked a dozen gold bars in the center of the courtyard. Lars had grinned at his people. "This is our cut, the gold Allistor has

Not needing to be stealthy at all, the trip back to Lars' people went quickly. Once there, Lars called them all together to discuss joining Allistor formally versus entering into an alliance. Initially more than half his people were in favor of remaining independent allies with trade agreements and a mutual protection pact. But as Logan, then Chris, and finally Lars spoke about what they'd seen and heard from Allistor and his people over the two days since they met, their people's opinion of Allistor rose. It didn't hurt that both his *Charisma* and *Luck* attributes had gone up since he'd left.

awarded us for helping him kill Paul – which we would have done for free – and clear the dungeon. Four gold bars for each of us. That's a hundred pounds of gold each, which right now is worth just under *two million klax.*" He paused for a second, then added, "Each. As in, two million for Chris, two million for Logan, and two million for lil ol' me. Not bad for a couple days' work, eh?" His grin was infectious, and when he took a knee, so did the others.

They returned to the Bastion, where Allistor made good his promise to those prisoners who wanted to return to their own Strongholds. As it turned out, there was at least one from each of the Strongholds Lars knew about in Denver. Allistor sent foragers out looking for mass transit, and they returned with a Department of Corrections bus that had been parked behind the courthouse. Seventeen of the eighty-five chose to leave the Bastion, and in no time at all they were all loaded onto the bus along with Allistor, Helen, Fuzzy, Amanda, Lars, and Logan.

One by one they approached the other Strongholds, honking the bus horn briefly to announce their presence, and asking to speak with the local leader as they released the prisoner or prisoners back to their homes. All but one of the Stronghold leaders greeted them politely, and agreed to a later sit-down to discuss an alliance.

The one that was less than friendly was a man named Matthew, whose family had been taken by Paul. He'd lost a wife and daughter, and only gotten the daughter back. She explained to her father that, "Mom died just a few days after they took us." But the old man wasn't listening. Allistor and his group left that Stronghold more quickly than expected, and without any hope that an alliance would include those people.

307

As they drove away, Allistor was already entertaining thoughts as to how they'd deal with the old man and his people, should they become hostile. It was dark by the time the crew returned to the Bastion, and they all settled down to a good meal followed by a relaxing night's sleep.

*****

For the next several months, Allistor stayed close to his people and his properties. They spent time securing themselves and their futures. Structures were modified to fit their needs, fields were planted, livestock rounded up and distributed.

Allistor went foraging with his crews from time to time, mostly gathering supplies needed for his various crafters. Any valuables, items, or edible food were considered bonuses. When fall turned into winter, the foraging parties went out less and less often, and the hunting parties increased. Only the hardiest and most experienced went hunting, though. Winter in the Rockies was no joke.

They were helped considerably when a thousand-strong herd of buffalo wandered into Cheyenne, cleverly using the abandoned buildings for cover from the biting cold wind and munching on the likewise protected and overgrown lawns, gardens, and parks that hadn't been buried in snow. In order not to scare the easy meat out of town with gunshots, Allistor and a few of the others would cast *Restraint* on two or three of the males, then someone would bang some pots together and shout, driving the others a short distance away. Still others would run in and slit the massive animals' throats while they were stunned. This job was normally assigned to the lowest level people in the group, to gain them what little experience the kills gave. Then the animals would be looted and butchered. Their hides made great leather gear for their people, or warm bed covers, once they'd been cleaned and treated. The humans also learned, mostly by accident, that if they were grouped in a party, each kill gave more loot. Instead of a single stack of maybe twenty pieces of buffalo meat an individual would loot from a kill, each member of a party would get ten to twelve pieces, as well as horns, hoofs, hide, et cetera. Then, they could manually harvest more from the corpse after it was looted. So, a group of six in a hunting party could take away three to four times as much meat from each animal than an individual. And the experience gain for the group members wasn't that much of a consideration, as buffalo generally didn't kill other creatures for food, thus remaining low level creatures.

Allistor or Helen accompanied every group, making sure they only took a few big males, so that the herd could continue to grow. There were plenty of cattle still roaming the fields and forests to supplement their people's diet, and no shortage of edible monsters to kill. Helen had unsurprisingly chosen *Ranger* as her class. Similar to some of the old stories and games, the class was more about being a steward of the lands than a fighter or scout. Though it certainly included those abilities. She got bonuses to her accuracy with every kind of ranged weapon, enhanced tracking skills, and boosts to her *Animal Husbandry* skill gains. In effect, the *Ranger* class mirrored her job description as a park ranger. It just made her the most badass park ranger ever.

Ramon and his people worked like madmen in the library, some reading through books, researching specific topics for crafters, or searching for useful spells. Others copied out hundreds of scrolls containing the various spells Allistor wanted all his people to have. Everyone learned at least the basics – *Light, Restore, Flame Shot*. He was determined that none of his people would go out into the world without at least those minimum preparations. Ramon had learned a few very interesting things from his reading as well. For example, they now knew that the aliens responsible for kidnapping Earth were an ancient race that had done the same to countless other worlds.

Those with an interest in fighting, clearing dungeons, or combat for various reasons along with the cowboys, hunters, and anyone else who regularly spent time outside the walls, were given more offensive magic if they had the stats for it. *Restraint, Erupt,* and *Mind Spike* were given to those special few who could use them. Many altered their builds as they leveled up, in order to obtain the magic.

And maybe most importantly, there were new weapons.

Allistor had given careful consideration to the two options given him as a reward for constructing the Bastion. After a little quick research on the open market, he determined that the ship with faster-than-light capabilities that could take him quickly to other worlds and other stars was the better option. But it wasn't an easy choice. His people needed tech right away – and the tech available was pretty amazing. There were actual plasma weapons that burned holes through all but the strongest substances, and equipment that could regenerate lost organs or limbs –

310

which normal healing wouldn't do, no matter how thick the nanites gathered. There were machines straight out of science fiction that could convert matter from one form to another. Scrap metal could be fed into it to be broken down and used to make tools or nails and screws. The production options were limited, of course. One could not use it to turn lead into gold. But it was great for producing everyday items for his people.

On the flip side, he could have used his reward to get all the tech, and simply purchased the ship with his billions at the end of the year. But Allistor wasn't one to gamble with such an important aspect of his people's future. There might not be a ship available to purchase at the end of the year. His gold could be stolen, or the market price could bottom out if they weren't careful to limit the supply. Better to use smaller amounts of gold now to get the tech they needed and be one hundred percent sure there would be a ship for them on what they had taken to referring to as 'Invasion Day'.

Allistor also made at least one trip per week to one of the local Strongholds, or invited their leaders to the Bastion, to try and build relationships and establish alliances. It was slow going. The leaders of each Stronghold were, by nature, independent, and not thrilled about possibly losing their people and thus their power. And they didn't know Allistor like Lars did, not having fought alongside him.

The accounts of the freed prisoners did lend him some credibility, which he attempted to boost by bringing gifts of food, or small alien weapons, skill scrolls, or even bags of gold coins depending on what each Stronghold needed most. The coins had the added benefit of being a hard, tradable currency that different folks could use to purchase things from each other. Paper money was a thing of the past, and credit was rarely offered.

And through all of that, he found time to visit his other properties and people via the teleport system. One of the things he purchased early was a pair of heavy-duty hover pads. They used some sort of magnetic force to lift themselves off the ground and remain there, where they could be moved horizontally quite easily. Allistor had purchased several smaller ones on a whim, and his people began using them to move butchered buffalo parts and other heavy loads weighing up to one ton. They worked so well that he purchased the industrial versions and took them straight to George at Luther's Landing. The things were the size of flatbed rail cars, and that's exactly how they used them. Taking them out to the train wreck, they were able to slide the flat pads under the overturned railroad cars and lift them. Then, by moving the pads over to the sloped gravel on either side of the track and setting them down, gravity did the work of tilting the heavy cars back upright. Not only did it give them access to more of the loot inside the wrecked cars, but it had the added advantage of clearing the wreck and potentially making the tracks usable again in the future.

Allistor also brought George one of the matter converters, which they fed all the scrap metal from the train into. The scrap was loaded onto a pad, the pad activated, and towed back to the Stronghold by one of the trucks. George. being who he was, went into the munitions business, converting the scrap into tens of thousands of bullets which they sold or traded to the other Strongholds in

312

Denver. And others Allistor and his people discovered along the way.

He built up the wealth of his tiny empire by selling off gold bars in small lots, from a single bar to a stack of ten at a time. He assigned Chris to the task, finding the man had a surprising facility for numbers, and a keen sense of the market demand. After just a month, Chris had manipulated the market so that they were receiving thirteen hundred klax per ounce for the single bars, and fifteen hundred for the bigger lots. He'd called the extra two hundred klax a 'convenience fee' for saving the buyers the trouble of bidding on individual bars over and over again.

Allistor began using the gold and silver coins to pay salaries to his support people, as promised. The teachers, gardeners, hunters, the guards, the folks who cooked and cleaned for the others. And he set up a system where the crafters could sell their 'practice' items of less than top quality to him at a slight discount. This gave them an option other than to break the items back down into component materials or throw them away. He in turn used them as gifts or trade items with other survivor groups.

Bjurstrom and his three team members became training officers, taking the lower level survivors outside the walls on hunting trips. They even located a few 'dungeons' while exploring caves and tunnels, or the city sewers and storm drains. Slowly but surely his people became stronger. Their crafting skills improved to the point where, after Allistor showed them the better quality samples, the folks in the other Denver Strongholds began to compete for the right to purchase them. Allistor was happy to oblige, hoping regular trade might be the road to successful recruitment or establishing alliances.

313

Through this whole period, Allistor awoke every morning and checked the countdown on his interface. Each day he did his best to help his people get stronger, feeling the pressure of the pending alien invasion. Each week he pushed himself harder, getting less sleep, trying harder to convince the other Stronghold leaders to join him.

His relationship with Amanda strengthened during those months as well. With him so often in or near one of their Strongholds, he was a short teleport away from spending evenings with her. It was almost as if he'd taken a nine to five office job that allowed him to be home for dinner most nights. For longer trips, she sometimes accompanied him, Helen, and Fuzzy.

By the time winter began to fade into spring, every single one of Allistor's people (except the children) were at least level ten and had chosen a class. Each of them had leveled up some sort of useful skill that contributed to the community, some of them more than one. Lilly, for example, had discovered during some long conversations with Michael that she could enchant the thread and other components of her leather goods to make them stronger, or add buffs. So, she spent a week or so sitting next to him every day, learning to do just that. Which was how she'd been able to create Allistor's awesome armor, and many other items just like it. He'd arranged to pay her a salary plus bonuses to experiment and create armor for as many of his people as she could, beginning with the fighters, hunters, and cowboys.

Allistor now had nearly four thousand people living in his various safeholds. Even his Outposts like the Gun Shop, Ranger Station, and the one north of Denver had regular patrols manning them as his people spread farther and farther out for hunting and foraging.

Some of his citizens had come from the other Strongholds in Denver, others had been found individually or in small groups out in the wild. Allistor had recruited a hundred people at once when they'd come across a Stronghold, run by a man named Hays, not far from one of Bjurstrom's dungeons. The group was doing well enough, but the snows had just started falling, and they were concerned about their food supply lasting the winter. It turned out Hays and many of his people had been part of a musical troupe, and they happily put on shows for people at the theater that had been attached to the mall in Cheyenne.

Nancy and Chloe had been busy as well. They claimed large spaces in every Stronghold, the Citadel, and the Bastion, and demanded that Allistor erect expansive greenhouses. Each one covered an acre at least, and featured stepped scaffolding that allowed two or three levels of planters to be growing vegetables and medicinal herbs at the same time. There was a mob of volunteers who wanted to learn to grow the crops in return for a salary from Allistor. Nancy interviewed and selected five or six for each greenhouse and trained them. Foraging trips were made to big supply stores to bring back seeds as well as mountains of bagged soil and fertilizer. In this way, each of the facilities became self-sustaining by the time the snows outside began to get deep. Most produced enough surplus to feed the nearby Outposts as well, and to gift or trade to other survivor groups.

*****

There were, of course, some setbacks. Not long after returning to Luther's Landing, George and his people tracked down what remained of Evan's settlement. After the losses the group had suffered, including George's son Luther, they'd sworn vengeance. And they went to get it. Allistor had been out with a hunting party at the time, and didn't hear about it until after it was done. Which he supposed was George's intent. He and his fighters had surrounded the encampment during the night. After their losses at Luther's Landing and the Warren, Evan's group had been reduced to a dozen or so armed men and women, and about twice that many civilians, mostly elderly and children. They didn't look well fed, and barely kept a watch during the night.

Their condition didn't matter to George. He waited till morning, when most of the survivors in the camp gathered for breakfast. As each one of the fighters emerged from a house, one of George's people was assigned to them. The group had pretty much settled down for their meal when George fired the first shot into the head of a man wearing a rifle. In seconds, ten of the fighters were dead or dying, and the rest were screaming and crying, flat on the ground or running for cover.

The remaining few fighters threw down their weapons and raised their hands, shouting, "Don't shoot!" or, "We surrender!" The others began to pick up the cry, and soon the whole group was begging to surrender.

George was the first to rise from cover and step into sight. The others followed suit, thirty of them with grim faces and raised weapons. On his orders, his people separated out the children and the infirm, any that obviously could not have participated in the attacks on

316

George's people, and herded them into a nearby building. That left him eight fighting-age and physically capable adults to deal with.

He pointed to the three he'd seen holding weapons. "Those three, move them into that house." He pointed behind him, and the three men were dragged away, begging for their lives. George looked at the remaining survivors sitting in front of him.

"Who among you participated in the raids on our community?" he growled at them. The four women and one man looked at each other, then up at him. All of them shook their heads.

"Any of you kin to Evan or his dumbass cousin? What was his name?"

"Justin." one of the women answered. "My husband. I'm guessin' it was you and your lot what killed him?"

George nodded. "After he and his people attacked us. Killed my son."

He watched as a sneer appeared on her face. "Good! Least he got a little payback for Evan." The others in line next to her nodded their agreement.

One of the men behind George, one who'd lost family in the raids on Luther's Landing, roared in frustrated rage. "Are you kidding me? You assholes came and stole from us, murdered our families, starved us very nearly to death!" He stepped toward the woman, but George held him back.

She spat on the ground at his feet. "You were cattle. The weak serve the strong, or die. If y'all were too weak to give us our due and still feed yerselves, then you deserved-"

Her thought went unfinished as a slug from George's shotgun entered her head between the eyes and sent her brain matter spraying out the back. There were screams from the children inside the building, who couldn't see what happened but had heard the shot.

Before the woman's dead body hit the ground, more shots rang out from George's people. The other four sitting next to her, and the three in the house behind them all perished in seconds. George blinked several times in surprise. He hadn't given the order to shoot, and hadn't expected it. He'd let his anger get the better of him. Now it was too late to do anything about it.

"Bring the others out here."

When the others had been brought to stand next to the bodies, the children whimpering and the adults not faring much better, George addressed them.

"These people attacked and killed our friends and family. For no other reason than they were too lazy to hunt, fish, or forage for themselves."

"You killed my mom and pop!" a boy of about twelve screamed at him. His eyes moved to two of the corpses and remained glued there.

The accusation stung George's heart, but he kept his face hard. "I'm sorry you had to see this. But they supported Evan and Justin in their efforts to kill our people.

318

Had I let them live, they likely would have picked up weapons and tried again."

"Damn right they would!" one of the old men shouted. He pointed a bony finger at George. "You'll get yours, you'll see!"

Just as all eyes went to the old man, the boy raised a hand holding a compact 9mm and fired three rounds point-blank into George's gut. Two more shots echoed between the buildings, and both the old man and the boy dropped dead as George's legs buckled and he fell to his knees.

"Stop!" he managed to call out, placing a hand on the ground to keep from falling on his face. "Stop firing, dammit!"

He felt a couple of heals wash over him, but the lead in his gut was still burning. He watched as his healing organs and skin pushed the flattened rounds out of his gut to fall with a clink to the pavement.

"What do you want to do with the rest of them?" the same man who had spoken before asked. From the tone of his voice, he was in favor of finishing them.

George grunted, then panted more than a little as he sat up and accepted help getting to his feet. He looked at the remaining adults. There were ten of them, most in their sixties or older. Three were young women, one pregnant. The rest of the survivors were kids ranging from about three to twelve years old.

"Any of the rest of you feel the same?" his voice came out hoarse, and he kept one hand on his gut, where there was still some significant pain.

All the heads in front of him, young and old, shook in unison. George looked around, a realization dawning on him. "This isn't a Stronghold. You folks been out here all this time?"

The eldest of the men, who looked to be George's age if not older, nodded his head. "Evan said if we wasn't strong enough to survive out here, then we didn't deserve to."

George shook his head. "And after he was gone?" The old man just shrugged.

George looked around. There was a police station half a block down the street. He walked down there, pulling the old man along with a wave of his hand. Stepping inside, he said, "Allistor left me in control of Luther's Landing. So I can use some of our resources to create a safe space for you. I'll do that, if you swear that none of you will raise a hand against my people, or any others, except in self-defense."

The old man raised his right hand. "I swear we'll leave ya be. I'm old, and tired, and I just want a decent night's sleep."

George pulled up his interface, and claimed the building. He quickly designated it as an Outpost. He turned the offices and holding cells into sleeping quarters. There was already a kitchen, and bathrooms with showers. After creating the wall, gate, power and water, he added the sensors.

"Nothing will spawn inside the wall. You can sleep safe in here. We'll leave you all your food and water." He paused, feeling a surge of regret. "With fewer of you now, it should last you longer. If you come by our Stronghold once a week, we'll give you some fruit and vegetables, but you'll need to hunt for meat. We'll leave your guns just outside the gate. Don't retrieve them until we're out of sight."

The old man offered his hand. "I'm sorry. For what Evan and them did to you and yours. He was a disturbed man, but he took care of us in his own way. Brainwashed some of these folks into doin' stuff they'd never have done, you know, before."

George nodded his head and walked out, not looking back. He called out for his people to gather up all the guns, and they left them outside the gate as promised, closing the doors behind the children as they were herded inside. George kept walking away, never once looking back.

When they reached Luther's Landing, he found Allistor there, waiting for him. As Earl, he'd received a notification about the creation of a new Outpost, one that George hadn't discussed with him ahead of time.

"Hey old man, did you just make yourself a fishing cabin or something?" Allistor greeted George as he sat down in the dining area across the table from him. Seeing the look on the old man's face, Allistor's smile instantly disappeared. "What happened? Did you get attacked?"

George sat there, his face expressionless as he told Allistor what they'd done. He expected his friend to explode, to preach about the value of every human life. He expected to be reprimanded, maybe even banished.

What he didn't expect was for Allistor to produce a .45 revolver and set it on the table between them. Initially alarmed, he reflexively moved a hand toward his own sidearm. But then he paused. His guilt had mounted as they'd traveled the few miles back. If Allistor felt he needed to die as punishment for his actions, he'd accept that.

Allistor spun the gun around atop the table. "I know how you're feeling right now. Taking the lives of other people, even murdering assholes, isn't easy. You're second-guessing yourself. Feeling guilty. Wondering if the ones you killed might have been redeemed somehow. Am I getting close?"

George just nodded, a lump in his throat preventing him from speaking.

"Let me be clear, George. I'm not happy you felt the need to do this without telling me. You are my representative here, my advisor. My friend. Did you keep it from me because you thought I'd prevent you from going after them?"

Again, George just nodded. His eyes fell from the gun on the table to his hands in his lap. His fingers absently picked at the bloody holes in his shirt.

"Do you remember when I first came here?" Allistor asked.

"I do." George's voice was still rough.

"I put a round through Evan's head the moment he refused my order to walk away."

"You did." George nodded, lifting his hands to set them flat on the table.

"I've killed a lot of humans since this all started, my friend. Some I knew for sure were murderers and rapists. But I couldn't always stop and check the level of guilt or innocence of everyone once the fighting started."

George looked up from his hands to find Allistor gazing at him. "Your people have been holding a lot of pain and loss inside them. What happened is not your fault. It sounds to me like the ones who died probably deserved it. But neither of us will ever know for sure. I can accept that. Can you?"

George didn't answer for a while, staring off into the distance as he replayed the morning in his head. He blinked and refocused when Allistor said, "Hey, listen." He shoved the revolver from the center of the table over to within an inch or two of George's hands. "I need to know that you can get past this. That you can handle things here. I need to know you're the tough old bastard who raised Luther to be a leader, and took his place when we lost him." Allistor paused, looking George in the eye. "Because if you're not, then maybe you're better off eating a bullet here and now. Save yourself and your people all the anguish of a slow decline."

"What? What did you just say to me, boy?" George was on his feet, his hands gripping the table so hard they turned white.

"There he is!" Allistor put out a hand to calm him, offering a regretful smile. "I'm sorry, my friend. I needed to snap you out of it. I've been where you were heading more than once, and I wanted to derail you here and now."

323

He scowled at George. "And don't look at me like that. Like you need my forgiveness for something. You did what needed to be done. You showed the survivors some charity, maybe more than I might have myself. Remember when we first found the Howitzers? I was ready to drop shells on those people that day. If we had, Luther might still be alive today, and there wouldn't have been a need for your actions this morning. You see, you're not the only one carrying around guilt. The secret is to accept the burden and then set it aside so you can deal with the day to day bullshit this place throws at you."

George sat back down and was silent for a while. Allistor retook his own seat and sat there, petting Fuzzy while he waited for the old man to work things out. Finally, the bear cub, who understood something was wrong if not the details, padded around the table and gently placed his Fibble doll in George's lap.

The old man broke down and cried, burying his face in Fuzzy's furry head as he hugged the cub. Allistor sat patiently, allowing George to get it all out. He really did know exactly how his friend felt. He'd agonized over too many human deaths. Amanda and Helen had both been there for him, helping him to work through it. And, of course, Fuzzy too."

Chapter 14

Where the Deer and the Lakota Roam

As spring continued to melt the snows, Allistor's people resumed regular foraging trips. Now with their higher levels, better weapons, and everyone having spells for both damage and healing, they felt much safer. More groups went out, and went farther out, often spending several days outside the safety of the walls before returning.

Though they had billions in gold to convert to klax or system points, Allistor never let them relax when it came to finding ways to earn money. They still gathered rare cars, weapons, vintage wines, anything that might earn big bids on the open market. The difference was that now Allistor granted them half of what their items sold for, split evenly among the party members who brought it in. This incentive proved quite effective, as it was simple human nature to accumulate as much wealth as possible, and his people were as human as any others. The cowboys were sent out to round up more cattle, and a team was assigned to the herd of buffalo as well. Helen said she knew of a great valley within Allistor's parkland where the massive creatures would thrive during the spring and summer, and be reasonably protected in the winter. It was on their agenda to go check it out and clear it of any dangerous predators.

One side effect of his people ranging farther and farther out was that they ran into more pockets of survivors. Some of whom had suffered through difficult winters. Well fed, healthy looking high-level survivors showing up at their doors with advanced weapons and food to share did a lot to recruit more people.

It had been August when the apocalypse struck Allistor's small town and he'd gathered his first dozen or so survivors together. By the first week of April, his total population was over four thousand, and growing quickly. Word was spreading, and it seemed new people were showing up at one Stronghold or another almost daily. Just a few at a time, a family here, a group of fifteen there. But the numbers were adding up. Each of them swore the oath before being allowed through the gates, and the system bound them to Allistor.

Nancy asked Allistor to visit the Warren so that she could show him something. Helen, Fuzzy, and Amanda joined him before they all left to head to his Thunder Basin parklands to check out the new buffalo grazing grounds.

When they arrived on the teleport pad, Chloe was waiting for them.

"Allistor!" She jumped into his arms, hugging him tightly. He immediately noticed she was taller and stronger than he remembered. It had only been a month or so since he'd been to the Warren, but he couldn't remember when he'd seen Chloe last.

"Wow! Look at you. You got big!" He grinned at her, booping her on the nose with his own. "What has Nancy been feeding you?"

She frowned at him as she answered. "Mostly vegetables. Ugh."

Allistor laughed and set her down, but her feet barely touched the ground before she leapt up into

Amanda's arms. "Amanda! You look so pretty!" Chloe kissed her cheek and wrapped her arms around the woman's neck. After a moment, she let go and reached for Helen, getting passed from one woman to the other.

"Oof!" Helen said as she took hold of the girl. "You're getting too big to hold. Picking you up is like trying to pick up Fuzzy!" she teased.

Chloe rolled her eyes. "I'm not *that* big!" She disengaged and dropped to the ground to wrap her arms around Fuzzy, who licked her face. She backed off and made a disgusted face for a moment – Fuzzy's breath wasn't exactly minty fresh – but decided to ignore the odor and resumed her hug.

"I've been leveling up!" she boasted, getting to her feet and taking Allistor's hand. She began to pull him toward the greenhouse as she talked. "You know we've been breeding the bunnies and the chickens. Ramon taught me how to slaughter them so they don't feel hardly any pain at all. At first, I didn't want to, cuz they're so cute and I helped raise them all. But if they need food, then so do we. And if we don't eat some of them, pretty soon we wouldn't be able to feed ourselves and all of them too. And we'd all starve. So, I learned how to do it right." the girl had gotten all of that out in one breath, and paused to inhale deeply before continuing.

"So anyway, now it's part of my job to kill the ones we're gonna eat. And I've killed so many of them that I'm already level three!"

Allistor froze where he was, causing Chloe to jerk at his arm when she continued on, then turn back to look at him. "What's wrong?"

He got down on one knee and pulled her to him, gathering her into his arms. Tears rolled down his face as he said, "Nothing's wrong, sweetie. I'm so very proud of you. I wish we didn't live in a world where you had to learn what you have. I'm doing my best to make sure you're safe, and you can have the kind of life a little girl should have. I wish…" He didn't finish the sentence, not having words that this special little girl would understand.

Amanda saved him.

"Hey Chloe… since the last time I saw you, Allistor has let like… fifty different monsters bite him, stab him, knock him down, throw him through the air, and stomp on him!"

Chloe's eyes widened for a minute as she pushed away and looked at Allistor's face. She was prepared to scold him about letting stuff bite him again, but when she saw the tears and mistook their cause, her face softened. She patted his cheek. "It's okay Allistor. Not everybody is good at fighting. Someday you'll learn how to do it the right way, and it won't hurt so much." She appeared to think for a moment, then grinned and added, "At least you have the prettiest doctor in the whole world to take care of you!"

Everyone laughed, and converged into a group hug that lasted until Chloe complained about being, 'smothered and smushed'. Allistor composed himself, and they continued on toward the greenhouse. To everyone's surprise, Chloe kept on going, right past the greenhouse and around the side of the main keep building. Last time Allistor had been there, it had still been paved parking area.

Now the ground was broken up, cleared, and sported row after row of tiny trees.

Nancy was standing in the middle of the field, maybe four acres total. Her eyes were closed, and her hands out to either side. As they approached, she hummed a little tune and slowly raised her hands, palms upward as if she were conducting an orchestra. The trees in a wide circle around her grew visibly taller and thicker before she stopped singing and dropped her hands.

"Wow!" Helen said as Nancy turned toward them. "I saw those saplings grow! Nancy that was *awesome!*"

Nancy smiled, looking tired as Chloe came and put an arm around her leg. She ran her fingers through the girl's hair. "Thanks. I've had a lot of practice over the winter. I've leveled the *Grow* spell so high that it branched off into two other spells. It's really very exciting!"

Allistor took his focus off the trees for a moment. "Nancy, I know you enjoy your work. But you need to get some rest, too. You look like you're about to pass out."

She waved off his comment. "I'm fine. Sleeping quite well, actually. It's just that growing so many trees at once takes a lot out of me. I'll be back to normal in fifteen minutes or so."

Allistor didn't look convinced, but he changed the subject. "Are these the reason you summoned me here, m'lady?"

"Ooh la la. Summoned. How fancy." Chloe teased. Allistor stuck his tongue out at her and crossed his eyes, earning him a giggle.

"I'm an Earl now, didn't you hear? I *AM* fancy!" He struck a ridiculous pose with one hand on his hip and the other pretending to hold a fancy cigarette.

Amanda mumbled, "Damn. Wish we still had working phones with cameras. Maybe I can get someone to paint you in that pose. Hang a life-sized copy of it in every Stronghold."

Chloe giggled again, and the ladies laughed while Allistor pretended to be horrified. He was enjoying this time with little Chloe, being able to relax and unwind a bit, and just be silly.

Nancy began to walk toward another section of the field, and they all followed along as she pointed to different sections. "Over there are apple trees. They take up the majority of the space, because they're hardy and the fruit can be preserved. Plus, Michael and Ramon put their heads together and figured out how to make apple brandy." She smiled just a touch when she spoke Ramon's name. Allistor was betting Chloe would have a little brother or sister soon.

"Over here we're trying oranges. This isn't really the climate for them, but if we can make it work by tenting them in plastic during the cold months, the vitamin C will do us all a world of good. Over here we've got some pecan and walnut trees. And there's a small peach grove back in the corner over there. We also planted a row of banana trees inside the greenhouse. Along with some raspberry and blueberry bushes that we'll plant along the outer edges of this field."

"This is great, Nancy." Allistor offered her a hand to shake. "I'm grateful to you for all your efforts. Without you and George, and your people, it would have been a hard winter indeed."

They chatted for a bit longer, Allistor catching them up on the happenings at their other properties. When Helen told her they were heading out to Thunder Basin, she asked the ranger to bring back any interesting herbs or mushrooms they might run across. "My *Herbology* and *Alchemy* skills have gone way up as well." She paused for a moment, giving Amanda a wink. "Having Ramon around so much has its benefits."

Allistor snorted at that. Ramon must be feeding her all the scrolls and training manuals that he found matching her skillsets in the library. He didn't mind one bit. In fact, that was exactly what he wanted. Nancy's efforts were helping to feed his entire little nation.

"We'll bring back as much as we can." he promised. Helen added that she'd make sure of it.

Leaving the mother and daughter after another round of hugs, and a promise to Chloe that he'd try and let stuff bite him less, then headed directly toward the motor pool. Allistor's pulse quickened slightly. One of his favorite bits of tech that he'd purchased from the open market was a small fleet of vehicles. They had lots of scavenged trucks, buses, RVs and such at each Stronghold, but these were special.

These ran on hydrogen.

The vehicle they were taking on their trip today was long and sleek, with a rounded front end and a tall body. It was longer than their usual ranger truck, and had three axles. The thing most resembled a bullet train car. It was made of a lightweight metal alloy that was stronger than steel and doubled as an insulator of both heat and sound. Its windows were very nearly indestructible. They'd learned that on a previous trip when some hostile humans fired at them without warning.

But the best thing about this type of vehicle, which he'd nicknamed the *Juggernaut,* was its engine. Nearly silent, it produced more power than a semi-truck diesel engine. And it ran on hydrogen. He'd purchased a small motorcycle with a similar engine for his people to take apart and try to reverse engineer. Allistor didn't quite understand the mechanics himself, but he knew the thing literally converted hydrogen molecules into energy. The engine was efficient, powerful, and all you had to do to gas up was pour water into the fuel tank. There were fancy removable battery packs that could run the thing for up to two days, but so far Allistor hadn't had to use them.

Water was literally everywhere around them in the form of snow, rain, condensation in the morning, and the thousands of rivers, creeks, and streams they passed. On the roof was a fold-out tin-foily thing that you could use to collect rainwater directly into the tank. Or it could be raised vertically and would harvest moisture from the air as they drove slowly. Allistor had tried setting it up once, and it made the *Juggernaut* look like a sailboat with wheels.

The vehicle had taught him some things about their new reality. For one, the interior systems were light years beyond Earth tech. There were sophisticated sensors that could detect life forms from a mile away. Some kind of superior radar that could provide 3D images of targets in the air. A wide array of communications options, from basic voice to real time 3D hologram images. In the event of a crash or an attack, there was some kind of foam that would fill the vehicle to prevent impact trauma, but still allow the occupants to breathe. He'd added an optional plasma gun mounted on a swivel on the roof that could be fired manually or operated from the cockpit. And the thing could hover for a short time, but that burned through the fuel tank in about ten minutes. The fact that it could run under normal conditions for most of a day on a single gallon of water suggested that at least some of the worlds out there suffered a shortage of water, thus the efficiency.

And the vehicles weren't that expensive, compared to some of the other available tech. He imagined that they were as common as pickup trucks in the system. The small fleet of *Juggernauts* had cost him two million klax. He'd gotten a discount by buying in bulk direct from a dealer named Harmon, of Harmon's Mahoosive Munitions & Emporium, who had contacted him via the market's messaging system soon after he'd begun spending large amounts on other items. That right there taught him that someone was tracking big spenders. He'd purchased ten of those vehicles, along with the motorcycle, a larger transport similar to an RV that could comfortably seat thirty people for long trips, several of the smaller hover pads, and the two industrial sized ones. Along with plasma rifles and pistols, and other items. The dealer had given him a twenty percent discount for such a large order, and a flowery-worded blessing nearly a page long that covered him, his people, his family, and future generations on into eternity. Allistor actually wished he had a way to print the thing and put it on a display somewhere. It was pure poetry.

When they reached the vehicle, Allistor laid a hand on the 'hood' and stroked it lovingly. Amanda rolled her eyes and looked at Helen. "Boys and their cars." He just grinned and moved to the back. Opening the back hatch with a touch of his hand, he retrieved one of the small hover pads that the hunters normally used to transport kills back to their vehicles. He slid it into the back and connected it to a handy port for charging. Fuzzy hopped into the seat behind the driver's seat, sitting upright like a human. The more the bear leveled up, the smarter and more anthropomorphic he became. Allistor had a bet with Amanda on whether he'd eventually learn to speak. He'd modified the seat from human dimensions to more of a bench configuration to accommodate the growing bear.

After a quick check of the vehicle's system via Nigel, who had taken over as the *Juggernaut*'s AI, they were on their way. The gates closing behind them, they headed north along the mostly deserted Highway 59, which would take them directly into Thunder Basin, one of the former National Parks that Helen had semi-accidentally awarded him when they'd first met.

It was maybe forty miles from the Warren to the southern edge of the parklands. Helen drove, as she knew the way. They took it slow, averaging about twenty-five miles per hour up the back road. There were occasional fallen trees, abandoned cars, and a jackknifed semi trailer that blocked most of the road about thirty miles up, which they stopped to investigate. After breaking the lock on the back doors, they found it was stocked with what seemed like an entire general store's worth of merchandise. There were hardware items – tools, rope, boxes of screws and nails – as well as pallets of canned goods, boxes of blankets and clothes, boots, fishing poles and tackle, stationary, cleaning products, and a hundred other things. Allistor made a note on his map and used Nigel's communication link to call back down to the Warren and have a foraging party sent up. With luck, they could get the truck running and just bring the whole load back to the Stronghold.

Just in case they were out longer than expected, the survivor in him caused him to grab some cans of beans and several boxes of pop tarts before they closed the truck up again.

Less than a half hour later, Helen pointed out a sign that said they were entering the Thunder Bluff grasslands. And it wasn't kidding. As far as Allistor could see there were rolling hills covered in the green of spring grass. Thousands and thousands of acres of it. In the distance to the west there were higher hills that could even be considered small mountains.

When he asked, Helen responded, "Those are the Bighorn Mountains to the west. They extend up from the Rockies to the southwest. There's a great big national forest there, too. If you want, I could sell it to ya real cheap." She winked at him. Then she pointed east at another set of rolling hills in the far distance. "Over there are the Black Hills. You know, Indian country?"

Amanda and Allistor both nodded their heads. Native Americans had been a big part of both of their lives growing up. The whole area had originally been Indian country, and there were still a lot of reservations nearby. Allistor himself had a little Lakota blood in him from a distant ancestor.

Helen continued. "Pretty much everything you see to the north and northeast of us is your land, *Earl Allistor*." as she spoke, she hit the gas and continued forward up the

335

highway for a ways. When they reached an intersection labeled with a sign that just read '450' she turned east. "Up ahead is a spot I was thinking about. For the buffalo, I mean. There's a coal mine there. Plenty of cover when the wind is whipping across the plains in the winter."

Amanda looked confused. "Uhm… You think our cowboys could herd a few thousand buffalo into a tiny mine entrance and keep them in there?"

Helen laughed. "Sorry, I should have specified. It's an open air mine. The Black Thunder mine is basically a huge series of great big holes in the ground. Like a quarry, with ramps leading down around the edges. Each one of them could hold a football stadium. You'll see in a minute."

True to her word, they soon came upon the mine. It was much, much larger than anything Allistor had expected. From the road it looked like a series of meteors had struck the grassland, burning away all the vegetation and leaving deep gouges in the earth. But as Helen drove them into the nearest hole, he saw the slopes cut into the rock that circled down into the pit several stories below.

Nodding his head, he said, "Okay, I get it. They can huddle down there out of the wind, and walk back up when they need to feed. And I'm guessing there's water nearby?"

Helen nodded and pointed toward the southeast. "There's a lake a mile or two that way. During the summer the herd can wander and get fat. They can be left to winter here, or herded to one of the towns to take shelter like they did this last winter." Allistor saw something dawn on her, and she began to talk a little faster.

"In fact, there is a little town northeast of here called Upton that is completely surrounded by the park. And if there aren't any survivors there, that probably means you own the town as well. Let's go check it out!"

She turned the *Juggernaut* around and got back on the highway. With a mischievous look, she said, "You want to test out this thing's off-road capabilities? We can get there on these roads, but I'm used to patrolling this area on horseback. Much shorter if we go straight across."

Allistor gave her a fist bump as his answer, and she immediately veered off the road onto the grass. The six wheels on 3 independent axles handled the rough terrain with ease. Helen proved she really did know the territory as she meandered between the hills and down gradual slopes into gullies that she'd follow for a mile or two before finding a drivable slope up the other side.

Allistor and Amanda enjoyed the views as they went. There were huge herds of elk roaming the prairie, and occasional stands of trees here and there. When Fuzzy indicated that he needed to get out and take care of some bear business, they discovered a colony of prairie dogs that didn't appreciate the grizzly invading their territory.

The trip took a few hours, as they were moving more slowly across the open fields and taking a zig-zag route. Eventually, buildings appeared on the horizon. A half hour later Helen rejoined a dirt road that led them into the town of Upton. As they drove in, Helen said, "Looks like somebody's still here." She pointed off to the north, where a plume of smoke rose into the air. "That's, uhh... I think that's the elementary school?" she guessed. "Been a while. There are two big buildings in town. The

337

elementary school and the high school. If I was gonna make a Stronghold, I'd pick one of those."

They passed a hardware store as they moved into town from the east. Then Joe's Food, which looked like a grocery store. Allistor liked the name. Simple and descriptive. A few blocks farther on, Helen turned left and headed roughly north through town. In just a minute they came upon a Stronghold.

"Yep, that'd be where the elementary school was." Helen pulled to a stop. The humans all got out, leaving their doors open. Fuzzy knew the drill by that time, and remained in his chair, seemingly bored. His Fibble doll lay balanced on his belly as he reclined.

Allistor called out toward the gate, not seeing anyone on the walls. It took a full minute and two more calls before someone appeared.

"Who are you? And what do you want?" a woman shouted down. She had the high cheekbones and jet-black hair of a native American. She didn't point a weapon at them, which Allistor took as a good sign.

"I'm Allistor! This is Helen, and Amanda. As for what we want... well, I guess we'd like to talk?"

The woman stared at him for a while, and a couple of other heads appeared on either side of her. "Talk about what?"

"Talk about maybe being friends? Trade? The weather? The usual stuff people talk about!" Allistor smiled up at the woman, whose poker face could have made a professional gambler nervous.

"I suppose you want to come inside." she stated, not really asking.

"Well, that would be easier than shouting back and forth, certainly. But I understand if you don't want to let strangers in. We could talk out here…"

A man to the right of the woman shouted, "What the hell kind of rifle is that?" He pointed toward Allistor, who turned around to look behind him before he realized he'd strung his plasma rifle over his shoulder.

Feeling foolish, he answered. "Plasma rifle. Alien tech. We bought it on the open market."

"Thought so. I seen one of them when I was shopping. Those things cost like a hundred thousand klax. You must be rich!"

"Allistor!" The other man slapped himself on the forehead. "That's where I know that name! Every time we leave town and head out to hunt, it says we're on your territory. And when we shoot an elk, it says we're poaching. What the hell man? With that rifle and that … car, or whatever it is behind you, you must be rich. There's like a million elk out there! You can't spare a few for hungry Indians?"

The other two on the wall suddenly looked decided unfriendly.

"No, no, it's not like that! I was awarded the park lands, and the system apparently is giving you some kind of automatic warning. I didn't tell it to do that! And no, I don't care if you shoot some elk to live on, I mean… look. Can we please sit down and talk about this? My neck's getting a little sore shouting up at you."

339

"My father is our tribal chief. He's out hunting right now. We really shouldn't let you in here until he says so." the woman called down, her face still scowling. "You can always go tell him he's not allowed to hunt. But I wouldn't recommend it!"

Allistor sighed. Helen and Amanda both shrugged. He had an idea. "Um… you mentioned your tribe. What tribe are you?"

The second man, the one who'd recognized Allistor's name, shouted, "What, we all look the same to you, white man?"

"To be honest, yes." Allistor called back. "I've got a little Lakota blood in me. I've been around natives all my life, and I can't tell the difference between a Lakota, a Cheyenne, or an Osage. Please, I'm trying to be friendly here. Would you tell me what tribe you're from?"

The first man stood straighter. "We are Lakota! Of the great Sioux nation!"

"Great! I'm pleased to meet my distant cousins. Now, let's resolve this whole hunting issue, okay?" Allistor puffed out his own chest, and called out, "I, Earl Allistor, hereby grant my cousins of the Lakota tribe the right to hunt on my lands within the Thunder Basin so that they may feed their families. I grant this right for as long as I shall live!"

A green glow surrounded him and the three people atop the wall. Their gazes unfocused as they read some kind of notification. When they returned their gazes to Allistor, they seemed a little less hostile.

"You still need to wait for my father to return!" the woman called out.

Allistor was getting tired of shouting at these people. "When do you expect him back?"

"Tonight, probably." she called out. "Come back in the morning."

Allistor wasn't looking forward to sleeping in the car overnight. That was the only place outside a Stronghold or Outpost where they could be sure a creature wouldn't spawn. Getting slightly annoyed, he called up to them again.

"Look. Uhh… I'm sorry, what is your name?"

"Call me Redfeather." the woman answered.

"Okay look, Redfeather. I'm up here with my companions scouting the land because we plan to move a herd of buffalo up here. And before you ask, yes. You can hunt the buffalo too, as long as you abide by Helen's rules for preserving the breeding stock. We want the herd to grow, not go extinct. Especially since there are so many elk to hunt instead." He paused to take a deep breath, and thought he saw looks of something approaching approval on the faces atop the wall.

"We're here in town because our cowboys are going to need a safe place to stay while they manage the herd, just like my friends and I are going to need a safe place to sleep tonight." He held up a hand to interrupt one of the men who had just opened his mouth. "I get it. You don't want to let strangers in. I totally understand. Helen here tells me this used to be the elementary school. And that there is a high school not far away. So here is what we're going to do.

We're going to drive over to the high school and turn it into an Outpost. We'll spend the night there, and come back to talk to you in the morning. How's that sound?"

The second man, the younger of the two, grew angry again. "That's our school! This whole town is ours!" He raised a rifle and set it atop the wall, not pointed directly at them, but in their general direction.

"I'm not trying to take your town from you. I don't need any of the resources here, except a building large enough to house my people and their animals, where they can sleep safely. I've already granted you hunting rights on my lands, when I could have been a dick about it instead. I'm trying here, guys. I really do want to be friends. But I'm taking that school. You can try to stop me, but I wouldn't recommend it."

The three Lakota put their heads together and whispered for a good long while. Allistor was tempted to just get in the *Juggernaut* and leave. But he didn't want to piss them off or scare them any more than he already had.

Helen helped the situation. "Redfeather! Your father is your chief? Would he be Chief Standing Bear?"

The three stopped whispering and turned toward Helen. "That's right. Why?"

Now it was Helen's turn to sigh. "I know your father! When he returns, tell him ranger Helen says hello! And tell him I said Allistor is a good man. He has even bound himself to a grizzly bear companion!" She turned toward the vehicle. "Fuzzy, come here."

Fuzzy half stepped half rolled out of the truck and padded over to Allistor, sitting next to him and licking his hand. Allistor, catching on to Helen's intent, took a knee next to the bear and began to scratch his ears, his back. After a moment he tackled the distracted bear cub, starting a wrestling match right there in the street.

After a few moments, Fuzzy pinned him, giving his face a slobbery lick before letting him go. Allistor got back to his feet, grumbling at the cub. When he looked up, the faces looking back were definitely friendlier.

Redfeather called down. "Can I... Can I come out and meet him? What did you call him? Fuzzy?"

"Of course! He won't hurt you, unless you try and hurt Allistor." Helen answered.

All three disappeared, and a moment later the gate opened. Redfeather stepped out accompanied by the older of the two men. The second man stood in the opening, rifle at the ready.

She approached them cautiously, and Fuzzy took a few steps toward them, moving slowly with a little bounce in his step, like a friendly dog meeting a new person. Allistor swore if the cub had more than a stub of a tail, he'd be wagging it. "It's okay, he really won't hurt you. He's a big slobbery glutton of a puppy dog. With horrible breath, so don't let him lick your face."

Redfeather halted a step away from the bear, who ignored her hesitation and stepped forward to give her a good sniff. After a moment, he plopped down on his butt, raised himself up into an upright sitting position, and waved one lazy paw at the woman.

She smiled, and raised a hand to give him a high five. When he dropped his forepaws back to the ground,

343

she reached and tentatively scratched above one ear. Fuzzy leaned into her hand and began to purr, enchanting her completely.

"He's so cute!" she gushed as she dropped to her knees and hugged him. She promptly paid the price for getting so close when he licked her face. Leaning back, she said, "Ugh, what do you feed him?"

"Well, a little while ago, some stale pop tarts and a piece of dragon jerky. But just the other day he ate some guy's face off…" Allistor smiled as she jerked back from the bear, getting to her feet and looking at them both warily. "Relax, the guy was trying to kill us. He took a shot at our shiny new truck there, and Fuzzy chased him into the woods."

Not exactly reassured, she took a couple steps back from Fuzzy. The bear cub took a minute to sniff at the man next to her, who calmly held his ground even though Allistor could see him gripping the handle of a pistol at his waist.

"If you don't draw that weapon, I promise he won't harm you. Or lick you. We really need to find some kind of breath mints for him, Helen."

The man relaxed, taking his hand off the gun and reaching down to pat Fuzzy's head. Amanda chuckled. "Fuzzy the Ambassador."

The man looked to Allistor. "Standing Bear will want to meet you. Both of you." He scratched Fuzzy's ear a bit. "Go, claim the high school if you have to. Return in the morning." The two turned their backs and walked back inside, the gate closing behind them with a metallic clang.

344

"You heard the man, back in the truck. Let's go back to high school."

Five minutes later they were parked in front of the main entrance of the school. It was a nice-looking building with a football field right behind it, and a large parking lot. The front doors were chained shut, and all the windows appeared to be intact, if dusty.

Allistor found a stick to use to hold the chain out away from the door. A single blast from his plasma rifle melted through the chain, and he pulled it free. Opening the doors, he and the others stepped inside. The trip had taken a good part of the day, and the sun was lowering toward the western horizon. But there was more than enough light to see inside the building. Each classroom had six-foot tall windows along one whole wall, which let in lots of light.

As soon as they were inside, Allistor pulled up his interface and tried to claim the building. Luckily for them, someone had taken the time to secure the building, and nothing had spawned inside. He was quickly able to declare the building an Outpost. It only took him a few seconds to designate his usual features – power, water, wall, and sensors. The school already had a large kitchen and cafeteria, as well as several bathrooms and a gym with showers. That would do for the short term. He authorized Helen, Amanda, and his other advisors to make alterations to the structure as needed. A quick check outside showed that the wall encompassed the football field and its stands, which could be used to shelter horses and other livestock with some minor alterations.

They sat down at one of the cafeteria tables for supper, then split up to get some rest. Fuzzy simply plopped down underneath the table and closed his eyes, while Allistor and Amanda claimed the teacher's lounge because it had a sofa. Helen pulled a few exercise mats from the gym into the coach's office and slept there.

Chapter 15

Betrayal and Exile

The following morning Allistor and company did a little sprucing up. The school had a pool, so Allistor filled it and added some chemicals to clean the water. Fuzzy didn't wait, leaping into the water and splashing around the shallow end like a child.

Helen went out back and looked over the bleachers. Standing underneath them, she accessed the interface and added walls at either end, and along the back. In the center of the long wall she put large barn doors that slid to the side, and a few windows with heavy shutters. Then she filled in the gaps above with a sloped ceiling. When she was done, she had a half-barn with room for a couple dozen horses, feed, tack, and more. She decided to leave it to the cowboys to construct individual stalls.

Which was pretty much what Amanda was doing inside the school. She was turning each classroom into a living area with half being a bedroom, and the other half being a sitting area. When she realized she couldn't get access to a market kiosk because the place was only an Outpost, she stuck her head out the door and shouted for Allistor.

He came jogging up, barefoot and soaking wet in just his boxers. Fuzzy jogged along behind him, equally soaked and dripping water everywhere. Shaking her head at the smiles on both of their faces, she said, "Children! You're both overgrown children."

"Yup! But this wasn't my fault. I was just watching Fuzzy play, and he pretended he couldn't get out. When I reached in to help him, he grabbed my arm and pulled me in!"

Amanda looked at the bear cub, who clearly shook his head no and did his best to look innocent. Looking at Allistor, she said, "And your clothes?"

Realizing he was busted, Allistor grinned. "Okay. Fine. I might have done a cannonball. Or three. I had to teach Fuzzy!"

With an effort Amanda suppressed a smile of her own. "Listen, mister cannonball. I need beds and stuff for this place, and the interface says we can't have market access here-"

"Because it's only an Outpost." Allistor finished for her, nodding his head. "We can always send up a truck with furniture and stuff. Unless you reeeally want the stuff today, I'd rather not waste the system points upgrading this place."

"No, I guess you're right. The cowboys and support people can bring up a load of stuff when they push the buffalo up here. Or maybe we can buy some stuff from the chief and his people. Pay them to let us scavenge beds from the houses around here." She nodded once, confirming the decision in her mind.

"Speaking of the chief, we should probably go see if he's back." Helen said as she walked up behind Allistor. "Nice boxers, boss. But uhh… they're a little see-thru when wet. Maybe put some pants on before we go meet our new friends?"

Allistor covered his private bits with his hands and dashed back to the pool, sliding a bit on the slippery floors. Fuzzy just stood where he was, giving the two ladies his best bear grin before he shook himself like a dog, showering both of them.

"Fuzzy!" Helen laughed as she scolded him. "Cut that out! No treats for you today."

Fuzzy's look went from amused to pathetic in a heartbeat. He tilted his head to one side and did his best to look sorry. It very nearly worked, but Helen held firm.

Allistor returned, fully clothed but still damp. They walked back out to the *Juggernaut* and made the quick trip over to the Lakota Stronghold.

Redfeather was waiting for them at the front gate, which stood slightly open. "Leave your fancy minivan there and come inside." she called out.

"Minivan? Minivan! This is a state of the art…" Allistor paused, trying to think of a good descriptor.

"Minivan is good." Amanda grinned at him, closing her door and walking toward the gate with Fuzzy in tow. Allistor shut his mouth and followed, giving Redfeather a dirty look for insulting his baby. She just snorted at him and closed the gate behind them before leading them into a building off to the left.

She led them to a room with a long table and had them take a seat. She waited with them for a minute or two before the two men from the day before entered, followed by her father, the chief. He was a tall man with wide shoulders and a trim waistline. His frame showed the kind of muscle earned from hard work on a ranch or farm.

Bright green eyes were framed by long white hair pulled back into a single braid that reached nearly to his waist.

"Welcome, Earl Allistor." he said as he entered. "Helen, long time. You look well." He nodded at the ranger. Then looked to Amanda. "And this pretty lady must be Amanda. And... Fuzzy? I am Standing Bear." He held out a hand to each of them as he greeted them, then let Fuzzy sniff him before he took a seat at the head of the table.

"I understand you've claimed the high school. Was all the land for thirty miles in any direction not enough for you?" his words were hostile, but his tone was neutral. Allistor looked at Helen, who nodded slightly.

"Though the grasslands are mine, that doesn't make them a safe place to sleep. We needed a safe place last night, as your daughter was understandably reluctant to invite us in here. And we'll need a place for our cowboys to sleep when they're here."

"Ah, yes. The alleged buffalo. Redfeather says you plan to bring a herd here."

"Well, not here specifically. Into the grasslands. Helen was thinking they might winter in the abandoned coal mine."

"Where do you think you're going to find a herd of buffalo?" Standing Bear asked.

"Oh, that." Allistor smiled. "They found us. Wandered into one of our cities over the winter and plopped down against the buildings to take shelter from the snow. Spent the whole winter mowing lawns and the grass in the parks."

Standing Bear nodded slowly as he thought over Allistor's words. "And this message I received about having permission to hunt the elk on your lands?"

Allistor was trying to be patient, to remain friendly. But Standing Bear had clearly heard all of this from his people, and there was no need for him to hear it again. Still, he started at the beginning.

"Look. I never asked the system to post any 'trespassing' or 'no hunting' warnings. I didn't even know about them. I never intended to keep you from hunting my lands. In fact, I had no idea you were here until yesterday. When I found out about this issue, I corrected it right away. But I'm sure your daughter already told you that. At least, I hope she did." He looked at Redfeather, who nodded once in affirmation.

"I came here in hopes of making friends and allies. We don't have a lot of time left before the aliens arrive, and we potentially have to fight for the survival of the human race. I have established several safeholds now, and have thousands of people who've sworn loyalty to me, to help protect each other and the human race. Together we are thriving. We have fresh meat, fruit, and vegetables enough to feed everyone. Our crafters are making great strides, producing items like this armor I'm wearing. We have enough resources to purchase alien tech like these plasma weapons, and the vehicle outside. And when the year is over, I will be taking delivery of an actual spaceship."

He stopped talking to take a breath and assess whether his words were having any impact. He decided to finish with one more point. "We're not here to steal from you. We don't need what you have. In fact, we can probably help you with some supplies if you need them. I'm here for your friendship, plain and simple. When the time comes, you're welcome to take a few buffalo, per Helen's guidelines." He looked up at Helen.

"Standing Bear knows them already. He actually knows quite a bit about maintaining the wildlife around here. His *Animal Husbandry* skill is probably higher than mine. Been hunting here for… what? Fifty years?" Helen looked at the old man.

He smiled at her. "It's not polite to remind an old man of his age, ranger. But yes, I know what you mean. Take only a few males, the oldest or the youngest, leaving the alphas and the females to mate and increase the herd."

Helen added, "And of course, please kill any of the canids or other monsters that might unnaturally thin the herds."

Allistor added, "In fact, if it will help you, I'll put a bounty on the canids and lanx, and other creatures that reduce our food supply. I'll pay you and your people one gold coin for each hide. Two if the hides are in usable condition for our crafters. Each coin is currently worth about twelve hundred klax." He did a little quick math in his head. "That would mean if you brought me usable hides for about 45 monsters that might have killed elk or buffalo, you'd earn enough to purchase one of these plasma rifles."

Amanda spoke up for the first time. "You know that we claimed the high school. We'll be needing beds and chairs and such for the cowboys when they arrive. We can send some up from our nearest Stronghold, but that's a bit of a pain. If you'll allow us to forage for enough

352

furniture for say, twenty room's worth of beds, dressers, tables, et cetera, here in town, Allistor will give you the rifle he's carrying."

Standing Bear shook his head. "I don't want any favors. You could loot the town, and there's little we could do to stop you. I won't risk my people over furniture we don't need."

Allistor thought about it for a moment. "I really don't want to fight you. The park may be mine, but I consider the town yours, except for the high school. If you don't want us to get the furniture here, we'll bring some up ourselves. But how about this. You and your people help us to round up furniture, and move it to the high school. In exchange you get this rifle. Or if you don't want it, we can arrange some other trade. For instance, if you prefer conventional weapons, we can provide you with those, and piles of ammo. Either way, we'll leave you with some fresh vegetables and fruit. And I've already given you my blessing to hunt in the park. In addition, we'll share with you all that we've learned about this new world and the system that governs it. I'm really trying to be your friend here, Standing Bear. I invite you to join me as my citizens. If you don't like the sound of that, then we can be allies, trade partners, or we can leave you alone and let you fend for yourselves."

Standing Bear looked at his daughter, and the other two. All three nodded their heads. "We have fifteen people here. Ten of us can help you move furniture. We have some pickups and a flatbed to move it with. We help you fill your rooms, you give me that rifle."

Allistor held out a hand, and Standing Bear shook it. "That's a start. We have a deal." Allistor looked at Amanda. "You want to take charge of that? Pick out the furniture to be loaded, and direct the unloading?" Amanda simply looked at him as if he were stating the obvious.

Helen looked to Standing Bear. "We could use a steady supply of feed for the herd through the winter, in case things go badly. I'm sure if you'd be willing to supply that, Allistor would compensate you for it. Likewise, if you were to claim Remy's Diner as an Outpost, get it up and running, I'm guessing the cowboys would pay for decent food and drinks while they're here. It's not like anyone's going to require liquor licenses anymore. And it's only a couple blocks from the high school, so they can stumble home if they overdo it."

The younger of the men behind Redfeather began to turn red. "So, you think we're just peasants to do your manual labor? Your cooking and field work? Pay the 'injuns' with beads and whiskey?"

Allistor bristled, getting to his feet. "No. Helen was trying to be helpful, to give you guys a way to gain extra resources. But since you put it that way, I reject Helen's idea. We are certainly capable of doing the work ourselves. I'm tired of whatever chip you have on your shoulder being vented at me. I've done nothing to deserve it. I've been nothing but friendly toward you up till this moment. We'll be leaving now." He opened his inventory and pulled out all the fruits and vegetables he had stored there, which created a decent little pile on the table. Amanda added to it, Helen didn't. She stood there giving dirty looks to the young man and Standing Bear.

When they were done, Allistor said, "A parting gift, to show our good faith. We'll instruct our people to stay out of town. They'll run the herds through the park, and stay at the high school when they're close by. You can, of course, still hunt in the park, and we'll still pay the bounty and purchase the hides from you. When you have some to turn in, just leave a sign in the window at Remy's, and one of our people will bring you the gold. Other than that, I suggest you, in particular, stay away from the high school." He stared at the loud-mouth. "I think its best if we just stay out of each other's way."

Turning to address Standing Bear, he said, "I'm sorry we couldn't work things out. I still hope we can someday be friends. But you need to know this:" He pointed at the young man. "If he or anyone else tries to enter my Outpost without my permission, their life is forfeit. I will come for them, and anyone who stands between us. I have already killed close to a hundred humans who have attacked me, my people, or others. Murderers, kidnappers, rapists. I value every single human life, but I will not tolerate those who do harm to, or steal from, others. I am the absolute authority in my lands, and I have no interest in establishing a jail system and feeding prisoners, so crossing the line means banishment or death."

Standing Bear stood, his face grim. "I apologize for my nephew. He's a moron who spends half his time drunk or high, and doesn't have enough brain cells left to realize when he should shut the hell up, or just say thank you." He shot the young man a look that promised a reckoning. Turning his gaze to Helen, he said, "Thank you. I know that you were trying to help us. And I apologize to you, as well."

Sitting back down, he looked at Amanda as he lifted a plump green pepper from the table. "And thank you, ma'am, for your generosity. I and my tribe are a proud people, and we sometimes have difficulty accepting help. We would be honored to help you furnish your Outpost, assuming Allistor will allow us to help you move the items inside." As he finished speaking, he put his hands in his lap and stared down at them.

"You are most welcome, Standing Bear." Amanda spoke softly.

Helen was a little louder. "We were all young and stupid, once. I have always considered you a friend, Standing Bear. From the first day we met, and you invited me to participate in a naked sweat with you." Her words struck home, and the old man's mouth twitched, threatening to smile. "Today changes nothing, you old rascal." she rounded the table, stood next to him, and placed a hand on his shoulder as she spoke.

"Allistor, I get why you're angry. But I would ask, as a favor to me, that you reconsider. If Standing Bear and his people are interested in working with us as discussed, or in other ways that might benefit us all, I ask that you consent."

Allistor was surprised by Helen's request, but also wasn't. He took a seat, and a couple deep breaths to calm himself, before he answered.

"Standing Bear, I apologize as well. I am still young myself, and my temper got the better of me. I should not have let the ignorant words of a fool goad me into losing a chance at friendship with your people."

This time Standing Bear did smile, at the same time that his nephew huffed and stomped out of the room. "Well said, young man. I accept your offer of friendship. If you'll give me half an hour, I'll round up my people and the vehicles we'll need to get your furniture." He stood and offered a hand, which Allistor shook. Then he shook with Amanda and Helen a well. Fuzzy got a head-rub too. "And if you'd like, we'll be roasting one of your delicious elk tonight, and you're welcome to join us." This time he grinned at Allistor.

"Ha! That sounds good. Maybe I can even help? I'm always trying to level my *Cooking* skill, and I don't currently know any elk recipes."

Redfeather took over as her father left the room. "Oh, that's easy. We use some herbs that you can find anywhere around here…"

*****

The furniture gathering took most of the day. A small convoy of trucks followed Amanda around as they went house to house picking furniture. She tried to choose items that were sturdy rather than decorative, either solid wood or metal bed frames. Which also meant that they were heavy. Allistor helped to carry the heaviest of the items, his increased strength surprising some of the Lakota. When the trucks were full, they made the short trip to the high school, and Amanda stood just inside the door directing traffic as items were brought in.

They didn't worry about arranging the furniture inside the rooms, other than to set up the beds. Amanda

357

decided to leave that to the cowboys. So the unloading went much more quickly than the loading. When they were done, Allistor invited everyone to take a cooling dip in the pool. Only a few took him up on it, stripping to their boxers and jumping in. That is until Fuzzy did a huge belly-flop in the center of the pool. Standing Bear roared with laughter, then leapt in after the bear cub, fully clothed. After that nearly everyone joined in.

A short time later the damp humans were loading themselves back into the trucks to return to the Lakota Stronghold. Allistor was about to get into the *Juggernaut* when Nigel called out. *"Lord Allistor, I have an urgent request to speak to you from Airman Redd at the Silo."*

The locals all started in surprise at the voice from nowhere. Allistor explained, "Sorry guys, that's Nigel. He's the AI that runs all my facilities. He came with the Citadel. Nigel, please put them through."

"Allistor, you there? Over." Redd's voice echoed around the parking area.

"Hiya Redd. I'm here. Uh, over? Can we dispense with that stuff, please?"

"Oh! Sure. Sorry about that. I've been on the radio nonstop and sort of got back into the… well, never mind. We found other people!"

Allistor smiled at nobody in particular in response to her excitement. "One of the foraging parties brought some people back?"

"What? No. I mean, we found *a lot* of people. With the radio. Thousands. Tens of thousands. There's a whole network of folks in different places who've been talking via short wave. And we found them! There's a guy in Detroit that says there are like fifty thousand people still alive there."

"That's great, Redd! Congratulations! Remind me to buy you a whole bunch of drinks when I see you!" He saw curious looks from all the faces around him. "Uh, you're on speaker here, sort of, and some new friends are listening in. What can you tell us about the folks you've found?"

"Hello, new friends!" Allistor could hear the smile in her voice as she acknowledged his hint to keep state secrets to herself. "It started with some guys on an Air Force base in Texas. I found them this morning, and they'd been talking to another group on an Army post in Kansas. A prison, actually. We got a three-way call going, and that started this whole sort of avalanche of people who were listening to us talk, then joined in. I've got two others in here with me, we're all on different radios getting locations, populations, monster stories, all kinds of info. But I thought I should take a minute and let you know. Cuz you're the boss 'n' such. I mean… sorry, sir!" Allistor could almost hear her sitting up straight and saluting the radio.

Helen and several of the Lakota laughed at that last part.

"You did great, Redd. Please continue as you were. Is there anyone that needs to speak to me urgently?"

"Uhhh… no, sir? Not really? Right now, there's no real formal conversations going on. We're just all sort of getting to know each other, and putting out calls for more people on as many channels as possible."

359

"Great. Because I'm about to learn how to roast an elk. Might take most of the evening. But if you need me for something urgent, don't hesitate to alert Nigel, and he'll get me."

"You got it boss. Have fun!" Redd signed off.

"Well, that was very cool!" Amanda hugged him. "I'm glad there's so many more people out there. That gives me a little more hope for our future."

"Sounds like military installations and big cities are doing better than our little towns out here." Helen observed.

"Makes sense." Allistor replied. "Half the airmen at the Silo were gamers, and I'm guessing it's the same with soldiers and sailors. And big cities would have a lot of gamers, too. Kids who weren't working farms or ranches in their spare time, with rich parents and high-speed web access."

"Not to mention that military bases are filled with trained fighters and weapons, and the bigger cities have thousands of cops, gangsters, and organized firefighters, et cetera. If they prepared quickly enough, they could have held out against the spawns."

Amanda spoke quietly. "We probably have more guns per person out here, but most of us were alone or in small groups. And there was only one sheriff's deputy for every few thousand people. Except like in Denver. We've found, what? Five thousand or more people there?"

Allistor shook his head. "Not quite that many. But you're all forgetting something. That monster that stomped our town, it was already at level ten on day three when it

360

attacked. It either spawned at a high level, or it had already killed a bunch of things before it reached us. Out here in the country, it could have slaughtered and eaten whole herds of cattle or sheep or whatever. And most of us humans were level one or two at the time. We didn't stand a chance. In the big cities and army posts, those folks probably put up more of a fight as soon as the creatures spawned. Killing them before they got too big. Or killing each other, and getting experience that way." He grimaced at the thought.

"A monster stomped your whole town?" Redfeather asked.

"Yeah, big ugly smelly bastard. Sixty feet tall. I'll tell you all about it over dinner." Allistor's voice relayed some of the sorrow he still felt at the loss of his family and friends.

They all drove back to the Lakota Stronghold, and Redfeather pulled Allistor aside as they prepped the elk for roasting. As he'd hoped, he learned a new recipe and got a +1 to his *Cooking* skill. Helen poked her nose in at the beginning to see what kind of herbs they used, taking notes so that she could pass the info on to Nancy. She bailed when Redfeather started showing Allistor what each of the plants looked like, as she already knew from her ranger training. Allistor learned the skill *Herbology* from the lesson, and rewarded Redfeather with a handful of gold coins.

Eventually the elk was put on a huge spit over an open fire, and the roasting began. It didn't take long at all for the delicious smell of cooked meat to permeate the air and make Allistor's stomach growl. They'd all skipped lunch while rounding up furniture, and he was hungry.

Before the meat was served, Allistor made a show of thanking Standing Bear for the hospitality, and for their help during the day. He presented the man with the plasma rifle, as well as a charger and extra battery pack. They all took a short trip out the gate, where Standing Bear picked a dumpster that stood near the front of an alley. He took aim and fired, and the white-hot round of superheated death burned right through the front of it.

Back inside, they all lined up as Standing Bear, Redfeather, and a few others dished out plates, cafeteria style. Allistor received a plate with a several slices of roasted elk, mashed sweet potatoes, a small amount of green beans, some small fried balls of something about the size of peas that he didn't recognize, which were covered in a sweet-smelling glaze, and a slice of freshly baked bread.

When everyone had been served and taken a seat, Standing Bear stood at the head of the table, gave a short blessing, and they all dug in. Allistor was sitting to the old man's left, with Amanda next to him, and Helen across the table next to Redfeather. They mostly ate in silence at first, Allistor appreciating the delicious meal. He lifted his cup to take a drink, and sputtered in surprise. "Is this…"

Standing Bear sighed. "Kool-aid. Yes. It's Redfeather's favorite, unfortunately. There's a pitcher of water right there if you prefer. Or we have beer, if you're old enough?" Several people chuckled at the question. Allistor had to think about it. His birthday was coming soon, but he was still only twenty.

"Actually, I'm not." The laughter got louder. "But Kool-aid is fine. It just surprised me, that's all." They resumed eating, and Allistor cleared his plate. Redfeather offered to dish him up some more, and he accepted.

"How did you like the prairie berries?" she asked as she got to her feet. "You want more?"

Allistor didn't notice most of the table quieting to hear his answer.

"Is that what those little things with the glaze were? They were good. I've never heard of prairie berries. Where do you find them? Nancy will probably want us to bring one of the bushes home for her greenhouse."

There was a general chuckle up and down the long tables in the cafeteria. Standing Bear coughed into his napkin, then smiled at Allistor. "They don't grow on a bush, my young friend. They have to be harvested, two at a time. Prairie berries are prairie dog testicles, fried in beer batter and served with a glaze made of sweet potato and sugar."

Allistor didn't catch on for a moment. When he did, his stomach felt a little queasy. He put one hand over his gut, the other over his mouth, and focused on keeping his dinner down. The Lakota roared in laughter, several of them getting up to pat him on the back and offer comments like, "I've never seen anyone ask for seconds."

Eventually, Allistor got himself under control, and took another drink of Kool-aid. It was fruit punch flavored, a classic.

Standing Bear thumped him on the back once, and said, "Sorry, boy. It's a sort of tradition going all the way

363

back to when the first white scouts and traders showed up on our lands. I couldn't resist."

Allistor waved a hand in dismissal. "I wouldn't have eaten them if you told me first, but they actually didn't taste bad. Though, I'll pass on seconds if you don't mind, Redfeather." He gave her a weak smile. Looking to Amanda and Helen, neither of them seemed to have any issue with having eaten the little rodent balls. Then something occurred to him.

"Did everyone eat these? How many little prairie dogs are running around without balls right now??"

This earned him even more laughter. Standing Bear answered while Redfeather went to dish up Allistor's plate. "We eat the prairie dogs, too. There were times in our people's past where that was the only meat available to us. We learned to eat many things. Roots, grubs, mushrooms, even boiled grass soup at times." He gave Allistor's hand a friendly pat. "You don't know enough of the history of your people, Allistor. When you have time, come back to visit for a while, and I will tell you stories."

"I'd like that, Standing Bear. Thank you."

After dinner, and Allistor's recounting of the void titan attacks, Standing Bear walked them back outside to their vehicle. "I am glad we met, young Earl. Chief to Chief, I offer you my hand in friendship." The two men shook hands. "My tribe is small. As far as I know, these are the last of the Lakota. We are not strong, but if you need our help when the aliens come, we will fight at your side."

"I hope it doesn't come to that, my friend." Allistor replied. He was about to say more when the *Juggernaut*'s version of a horn honked, and the lights flashed once. They all ran over to the vehicle, and Allistor opened the door.

"What's wrong, Nigel?"

"My sensors have been tracking a single humanoid who has infiltrated the High School Outpost. I have been unable to alert you until now. He scaled the wall using a rope, and is currently sitting in a maintenance closet near the front door. Shall I lock him in, Lord Allistor?"

"Yes, please do, Nigel. We'll deal with him shortly."

Allistor turned to give his apologies to Standing Bear, but paused at the look on the old man's face.

"My idiot nephew. It has to be him. I noticed he wasn't at dinner, but thought he was just sulking. I'm sorry."

Amanda spoke, her voice cold. "If he's hiding in that closet, he is planning to ambush you." Allistor looked at her, then at Helen, who nodded.

Standing Bear sighed. "I think you are correct, Amanda. The little shit is probably planning revenge for what he perceived as insults this morning." He turned to Allistor. "What do you want to do? He heard your warning this morning. He knows the penalty for his intrusion and any attack he makes could be death."

Allistor studied the old man as he spoke. His voice was thick with emotion, and his eyes reflected great despair. But there was steel resolve in the set of his mouth, and his shoulders. He was prepared to let his nephew die if necessary.

Allistor shook his head. "What the hell is his problem?"

Redfeather had joined them, planning to say goodbye, but hearing Nigel speak and the subsequent exchange. "He doesn't have a real problem. He's a miserable little shit that imagines the whole world is against him. If you weren't mostly white, he'd have hated you for being wealthy. Or for not being Lakota enough. Or having a better looking girlfriend, a cooler car, better weapon... he doesn't need a real reason. He's had an easy life, and wasted it on drugs and booze."

Standing Bear gave her a stern look, and she stopped talking. "He is still your cousin, girl!"

She lowered her eyes and spoke quietly. "I'm sorry, father."

Allistor decided. "I don't need his life. But I can't excuse him trying to take me out so soon after being warned. Why don't you and a few of your people come back with us. If I can get him out of the closet alive, I'll leave his punishment to you."

Standing Bear just nodded, giving his daughter a look. She sprinted back into the building, and returned a minute later with three men. All three held weapons in their hands. The Lakota piled into a pickup and followed Allistor's group back to the high school. Nigel opened the gate for them, and closed it behind.

Allistor motioned for the others to stay back as he approached the front doors. He spoke loudly to Amanda, to be sure the fool in the closet heard him coming. "It'll be good to get a full night's rest after that big meal..."

Casting *Barrier* in front of himself, he pulled a shotgun from his inventory and stepped through the double door, which Nigel obligingly opened. He stomped his feet slightly, the hard soles of his boots thumping against the polished stone floor as he passed the closet. There was a rattling of the doorknob, then some cursing when the locked door didn't open.

"We know you're in there, genius." Allistor moved closer and called out. Standing Bear and his men hovered near the front door twenty feet away. "Put down whatever weapon you have, and I'll let you out. Your people are here to take you home."

"Liar! You said this morning you'd kill me. You want my life, come in here and get it!" As he finished speaking, a shotgun blast erupted through the door, shattered the magic barrier, and knocked Allistor backward. The buckshot had peppered his left arm and side, and he was bleeding from multiple wounds. He was about to cast a heal on himself when Amanda and Helen beat him to it.

Grunting in pain, he pushed himself with his good arm and legs to the side, out of the line of fire. Seeing Standing Bear and his men approaching, Allistor raised a hand to stop them.

"You moron! Standing Bear is right here, and I had told him he could take you home and punish you his way!" Allistor shouted at the hole in the door. He heard the man reloading inside.

Standing Bear shouted too. "He's telling the truth! You never think anything through, do you? Everybody's always picking on you, right? Lying to you? Did you think you could kill all three of them, and the bear, and get away clean? Now if Allistor doesn't kill your cowardly ass, I'll do it myself! You have no honor! You are a disgrace to our people, and if your mother was still alive, she would be ashamed!"

Allistor heard sobbing from inside the closet. There was no light inside, and he couldn't tell where the man was. He whispered, "Nigel, please open the door."

The door swung open, and the light from the hallway revealed the man crouched against the back wall of the closet, gripping his shotgun tightly. He began to aim it toward Allistor again. Allistor cast *Restraint*, freezing him with the barrel still pointed toward the floor.

"Quick, get his gun. He can't move." Allistor called out. One of the men ran into the closet and yanked the weapon free, careful not to let a frozen finger pull the trigger. As soon as he had the gun in hand, he used it to deliver a vicious blow to the still stunned face. The young man's nose shattered, and blood poured down over his mouth to soak his shirt.

As he unfroze, he wailed in pain and covered his nose with both hands. The other man stepped away, and Standing Bear moved into the closet. His face was a thunderstorm of anger and shame. Grabbing the boy by the hair, he yanked him to his feet. The old man's strength as he raised his arm had his poor nephew tippy-toeing across the floor even as he screamed in pain. Standing Bear thrust

368

the boy forward, letting him loose to stumble into the arms of the other three.

All three men acted without a word. One punched the boy in the gut, doubling him over and knocking the wind out of him, stopping his cries of pain. The one who'd taken the shotgun slammed the stock into his bent spine, driving him to his hands and knees, causing him to leave bloody handprints on the floor. The third man kicked him in the face, the force of the blow snapping his head back with an audible crack, and Allistor couldn't tell if it was his spine or his jaw.

Standing Bear ignored it all, turning his back on the beating and offering a hand to help Allistor to his feet. "I am sorry, Allistor. I am ashamed."

"Not your shame, nor your fault, Standing Bear." Allistor offered, trying to focus on the old man's face rather than the beating happening behind him. "This will in no way hurt our friendship."

On the other side of the fight, Amanda shouted, "Stop! Please."

The three men paused, turning to look at her as the young man collapsed, gasping for air and moaning. It looked like someone had broken one of his arms in the few seconds Allistor wasn't watching. There was a growing pool of blood on the floor.

"Please don't kill him. I know both Allistor and Standing Bear think he should die. But he's just a kid." Amanda's eyes reached Allistor, pleading. There were tears already running down her cheeks.

Allistor looked at Standing Bear, whose face was hard as stone. "As I said, I don't need his life. Maybe this beating will teach him a lesson."

The three men looked to their chief for guidance. After a long moment, he waved them back and stepped in close to his nephew.

"You will get on your feet, and walk from this place. From this town. You will not return." He turned his back on his nephew, who was now struggling to get to his feet. Eventually, after he failed several times, two of the men grabbed his arms and lifted him to his feet. They marched him to the door, and pushed him through. Both watched as he stumbled, holding one arm with the other and dripping blood, out the gate and into the darkness.

Chapter 16

The Bigger They Are...

The following morning, Allistor and company returned to the Warren. They'd said their goodbyes to Standing Bear, with promises of future trade and bounties to be claimed. Rather than go cross-country again, Helen drove the roads on the way back.

When they ran across some of their people getting the abandoned semi back on the road, Allistor changed his plans. "Please take this north to Upton. Helen will give you directions. When you get there, you'll find the Lakota Stronghold. Give them this truck and everything in it. I'll still pay you all your shares out of common funds. If you like, we have our own Outpost there as well. You can spend the night and return in the morning. There's a nice swimming pool. Oh! And on your way back, please stop and shoot maybe half a dozen elk to take back to the Warren."

With that done, they continued on to the Warren. Driving through the gates, they found Bjurstrom, and some folks Allistor didn't recognize, stepping off the teleport pad. He waved to them, then jogged over.

"Hey Allistor. Pretty cool news, finding all those other people, right?"

"Very cool! I was just going to head to the Silo and talk to Redd, get a better update. What's going on here?" He motioned toward the group near the pad.

"Ramon told me about the vermin warren you cleared out in the sewers here back in the early days. I figured it might have been re-occupied by now, so yesterday I sent one of my guys to check. There's a whole mess of those mutant lizard-dog things down there now, mostly level ten to fifteen. So I brought over a party of our lowest level noobs to get some experience and level up a bit."

"Great work, man. Thanks!" Allistor thumped him on the back. They pulled their gear from the *Juggernaut* and headed for the pad. Allistor greeted the party on his way past them, wishing them good luck.

They were just about to step on the pad when Helen stopped them. "Shit! I forgot to give Nancy this herb stuff and the elk recipe. Hold on." She dropped her gear and began to jog toward the greenhouse.

Allistor called after her. "Ask her to send a load of produce up to Upton, please!" She waved over her shoulder in acknowledgement as she disappeared into the greenhouse.

Ten minutes later they were back at the Citadel in Cheyenne. Helen set off to find Nathan, whom she had not yet kicked to the curb despite her protestations months before. Fuzzy wandered off to find a secluded patch of grass to take care of some bear business. Allistor and Amanda hit the open market kiosk to pick up a few things. He needed to replace the plasma rifle he'd traded to Standing Bear, and she was looking for a spell scroll that might complement her *Internal Analysis* ability. She'd been using the spell at least once per day since she'd learned it, and it was getting harder and harder to achieve level increases. She was also on the lookout for a better healing spell that would do more than *Restore*'s one thousand points.

With all their great achievements, their dedication to getting stronger and learning more, Allistor and his people were all still low level compared to what he expected the aliens to be. If it came to a fight, they were going to have to rely on sturdy walls, alien weapons, and plain old heart to win the day. He had nightmares about a single alien land-grabber blasting through his gates with ease and slaughtering his people to claim the Citadel, or the Capitol.

As if his thoughts summoned the reality, they were interrupted by a sound he knew he'd never forget. It rumbled across the landscape to vibrate through the walls and into his soul, where it created fear and repulsion simultaneously.

The closest thing he could compare it to was a mechanical monster that appeared in an old, turn of the century MMO. It was found in a place called Hellfire, and when it approached, everyone fled. Players would be minding their own business, running about collecting quest items or battling mutant pigs, and suddenly the ground would shake, and a deafening noise that sounded like a foghorn mixed with the howling of a tornado would echo across the area. Those that didn't run were stomped into oblivion.

Allistor had that feeling now. "Void titan." he said to himself. Then louder, he shouted, "VOID TITAN!" to anyone who would listen. His memories of their previous battle with the monster outside the Warren made his tongue go dry. He'd been trapped in the giant monster's armpit, and the stench had given him an actual physical debuff.

"Nigel! I need Sam and George, right now!" he shouted toward the nearest wall, even as he ran toward it to climb the stairs. By the time he got to the top, they were connected.

"Go ahead, Lord Allistor."

"Sam! George! We got another void titan! Coming at the Citadel this time. I need you and your Howitzer crews here right away!"

"Shit!" Sam's voice answered first. "It'll take maybe ten minutes to get everyone together and get there."

"I'm on my way. Our gun's already there, but my crew is scattered. I'll get Nigel to alert everyone and we'll meet you there." George responded.

Allistor didn't need to alert everyone at the Citadel, the roar of the approaching monster had everyone moving already. Even those who hadn't fought one of the giant monsters before recognized the sound as bad.

Reaching the top of the wall, he pulled the .50 cal sniper rifle from his inventory. Leaning against the parapet, he scanned the area. The Citadel sat on a rise above the city, and the extra elevation of being atop the wall gave him a commanding view of their surroundings. It only took him seconds to spot the beast moving in their general direction. It towered above the trees in a patch of forest to the south of him, on the other side of the airport.

A sharp whistle from behind him caused Allistor to turn. Another directed his gaze upward, where he found

Dean waving at him from the guard post atop the tower. He had the .50 cal that Allistor had given him when a dragon attacked the Citadel. Dean pointed toward the oncoming monster and shouted, "That thing's at least eighty feet tall!"

Allistor thought he was about right. It was significantly larger than the one they'd battled before. Both in height, and in bulk. This one had a wider head, with twin sets of horns that curved backward from the top and sides. When it opened its mouth, the jaws were lined with dozens of sharp teeth, each the length of Allistor's arm or longer. Its legs and lower body were obscured by the trees, but Allistor could see bulging shoulders and biceps rippling with muscles. It appeared to have moss, shrubs, and even a small tree growing across its back. Dark leathery skin stretched tight over its massive rib cage as it took in a breath and roared again. Allistor felt the wall vibrate underneath him. A wall that five minutes ago had felt impenetrable and secure.

Now, looking across a mile of open land at the thing, Allistor thought maybe it could simply step over his wall if it wanted to.

Using his rifle scope, he took a closer look.

Xar' Dakra
Void Titan Elite
Level 30
Health: 187,000/187,000

Even as he *Examined* the monster, it stepped out from the trees, smashing a few of them to the ground like they weren't even there. The thing was a walking tank,

375

with an enormous health pool, skin that looked tough as iron, and sharp claws at the end of its fingers and toes. Its arms stretched down past its knees, giving it a reach of maybe fifty feet or more. Allistor continued to watch it through his scope as it stepped out onto the airport grounds and crushed a service truck under one foot.

Allistor heard a shot from above. The creature was well within range of Dean's weapon, being about half a mile away and moving closer. He observed the monster pause as the round struck it in the face, carving a divot out of its cheek. Black blood began to ooze down its face as it roared again and beat one of its three-fingered, clawed hands against its chest.

What came next surprised and terrified Allistor.

The monster's roar of pain turned into words.

"Yyyyooou will diiieeeee!"

Allistor and everyone else within miles of the creature froze. His heartrate doubled, his stomach sank, and, somewhere in his core, his soul shuddered with fear. Of all the monsters they'd encountered since the apocalypse, none of them had been capable of speech. They'd seen no evidence that any of them were even sentient, or operating at a level above the instinctual need to hunt and feed, and simple self-preservation when they fled.

A moment later Goodrich joined Allistor atop the wall. "Holy shit, did I hear that thing talk?"

Allistor just nodded, his mouth too dry to speak. He set the bipod of his rifle atop the wall, chambered a round, took aim, and fired. He watched through the scope and his round shattered a tooth in the monster's open mouth. Goodrich fired several rounds from his own rifle, as did several others who'd joined them atop the wall. Another blast from Dean up on the tower, and Allistor reloaded and fired. This time his round struck just above its right eye, causing blood to ooze down onto the orb.

> *Xar' Dakra*
> *Void Titan Elite*
> *Level 30*
> *Health: 185,100/187,000*

At this rate the thing would reach them and demolish the entire Citadel before they even whittled away half its health. Every second, more people were joining him on the wall, firing as rapidly as they could. Allistor realized that for most of them, it was still out of range.

"Nigel, loudspeaker please." He waited a moment, then shouted, "Hold your fire!"

Nigel transmitted his words up and down the line, and the firing quickly ceased. Allistor continued. "I know it's a big target, and hard to miss. But for most of you he's out of range. Hold your fire until he reaches the base of our plateau here. For those using hunting rifles with better range, aim for its face!"

Sporadic fire resumed as his people with long guns that had the proper range began to focus on its face.

Allistor took another look, seeing multiple lines of ichor dripping from tiny holes, so small on the giant visage as to look like pinpricks.

"Nigel, put me through to every one of our facilities, loudspeaker please."

"Go ahead, Lord Allistor."

"Listen up people! We've got an eighty-foot tall void titan attacking the Citadel! I need every available fighter here ASAP. Leave a guard force at each Stronghold, and bring whatever big guns you have. Including your plasma rifles."

Another quick look at the approaching titan to gauge its speed, and Allistor took off down the stairs. Helen and Nathan were charging up toward him, and he turned them around. "Come with me! We need to distract this thing."

The three of them ran to the motor pool, where Allistor scanned the vehicles. His first instinct was to use one of the *Juggernaut* style vehicles. But there was a good chance they were about to get stomped, and he didn't want to waste the expensive tech. So, he chose one of the Humvees with a machine gun mounted on top. "Nathan, you're on the gun. Helen, you drive." He hopped in the passenger seat, and they took off. Nigel opened the gates for them, and they shot down the switchbacks as fast as Helen could manage it without tipping them over.

The creature was very nearly at the base of the plateau when they reached it. Helen gunned the motor and aimed the vehicle straight at the monster's massive right foot, which was already planted as the left foot raised in the air. Nathan tilted the gun as high as it would go and shot up into the creature's crotch as they approached, then switched to the foot when he lost the angle. Allistor fired his brand-new plasma rifle out the passenger window at the right foot as well. Just before they reached it, Xar' Dakra planted his left with an earth-shaking stomp and began to raise the right foot. The heel was barely off the ground when they shot past it, rocketing down the road behind the monster.

Allistor leaned back and shot the giant in the ass with a couple rounds of plasma before they got out of effective range. The weapons did a lot of damage, but they were short distance weapons, a few hundred feet at most.

"Head over to the airport!" Allistor shouted over the gunfire as Nathan emptied a belt into the monster to hold its attention. "We're gonna kite this thing for a while, until our people can get the big guns set up. Maybe tire it out a little! And honk the horn if this thing has one!"

Helen did as instructed, yanking the wheel toward the airport entrance while pounding on the horn in the center. Xar' Dakra roared in answer as he clumsily spun around to follow. Helen didn't let off the speed as she extended the distance between them. Allistor didn't blame her one bit. It was like having a high rise with claws and sharp teeth chasing them.

And when it finally got turned in their direction, its long loping strides quickly began to eat away at their lead.

Nathan, no longer firing as he needed to reload, began to panic. "Uhh... Helen? Need to go faster. Punch it! This thing can run! Like, seriously, go faster!"

She punched the accelerator and the engine screamed as the heavy armored vehicle increased speed. Finished with his reload, Nathan fired a few test rounds to be sure the weapon worked properly, and to keep the giant's attention.

They blasted through a closed chain-link gate and tore past a few private hangars out onto the runways. Helen slowed and turned to the left, watching in her mirrors as the titan turned as well. His inside angle meant that he caught up a little more, and the wheels began to skip with the impact of its every step.

Nathan began to fire up at its crotch again, which seemed to annoy Xar' Dakra quite a bit. It roared and put on even more speed, clearly planning to stomp them into fertilizer. Allistor reversed himself, sitting on his knees in the shotgun seat and leaning out the window to fire back at the titan. Helen watched the mirrors closely, maintaining her course until Allistor and Nathan were both screaming for her to do something. She could see the shadow of a massive foot block out the sun above them, and shouted, "Hold on!" before she cranked the wheel to the right as she pressed the brake.

The effect was amazing. The Humvee slowed and turned, making the monster's foot overshoot and come pounding down on their nine-o'clock as Helen punched the accelerator and zoomed off behind Xar' Dakra once again.

It roared in frustration even as both men cheered and fired at the monster's backside. Allistor knew they weren't doing much damage, but their intent here was to buy time, not kill the thing.

Xar' Dakra
Void Titan Elite
Level 30
Health: 171,050/187,000

It bent and took a swipe at them with its right arm even as it started to pivot. The claws on its three fingers raked deep furrows in the runway surface as they passed just behind the Humvee. Allistor took advantage of the fact that it was bent down to shoot it in the face. A lucky crit burned into the monster's eye, causing it to jerk upright and place both hands over its face. Helen sped away, honking the horn like a madwoman.

At this point, all three of them were nearly deaf from the monster's foghorn of a roar, and Allistor's throat was getting sore from screaming over it and all the gunfire. He tapped Helen's arm and pointed toward one of the hangars. "Drive in there!"

She followed his pointing finger and nodded her head. The Humvee sped toward the structure and into one of the open doors. Allistor immediately regretted the choice, as they all went temporarily blind while their eyes adjusted to the darker interior of the building. Helen slammed on the brakes, and managed to stop the vehicle before it collided with the tail of a private plane.

"Shit! I didn't know there was a plane in here. Back outside!" Allistor shouted. He didn't want the monster crushing the plane for two reasons: First, it might explode and take all of them out with it. And second, if they had anybody who could pilot that thing, it would widen their scouting range considerably. All of this processed through his mind in the few seconds it took to scan the interior.

Helen cranked the wheel around again, and they paused for a second just inside the doors to see where Xar' Dakra was. He was less than a hundred yards behind them, which for him was only a few steps.

"Hold on, this is gonna suck!" Helen hit the gas even as Nathan began firing again. He cackled gleefully as he sent round after round into the monster's crotch. "No baby asshole titan monsters for you!"

He stopped laughing as Helen weaved sharply to avoid a kick as they approached, then weaved back again to avoid another swipe, driving directly under the giant and drenching Nathan in the foul-smelling black ichor that was raining down from its crotch. He abandoned the gun on the roof, dropping down into the vehicle and puking his guts out. As he tried to wipe the stuff from his head and face, Allistor sympathized. He'd been covered in the stuff after the last void titan battle, and already his own stomach was roiling from the stench.

It wasn't just Nathan. The whole Humvee was showered in the stuff. It covered the windshield, leaked down through the gun turret hole, and even splashed in through Allistor's open window onto his arm and leg.

"Gah!" Nathan wasn't capable of speech. He pulled what looked like sweatpants from his inventory and began trying to wipe out his mouth, soiling the garment with vomit and ichor both.

"Stink attack! Damn, that's awful!" Helen shouted, giggling wildly even as she tried to cover her nose and mouth with one hand. Allistor was pretty sure she'd gone insane. Her foot was pressing the accelerator to the floor as they zoomed down another runway. The monster had turned once again, bloodied and angry at its inability to stomp the fast-moving menace.

"Noooo Runnn!"

Its booming voice aimed directly at them made the Humvee vibrate, and pretty much finished off Allistor's hearing. Which is why he didn't hear Helen screaming as she saw Xar' Dakra in her mirror pick up a parked compact car and fling it at them. Allistor shit himself when the car crashed down not three feet to his right, rolling end over end and actually grazing his side of the Humvee before losing momentum and falling behind them.

"What the hell?" he screamed, barely able to hear his own voice. "Did he just throw a car at us?"

Nathan, looking a very sickly shade of green, stuck his head back up and took control of the gun. He squeezed off a few rounds, screaming at the monster. "You dirty, nasty, stanky piece of shit! You're gonna pay for that!"

When the ammo belt reached its end, he frantically began to disengage it and reload. His hands kept slipping on the goo, which got inside the gun when he opened it.

Allistor looked back, seeing that the monster was out of range of his plasma weapon. He decided it was angry enough at them anyway, he could save his battery charge. When he looked forward again, he noticed they were quickly running out of runway. Helen was wide-eyed and emitting this sort of wordless wail, her grip on the wheel so tight her knuckles were white, and the pedal to the metal. A quick look ahead of them revealed a high pile of sand directly in their path, placed there to stop runaway planes as safely as possible.

"Helen! Stop! Need to turn!" he screamed, shoving her shoulder with considerable force. The action snapped her out of whatever vision she was having, and she hit the brakes.

Hard.

Allistor cursed as he slid off the passenger seat, his head slamming into the dash even as his legs and butt bunched up in the footwell underneath. An accidental pull of the trigger burned a hole in his door, and the smell of burning titan ichor finally made him puke. He managed to get his head out the window first, which he thought he deserved a medal for.

When the retching stopped, he noted that Helen had turned them around and was now racing down a different runway at an oblique angle. The titan didn't have to worry about going off-road, and was quickly closing the distance between them.

A moment later Helen shouted, "Shit!" and leaned toward Allistor even as an impact on her side sent the vehicle into the air. Nathan screamed as his ribs were crushed from the impact and sudden change of direction, and Allistor was very nearly thrown through his window.

Nathan's scream ended abruptly as the Humvee landed on its roof, then rolled several times before coming to rest on its wheels. Both Helen and Allistor were dazed, their health bars low and still dropping from bleed effects. He cast a heal on her, then one on himself, managing little more than to stop the bleeding. They were both down to about a quarter of their health pools.

Even worse, Allistor couldn't hear Xar' Dakra. There was a muffled thump, then another, but he didn't feel the ground shake. Had he not already voided his bowels, he would have done so right then, picturing one of the massive feet descending upon them right then.

Instead he heard a muffled version of the titan's roar, *then* felt a couple of vibrations from its footsteps. With each one, he expected the roof of the Humvee to cave in and crush him.

He cast another heal on Helen and himself, then looked toward the back. Nathan was back there, his head and upper torso crushed into pulp, smeared against the opening in the roof. The gun and turret had been bent back so that they melded with the mangled body. Allistor retched some more, but there was nothing left in him.

Taking hold of his rifle, he searched everywhere that he could see for the monster. His heart was racing and there was a ringing in his head that suggested he was concussed. Finally, he spotted it moving toward the Citadel.

Pushing himself out of the vehicle, he fell onto the pavement face-first. The passenger door was missing, lying several feet away where it was flung as the Humvee rolled. Holding onto the frame, he pulled himself to his feet and stood there a moment, steadying himself. Then he used the truck as a crutch, working his way around to yank open Helen's door and pull her out. He cast another heal on her when he saw that her entire left side looked broken. Her arm was at a strange angle, and two of her ribs were poking through her shirt underneath the arm.

Quickly pulling a healing potion from his ring, he poured some of it directly onto the protruding ribs, then the rest down her throat. When she didn't swallow, he pushed her mouth closed and held her nose. After a few seconds her body took over and gulped down the liquid, then gasped for breath when he let her go.

She awoke screaming, the pain from her ribs and arm excruciating. Allistor held her shoulders against her seat to keep her as immobile as possible. Sometime during the struggle, she appeared to remember what happened, and tried to turn back and look for Nathan.

He let go of her shoulders and took hold of her head with both hands, using his strength to keep her facing him.

"Nathan's gone. You don't want to look back there. Trust me."

She stared into his eyes as tears rolled down her face. He held her there for a while, wanting to hug her but knowing it would only damage her more. He cast another heal, and she screamed again, then passed out. Finally letting go of her head, he collapsed onto the tarmac. Every bit of him hurt. He'd gotten Nathan killed and nearly killed Helen and himself with his foolish idea.

As he sat there, watching the titan stride back toward his people, he heard another of the thumps from before. When Xar' Dakra's torso jerked backward and a hole appeared in his back, Allistor wanted to cheer.

"The Howitzers!" he gasped, unable to get enough air to shout. He didn't hear a word he said, and was sure Helen didn't either. After casting another heal on them both, his hearing improved a good bit. He heard gunfire, the sound of plasma weapons, and the sweet, sweet sound of a Howitzer round firing.

He pulled himself up again, he legs a little steadier this time. Though his health bar was back to full, he still felt damaged inside, concussed and weak. He checked Helen's injuries, finding that her ribs had retreated and her flesh showed a fresh scar. Patting her cheek a few times, he said, "Come on, lady. On your feet. That thing's not dead yet."

*****

Andrea was atop the tower with Dean, observing the fight through a rifle scope just as he was. Her guys, except for Bjurstrom, who was off in some rat dungeon with the lowbies, were spread out along the wall to help coordinate fire. Her heart leapt into her throat as the giant delivered a vicious kick to Allistor's Humvee and sent it flying. It landed on its roof fifty feet away, crushing Nathan before log-rolling several times.

She was sure that all three of her friends were dead. Nothing could have survived that. And the monster was moving forward to finish the job. She began to sob, even as she heard Dean cursing up a storm next to her.

"That son of a bitch killed them! Did you see? I'm gonna cut its god-damned nuts off and hang 'em from this tower! I'm gonna shit in its eye socket! I'm… Oh, shit! He just rolled out his door! Allistor's alive!" He keyed his radio, screaming into it. "Allistor's still alive! Shoot that thing! Get its attention! Right fickin' now!"

Sam shouted back through his own radio. "Already on it!" and both Howitzers boomed within about a second of each other. One round struck the ground very close to the monster's feet, causing it to stop and look down. The second round blasted into its hip, staggering it.

Dean fired with his .50 cal sniper rifle, the monster still well within his range. Andrea heard a few sporadic rifle shots from below, as well. She held her breath as the thing turned away from Allistor and started back toward the Citadel's walls. It was clearly limping, and moving more slowly than when it had been chasing the Humvee.

Andrea wept even as she raised her own rifle and took aim. A deep breath to calm herself, and she squeezed the trigger. She thought her round bounced off one of the thing's teeth as it opened its mouth to roar. Sliding the bolt back and chambering another round, she fired again.

Down on the ground, George and Sam were shouting at their gun crews as they reloaded and adjusted the Howitzers. They were a little rusty, not having practiced in several months. Sam vowed that would never happen again. If they'd been two seconds slower just a minute ago, that big monster would have stomped Allistor flat.

"Move your asses! You see that mountain moving our way? He's coming to eat you!" he roared at his guys, even as they shoved the new round in and secured it. When his guy on the sights gave him a thumbs up, Sam fired. George's crew were only about five seconds behind.

Not having a way to get the massive guns up on the wall, they'd settled for opening the gates and backing the weapons up so that they were aimed toward the airport. The radio in his ear gave him a play-by-play of Allistor and company dodging and teasing the giant while he and his guys prepped their gun. He was just preparing to fire when Dean screamed at them through the radio.

He loved Allistor like the boy was his own son. He'd felt a dagger in his soul when the radio screamed that the boy had been killed, his gaze instantly finding the still-rolling Humvee. Blind rage had him promising a painful death for Xar' Dakra and all his kind. When he heard

389

there was a chance to save Allistor, he'd have sprinted down and thrown the round at that monster if he had to.

Which is what he thought the air force guys were doing as they ran past him out the gate. "Hey! Where you going?"

McCoy held up a claymore in each hand. "Gonna leave a few surprises for the big fella!" Sam saw the other six airmen each held two of the anti-personnel charges.

"You know those won't kill it!" Sam shouted at the man, who was already turning to catch his friends.

"Nope! But it might hold still for a second, so you can shoot it!" McCoy grinned back at him, leaping down over the edge of one of the switchbacks and disappearing.

Sam chuckled even as his guys called out that his gun was ready to fire. He looked to his gunner, who was adjusting to sight on the monster. The moment he saw the thumb go up, Sam fired.

This time his round blasted into the thing's side, where a human kidney would normally be. Sam saw a spray of black blood behind the monster as the round exited its back. A quick glance over at the Humvee showed Allistor getting to his feet and reaching into the driver's seat. He hoped that meant Helen still lived as well.

*****

Allistor was about to lift Helen out of the driver's seat when he changed his mind. Reaching for the gear

390

shift, he put the Humvee in neutral and took hold of the ignition key, he turned it to the off position, then cranked it. After some sputtering, the engine came to life. It didn't sound good, but it was running. A quick glance told him the vehicle had at least one flat tire, and possibly a bent or broken axle. It didn't matter – they were never going to get back into the fight walking.

As gently as he could, he lifted Helen and moved her over to the passenger's seat. Then he climbed in and put the truck in gear. It lurched forward, two flat tires thumping as something metal under the hood squealed. The ride was rough, but not as bad as it would be if he had to carry Helen and try to catch up with the monster.

The Humvee thumped and bumped and squealed its way down the runway, at its best speed of maybe twenty miles per hour. He couldn't tell exactly because the speedometer was shattered. He kept his focus on the Xar' Dakra as they inched closer to his back.

> *Xar' Dakra*
> *Void Titan Elite*
> *Level 30*
> *Health: 90,750/187,000*

The elite monster was below half health. Allistor had to assume it was because of the hits it took from the big guns. He could see the two batteries sitting side by side in the middle of the open gate. Even as he approached the titan from behind, one of the guns fired again. The round clipped the titan's leg, the glancing blow still enough to

391

shatter bone. Allistor gasped as the round ploughed up the dirt not thirty feet to his left.

Xar' Dakra roared, "*Eaaat yourrr soulsss!*" and pointed toward the gate, identifying the source of his pain.

The second gun fired, and this time the round impacted someplace more solid. Based on the titan's step backward, Allistor thought maybe it was the chest. No round came out the back like before, and he was sure he heard the giant wheeze after the impact.

While it was distracted, he drove up as close behind it as he could. His plasma rifle was on the floor someplace, but Allistor was now within range to use magic. He cast *Mind Spike* at the titan, but it appeared to fail completely. There was no reaction at all as it recovered its balance and started forward again.

Following behind, Allistor focused on his *Erupt* spell. Rather than cast it outright, he tried to imitate what he did with *Flame Shot*, building up the spell with more and more power before launching it. It seemed to be working, and he increased the juice he put into it for a full ten seconds before focusing on the ground where the thing was about to step.

He released *Erupt* with all the spirit and focus he could muster behind his intent. A stone spike the size of a Christmas tree burst from the ground just in time for Xar' Dakra to put his full weight down upon it. As big as it was, it barely penetrated all the way through the foot, with just the very tip protruding from the top and making black blood well out around it.

Xar' Dakra screamed, the sound threatening to shatter the wall ahead of him even as people along the top of it covered their ears and wailed at the pain. The titan gingerly stepped forward with its unimpaled foot, then tried to lift the one with the spike in it. The spike held just long enough to throw him off balance. He fell forward, both hands and one knee hitting the ground.

While it was down, Allistor used the last of his mana to hit its eyes with a built-up *Flame Shot*, only to be disappointed when the flames struck, but appeared to do it no harm. In fact, Xar' Dakra managed to get back to his feet, snap the stone spike, and continue toward the Citadel, still not noticing Allistor in the Humvee. It wheezed again as its torso expanded, and a light of hope bloomed inside Allistor.

Not having taken time to grab a radio, he had no way to communicate with his people up on the wall. Which made him feel foolish. He stopped the truck for a moment and located his plasma rifle. The brand-new weapon was scratched and slightly dented from the Humvee's roll, but, as far as he could tell, it was still functional. It was the only thing left in his arsenal, other than his sniper rifle, that could hurt the thing. He was ready to sacrifice himself to slow the thing down long enough for Sam and George to get in a few more shots.

Xar' Dakra had left the airport behind and was now limping toward the first switchback leading up to the gate. Being eighty feet tall, he didn't need to follow the road. He simply stepped upward with his good leg, pulling himself up one level like it was a set of stairs.

The moment he did, both guns fired. The dual impacts knocked the titan off balance, and it was forced to step back down, arms waving for balance, to keep from falling. When it stepped back with its weakened leg, the remaining bones snapped and the leg gave way. Xar' Dakra tumbled backward, landing with a tremendous thud and raising a dust cloud with the impact.

Seeing his chance, Allistor pushed the Humvee as fast as it would go. Which was still painfully slow as he drove past the prone monster, steering with one hand and firing his plasma rifle with the other. He got up the first ramp and was working his way up the second when Xar' Dakra began to move. The monster sat up, bending forward at the waist and trying to grab the Humvee moving above. Allistor leaned forward against the steering wheel, trying to use body english to make it move faster. He was saved by a hail of plasma rounds falling onto the thing's head from atop the wall.

Making the next turn, he had to slam on the brakes as McCoy and three other men jumped in front of the Humvee with the arms raised. "Stop! We just set up some mines!"

They rushed to the Humvee, McCoy helped Allistor out and began to lead him up the slope along one side as the others grabbed Helen and lifted her. A quick glance told them there was nothing they could do for Nathan, and they worked together to carry Helen up the slope. Both teams avoided the traps they'd just set, moving as quickly as they could. People on the wall shouted encouragement as, behind them, Xar' Dakra was pushing himself up and beginning to crawl after them.

*"**Noooooo! Dieee!**"* he wheezed as he clawed great gouges in the earth, collapsing the bank of the slope below them. When the abandoned Humvee rolled down the bank toward him, he snatched it up and hurled it toward the wall. The shouting turned to screams as the armored vehicle struck the top of the wall, crushing several people before exploding, flaming gas billowing out to burn many more, both atop the wall and down below.

Another Howitzer round struck him in the shoulder, pushing him back and snapping bone. More plasma rounds rained down on him. The repulsive smell of burning titan blood wafted up the hill, making everyone nauseous, even as they fled for their lives.

One of McCoy's airmen, whose name Allistor couldn't remember, popped up as they cleared the next level, reaching the last upward ramp before the gate. He had an RPG launcher on his shoulder, and winked at Allistor as they limped past. As soon as everyone had cleared his line of fire, he pushed the trigger.

The rocket shot forward at nearly point-blank range, flying directly into the open mouth of the crawling titan. Striking the back of its throat and detonating, it blew massive chunks of tissue and teeth outward. The airman who'd fired the shot was peppered with nasty ichor and bone shrapnel. He fell backward with a cry of pain.

McCoy abandoned Allistor, pushing him upward toward the gate before he turned and ran down to retrieve his comrade. Allistor quickly checked his mana, seeing that enough had regenerated for him to help. He cast *Levitate* on the injured man, and McCoy was able to easily drag him back up the slope. Allistor turned and tried to keep up with the others, still a little unsteady from getting his head bashed around. McCoy caught up to him and helped both men into the gate.

A moment later, several explosions went off as Xar' Dakra reached the claymores. There were muted cheers from the wall as the entire place rocked with the combined explosions. Allistor could see Sam and his guys rushing to reload the big guns, even as he heard more plasma rounds being fired above.

Exhausted, wounded, and out of mana, Allistor put his back to the inside of the wall to one side of the gates and slid to the ground. His people had already set Helen down there, along with a few dozen of his people wounded by the Humvee, and both Amanda and Nancy were tending to them as Dawn stood guard, watching the open gate like a hawk. With a groan, Allistor produced and gulped down a mana potion. He cast heals on each of his people, one after another down the line until he ran out of mana again.

Sam's crew was first to be ready, but they waited for George's crew. When both were set to fire, Sam called out, "Hooooold... wait for it to look right at us... FIRE!"

The guns both rocked backward as the kinetic rounds raced out of their barrels. Allistor couldn't see where they hit, but a moment later he and everyone else in the Citadel leveled up. There were cheers from up on the wall, down by the gate, and especially up on the tower where Allistor heard Dean yelling, "Yeeeeehaw!" and saw him waving his hat.

Allistor's interface was flooded with messages, but he didn't care. He simply closed his eyes and leaned his head back.

Chapter 17

Aftermath

When Allistor opened his eyes, he found Chloe standing in front of him. Her head was tilted to one side, her arms crossed. Fuzzy sat next to her, looking from Allistor to the little girl and back again. He had his Fibble doll in his mouth, and it was covered in crumbs that Allistor suspected used to be cookies.

"Hi there, Chloe. When did you get here?"

"Just a little while ago. Mom had Nigel ask us to bring a bunch of herbs for her to make potions. You've been asleep for a while. And you look like shit."

Fuzzy's eyes widened as he looked at the girl, who covered her mouth and giggled, looking over both shoulders to see if her mother was nearby.

Allistor snorted. "Thanks. That's about how I feel, too. I don't know if they told you, but that big void titan punted us like a football."

Chloe's face grew sad. "Yeah, they told us. It killed Nathan. And a bunch of others. This was a bad one, huh?"

Allistor nodded, motioning for her to come closer. He gathered her into his lap and hugged her. She made a face at the smell, but relented. "Yeah, this was a bad one. But we're still here. And even though we lost some good people, we'll remember them and what they did to help the rest of us stay alive."

Chloe just nodded. Looking around, Allistor counted eleven covered bodies laid out farther down the wall. He assumed there were at least a few more that weren't recoverable. After a deep, calming breath, he looked back at Chloe.

"So, you should be proud of me!" He poked at her belly, causing her to squirm.

"For what?"

"I didn't let that thing bite me! Not even once!"

She rolled her eyes at him. "But you let it kick your ass. Like, actually kick you. Hard."

"Well, you didn't say anything about not letting monsters kick me. Only bite me. You mean now I have to keep them from kicking me, too?"

She leapt up out of his lap and turned to face him, hands on her hips. "Yes! Kicking, biting, scratching, shooting, umm... stomping!" She paused to sniff at him. "And pooping! No more letting them poop on you!"

Without another word, she turned and stomped away. Fuzzy watched her go for a moment, gave Allistor a sniff from a safe distance, then shook his head and followed the little girl.

"Traitor!" Allistor called out before sniffing himself. "On the other hand, I don't blame you." He leaned forward and pulled off his shirt, which had absorbed the majority of the titan blood that had splattered him.

Leaning back again, he pulled up his notifications. He'd received a huge amount of experience and Fame Points. There was experience for killing the titan,

399

experience for defending the Citadel, even more experience in the form of a bonus for defeating an elite monster twice his level. All of it combined had raised him up to level twenty! He felt elated for a moment, until he looked over at the bodies nearby and remembered the price.

As he looked around, he saw that thousands of his people had responded to his call. Some only just arriving as the fight ended, as there were limits to how many could teleport at one time. But based on the vacant stares he saw, even those who arrived before Xar' Dakra died, but hadn't made it up onto the wall to fire a shot, still leveled up. He'd ask Nigel about it later.

Getting to his feet, he walked over to where Sam and the others were cleaning up spent shells and preparing to retire the big guns. Allistor called out, "Great job guys! You saved us all, no question. And especially me! If you hadn't fired when you did, I'd be a pancake right now. So thank you."

He held out a hand to Sam, who sniffed conspicuously in his direction, made a face, and declined. "You're welcome, boy. I'll shake your hand after you've had a shower. No offense, but you reek." The others all chuckled, giving him thumbs up or salutes from a few steps back.

With a sigh, he lowered his hand and said, "I take it back. You guys suck. I'm gonna go loot this beast, and I suggest you join me. Gotta be some epic drops for a level 30 elite."

He turned and walked out the gate, the gun crews and the folks who'd come down from the walls to loot all giving him a wide berth. He was almost glad they could only smell the monster blood and not the load in his pants. As he was walking toward the corpse, he muttered to himself, "Too bad we don't have cameras anymore. This would make one hell of a group photo."

Approaching the monster, he saw that both of the final Howitzer rounds had slammed into its face. The once terrifying visage was now a mostly pulped mass of shattered bone, torn flesh, broken bits of teeth, and the black ichor. Not bothering to hold his breath as some of the others were doing, he reached out and touched a clean spot on its shoulder.

Immediately his entire interface was packed with loot notifications. He received ten thousand klax, twenty vials of the stinky blood, one of the eyes, one of its claws, a stack of void titan hide, and not just one, but *three* purple glowing items. The first was a scroll, which he set aside. The second was a bow. It was jet-black in color, with a string that glowed the same blue as Xar' Dakra's skin. It came with a quiver made of its actual skin, that also glowed purple and was filled with two dozen black arrows.

> *Titan Bow*
> *Item Quality: Epic*
> *Attributes: Stamina +3, Strength +3, Agility +2, Dexterity +2*
> *This bow was fashioned from the bone and sinew of Xar' Dakra, a void titan elite. Lightweight yet strong, the weapon is nearly indestructible. The sinew bowstring is immune to all but fire damage. The quiver made of the titan's hide adds +2 to user's armor, and +2 to magic resistance. Each of the black arrows in the quiver are fashioned from shards of the titan's long bones, and tipped with*

fragments of its teeth. The arrows will not shatter on impact, and can be re-used indefinitely. This item is bound to Earl Allistor.

Allistor took a moment to admire the bow, then put it away. He unrolled the scroll to find it was a letter with a scroll wrapped inside it. He read the letter first.

Earl Allistor,

My congratulations! If you are reading this, you have defeated the Elite Xar' Dakra. That is no small feat for a being only partway through their Stabilization period. Your victory is a credit to your strength, adaptability, and leadership. As a reward, I have enclosed a spell scroll I am sure you will find helpful in your future endeavors.

Know that we are watching you, and that we are impressed with your achievements. Your ruthless pursuit of justice, the killing of fellow humans despite your belief in the value of all human life, and willingness to do what must be done have served you well. We look forward to your future adventures.

-An Admirer

Allistor gripped the parchment and gritted his teeth, his face turning red. He wanted to tear the letter to shreds, then the scroll that came with it. The anger surged through him as he pictured some alien overlord watching him on a holoscreen and laughing as he was forced to take human lives.

Amanda came and put a hand on his back, leaning in to whisper. "I don't know what has set you off, but people are watching."

Allistor glanced around, seeing hundreds of people with their eyes on him as they moved forward to loot the monster, then retreated. He decided it wouldn't hurt to motivate them a little bit as well.

"Nigel, loudspeaker please, in every facility."

"Go ahead, Lord Allistor."

"For everyone who hasn't already heard, we've achieved a great victory today! A level thirty, elite void titan attacked the Citadel, and we managed to kill it. We paid a heavy price, though. A dozen of our own people won't be returning to their homes tonight."

He paused to take a couple deep breaths. "When I looted the monster, I received the following letter from, I have to assume, one of the aliens who stole our world and brought it here. This is what it says."

He read them the entire letter, word for word, his voice thick with emotion and anger. When he was done, there was nothing but silence from the crowd around him. He held the letter in the air, the parchment flapping in the breeze.

"*THIS* is why I'm pushing all of you so hard. We're nothing but NPCs to these alien bastards. Game pieces that they throw monsters at to see what happens. Trained monkeys to amuse them as they sit with their feet up eating popcorn!" There was some angry grumbling among the crowd.

"We lost good people today! Fellow survivors who just wanted to live their lives in the best way left to us. Humans willing to stand on a wall and put their lives on the line for you and me. Who ultimately paid with their lives so that we might live on. I don't know about you, but as soon as I can, I'm gonna take the fight to these bastards! I'm gonna make them pay for the twelve lives they so carelessly took from us today. And the millions or billions they've taken since the apocalypse!"

The crowd erupted in a roar of approval. Guns were thrust into the air, and all around him feet began to stomp in a slow, steady cadence.

"*YOU* are our future! You are the best hope of the human race! Every one of you are my brothers and sisters in this new world of ours. I have pledged my own life to protect yours-"

George cut him off there, shouting, "Yeah and ya damned near accomplished that today, ya crazy fool!" to which the crowd cheered in agreement. Most had seen Allistor and the others charge toward the monster to distract it. And seen the Humvee get punted.

Allistor grimaced, blushing slightly. "Okay, maybe that wasn't the wisest move. But we needed time for our reinforcements to reach us. My foolish act got Nathan killed, and I will bear that burden to the end of my days. But even had I known the outcome, I would have done the same. Three lives to protect thousands isn't even a close call. If that thing had reached here, it would have killed hundreds, if not thousands, and destroyed our home. Just like the first one we fought destroyed my entire hometown."

The people around him were silent, some looking at him, others gazing at the dead giant, or the broken and burnt section atop the wall.

"Alright. Those of you who wish to stay and pay your respects, we'll hold a ceremony for those we lost after dark. You're welcome to stay and eat, heal up, maybe get some equipment or scrolls while you're here. Those of you who are needed back at your own home bases, thank you all for coming to help us. And know that we'll be there for you when you need us."

Allistor left them, crossing back inside the gate and glancing over to see that Helen was awake. Tears streamed down her face as Nancy sat holding her hand. Amanda moved to join them, and Allistor started to follow, but Amanda stopped him with a shake of her head. "Give her some time."

He just nodded, gave Helen a sad smile when she noticed him, then turned away to go hit the shower.

*****

Freshly cleaned and wearing new clothes, he took a moment to look at the scroll that was included in the letter.

Scroll of Titan Summoning
Item Quality: Extremely Rare
This scroll teaches the user the ability to summon a Titan from the void. The summoned titan will be soulbound to the summoner, and unable to harm the spellcaster or their allies unless ordered to do so by its master. Size, strength, and level of the titan summoned is determined by the level, attributes,

405

*and ability of the summoner. Minimum spell
requirements: Level 25; Intelligence of 20 or
higher. Will Power of 20 or higher. Spell cost:
2,000 mana. Cooldown: 24 hours. This scroll is
bound to the soul of Earl Allistor.*

Allistor put the scroll back into his ring. He didn't
have the level or stats to be able to use it yet. And he
wanted Ramon to do some serious research into the rules of
summoning before he even attempted to use it. He had
zero trust in the entity that had awarded him the scroll. In
fact, as he'd been showering, the thought struck him that
since the titan was carrying the letter and scroll, there was a
strong chance that the letter's writer was the one who sent
the monster.

Dressed in a pair of jeans and a T-shirt, he took his
badly torn and soggy leather armor down to Lilly, who was
working out of her own shop at the Citadel. He'd tried his
best to wash away all the titan blood stench while he'd
been in the shower, but Lilly still made a face when he
handed it to her. That changed a moment later when he
also handed her the stack of titan hide and bits of tooth and
claw.

"I can make you some even better armor with
these!" She was getting excited as she pulled, poked, and
bit the material. He offered her the eye that he'd been
given as well, but she threatened to poke him with sharp
needles if he didn't get it out of her shop. He took the hint
and left. Spotting Nancy in the food court area, he offered
her the eyeball and the bottles of blood. She took them,
saying she had no idea what they might be good for, but
she'd keep them for later or find someone who could make

use of them. He was just happy to get them out of his inventory.

When he got back outside, some people had hitched chains to the twisted and burned husk of the Humvee to pull it from the courtyard over to the motor pool. They had some mechanics in their group, and Allistor hoped they could rebuild it. Though, he wasn't sure he'd ever want to ride in it again. Maybe it would be better just to salvage the parts for repairs on their other Humvees.

He walked around, talking to his people, hearing their perspectives of the fight, and how many levels they'd earned. A few of them spoke about friends who'd been killed, or the families they left behind. Allistor reminded himself to make sure those families were compensated. He'd put Chris on it right away.

As the sun began to set, the food court area filled up, then overflowed with people who'd stayed to pay their respects to the fallen. Logs were dragged in and pickups pushed closer to the building for people to sit on. More wood was stacked in a funeral pyre with the bodies laid on top. When everyone had eaten and the sun was below the horizon, Allistor spoke to the crowd. Once again, he had Nigel transmit it to all his people.

"Tonight we honor those who perished fighting for all of us. We remember them for who they were, and grieve for the people they might have become. I know many of you here knew them better than I did, much to my regret. Please, come up here and tell us about them." He waved at one of the women who'd been close to a man on the wall.

For more than an hour, person after person stood up to tell a story about one of the lost. Sometimes it was a funny story, other times one of strength, or courage. All of it was heard by every human survivor among Allistor's people.

The last to speak was Helen. She had tears streaming down her face as she began to speak. "Nathan and I had been... dating for a few months now. I'm not a good one for relationships, and I always kept him at a distance. I shouldn't have done that. I should have told him how I felt about him every day. I know he... I know he loved me. And I think I loved him too. He was strong, and funny, and he danced like a drunken monkey with its pants on fire." She paused, a small smile forming for just a moment.

"He was a good man, and I miss him. I hope he's found peace, a good horse, and open prairie wherever he is now." Everyone was silent as Helen sat back down. Nancy and Amanda hugged her from either side.

Unable to speak after that, Allistor simply called down a *Flame Shot* on the pyre. They all sat in silence, except for the sounds of weeping, as the bodies were reduced to ash. Slowly, the crowd drifted apart, a few at a time. Small groups remained to share more stories or support those who'd lost friends. A few kegs were tapped, and toasts were raised. A young man with shocking blue hair began to play a guitar and sing. Allistor remembered him as one of the Laramie survivors he'd interviewed months before. He remembered the man's name was Scottie, that he liked peanut butter and banana sandwiches "just like Elvis", and he fancied himself a bard. At the time, Allistor had laughed. But a bard seemed to be exactly

408

what people needed at the moment. The man sang a mixture of sad songs, lively songs, and even composed a tribute to the fallen and their heroic deeds on the spot. He made a note to thank the man personally for his efforts.

Allistor eventually found himself face to face with Helen. She sat on one of the logs, staring down into a mug she held with both hands. Allistor sat next to her, wanting to put an arm around her but not daring. He tried twice to speak before his throat opened up enough to make sound.

"I'm so sorry." he began. "If I hadn't brought you two with me… God, Helen. I got him killed. And nearly got you killed too. I'm so sorry." His voice broke and his shoulders shook as he sobbed quietly next to the woman who was probably his best friend in the world. All the guilt for Nathan's death, and all the others from the first day till that moment, pressed down on him.

The two of them sat there in silence, inches apart but not touching each other. After a long while, Allistor got himself together, taking a few deep, cleansing breaths. Still, he didn't speak again. He was waiting for Helen to vent at him. To rage over her loss, to blame him.

"He went out exactly as he'd have wanted to." she whispered.

Allistor looked up at her, meeting her eyes. She went on. "I mean, he went quickly, and died fighting that big-ass monster. Did you hear how happy he was? I mean before the stink and the puking? When we were racing that thing, and he was shooting it in the nuts? If he was still here, he'd have said that was the best time of his life."

Allistor couldn't help but smile slightly as he recalled the man whooping and laughing as he fired on the titan, or yelling for Helen to go faster.

"Yeah." was all he could manage. Then he said, "I didn't know you two were so serious. It wasn't that long ago I thought you were going to push him off on Dawn."

Helen grunted. "I was, too. I mean I was ready to dump him at least a dozen times. But he always did something that made me want to keep him around a little longer. Stupid things. He named his damn horse after me, thinking it was some kind of big compliment. I didn't have the heart to tell him otherwise. That was just Nathan. He lived his life by the seat of his pants, never worried much about anything. I don't think the man ever told a lie in his life. He just didn't see the point." she sighed, leaning into Allistor.

"I don't blame you. I know you think I do. And I know you blame yourself. It was just fate that we found you just as you were charging out there to be a hero. And to be honest, if you hadn't asked us, I'd have made you take us along. It was the right thing to do, Allistor."

He echoed her lean, pushing his shoulder against hers. "Would it be totally awkward if I hugged you right now? Cuz I'd really like to hug you."

She shook her head, and he wrapped his arms around her, squeezing tightly. They stayed that way for a few minutes, neither of them speaking. When he finally let her go, they both had tears in their eyes again. Needing to change the mood, he said, "So I was thinking it's time to go out and do some more exploring. You told me once about that place... Savage Run? Maybe stop there and take Fuzzy fishing. Any chance you'd like to join us?"

As if summoned, Fuzzy came lumbering out from behind a truck. He padded toward them, sitting a few feet away and sniffing. When he decided it was safe, he stepped forward and placed his head directly in Helen's lap, demanding ear-scratches with a huff. She absently complied, not really even looking at him as Allistor spoke. "Seems Fuzzy is up for it. We can take a *Juggernaut*, it can handle rough terrain."

Helen nodded, only half listening. Her gaze was unfocused, and he thought she was probably remembering something. Eventually, she spoke. "I know a good spot to build an Outpost there. It's up on a bluff, overlooking the lake. Mountains all around, and the passes are blocked by snow for a good part of the year. It would make a good retreat, a place for our people to do a little R&R. Plenty of fish in the lake, woods to hike through. They can even pan for gold in the feeder streams. There's a pavilion atop the bluff now, and campers used to set up around it during tourist season."

"Sounds perfect. How 'bout we leave in the morning?"

Helen nodded and gave Fuzzy a hug just as the teleporter flashed. Bjurstrom and his group emerged, looking dirty and disheveled, armor and clothing torn. The man trotted over to Allistor, taking in the somber mood of the crowd and the ash of the funeral pyre.

"What'd I miss?"

Chapter 18

The Wilderness Is Full Of Murder Chickens

Amanda elected not to join them on their trip into Medicine Bow National Park. She gave an excuse about wanting to study those who'd been injured in the monster fight, and those injured among Bjurstrom's noob dungeon runners. Allistor suspected she was just giving Helen and himself time and space to work out any awkwardness between them.

The three of them had an early breakfast in the dining area, where Fuzzy managed to mooch a good bit of sausage, bacon, and fruit slices from the cowboys and early risers who were having their own breakfasts. Each of the cowboys made a point of stopping to put a hand on Helen's shoulder or give her a hug and speak a few words. The more she heard about how Nathan had spoken of her all the time, and how much he'd cared for her, the more silent tears flowed down her face. Fuzzy even abandoned his quest for bacon to sit next to her and put his head on her lap.

They escaped the crowds eventually, loading up supplies and grabbing one of the *Juggernauts*. After a final check-in with Andrea and Dean, Helen drove them out the gates of the Citadel and headed west. The area in question was toward the west side of the Medicine Bow National Forest, part of Helen's old territory as a ranger. She knew all the trails and back roads. From Cheyenne they took the route Allistor's people had established to Laramie, clearing cars and other debris to make the trip faster and safer.   A quick stop at the Stadium to check on folks there, and they were on their way again.

Medicine Bow was actually several forests in different locations combined into one National Park. The section they were looking for was almost directly west of Laramie, in an area of deep forest and plateaus. Helen used the *Juggernaut*'s hover ability several times to cross creeks filled with fish after weaving through narrow trails in old growth forest. After the second creek, Fuzzy's nose remained stuck out of one of the windows, and he complained so much that they stopped at the next one.

The moment Allistor opened one of the side doors, Fuzzy was out like a shot. He bounded down the bank and leapt far out into the creek, executing a nearly perfect bear cub cannonball.

Puffing out his chest, Allistor grinned at Helen. "I taught him that!"

Helen, ever the ranger, had her shotgun in hand and was scanning the area on both sides of the creek even as she laughed at the bear's antics. Fuzzy dunked his head under the water and came up with a fish, proudly slogging back to the bank to plop down and consume it.

"We might as well do a little fishing while we're here." Helen said, putting away her weapon and pulling a pole, tackle box, and net from her inventory. "There are some tasty brook trout in here. We can cook some up for dinner, maybe smoke some for later."

Allistor followed her lead, grabbing his pole and approaching the bank. It was steep enough that the humans could lean back comfortably and enjoy the sunshine as they

413

waited for hits. Which didn't take long. Allistor was first this time, pulling in a feisty little fish that weighed maybe two pounds. Helen's first one was slightly smaller. These weren't the monster lake trout they'd caught before. Each one was just a mouthful or two for Fuzzy, or would make a decent meal for a person.

Fuzzy finished his first snack and strolled back into the water. After standing still for a moment, he lashed out with a clawed forepaw and scooped another fish right out of the water. Taking it in his mouth, he flung it up onto the bank, then reset and waited for another one.

"Lazy old bear!" Helen called out to him. Turning to Allistor she said, "Watch, he'll make a pile of them before he drags his overweight butt out of the water to eat them."

Fuzzy didn't disappoint, stacking up half a dozen fish before plopping down on his rump and sitting upright like a human on the creek bank. He daintily snagged a fish with one claw, brought it up to hold between his paws, and gnawed the head off it. Allistor couldn't help but laugh. His bear looked almost like an oversized raccoon eating its meal.

"There will be much bigger fish in the lake, I'm sure. Well, it's more like a glorified beaver pond. But there are fish that have lived in there for years, maybe decades. They've had months now to eat these smaller fish and get bigger. Still, these will do just fine for dinner." Helen held up her third catch. It was about the length of her arm from fingertips to elbow.

When Fuzzy had consumed a couple dozen fish, and the humans had each landed a dozen or so, they packed up and got ready to go. Fuzzy shook himself, then rolled around in the tall grass a bit to dry off. When he got back into the vehicle, he plopped down on the bench seat, gently retrieved the Fibble he'd left there, and closed his eyes.

Back on the move, Helen expertly guided them through the forest. They spotted a bull moose that stood easily eight feet tall at the shoulders, with a set of horns that must have weighed a ton. Helen paused the nearly silent vehicle, and they watched it move through the brush, stepping over smaller bushes and simply pushing through the larger scrub trees. Just out of curiosity, he *Examined* it.

> **Bull Moose Alpha**
> **Level 11**
> **Health: 6,100/6,100**

"Wow, level eleven. Can animals level up from eating plants? Or has this thing been killing other animals?" Allistor asked Helen.

"Moose generally don't attack, unless threatened, or mating. It's possible he killed a rival moose. Or maybe fought off some wolves or canids or something? Defending itself or its herd." She paused to check the surrounding brush. Not seeing anything, she made a disappointed face. "The newborns should be coming about this time." Helen whispered as the massive alpha male strode past. "They're so cute with their gangly legs and little round snouts."

Allistor just smiled to himself, watching his friend enjoy herself in her element. For the first time in a long time, he was content to just sit back and enjoy nature for a few days. His people could take care of themselves, barring another elite monster attack.

When the bull had moved on, Helen continued up a gradual rise thick with pine trees and brush. Allistor was just closing his eyes to join Fuzzy in a nap when they emerged onto a mostly open plateau. "This is it! We're here." Helen stopped the vehicle.

Allistor leaned forward, scanning the area. He looked at Helen and raised one eyebrow, not overly impressed with her chosen location. The pavilion was there, as she had described it. A long, pitched roof sitting atop two rows of eight columns each. There were ten long picnic tables and benches set up underneath, easily room enough for a hundred people to sit and eat. Allistor doubted there had ever been that many there at one time. The rest was just mostly open grass with scattered trees, scrub brush, and bbq stands. While it was pleasant enough, he didn't see the allure.

"Just wait." Helen got out of the vehicle and began to walk toward the structure. Allistor followed, while Fuzzy snored contentedly in the back. As he got closer to the pavilion, he saw that they were indeed on a high plateau, and that about twenty feet beyond the structure the ground dropped off. Nearing the edge, he whistled.

Below them was Helen's beaver pond. A section of the flowing creek that had widened into a small lake filled with crystalline water. It dropped off in a small waterfall at one end, the pleasant burbling sound reaching them atop the plateau. Beyond the water were rolling hills covered in ancient trees that grew in size the farther away they got.

And in the far background were snow-capped mountain peaks.

He walked right to the edge, standing on a bedrock outcropping and looking straight down. The fall was about a hundred fifty feet to the narrow, pebbled shore of the lake where it butted up against the bluff.

Helen elbowed him, causing him to lose his balance slightly and sending a surge of adrenaline through him. She steadied his arm, and snickered.

"The only approach is the way we came up. Steep walls on the other three sides, all sheer climbs. You could put a wall across the incline, and this place would be hard to assault by land. And if we had to, we could throw fishing lines or nets on long lines right over the edge here." She looked down, and pointed. "See that dark spot in the water? It's an underwater cave entrance. Some softer limestone down there, and the water has worn it away over millions of years. That hole goes down nearly sixty feet, and feeds into a whole cave system. So, if you ever get the urge to jump from up here, aim for that dark spot."

Allistor bent to pick up a pebble, tossing it over the edge. He watched it arc out over the water and plunge below the surface, sending out a ring of ripples that only lasted for a short while before the gentle current pushed them away.

"Okay, you were right. This place is beautiful. Perfect place to come and relax. But I think you're wrong about the Outpost."

When Helen looked sideways at him, opening her mouth with a question already on her face, he added, "I think we should put a full Stronghold here. As you said, it's a defensible position, plenty of fish and wildlife to hunt. Deep inside our territory, and secluded enough that nobody's going to just stumble across it. The tall trees on the rise would hide it from any ground scouts. And who's going to be flying around way out here?"

Helen poked him in the ribs. "We can put one of your teleport pads here, and make this a fallback position for our people if they need it. Until then, it can be our vacation resort!"

Allistor agreed. But he didn't set up the Stronghold right away. Something inside him didn't want to disturb the natural beauty of the place just yet.

"Let's camp here tonight. We can move some of the tables and park under the pavilion. Sleep in the *Juggernaut* where it's safe. Maybe spend a couple days here. Then I'll build the Stronghold."

Fuzzy woke up as they were moving tables around. He got out and gave everything a good sniff, whining slightly as he peered over the edge at the water below. Backing up, he moved off into the trees to take care of some bear business.

When the *Juggernaut* was parked, Helen and Allistor used one of the tables they'd moved outside to clean the fish, leaving a pile of heads and guts for Fuzzy. Allistor gathered firewood while Helen pulled some seasonings from her ring and prepared the fish. Using one of the dozen or so grills set on poles around the pavilion, they cooked about half the fish. While the meal was cooking, Helen showed Allistor how to weave and bind some small, flexible branches into a sort of cage, then

418

weave in even smaller ones until she had a semi-airtight smoker, which she hung high over the fire from a tripod of larger branches. She laid out the rest of the fish inside, and stoked the fire with some slow-burning hardwood that Allistor thought was probably hickory branches. The smoke from the fire increased, drifting up into the bottom of the smoker cage and staying there for a while before leaking out between the sticks.

The smell was incredible, and Allistor's mouth was watering by the time their meal was ready. He burned his fingers tearing into the tender fish to pull it off the skin. Twice they had to stop Fuzzy from pulling down the smoker and eating the fish inside.

Having eaten two fish, Allistor's stomach was full, and he tossed a third one to Fuzzy after making sure it had cooled enough. He was sitting on the grass, his back against a log that had been laid out for sitting. "Ahhh, that was amazing. Thank you, Helen. Can you teach me how to cook these tomorrow?"

"Sure! It's not complicated. Probably won't even level your cooking skill. But it's a good, simple recipe using readily available seasonings. Handy one to know when you're living near the water."

Allistor only heard half of her reply, already drifting off to sleep. Helen let him nap as she stowed the rest of the cooked fish in her ring, and watched the smoker do its thing as she relaxed and let her thoughts drift. She was half asleep herself when Fuzzy began to growl.

She was on her feet a moment later when she detected a rustling of leaves beyond the tree line. It was getting dark, the sun having already fallen behind the peaks to the west. The fire in front of her was still burning bright enough to impair her night vision when trying to look into the darkness. She cast *Light* and pushed the globe down the slope toward the trees.

"Allistor, get up. We've got company." She nudged him with her foot as she spoke. He too was instantly on his feet as Fuzzy stood and bared his teeth in the direction of the trees. He let out his best bear cub roar and stepped forward, hackles bristling.

Several deep growls answered him, echoing from out of the darkness up the slope. Fuzzy took a step back, his tail lowering and his head shifting left and right, less sure of himself now that it was clear he faced several foes.

"Don't worry, buddy. We got this." Allistor was confident they could handle a pack of canids. At their levels, most animals in the forest would be no real challenge.

But what walked out of the trees into the light weren't canids.

They looked like chickens. Or, more likely, the dinosaur version of what chickens used to be. Each one stood a good eight feet tall, with grey-green reptilian skin in place of chicken feathers. Their wings looked vestigial, the folded flaps of leathery skin too small to support their large bodies in flight. Red eyes were set wide on their heads behind sharp ebony beaks, large enough to sever a human limb with ease. Helen *Examined* the closest.

> ***Kylling Hunter***
> ***Level 17***
> ***Health: 9,000/9,000***

"Are you kidding me? Giant murder chickens?" Allistor grumbled as another, and another, stepped into view. He could already see five of them, and more seemed to be moving in the dark beneath the trees.

Helen snorted. "Regular chickens are murderous little shits. People just don't notice cuz we're so much bigger. They don't often attack us."

The nearest one took another step forward on its oversized chicken feet, the three wicked front claws reflecting the light briefly before digging into the ground. Its growl was completely unchickenlike, sounding more like a wolf or bear. Altogether, Allistor estimated the thing weighed about two hundred and fifty pounds.

"The smell of the cooking fish must have drawn them. Stay close to the fire." Helen said as she piled some wood on to it. "If they're anything like our chickens, they'll fear the flame."

"Let's find out." Allistor quickly cast *Flame Shot* on the frontrunner, the standard sized fireball racing forward to impact the creature's chest. It squawked in terror, sounding much more like a chicken now, and fell over backward, its feet scrabbling at the air as it burned. Without feathers, the fire didn't spread as Allistor had hoped, but it still did some damage and slowed the mob's approach. The other kyllings hesitated, looking at their packmate. But the surprise didn't last. As it got back to its feet, they all began to move forward slowly, stalking their prey."

421

"I'm not gonna get eaten by giant dino-chickens."
Helen gritted her teeth. Raising her shotgun, she took aim
and fired at the wounded kylling. The buckshot round tore
into its head and neck, causing blood to spout and knocking
it down again.

Kylling Hunter
Level 17
Health: 4,200/9,000

Allistor fired as well, his shotgun loaded with slugs.
He aimed for the downed murder chicken's chest, and the
round punched right through. The reptilian hide didn't
seem to give them much in the way of armor protection.

As if his shot had been a starting pistol, the four
others charged forward at surprising speed. They moved in
a rough line, fanning out so that they formed a sort of half
circle around their prey. Three more kyllings emerged
from the trees to join the formation. All seven of them
closed rapidly.

"Oh, shit!" Allistor shouted, firing at two on the left
flank, knocking down first one, then the other. Fuzzy
rushed forward and latched onto the neck of the first to fall,
shaking his head savagely and snapping its spine. The
other pecked at the bear cub even as it struggled back to its
feet. The nasty beak opened wide wounds in the bear cub's
side. Allistor took a second to cast a heal on his bear cub,
then fired again at the monster attacking him. "Leave
Fuzzy alone!"

Helen was calmly chambering and firing round after
round. As they got closer, her buckshot was tearing into

more than one of the kyllings at a time. But the shots weren't killing them, and they either fell and got back up, or simply stumbled and continued on.

Allistor panicked. Having nearly lost Helen so recently, he couldn't think of anything else as the monsters charged her. Each of them towered at least two feet above her, yet she held her ground. He cast *Barrier* in front of her, hoping to stop at least one stab from those nasty beaks.

One of the kyllings leapt at her, its clawed feet extended, intending to rip her to pieces. She raised her weapon and shot it directly in the face, removing most of its head. She ducked as the corpse tumbled past her, one of the claws catching her shoulder and spinning her around as it ripped into her flesh. She screamed and fell, and Allistor lost his mind.

He cast *Flame Shot* twice in rapid succession on two different targets. The screaming squawks distracted their companions for a second, giving him time to fire a round into the kylling nearest to Helen. The impact knocked it down, and from out of nowhere an enraged Fuzzy charged in. He stomped and clawed at the downed bird, pinning its legs with his bulk and trying to bite its neck even as it pecked at his head.

With three more of the birds closing on Helen, Allistor didn't have time to help the bear. He cast another heal on Fuzzy and turned away, hoping his cub could handle the fight.

Stepping over Helen, and placing himself between her and the advancing monsters, he cast *Erupt* in front of one. The spike shot up from the earth and impaled its breast on one side. The wound didn't kill it, but it did stop it in its tracks, causing a bird behind it to smash into it and fall over. He hit that one with *Flame Shot*, and left it to burn for a moment.

Turning to his right, he caught one charging in with its head down, intending to snap Helen's arm off as she attempted to push herself back to her feet. He cast *Mind Spike* on the bird, hoping its tiny chicken brain wasn't too small for the spell to have any effect.

The murder-chicken went berserk.

It roared in anger, its eyes flashing red as it used one clawed foot to dig at its own head. After doing some significant damage, it stopped clawing and charged at a fellow kylling, leaping at it claws first. The kylling that the berserker attacked was the same one Allistor had burned after it crashed into the shish-kabobbed bird. Confused at first, it quickly began to fight back. The two of them tumbled to the ground, biting and slashing each other.

Allistor reached down and helped Helen to her feet. She'd healed herself, and was almost back to one hundred percent. A quick look around showed him Fuzzy limping away from another dead bird. But the bear had paid an awful price. His face was a bloody pulp, and he bled from several ragged wounds in his neck and chest. Allistor and Helen both cast heals on the whimpering bear as he limped toward a picnic table and squeezed his bulk underneath to hide.

That was all Allistor had time to see as another of the birds dashed at him from his right. Changing tactics, he dropped his shotgun and reached into his inventory to pull out his trusty rebar spear. As the bird charged in, Helen fired a round of buckshot into its torso. It stumbled toward

424

them, and Allistor stepped forward. With a home run swing, he whipped the heavy rebar spear around and knocked the legs out from under the kylling, both of them snapping under the impact. When it struck the ground, he flipped the spear around and jammed the sharp end through its skull, pinning it to the ground as the broken legs and tiny wings twitched.

Allistor's chest heaved as he gulped down deep breaths. His head whipped back and forth, seeing only dead or dying murder chickens. The one he'd impaled on the spike was still struggling, until Helen stepped forward and blasted its head from its neck. The berserker chicken had been mauled by the one Allistor had just pinned to the ground, but wasn't quite dead. He jerked his spear free and slammed it through that one's skull as well.

He, Helen, and Fuzzy all leveled up, golden glows surrounding each of them. When they were sure there were no more of the kyllings in the woods, both of them went to check on Fuzzy. They had to coax the ferocious bear cub out from under the table, offering him bits of burnt chicken. As the traumatized bear gnawed on the crispy meat, the two humans looted all the mobs. They each received a total of three thousand klax, eight stacks of meat, several claws and beaks, four sets of eyes, and some kylling hide.

Helen sighed. "We need to dispose of these before they draw any more monsters. I've had enough for one day. But we shouldn't waste any of this. We're going to have enough murder chicken meat for a bbq at the Citadel." She grinned at him, producing her knife and proceeding to harvest the nearest corpse. Allistor pulled his own knife from inventory and got to work as well.

Fuzzy helped himself to the leftover scraps until his belly was full. Then they convinced him to help by dragging the unused bits over and dropping them off the cliff into the lake, where a feeding frenzy immediately began.

Helen made sure Allistor harvested the beaks and claws that weren't included in their loot, and as much of the hide as possible. And of course, the meat. When they were done, they had nearly a thousand pounds of meat in total.

It was fully dark by the time they finished harvesting the murder chickens and Helen had taken down the smoker. All three climbed into the *Juggernaut* and settled down. Allistor chose the driver's seat, which reclined to an almost-horizontal position and was comfortable enough to sleep in. Helen chose to curl up in the back, using Fuzzy as a pillow, the two of them quickly snoring. Allistor wished for about the hundredth time that they still had working video cameras to record the moment. Eventually, he too drifted off to sleep.

*****

Morning came sooner than Allistor expected. Fuzzy's full belly and gastrointestinal eccentricities eventually filled the vehicle with a stench so intolerable it woke the sleeping humans well before dawn. They evacuated the vehicle, loudly scolding the bear cub, who didn't even wake up.

Sitting on one of the tables as the *Juggernaut* aired out, Helen grumped. "I want coffee."

Allistor started to rise to restart the fire, but she gripped his arm and pulled him down. "The coffee and the coffee pot are in the truck."

Laughing, Allistor sat back down. "We should know better than to feed him so late in the day. Or let him sleep inside with us after eating a hundred pounds of chicken brains and guts."

Helen nodded. "He needed the protein. Both to replenish all the blood he lost, and because he leveled up and got bigger."

"Only thing I noticed him leveling up is his gas attacks." Allistor mumbled, making Helen smile.

"So, what do you want to do today?"

"Well, I was thinking just a nature day. Sit in the sun, do a little hiking, maybe some fishing. But now I'm thinking we should go ahead and set up the Stronghold and get back."

Helen looked at him for a long moment. She stared into his eyes as he did his best to look innocent. Finally, she smacked his shoulder. "You just want to go mess with Nancy!"

"You betcha!" He beamed. "How do you NOT want to? We've been giving her shit about fast-growing those baby chickens and bunnies since almost day one. And now we just fought a herd of giant, killer murder-chickens! No way I'm passing up this chance!"

Helen snort-laughed at his enthusiasm. It felt good to just be silly and childish for a few minutes. What better time than right after being chased from your bed by a bear cub with weaponized farts?

"I just hope we can find more of them. Maybe capture a few and start raising them. I mean… two hundred pound chickens can feed a lot of people." Helen winked at him.

"Heyyyy! We should *totally* do that! I mean, we have all this space, right? We could raise herds of dino-chickens right along with the elk and buffalo. And these things are big enough to ride! Imagine going into battle on murder-chicken mounts with… with lasers on their heads!" He paused for a minute, both of them belly-laughing.

"Let me build the Stronghold, then let's see if you can track them back to their nests or whatever. Maybe there are eggs?"

"Yup. Let's do that. And speaking of eggs… when was the last time you got an update on the dragon eggs?"

Allistor's expression changed from enthused to grumpy. "Amanda has been examining them every week. The dragons inside are growing, but very slowly. That first day when we killed their mom, she thought they were about eighty percent developed. After all these months, she says they're maybe eighty five percent now. She enlisted a guy named Daniel to help monitor them every day. He talks to the eggs. Like, has entire conversations with them. He has named them and everything. It's a little strange."

Helen nodded. "I was thinking maybe you should modify the design of the Strongholds a bit. Maybe add in a landing pad? Somewhere up high, like on a tower or connected to the walls or something."

"Landing pads for dragons?" Allistor's voice went wistful as he stared up at the sky, imagining patrols of dragons and riders landing.

"Well, sure. Maybe. But also for airships. Spaceships. Whatever."

"What? Oh, right. I see what you mean." Allistor abandoned his dragon fantasy. "Sure, we can do that. Hold on to your britches, here we go." He closed his eyes and pulled up his interface, selecting the Stronghold option. As always, the area around them became invisible, with the contour of the land underneath them laid out in a grid that showed dimensions as well as topography. Allistor placed the structure so that it pushed right up to the edge of the plateau on the steep sides, with the gate facing the gradual slope. He constructed a main building, high walls that stretched across the entire low side, and added the usual power, water, and sensors. He built a greenhouse, placed the fifth of his six teleport pads, then added several towers spaced around the outer edges. The tops of some of the towers he flattened to allow for ships, or dragons, to land.

When it was done, and the blinding light had faded, they were sitting on their table in the center of a wide dining area, the pavilion having remained inside the new walls. Fuzzy, awakened by the light, came sniffing around. He took in the new structure without much reaction, instead focusing on getting ear scratches from Helen.

"Oh, no you don't, Sir Fartsalot! I haven't forgiven you for the nasty wake-up this morning. I think I can still taste it in the back of my throat!" she scolded the cub, who was doing his best to look innocent. He gently placed his

Fibble doll in her lap, then nudged it with his nose as if offering to let her play with it.

"Oh, so your way of making up is offering me your dirty, slobber-soaked doll?" She looked down at him, doing her best to maintain a cross expression. When he sat back on his rump and huffed at her, his head tilted to one side as if confused by her lack of enthusiasm, she couldn't take it anymore. "Alright, ya big smelly teddy bear. Come here 'n' get some scratchin'. But the next time you stink up the vehicle, you're walking home!"

Fuzzy placed his head in her lap, not believing her for one second. Neither did either of the humans. She handed him back his gooey doll, which he took from her as gently as if it were a living thing, then gave him a good thorough ear, neck, and snout scratching.

The three of them puttered around the Stronghold for a few minutes, Allistor claiming the master suite at the top of one of the towers for himself, Amanda, and Fuzzy. Helen asked Nigel to reserve a nearby room on a lower floor for her. With that taken care of, they took some supplies out of their inventory to stock the kitchen for the first few survivors who showed up, leaving about a week's worth of food for two people.

Allistor didn't want to leave the place empty, on the off chance that someone else was roaming the wilderness and might try to claim the Stronghold. "Nigel, can you put me in touch with Andrea please?"

"Of course. One moment, Lord Allistor."

They only waited a few seconds before Andrea's voice came through. "Allistor? What's up?"

"Not much, just been fighting a herd of giant murder chickens. Probably one of Nancy's experiments gone wrong." He winked at Helen. "Anyway, we have a new Stronghold. Let's call this one… Wilderness. Helen and Fuzzy and I are going to track the big birds – they're called kyllings, and today was the first I've seen of them – and I would appreciate it if you could send a few guards here to watch over the place? Lots of room here, and it's beautiful country. So if some others want to come hunt or fish or craft or whatever, that's fine too. Oh! And let Nancy know there's a new greenhouse to play with?"

"Sounds interesting. I'll come check it out myself. We'll take care of it, boss. And… murder chickens?"

Helen laughed. "Think eight-foot tall dino-chickens with scales instead of feathers. And claws as long as your forearm."

Allistor added, "Don't tell Nancy, but we're going to see if we can track them back to a nest and find some eggs. Raise a whole pack of them. We got about a thousand pounds of tasty chicken off just the ones we killed here."

"Damn, boss. Leave some in the kitchen, will ya? We'll have some bbq ready when you come back."

"Already done. See ya then." Allistor concluded the communication.

The three of them exited the gates, Nigel closing them automatically as they walked away down the slope. Helen quickly picked up the trail. "Turns out a pack of giant dino-birds isn't that hard to track." She pointed to

431

deep gouges in the earth where the running chickens had passed.

Nearly half an hour later she slowed the pace as the tracks converged into a tight passage between some rocks. There was evidence of many more tracks, some old, some fresh, leading in and out of the narrow opening. Without speaking, she motioned for Allistor to go first. And a finger held to her lips told him to go quietly.

Casting *Barrier* on himself, he crouched low and moved through the space. He gripped his shotgun loaded with buckshot, intending to mutilate anything that came at him around a corner. The rocks on either side of him rose steeply upward, and were probably climbable. But he'd need both hands to do so.

Stepping out of the narrow passage on the other side, he found a wide hollow in the side of a cliff face. Not quite deep enough to be considered a cave, it extended maybe thirty feet into the stone, and was at least a hundred feet wide. The ceiling at the front was twenty feet above, and it sloped downward to less than ten feet at the back. Almost as if a giant axe had swung into the side of the hill and carved out a wedge.

More importantly, scattered around the interior were more than a dozen nests.

They didn't look like chicken nests. There was no hay or twigs woven together. These nests were constructed of small branches, bones, hides, and leftover bits of whatever the murder chickens had been killing. The place reeked of rotted meat, and Fuzzy flat out refused to approach. There were no kyllings visible.

"Cover me, I'll check the nests." Helen whispered. She strode forward, watching the ground to avoid stepping on any twigs or bones that would snap loudly. Peering into the first nest, the edges of which were built up about three feet above the ground, she shook her head. Moving on, the second and third nests she checked were also empty. But she paused at the fourth nest, one near the back wall, and gave Allistor a thumbs-up. She carefully reached down and lifted a white mottled egg that looked very much like the eggs found in the hen house at the Warren, only about twenty times as large. She made the egg disappear into her inventory, then reached for more. When she'd emptied three eggs out of that nest, she moved on.

Allistor had counted eight eggs retrieved when a low growl from Fuzzy alerted them both. Helen was still near the back of the nesting area, and as she looked toward Allistor and Fuzzy, her eyes grew wide. Turning as quickly as he could, Allistor instantly regretted their little egg hunt.

Kylling Brood Mother
Level 25
Elite
Health: 39,000/39,000

The murder-chicken bosslady was easily a third again as large as any of the ones they'd already fought. Over ten feet tall, she made the others look like cuddly peeps in comparison. Her eyes glowed a deep red, revealing an intelligence that concerned Allistor. He noted a constant low growl rumbled from her chest, lowering in pitch as she stared at him. She had a larger set of wings

433

that, as she unfurled them to either side, looked almost large enough for her to be able to fly. Her beak dripped with blood, as did the half of a wolf carcass she held in it.

Her wingspan was easily thirty feet, and with both of them open, she effectively corralled them inside the nest area. Helen moved forward to join Allistor and Fuzzy, abandoning her egg search. "Probably better to leave a few anyway. In case we killed the only male."

Allistor barely registered what she was saying. He was watching the brood mother, who tilted her head and listened as Helen spoke. A moment later, she let out a half-roar, half-squawk that echoed so loudly in the stone chamber that Allistor covered his ears.

To his dismay, when the echo died down, he heard several answering calls. In moments, six more of the normal-sized murder chickens appeared behind the brood mother.

"This is very bad." Helen muttered, causing the boss chicken to tilt her head again. "We need to run and climb a tree or something." There was the beginning of panic in her voice.

Allistor shook his head. "They're faster than us. Our best hope is to get back to that narrow spot ahead of them, and hold them there. Hope they don't figure out to go around some other way and come up behind us. Or down on top of us." He didn't like their chances, but he wasn't about to give up.

The first thing he needed was to get past the boss and her wings. The others were holding well back behind her, as if waiting for some command. Allistor intended to make sure that command didn't come. He began by casting *Mind Spike* on the brood mother. She shrieked in pain, the sound hurting the ears of both the humans and bear. Her wings furled, and she spun around, ripping the earth to shreds with her claws as she thrashed her head and tried to pry the spike from her brain with her wings.

"Now! Go!" Allistor cast Flame Strike on the kylling nearest the path to the choke point. It screeched much like its matron, flapping its vestigial wings and bumping into its nearest cousin. Fuzzy led the charge, outpacing the humans with his four legs. Helen was right behind him, and Allistor brought up the rear.

The rest of the kyllings charged, shouldering past the burning chicken or dodging around it. But the distraction had bought Allistor and company enough time. Fuzzy and Helen passed through the narrow spot, and Allistor slid to a halt just on the other side, turning to face the oncoming monsters. He cast *Erupt* into the narrowest spot just as one of the murder chickens was about to push through. The stone spike shot upward, bursting through the kylling's foot and into its gut, stopping its momentum completely. Two others ran into it from behind, pushing it farther onto the spike and jamming its writhing body into the choke point. For good measure, Allistor cast *Flame Shot* on it, causing it to burst into flame and scorching the two behind it as well.

Helen had her shotgun out and pushed him aside, blasting the trapped kylling in the face from three feet away. Its head disappeared in a cloud of blood, bone, and a tiny amount of brain; the buckshot and bone shrapnel continuing on to damage the kylling behind it.

The others immediately began to pick at the body, tearing off chunks as they attempted to pull it out of the way.   A moment later they were joined by the brood mother, whose head towered above the others.

Kylling Brood Mother
Level 25
Elite
Health: 36,200/39,000

"We should run for it!" Helen shouted, much louder than necessary. Allistor was right next to her. Something about this fight was unnerving her. He shook his head. "It won't take them long to get past this. We need to kill them now." He paused, then grinned. Turning to face Helen, he put a hand on each shoulder. "Deep breath. We'll get through this. I've been waiting for a chance to use that scroll."

He pulled the *Storm* scroll from his inventory and opened it. The magic flowed into his head, knowledge of the formation of clouds, water condensation, the buildup of friction between the positive and negative ions in the clouds, and the release of the charge. To his surprise, he learned that lightning actually originated in the earth nearly as often as in the clouds, when the positive charge in the earth reacted to the negative charge in a cloud and a visible bolt was released.

All of this absorbed into his consciousness in a matter of seconds, and he felt a little dizzy as Helen continued to massacre the kyllings that were trying to clear the path. She fired once at the brood mother's face just to keep the beast back. Allistor saw tears running down his friend's cheeks.

Looking upward, he teleported himself to the top of the rocks to the right of the path using his *Dimensional Step* ability. Now looking down at the flock of murder chickens and their scary-as-hell mom, he focused on her and began to channel *Storm*. He had nearly three thousand mana left after the spells he'd already cast, which would give him up to thirty seconds of lightning damage. He hoped that would be enough.

A light cloud gathered above him, drawing in wisps of other clouds and getting darker as it grew larger. It began to rotate, small sparks of electricity flashing here and there as it built up a charge. It was nearly ten seconds after his initial cast that the first lightning bolt struck. Since he'd targeted the brood mother, the bolt hit her. Her roar of frustration turned into a surprised squawk that lasted only a second before she was stunned. More bolts began to strike around her as Allistor continued to channel the spell. The other kyllings were struck as more mana was poured into the storm. First a few here and there, then all of them were struck repeatedly as the number and frequency of the bolts increased. Allistor gritted his teeth at the twenty-second mark. The rapid and extended drain of mana from his system was almost painful. And the heat that rose up to wash over him along with the smell of ozone and burning flesh was getting uncomfortable.

At twenty-five seconds, he stopped channeling. He didn't want to drain his mana completely, and all of the kyllings were down. Including the boss. She wasn't dead, just badly burned and stunned unconscious from the multiple strikes.

Kylling Brood Mother
Level 25
Elite
Health: 5,180/39,000

He was raising his shotgun to put a few rounds in her head when Helen called up. "Don't shoot!" When he lowered his weapon, she pulled out some rope. "If we can take her back, she can raise us our herd. We have no idea whether these eggs will be male or female. Or if they'll even hatch."

"How the hell are we going to take her back? She weighs something like five hundred pounds. And the moment she wakes up, she'll eat our faces."

Helen just grinned. "Get down here and help me."

Allistor hopped down from boulder to boulder until he reached Helen. Fuzzy was going around the other birds, crunching necks and making sure they were dead. Allistor was surprised to see that he was receiving loot each time Fuzzy touched one of the dead birds. Ignoring that development for a moment, he stepped next to Helen. "What can I do?"

"Hold this." She looped one end of the rope and handed it to him. She took the other end and began to tie the brood mother's feet together. When she had them tightly secured, she returned to Allistor. "Okay, pull as hard as you can up toward her head. Don't worry, you won't hurt her. Chickens are very flexible."

Allistor pulled on the rope, causing both knees to bend up toward the chicken's belly, and its feet to press against its tail end.

"Okay now wrap the rope one time around its neck, then put the loop over its beak. Make sure the rope is up behind that ridge at the top." Allistor did as he was told. Once the loop was on, he saw for himself where he could pull the loose end and tighten the loop. It was a simple slipknot.

When he was done, the monster was effectively hog-tied. Helen went behind him and tightened the rope slightly, less forgiving than he was. Then she tied off the loose end to make sure the knot couldn't be undone.

They took some time to loot and harvest the bodies, adding a few hundred more pounds of murder chicken meat to their store. Since they had the brood mother, Helen went ahead and collected the rest of the eggs. Assuming they'd killed the entire flock now, the eggs were doomed if she left them.

"Alright, I'm going to run back to the Stronghold and get the hover cart from the truck. You start dragging this big momma back in that direction, and I'll meet you in between." Helen smirked at him. When he opened his mouth to protest, she added, "Don't tell me a big strong man like you can't handle it. I mean, with your strength stat, you should be able to throw her over one shoulder and carry her back."

Allistor stuck out his tongue and crossed his eyes. "Just hurry. And be safe. If you see anything, like more murder chickens, run or hide. I'll see you soon."

Helen took off, and Allistor turned to look at the kylling elite. She was awake and growling, occasionally struggling against her bonds. She'd been awake for several minutes, and was much calmer now. At first, she'd thrashed until the knots tightened. Allistor had worried she'd break the rope, but Helen had reassured him that it was twenty-five-hundred pound climbing rope, and would hold just fine.

With a sigh he reached down and grabbed ahold of the rope at her feet, walking back toward the Stronghold and dragging her behind. She gave a few muted squawks of protest and struggled a bit more at first. But she soon realized she wasn't going to be able to break free.

He pulled her down the slope from the nest and across a wide meadow they'd passed before. At the end of that, he began to head back uphill. Helen had been right. With his improved strength, he probably could lift the kylling and carry her. And pulling her was not much of a strain, though it did require some effort.

He'd gone about twenty minutes when Helen appeared with the hover cart. Fuzzy helped lift the creature up onto the flat surface, and Helen took over. She pulled the thing the remainder of the way, being careful not to snag on any brush and tip it over.

Back at the Stronghold they found Andrea and half a dozen others settling in. When they saw the brood mother bound on the cart, eyes widened and curses were whispered.

"Holy crap. I thought you were joking when you said murder chickens. That thing is nightmare fuel."

Allistor grinned. "Right? And I plan to blame the whole thing on Nancy!" The others chuckled. "We've got a bunch of eggs, too. Gonna put her someplace she can't hurt anyone and see if we can domesticate these bad boys."

He and Helen left some more of the kylling meat for the folks who were staying the night at Wilderness. One of them was already preparing a bbq sauce recipe that they swore was the best in the west. Allistor wished them luck, and they loaded up the vehicle with the hover pad in tow, drove it onto the teleport pad, and transferred to the Warren.

There was a big ruckus when they arrived with the brood mother. Allistor immediately pulled off the pad and drove toward the center of the compound. The moment he got out, he started calling, "Nancy! Where's Nancy? You see? I told her what would happen if she kept fast-growing those chickens!" and, "Imagine what'll happen with those bunnies!"

Eventually Nancy came stomping out of the greenhouse. "What is this nonsense about me making mutant chic-" Her voice trailed off as she saw the furious brood mother struggling on the cart. "What the hell is that?"

Allistor's smile couldn't have been bigger as he waved toward the helpless mob. "You tell me, miss. You said it wouldn't hurt to grow the chickens faster."

"Stop that! You know I didn't do this. If you were younger, I'd put you over my knee, you little shit!" she scolded him, but she was smiling as she did it.

441

"You're in trouble now!" Chloe, who had been hiding behind her mom's leg and staring wide-eyed at the giant murder chicken, said. "I always get a spankin' when she calls me a little shit!"

"Chloe!" Nancy looked down, and the child covered her mouth, giggling. "You're gonna get one tonight if you don't behave."

"Why do I get a spankin'? Allistor's the one that brought the monster you made!" The girl half-pouted, watching carefully to see if her ruse worked.

"I did *not* make that big chicken monster!" Nancy nearly growled. "Do you think I would let you take care of the chickens downstairs if they might hurt you, sweet one?"

Chloe beamed at her mom. The term of endearment almost certainly meant her spanking was forgotten. She looked up at Allistor, who winked at her. "She's right, Chloe. We found these far, far away. It's not one of your mom's special chickens. But did you see how red she got when I said that? I'm probably gonna get a spanking, but it was worth it!"

Nancy smacked him on the shoulder the same time that Helen smacked him on the back of the head. Most of the folks gathered around were smiling and chuckling.

"So, I think this would be a good place to set up a corral for these things. We've got the big momma here, and Helen has a bag full of eggs. They're carnivores, so maybe feed them some of the rabbits and whatever the hunters can bring in? Some elk? See if you can tame her and her offspring? We can herd them like the buffalo."

Michael came walking up as he spoke. "Or we could totally train them as battle mounts!" he called out, his grin matching Allistor's as the two bumped fists.

Somebody else shouted, "Murder chicken mobile infantry!" and Allistor looked around to see if he could identify them for a fist bump too.

Another voice that he thought came from near the motor pool shouted, "Gnomes Rule!"

Ignoring the childishness, Helen added, "I think I'll stay here a while. My *Animal Husbandry* skill might come in handy, and maybe I can level it up." She looked at Allistor with her hands on her hips and an expression that brooked no argument. "Come on *Lord* Allistor, make with the hand-wavyness and make me a place for these things."

Allistor could get behind that. "You want it up here? Or down below?"

Nancy spoke first. "She looks like maybe she can fly? Wherever it is, we probably need to put a roof on it."

Helen nodded. "They built their nests under the cliff face, so they don't mind something over their heads. But they also need room to run. So, let's set up something outside the wall. Maybe some kind of add-on like you did at the Citadel. A covered area for nests, and a wide open area for them to run. I'll clip her wings so she can't fly."

Allistor nodded and stepped out the gate. Several of the others followed, some with weapons to keep watch, others just curious. He opened his Stronghold interface and began to scroll through the options he had for different structures. Eventually, he found something called a *Menagerie* that looked like it would work. It had a series

443

of cages along a lengthy U-shaped corridor, and one end opened with a wide set of doors large enough to bring an elephant through. The interior courtyard could be covered over easily enough to create a large area for the brood mother to roam, and they could enclose an even larger area with a wall.

He selected the structure, then added enough walls to enclose a ten-acre space. Nancy and Helen both assured him that would be enough for a small flock of the giant chickens. Hopefully by the time they got larger, they'd be trained enough to be herdable and could be let loose in the grasslands, or a section of forest to be set aside.

When it was done, Helen had a couple of the guys help her dig a wide hole about three feet deep, where she placed the eggs. Then they pushed the hover cart into the enclosure, and everyone but Allistor backed out.

He stood next to the brood mother, the two of them eyeing each other. He held a long knife in one hand, and began to speak to her in a soothing voice.

"Okay, there are two ways we can do this. You can behave yourself, and let me cut these ropes. Then I'll leave quietly, and somebody will toss you a few tasty bunny rabbits to munch on. Or you can try to kill me, and I'll step outside and hit you with fireballs until the ropes burn off. What's it gonna be?"

She eyed him for a good long while, but didn't struggle against the ropes. He noted that her gaze occasionally flicked to the nearby clutch of eggs. "Okay, good. You want to take care of the eggs? Let's try this."

He decided to start at the feet, expecting that if he freed her head first, she'd simply decapitate him with her beak. So he very carefully cut the rope where it bound her feet together. As she straightened out her stiff legs, probably trying to restore some circulation after being bound that long, he quickly untied the knot securing the other end of the rope. After that, a quick tug on one side of the slip knot, and the kylling was free.

Allistor didn't waste time sitting around to see what she'd do. He took hold of the hover cart, used his improved strength to tilt it and dump the brood mother ungracefully on her face, then made a run for it while pulling the cart behind him. His people laughed and cheered as he hauled butt toward the gate, not caring how it made him look.

She gradually got to her feet, roaring at him and the others and starting toward them with murder in her eyes. But she quickly saw that she wouldn't catch him, and changed her path. Trotting over to the eggs, she nosed at the hole a bit, then looked around the enclosure as if searching for something.

Helen immediately said, "Grab some hides. The messed-up ones, not good for much. Especially scraps, bones, whatever we might have. Maybe grab some left-behind clothes or rugs from what's left of the houses over there." She pointed toward the closest ruined homes. "Their nests were made up of that stuff. Probably helped keep the eggs warm. Toss her some carcasses too." Several people ran to carry out her orders.

The rest of them watched as she settled atop of the makeshift nest, never taking her eyes off the people standing in the doorway. Allistor had Nigel set a new ring of sensors around the walls to let him know if anything managed to climb up. He put two sets of stairs on the outside of the wall for his people to use when feeding the murder chickens.

And with that, it was time to call it a day.

Chapter 19

Darwin Was Right

The next few months were spent securing their holdings. Foraging and hunting parties continued to find stray survivors and bring them in. A few were attacked by the humans they encountered, and forced to eliminate them. Seven more of Allistor's people died in these senseless attacks. Nineteen ambushers died as well. All of them were people who could have contributed to the new world, become part of something bigger, but chose to murder and steal instead.

One of those rescued was a small boy whose family was attacked as they traveled toward Cheyenne. They'd heard of Allistor's Citadel and were looking for a safe place. Waylaid along the road, the boy's mother had been killed quickly, and the father was still fighting when one of Allistor's hunting parties heard the commotion and showed up to help. Unfortunately, the father was also killed before the fight was over. The hunters had been from the Warren, and brought the boy back there with them.

Meg and Sam immediately adopted the boy, who didn't speak for several days. When Meg finally coaxed him into saying his name, he mumbled, "Cody."

"Well, now! Nice to meet you, Cody!" Meg hugged the boy, and Sam patted him on the shoulder. "You're gonna stay with us now, if that's okay? We'll look after you. Make sure you eat good. Teach you what you need to know." Meg hugged him again. "Can you tell me how old you are?"

"I'm… this many." Cody held up a hand with all five fingers opened up.

"Five? You're five years old?" Sam asked.

Cody nodded.

Meg ruffled his hair a little, the blond locks sticking up afterwards. "Do you know when your birthday is?" Cody nodded, but didn't say a word. Rolling her eyes and grinning at Sam as she realized she was going to have to word things more clearly, she said, "Can you tell us when your birthday is?"

"Fireworks day." Cody mumbled, his hands fidgeting.

Sam asked, "You mean the fourth of July?"

"Yep. That one." Cody answered, his head bobbing.

"Well, I'll be damned." Sam mumbled.

"Sam! Not around the boy." Meg slapped his arm.

"It's okay miss Meg. My daddy said that word all the time. And shit, too." The boy looked up at Sam with a half-smile, as if by saying bad words together they shared some kind of secret.

Chuckling, Sam put a hand on the boy's shoulder and said, "Damn right, son." He saw the look Meg was giving him, and added, "But let's just save it for when it's just us men, alright?"

Cody nodded again, giving Sam a full smile this time.

It wasn't long before Chloe adopted Cody, though the boy was older and larger. She scooped him up on the way to go tend the chickens and bunnies, and from that point on the two were inseparable. They played tag with Max, the big dog bowling them over and licking them into giggling spasms before taking off for them to chase him. The three of them would wear themselves out, report to Meg for a snack, then the kids would use Max as a pillow while they all napped.

Helen leveled up her *Animal Husbandry* skill working with the kyllings. She began feeding the brood mother by hand, always with at least two others guarding her back. The eggs hatched after a few weeks, and the humans began feeding the little ones immediately. The brood mother didn't like it at first, snapping at the humans who tried to get close. But eventually she learned that humans meant food for her and the little ones, and she relented.

Helen began whistling at the giant murder chicken as she fed her, getting her used to the sound. Eventually, through the use of reward feedings for correct behavior and a rope, she could get the brood mother to move at her direction with a whistle and a tug on the rope. At the end of two months of daily practice, she didn't need the rope anymore. And Helen could approach her alone, with no guards. They weren't bonded, but it was progress.

The kids took to gathering atop the wall around the kyllings' enclosure, watching as Helen worked. To their delight, when the little kyllings became steady enough on their feet, they began to mimic what the brood mother was doing. Soon enough, when Helen gave two short whistles, the entire flock would make a right turn, and a left turn for three.

The adults would stop by and marvel at the sight as well, fist-bumping each other and whispering about murder-chicken cavalry. The cowboys even tried to convince Helen to let them start saddle-training the little ones. She told them to wait until they were a bit larger, but to go ahead and have the leatherworkers start designing and creating saddles. This announcement was cause for a big celebration at the Warren, where they served – what else? – bbq kylling meat.

Allistor spent a lot of time on the road over these months, joining the hunting parties and undertaking diplomatic missions to the other Strongholds in Denver. By the time July 4th came around, he had established solid alliances with all but one. The lone holdout was Matthew, the same man who'd all but kicked Allistor out of his Stronghold after Allistor had rescued his daughter from Paul at the depository and returned her. Despite assurances from many survivors who'd been there, the man continued to blame Allistor for his wife's death.

And Matthew didn't just refuse an alliance. He was openly hostile whenever Allistor approached. His hunting parties twice attacked others, one of Allistor's and one belonging to an allied Stronghold. There were no fatalities, fortunately, but with live rounds flying it was only a matter of time until someone was seriously hurt or killed. Matthew also lobbied the other Stronghold leaders, whispering to them that Allistor was taking advantage of them. That the whole alliance was just about gathering power for himself, and that everyone would end up as little more than his slaves. He spread rumors of Allistor taking young women from other Strongholds and adding them to his harem. And he kept making a more insidious suggestion.

That if they banded together, they could seize the Bastion and share all that gold.

Allistor had, of course, heard from the other leaders of Matthew's efforts. He had let the man be, despite all the attacks, both physical and verbal, wanting to avoid a conflict with Matthew's Stronghold if at all possible. But his attempts to organize an attack on the Bastion couldn't be overlooked. With less than a month before the Stabilization was over and the aliens arrived, he couldn't afford to let it go any longer.

Allistor took Bjurstrom, McCoy, Goodrich, and Campbell with him in one of the *Juggernauts* to Matthew's Stronghold. Parking a hundred yards from the gate, he used the loudspeaker feature to call out. "Matthew, this is Allistor. I want to speak with you, peacefully."

"Screw off!" a voice rang down from the wall. It wasn't Matthew's voice. Allistor waited, the guys in the back looking grim and checking their weapons.

"Hey, boss. Not that I'm complaining or anything, but if we're gonna take on a whole Stronghold, shouldn't we have brought one or two more guys?" McCoy asked, earning nervous chuckles from the others.

"What? I just brought you guys to guard the vehicle." Allistor joked with them. "I mean, usually Helen and Fuzzy handle it themselves. So, if you think we need to go back and get them…" There were a couple snorts, and things quieted down as they continued to wait.

After nearly twenty minutes, the gates opened and Matthew emerged, with six armed men behind him.

"That's what I'm talkin' 'bout!" Goodrich slapped his knee. "Seven against five? They shoulda brought more guys!"

Allistor opened his door. Stepping out, he said "You guys stay behind cover. There are sure to be snipers up there."

Bjurstrom shook his head. "You expect us to lay low while you hang your ass out there to be shot full of holes? We should be *in front* of you. Our job to is take those bullets, keep your royal hoity toityness alive."

"He's more highfalutin than hoity toity." Campbell observed. The other two nodded their agreement.

Bjurstrom rolled his eyes. "Regardless… we can't just sit here and watch you get killed. Amanda would have our nuts in a jar by nightfall."

Shaking his head, Allistor said, "Guys, he's waiting. And this isn't the most patient man on Earth. Just do what I say. This has to be between Matthew and me. If fighting starts, dozens or even hundreds of people could die. I don't want that. One of you get behind the wheel, and keep the engine running. If necessary, I'll pop back here and jump in the side door. Deal?"

Not waiting for them to answer, he began to walk toward Matthew. He did so with his hands up and empty, meant to show that he intended no harm. Matthew didn't buy it.

"We all know you don't need a weapon to kill, boy. Why are you here? You have two minutes."

"I'm here to talk to you, Matthew. To work out whatever issue you have with me, man to man. To stop these threats you're making against me and my people." he shouted loud enough for the people on the wall to hear. His best hope was that, if he had to kill this man, his people wouldn't be inclined to seek vengeance.

"What threats?" Matthew put his arms out wide in a pose of innocence.

"Your attempts to get others to help you attack the Bastion." Allistor stepped closer. "I've tolerated your bullshit, the rumors you try to circulate, the accusations. But I will not tolerate any plans to attack my people. What is your problem with me? I've done nothing to harm you. My people and I saved your daughter and returned her to you. What is my crime?"

"You're trying to take over!" Matthew screamed at him, going from calm to raging in seconds. "You want to take my Stronghold. You turn my people against me! You brainwashed my daughter! She's constantly 'Allistor this' and 'Allistor that'!"

"I barely met your daughter before we brought her back to you. And I'm not trying to take your Stronghold from you! Have I taken any of the others'? I asked for their friendship, and offered mine in return. It's that simple."

"You stole Lars' Stronghold!" Matthew accused.

"You're a damn moron. Have you spoken to Lars? He *requested* to join me and my people. His people

453

unanimously agreed." Allistor lost his patience. He knew in his gut this man was never going to change his mind.

"I'm a moron? *I'm* a moron!?" Matthew nearly foamed at the mouth. "That's the best you can do? That's how you plan to undermine me in front of my people?"

"I have offered friendship. I've offered assistance. If you didn't have such a stick up your ass, your people would be better off than they are now. Our year is almost over! The aliens will be landing before we know it! We humans need to stick together! Not plot against each other, kill each other off, because *one of us* can't stop being a dick!"

He stopped talking as Matthew turned and grabbed a weapon from one of the men behind him. Allistor held up a hand. "Matthew, stop! If you attack me, I'll be forced to kill you! Despite all your bullshit, I still mean you no harm! Just stop attacking my people, and the others here in Denver. That's all I need from you!"

Matthew's face was bright red as he struggled with the shotgun he'd grabbed. He apparently wasn't familiar with it. Allistor cast *Barrier* in front of himself, then prepared to cast *Dimensional Step*.

"The rest of you! Stand back! I don't want to hurt anyone, but if he points that thing at me, he's dead. Move back!"

All but one of the men behind Matthew did just that. They all took several steps back. The only one that didn't move back was the man he'd grabbed the gun from. Instead, he stepped forward to help his boss with the weapon, pointing out the safety.

Matthew stepped forward, raising the gun to point it at Allistor. His target disappeared just as he was pulling the trigger, and the buckshot ricocheted off the vehicle behind where Allistor had been. A second later, blinding pain ripped through his brain as Allistor cast *Mind Spike* from right behind him.

Drawing his knife from his belt, he stepped forward and wrapped his left arm around, grabbing Matthew's forehead and pulling his head back while putting the knife in his right hand to the man's throat. He spun them both around to face the men behind them, and those on the wall.

"Matthew is a dead man! You all heard me! I've given him every chance to back off, and he just tried to kill me! For no damn reason!" He paused, looking at the men nearby, then the folks on the wall, and those gathered in the open gateway.

"The question is, how many of you are willing to die with him?" He stood there, holding the knife as the spell wore off and Matthew began to shout.

"Kill him! Shoot him! What are you waiting for? Shoot him!" Spittle flew from the man's mouth.

The men who'd walked out with Matthew lowered their weapons. One of those who'd stepped back said, "We don't want any trouble. You're right, he's obsessed. He came out here, planning to kill you."

"Please, don't kill him." a woman's voice called from the direction of the open gate. Allistor turned himself and Matthew to face her. He didn't recognize her initially, but as she walked closer and continued to speak, her identity became clear. "My father doesn't deserve to die like this. He… he just can't face what happened to my mother. It broke his mind. Somewhere in there he knows it wasn't you, but he can't punish Paul now that he's dead, and it was you who brought me back without her, so his mind makes the only association it can. Please."

Allistor spoke the words, even though his mind already told him it would make no difference. "I didn't kill your mother. Paul did. From what I understand, it happened long before I even came to Denver."

The man who'd answered before spoke again. "We know. Matthew and a few of us here had been going out hunting Paul's people whenever possible. We captured one and questioned him. He told us that Paul raped and then killed Matthew's wife." The man paused, lowering his eyes and shuffling his feet. "He… took great pleasure in giving Matthew all the details. And Matthew couldn't help but listen. It pushed him over the edge. The way he killed that man…"

Again, the man paused. When he'd composed himself, he raised his head and looked Allistor in the eye. "Look, I know he just tried to kill you. And you're right about his lying and plotting. All of it. But please don't kill him. He was a good man. He personally saved the lives of many of us here. And the rest owe him a debt for taking us in and providing a safe place when we were dying off like flies. You don't know me, and you don't owe me a thing. But from what I've seen and heard, you're a good man who values human life. So I'm asking you, on behalf of all of us here, spare his life. We'll make sure he can do you no harm."

"You worthless cowards! Somebody, shoot him!" Matthew roared. His enraged strength was still not enough to overcome Allistor's. With the buff from Lilly's armor, his *Strength* attribute was a seven.

"I don't want to kill him. I came here to talk to him. And, frankly, I could have killed him a dozen times since we've been standing here. But I also can't just let him go. If word gets out that I forgave an attempt on my life, the details of the situation won't matter. It'll be open season on me."

The man nodded his understanding. Matthew's daughter spoke up. "I don't know if you even remember me. My name is Linda."

Allistor nodded. "I remember you, Linda. From the day I brought you back here."

"I love my father. He was a wonderful dad, and has been like a father to many of the folks here. If you'd met him before Paul took my mom, I'm sure you'd have been friends." Tears streamed down her cheeks as she spoke. She reached out a hand as if to touch her father, then hesitated before lowering it again. "But I know that he's not that man anymore. I've spent all the months since you brought me back trying to get through to him. I can't make him understand. He's lost in the pain, and I don't know if he'll ever come back to me." She paused, looking at the people up on the walls and gathered nearby. "I'll swear an oath. You know, like the one some of the others swore to you that day you freed us. I'll have every person here swear it as well. We'll join you, and we'll keep my father under control. Even if that means locking him up."

Allistor was surprised by the offer. More than surprised. Shocked. He'd come here hoping that, best case, he could convince Matthew to stop the campaign against him. He didn't expect to gain a thousand or more followers in the process. He still didn't like the idea of letting the man live, but it was suddenly worth considering.

"You can deliver on that promise? All your people will swear the oath?" Allistor asked, his tone of voice revealing his doubt.

She simply looked at the men surrounding them. Each one of them nodded his head. The one who'd been pleading for Matthew's life said, "All of us. Even if we hadn't heard good things about you, we'd do it to save Matthew. We'll swear the oath."

"The hell you will!" Matthew shouted. With a sudden surge of strength, he slammed his head backward into Allistor's face, crushing his nose and causing blood to pour out. Surprised and stunned, Allistor loosened his grip and Matthew broke free. He reached down and pulled a hunting knife from his boot and slammed it into Allistor's gut up to the hilt. Still stunned from the blow to the face, Allistor was too slow to defend himself. He doubled over in pain, the knife blade inside him causing even more damage as he did so. When Matthew ripped the blade free, Allistor fell to his knees, placing both hands over the wound, instinctively trying to stop the bleeding and hold his guts inside.

"Noooo!" Linda shouted, reaching for her father even as two of the other man stepped forward to grab him.

Matthew kicked Allistor in the face, knocking him backward off his knees to sprawl on the ground, still trying to stop the bleeding. Allistor's mind was screaming at him to heal himself, but he couldn't quite manage it. It was as if the spell was hanging there in front of him, just out of reach.

"I did it! I killed the bastard!" Matthew was shouting even as he raised a foot and stomped on Allistor's head. His health bar dropped to below fifty percent, then ticked a bit lower from the bleed effect caused by the knife wound. When the blow didn't finish him, Matthew raised the foot again.

A single shot rang out, and the boot came down. But it landed without much force, and hit the pavement next to Allistor instead of his head. He felt a heal land on him, then another, and his head cleared enough to see Matthew lying on the street next to him, most of his own head blown away.

Allistor tried to sit up, but his stomach rebelled and he barely managed to turn his head before he vomited up his breakfast along with a considerable amount of blood. Another heal washed over him, but he just lay back down. He could hear people talking above him, but his head was still fuzzy, and the words didn't make a lot of sense.

He could tell that Bjurstrom and the others had joined him, and all had weapons raised.

"I'm sorry." Bjurstrom said. "He was killing Allistor. I had no choice."

"I know." Linda said, on her knees next to her father's body. "You did what you had to. I think... I think maybe he wanted it this way." The men from her

Stronghold gathered behind her, lowering their weapons and bowing their heads.

Bjurstrom and the others lowered their weapons as well. Campbell took a knee next to Allistor and asked, "You okay, boss?" He slapped Allistor's cheeks a few times, as if that would bring him around.

"Stop hitting him, genius. The man probably has a concussion from bein' stomped." McCoy pushed Campbell away and took his place. He examined the wound in Allistor's gut, then cast another heal on him. "He'll live. The gut damage is healing. I don't know about his brain."

Allistor managed to sit up this time, though he was still dizzy. McCoy reached out a hand and helped him to his feet, then steadied him when he wobbled. "I'm sorry, Linda." Allistor's words came out slightly slurred and slower than normal. He shook his head, instantly regretting it when he became nauseous again. After taking a moment to cast a heal on himself, he continued. "I didn't want this. And I'm sorry it happened this way. But I can't apologize for my guys defending me."

The man who'd been speaking for Matthew stepped forward, his hand out. "We know. My name is Dillon. I know that you were going to spare his life. I saw it in your eyes before he... well, before."

Allistor shook his head, even that small motion making him feel off balance. He resisted the urge to shake his head again.

"Good to meet you, Dillon. I wish it were under better circumstances. I want you to know that there are no hard feelings on my part." He rubbed his still-sore gut where the knife wound had closed. He decided to ignore good sense and decorum, and push things a bit. The aliens were coming soon, and the big picture was more important than being sensitive.

"Linda, Dillon, if you and your people are still willing to take the oath, I'll do my best to look after you the way Matthew did before he changed. I know now may not be the best time to offer this, but our time is short. We have a lot more preparing to do before the aliens arrive."

Linda didn't seem to hear him. But Dillon shook his head. "You're right, this is not the time. We need to burn Matthew's body and talk things over. If it were up to me, we'd swear the oath right now. But I can't speak for the others after... this." He nodded toward Linda and Matthew.

"I understand. We could stay and assist with the funeral if you like." Allistor offered.

Linda spoke this time. "No, thank you. I think it'd be best for you to go and let us take care of things. Come back tomorrow, and we can talk then."

Allistor felt horrible. He'd been prepared to kill Matthew himself, and though he would have regretted the need to do so, he could have lived with it. Somehow, the fact that one of his men had to do it for him made it harder to accept. Despite the certain knowledge that had Bjurstrom waited another second or two, Matthew would have finished him. He could find no blame for anyone other than Matthew, but his gut still ate at him. And not because of the knife wound.

"Of course. We'll return tomorrow, around noon? And again, I wish things had gone differently. I truly do."

He turned and led his men back to the vehicle. They piled in and backed away from the Stronghold a ways before Goodrich turned the *Juggernaut* around and drove away. Allistor sat in the passenger seat, supporting his head with both hands as he leaned forward.

"You okay, boss? He stomped you pretty hard." Campbell asked.

"My head is clearing, slowly. Hurts like hell, though. I'm still a little dizzy, and I feel stupid."

Grinning, Goodrich replied. "Hope it didn't kill too many brain cells, boss. I mean, let's face it. You weren't a genius to start with." The others chuckled, and he added. "Amanda and Helen would be pissed if we brought you back needing to be fed and diapered from now on."

"If that happens, Goodrich, I'll tell Andrea to make sure you're on permanent diaper duty." Allistor responded without moving his head. That earned some outright laughter as well as a groan from Goodrich.

The vehicle quieted instantly when Allistor continued, his voice barely audible. "I didn't want to have to kill him. I'm so tired of killing other people. If this were still the world we grew up in, I'd be labeled some kind of serial killer or terrorist for what I've done. But no matter how often I look back at it all, I can't see any other way things could have gone. At least, not without risking even more lives."

The others all stared at him, or down at their own hands. Goodrich focused on the road ahead.

"We have… what? Three weeks left before our year is up? Then we can start killing aliens instead of other humans. Get a little payback for what they've done here. What they've turned us into."

Bjurstrom's voice was just as quiet. "To be fair, boss. Some people were assholes, rapists, and murderers before the apocalypse. It just freed them to be themselves without the usual consequences."

Allistor knew he was right. But like Matthew, his anger was so focused on the aliens who'd caused the apocalypse and killed his family that he didn't truly acknowledge the point. Instead, he changed his train of thought to something more practical.

"Nigel, please contact Andrea. Tell her I'd like her radio crew to set up a nationwide conference call for tomorrow morning, 9:00am our time. Include everyone we can reach. And call our leadership together for a 7:00am meeting."

"Of course, Lord Allistor."

Chapter 20

Big Promotion

The following morning, Allistor was up early to meet with his own leadership. Rather than try to squeeze everyone into a conference room, he called them all to the nearly empty Wilderness Stronghold and set up in the dining area. His core group were there, Sam and Meg and the other original survivors from the Warren, as well as George, Virginia, Bob, Richard, Dean, Andrea, Lars and Logan, and most of the leaders of the allied Strongholds or their representatives. In all, there were nearly fifty people attending.

"Thank you all for coming so early. In a couple of hours, we're going to have a conference call with every major group of survivors we've managed to contact over recent months across the US, Canada, and Mexico. Our radio teams have been doing a great job of seeking them out and handling the 'getting to know you' bits, so that we're on at least a friendly basis with most of them. Now I think it's time for us to start the more serious discussions about how to deal with the pending invasion, and how best to work together with all of them to improve everyone's chances of survival, and even continued expansion going forward."

He paused, giving them all a chance to absorb what he'd said. When all eyes refocused on him, he continued. "Some of the folks have their shit together, maybe even better than we do. Others are just barely hanging on. We can help those folks to some extent, but our time is limited. My people and I will do for them what we've done for some of you – that is make sure they have access to healing spells, some offensive magic, the formulas for health and mana potions, and maybe some of our cast-off gear that we have replaced with newer, better stuff."

The reason I've brought you all here is to discuss what we think the priorities should be over the next few weeks. I have my own opinions, but I'm not foolish enough to believe that I have thought of everything. Among this group are folks from more than a dozen different Strongholds that faced different challenges and circumstances as they grew. So, let's pool our experiences and see if we can agree on the best steps to take between now and the end of Stabilization."

Seeing heads nod around the room, he motioned to Ramon, who took over.

"We've been cranking out and stockpiling scrolls for distribution. As Allistor mentioned, the priority has been on healing spells and the low level offensive spells. I've also made fifty copies of scrolls with Nancy's *Grow* spell to help folks feed themselves with crops. And our research into using it on crystals has paid off. We have grown thousands of small crystals into medium and large crystals that can hold significant enchantments. We're still working out how to make practical use of these crystals, but I think we're close.

One of the Denver leaders raised a hand, and Ramon nodded at her. "What about the higher level spell scrolls? Do you have some of them for those of us with the stats to use them?"

Ramon nodded his head, but looked uncomfortable. He glanced at Allistor, who took the floor again.

"The short answer is yes. But those are significantly more expensive to make, in terms of both materials and time. We'll be making them available for sale at prices that cover the cost of production and provide a small profit to our scribes. Those prices will still be considerably lower than what you'd have to pay for them on the open market."

There was some quiet mumbling, but no outright protests. All of these people had benefited from Allistor's generosity in some form, and were grateful.

"Which brings us to another aspect of necessary preparations. Economic strength. Chris has been handling most of the trading and finances for my people and myself since he joined us. I'll let him talk about this. And please, feel free to speak up with questions or suggestions. That's why you're all here."

Chris stood and cleared his throat. "Our radio teams have been passing on certain information to the people we talk to. Including how to identify and sell rare and valuable items on the market to generate klax for the Strongholds. Because there are things we'll need that we just can't salvage here, or make for ourselves. Like the plasma weapons. Or teleport pads, vehicles with the hydrogen fuel engines, and so on. We have no idea what level of wealth the colonizing aliens will bring with them, so our theory at the moment is simply that we need to gather as much wealth as we can in the time that we have. And then try to spend it wisely on items that will be most useful. That's part of what we wanted to ask all of you."

Richard spoke up. "The vehicles are vital. Being able to travel between our allied Strongholds without having to carry large gas cans or siphon fuel from vehicles along the way is huge. Especially if we're going to start expanding our travels to visit allies in other regions."

Dean added, "The plasma rifles allowed us to take down that elite void titan at the Citadel. If we'd still been firing our Earth weapons, that fight might have gone differently."

Sam continued Dean's contribution. "And we can be certain that the aliens will have weapons at least that good, if not better. We don't know how hostile they'll be when they arrive, but we need to assume we'll need to defend what we have."

Amanda stood up next. "Don't forget the medical machines we bought that can regenerate severed limbs and destroyed organs. If we're going to have large scale fights on our hands, those are the best way to keep our people combat effective. Healing potions and spells are great for minor wounds, but without those regeneration machines, more serious wounds are going to whittle down our forces quickly."

Allistor shook his head. "Most of the others are not going to be able to afford those anytime soon. Maybe we can structure some kind of loan program to provide one at each major holding? I think they were something like seven hundred thousand klax each?"

Chris nodded his head. "We can get a discount if we buy them in bulk, but then we have delivery issues. I'll work with the vendor and see if we can arrange shipment to multiple Strongholds from one order. But we should bring

467

that up in the call later. Assuming every one of the sixty-five Strongholds we know of wants one, that would cost us…" He paused to do some quick math. "Somewhere between forty and forty-five million klax, depending on the discount." There were a few whistles from among the leaders in the crowd. Most of them didn't currently have even a million klax in their accounts. What they earned, they generally spent on some of the same gear they were discussing here.

Allistor looked around the room. "Obviously, those of you who don't have one of these machines yet can participate in this loan program. I'm thinking one year to repay the cost, at one percent annual interest. Any of you interested?"

Five hands went up in the air, representatives from most of the other Denver Strongholds. Lars already had one at his place. And Matthew's Stronghold wasn't represented here.

Lilly stood up. "I think we should add in crafting recipes and training scrolls."

Allistor nodded. "There's not a lot of time left for their crafters to level up, but you're right. Every little bit of buffed gear might help. Those are more expensive than the spell scrolls, but we can offer them at the same discount."

Logan raised a hand, and Allistor gave him a nod. "I've been doing some reading on the Stronghold construction and defense options. None of us has really explored this much, but the system does offer the option to construct automated defensive systems, even on structures as small as Outposts. Wall-mounted batteries, anti-aircraft, shield bubbles, even land mines and similar traps for outside the walls."

Allistor had noticed them when he first built the Warren, but they had been priced so far out of his range that he'd mentally written them off and forgotten about them. And that was Logan's next point.

"They're expensive as hell. But if the aliens are hostile, they might be the one thing that can save us." He pulled up his interface and read off some numbers:

> *"Wall-top plasma cannon emplacement: 500,000k*
> *Anti-aircraft disruptor battery: 800,000k*
> *Shield dome generator: 400,000k for 500 meter*
> *diameter.*
> *Each additional 500 meters: 200,000k*
> *Anti-personnel mines: 100,000k per dozen"*

He looked around at the other Stronghold leaders. "These are the basic units. Just like with everything else, there are upgrades available that reach into the tens of millions in cost. And the arms dealers sell things like tanks, fighters for both air and space use, sea vessels from small armored torpedo boats all the way up to something called a *Leviathan*, even battalions of battle droids."

Allistor wasn't the only one who found himself drooling. These were things straight out of sci-fi movies and VR games that every kid dreamed of. And now, with the invasion pending, he intended to buy as many of them as he could afford.

Bob spoke up while everyone else was daydreaming of droid battles or driving tanks. "With price tags like these, we should be encouraging people to push hard on gathering resources. And I don't mean foraging. Like, finding gold or silver mines, or large depositories like the one we claimed. How valuable are diamonds on the open market? They should be exploring what big caches of valuables they can get their hands on quickly. And for long term income producers like the mines, my guess is that with a system as advanced as this one seems to be, there will be an opportunity to borrow needed funds from some kind of bank against future mine proceeds."

"That's a very good point, Bob. Thank you." Allistor grinned at the man.

George cleared his throat. "I hear that a bunch of the folks you contacted are on military installations. Those guys should focus on the big weapons. Tanks, cannons, missile launchers, fighter planes, drones. If they would be willing to send a couple tanks, for example, to the smaller Strongholds that don't have the funds for plasma cannons, it might make the difference in whether they stand or fall. And if they leave now, they should have time to travel before our clock runs out, even stopping to siphon gas if necessary."

Helen raised a hand. "I've been thinking. Since I was able to grant you the National Parks in this area, I might be able to do the same for them. Like, grant each of them a park near their location, if there is one. That might enable a few of them to get titles like yours, and upgrade their Strongholds to Citadels. And give them space for their people to raise crops or hunt, or whatever, that the aliens can't claim."

"Damn. You're right. If you have that authority, we should have been using it already. Let's get out some maps and get to work on assigning all the parks. We can get our allies to start sending people there to create Outposts or whatever and protect those claims. Every square mile we can claim now, we should. I wish we'd had this conversation earlier!" Allistor felt like smacking himself in the head.

Amanda poked him in the side. "Don't be so hard on yourself. We haven't known about the others for very long. And while I commend you on your intent, you need to consider that plan a bit more from a long-term perspective. Everyone here is an ally, and trustworthy. But those people on the radio... well, humans are greedy by nature. If you just give them all these resources, what's to stop them from using those resources against you at some point? Just because it's us against the aliens right now doesn't mean it will always be that way."

Allistor bristled a bit at those words, and there were some thoughtful murmurings among the crowd. But as he considered what Amanda had said, he found wisdom in it. Calming himself, he answered. "You are absolutely right. Helen, maybe we figure out a way to claim all the parks immediately, then distribute them to those we trust as quickly as we can. Can you maybe do some research into that?" She nodded and began to write on a pad in front of her, giving him a 'we need to talk later' look.

Michael stood up next. "This is a little off topic, but since we're all here and talking strategy..." he broke off and looked at Allistor with a question on his face. Allistor nodded, and he continued. "You have one teleport pad left. And I'm thinking you should put it somewhere far away. Like on one of the coasts. Where we can establish a fishing fleet, maybe even a navy. There are plenty of lakes and rivers here with enough fish to feed all of us. But with the aliens coming, who knows how they'll treat those resources? They could drain the lakes, dam the rivers, and harvest all the fish in a week for all we know."

There were alarmed looks from nearly everyone in the room. Clearly none of them had considered that possibility. What if the aliens came to basically strip mine the planet's resources and then leave the humans with a depleted wasteland?

"I... think you're right, Michael. And maybe it's worth spending the funds to buy a few more teleport pads. Our hub can handle up to a dozen. The question is how we get to the coasts to execute your plan."

Andrea spoke up. "We have helicopters at the Silo. Nobody who can fly them, but if one of the other bases has pilots, maybe they'll lend us one? Hell, they might have planes, too. Or there are some National Guard planes still at the airport in Cheyenne. I'm sure Denver has some as well."

The conversation continued with input from almost everyone present by the time they were done. It was 8:45am and Allistor wanted to speak to the folks at the Silo for a bit before the scheduled call. He wanted a refresher on who they were speaking with and where. The thought of squeezing into the cramped radio room at the Silo got him thinking, and he asked, "Nigel? Can the radios at the Silo be tied into your communications system?"

"They already are, Lord Allistor."

"So, could you broadcast the entire thing here in this room, and let them hear us as well?"

472

"Of course, Lord Allistor. Would you like me to make it so?"

"Yes, please. And patch me through to Redd in the radio room. Thank you."

*****

The conference call turned out to be quite difficult to manage. With so many voices in different places, and the delays caused by long distance radio transmissions, there was initially a lot of talking over each other. This meant a lot of repeating questions or replies, and some hard feelings in a few cases. There were a couple of groups in Mexico that needed translation in Spanish, and one group in Canada claimed to only speak French, though the general consensus was that they were full of shit. It turned out Nigel could translate the broadcast for everyone, and eventually the military folks whose radio operators were more professional managed to work out a system that minimized the other issues, and the call became more productive.

The main call lasted nearly three hours, and Allistor was giddy over how well it went. The amount of information shared, the willingness to cooperate and help each other, and the news of just how many hundreds of thousands of human survivors were still out there and accounted for made his heart thump in his chest. Just the groups they'd managed to make contact with had a combined total of nearly two million survivors. It turned out they'd been right about the military posts and large cities doing better. Houston, for example, had a dozen

Strongholds and a Citadel, and more than a hundred thousand people. It gave him real hope.

The call eventually ended, but spawned several smaller calls with specific Strongholds or groups of allied Strongholds, and the result was nearly two whole days of scheduled calls on the radio.

Allistor had to delegate a large chunk of the immediate secondary calls to his leaders, as he was expected back at Matthew's Stronghold at noon. By the time he teleported to Denver, grabbed a vehicle, and drove across town, he was an hour late. But when he and his crew from the previous day arrived, the folks who greeted him didn't seem to mind.

Linda awaited him at the gate, which was opened as they approached. Once again, they parked a short distance away, and Allistor walked the rest of the distance. He saw Dillon standing behind Linda, along with the same group of men who'd walked out with Matthew the day before.

As soon as they'd shaken hands and said hello, Dillon got right to the point. "I'll save us all some time. We're not going to be swearing the oath and joining you as your citizens." the man looked annoyed as he spoke.

Linda stepped in to explain. "We spoke about this for several hours last night, and again this morning. Despite our assurances, there are still some people who believe my father's accusations about you. And some of them circulated more rumors last night that you murdered him in cold blood yesterday. We've talked to them until we're blue in the face, told them the truth, but they refuse to accept it. And a hundred or so have threatened to leave if the rest of us take your oath."

Allistor shook his head.   It amazed him how much damage a single deranged individual could do. And what cattle mentality some groups of people could display. Even before the apocalypse, the masses believed what they saw on holovids or supposed news media sources, regardless of whether there was any truth to it. Most never bothered to check for themselves.

"I'm sorry to hear that." He reached out a hand to Linda, aware that a large number of the Stronghold residents were watching. "And again, I wish things hadn't gone the way they did with your father. I wish you all good luck."

Linda shook his hand, looking confused. As Allistor stepped away, Dillon stepped forward, holding out a hand to stop him from leaving.

"We, umm... were hoping your offer of alliance was still good? Our people will accept that, as long as Linda and I are still in charge. We know you've made similar offers to others." he let his voice trail off, clearly uncomfortable.

Allistor perked up some. "Of course!" He turned and favored Linda with a grin. "I'm sorry, I thought you were rejecting me altogether. I misunderstood. Of course I'd like you to be allies! We've got a lot to discuss." He looked around the inside of the Stronghold. Most of the faces were smiling, but here and there were pockets of scowls and frowns.

"I don't want to cause issues with the folks who dislike me here. So, I invite you two, and whatever advisors you want to bring along, to join us at the Citadel in Cheyenne. We've just spent the morning talking to groups across the continent, and there's lots of news to share. That's why I was late, actually. Sorry about that."

They accepted, and fifteen minutes later Linda, Dillon, and three others were climbing into the *Juggernaut* with Allistor's crew, and they headed for the Bastion. He sat in the back with them and told them all about the vehicle, its hover capabilities, and the hydrogen fuel engine. They were impressed with the tech, and though he felt a little guilty about it, Allistor purposely didn't warn them when Goodrich drove up onto the teleport pad and they were instantly transported to Cheyenne.

"Holy crap!" Linda gasped when the view outside the windows changed. "Was that magic?"

Allistor thought about it for a moment. "More like advanced tech. Our whole world is sort of ruled by it now. I tried to tell your father some of this, but he kicked me out. Since I don't know how much he allowed the other Strongholds to share with you, we'll start from the beginning…"

*****

Over the next few days, the radio calls were completed, and Allistor's people began to distribute the scrolls and supplies they were sending to other groups. They solved the transportation problem for most items simply by using the market kiosks to sell items directly to specific buyers for minimal charges of one hundred klax.

Allistor participated in most of the secondary calls, getting to know the other leaders, spending a little extra time with the fifteen who had managed to create Citadels.

476

They exchanged information and advice, as well as making arrangements for supply exchanges. Allistor was particularly proud of brokering a deal for three tons of fresh oranges from just outside Orlando in exchange for purchasing them a crate of anti-personnel mines. The folks in Florida got the better end of the deal by far, but Allistor took great pleasure in passing out some of the oranges when they arrived. Mostly because he could tell his people that they came from the Disney World Citadel, which tickled him for some reason. He pictured thousands of people living in the princess' castle and running around with mouse ears on their heads.

The only people he shared that particular visual with were Chloe, who giggled and called him silly, and Amanda. His girlfriend had looked at him like he was an idiot and rolled her eyes, but he caught her smiling as she turned away.

At the end of the second day, just as he was retiring to his quarters at the Bastion with Amanda, Helen knocked on his door. When he let her in and the three of them got comfortable in the sitting room, she took a moment to grab a decanter off the coffee table and pour them each a drink. Leaning back, she said, "So I've been doing the research you requested. Ramon helped a good bit. From everything we've read, I should indeed be able to grant ownership of all the national parks to the owner or owners of my choosing. The fact that I was able to grant the first few to you implies that I'm the highest ranked living member of the Park Service at least, and possibly of the Department of Agriculture. But we should dispose of the parks quickly, in case there's still a president or someone out there who could appoint a new person with a rank higher than mine."

Allistor leaned forward. "Okay, how do you want to do this? Do you have a map or something?"

Helen nodded. "While you were gabbing on the radio, I took a few of Andrea's guys and we ran up to the Ranger Cabin Outpost. There were books and maps there. They brought me locations of all the groups you've been talking to, and we marked up a map in the library to show parks close to each group."

"Wow! That's awesome, Helen!" Allistor got up and gathered her into a hug. Amanda looked less enthused. Allistor was reminded of her caution from their previous meeting.

Helen sat back down, a Cheshire Cat grin on her face. Allistor asked, "What aren't you telling me?" she took a long, slow sip of her drink before answering.

"Well, according to Ramon's research, I have the power to make you an even bigger ass than you already are."

"What?" He leaned back on the sofa and crossed his arms, giving Helen a dirty look. Amanda, quicker on the uptake than her chosen mate, started laughing.

"Yep!" Helen continued, pulling a book out of her inventory and opening it to a marked page before sliding it across the table between them. "According to this, if I grant *all of the parks* to you right now, it should promote you to what they call a *Planetary Prince*." She chuckled as Amanda's laughter turned into a cough and she had to take a drink.

"A what?" Amanda asked as soon as she was able. Allistor was busily reading the page Helen had indicated.

478

"Yep. Lord Fancypants here will become Prince Fancypants. And once the title is bestowed, he can award some of the lands to his *vassals,* granting them titles like he got that first day. And he gets to keep his title of Prince. The only higher title on a planetary scale is Emperor. And Ramon says to earn that you'd pretty much have to rule the whole Earth. There can be up to twelve Princes on a planet." Helen sat back, looking very pleased with herself.

Amanda looked at her, then started laughing again. "You're thinking about keeping all the parks and making yourself an actual Princess, aren't you!"

Helen nodded, bursting out in laughter as well. "I did think about it! I mean, come on. A real-life Princess! Lord Fancypants here would have to bow to me at court. I could make Fuzzy my Chancellor!" The two women collapsed into helpless laughter, which Allistor mostly ignored. He was still reading and absorbing the information in the book. He'd moved on from the page Helen had marked, and was finding some interesting facts that he doubted she'd read far enough to see.

Eventually, he closed the book and set it down. "So, Princess Helen… what's it going to be? Are you going to keep the parks yourself?"

"Oh, hell no!" Helen sobered up a bit, pouring herself another drink. "I became a ranger because I enjoy solitude and as little responsibility as possible. I've seen all the headaches you deal with just with your few Strongholds. That's not for me. They're all yours, all four hundred of them." she paused, the serious look on her face turning to one of mischief.

"In fact… I Helen Rodgers, last of the Rangers of the National Park Service, hereby grant you, Earl Allistor of Earth, all rights to every National Park in the United States and its territories."

Allistor, who had held up a finger and opened his mouth to stop her when he realized what she was saying, was nearly blinded and deafened at the same time. Golden light filled the room, and every room in every one of his properties, and the air resounded with trumpets, chimes, and angelic choruses singing in celebration. Fireworks exploded in the air above, and Allistor nearly passed out from the sensation that poured through his body.

And, of course, the obligatory system alert popped up on everyone's interface.

World First!

Earl Allistor has gathered sufficient resources to become the first to earn the Title of Planetary Prince of UCP 382!

Congratulations, Prince Allistor! May you rule long and wisely!

There was a solid wall of other notifications filling his interface, but Allistor closed it for a moment as he stared across the table at Helen. Her eyes were wide, as was her open mouth. "Damn. I mean, I knew you were gonna get a promotion, but that was…" Her eyes unfocused as she looked at her own interface. Her mouth dropped open again. "Uhm, it seems that the National Park Service is now a ministry within Allistor's Princedom, since he now owns them all. Also, I just picked up six

480

levels' worth of experience and the Title of Minister…" her voice faded as she continued to read.

Allistor shook his head. "A little warning would have been good. I feel like I just had a two-minute orgasm that spread through my whole body."

Amanda snorted. "Well, now I'm jealous." She laughed as Allistor blushed slightly.

Helen refocused on Allistor. "It says here I should negotiate a salary package with you." She grinned. "I'm gonna want *a lot* of moolah, and like, ten weeks of vacation time every year."

Allistor scowled at her. "What? You just promoted yourself to Big Boss Ranger Lady. You've got 400 parks to manage now. No vacations for you!" The scowl converted to a wink after a moment. "Seriously, thank you for this. You've pretty much single-handedly turned me into an NPC boss. Maybe even a dungeon boss?" He got up and pulled her to her feet, giving her another hug. "And Fuzzy would have made a lousy Chancellor."

Helen gulped down the rest of her drink. "You're welcome. Now give away some of those parks to people who can defend them. I'm going to go join the celebration I hear downstairs."

Allistor cocked his head, listening. Sure enough, the sounds of a large party were drifting up from below. Helen added, "You should probably make an appearance as well. People are going to want to like, bow down to you, or something." As she got up and walked out the door, she called back over her shoulder, "The map and list are set up in the library if you want to go over them!"

Allistor sat back down, reaching for Amanda's hand and gripping it tight. "Hang with me for a few minutes before we go down there? I've got like a hundred notifications to get through here."

She squeezed his hand in return, saying, "Of course, Prince Fancypants."

Opening his interface again, he started reading the ones that were highlighted in bold text first. It seemed he too had gained several levels.

> ***Level Up! You are now Level 22. You have earned two attribute points.***
> ***Level Up!...***
> ***Level Up!...***
> ***Level Up! You are now Level 30. You have earned two attribute points.***

With nine new levels, he had a ton of attribute points to assign, but he decided to deal with that later when he'd calmed down a bit.

> ***Congratulations! You are the first human to secure the Title of Planetary Prince. Reward: 10,000,000 experience points; 10,000,000 klax; Prince's Seal***
>
> ***You have earned the Title: Planetary Prince***
> *By securing land holdings of one hundred thousand square miles or more, you have earned yourself the title of Planetary Prince. As a Prince, you have the right to levy taxes on any citizens in residence upon your land. Further, you may sell or grant portions of your land and accompanying titles up to the level of Earl to those who pledge themselves to your*

service. You may not compel any citizen to pledge to you, but those who refuse can be evicted from your holdings. Further rights and benefits will be bestowed upon completion of the Stabilization period.

Just like the previous Seals he'd been awarded, the Prince's Seal granted some buffs. But again, he put that information aside to absorb in detail later.

There were dozens of notifications with little red stars next to them. Reading the first of them, he saw it was a notification that intruders were encroaching on his sovereign territory at one of his parks. Scrolling down, he noted that they all seemed to be simple notifications. None of them said he was in any danger of losing title to the parks. Which made sense, as he hadn't lost the Thunder Basin park when the Lakota had hunted on his territory.

Allistor grimaced to himself as he imagined all those people in all those parks getting pissed at him over notifications that they were intruding on his turf.

The last notification that he took time to read was in large gold and silver letters with flourishes at the end. It wasn't a surprise, as he'd just read about the requirements in the book Helen had given him.

Congratulations! You have amassed the resources and achieved a sufficient Noble Rank to unlock the ability to construct a Capital City! See the Capital City tab in your interface for detailed information.

Allistor waved away the rest of the notifications as he got to his feet, pulling Amanda with him. He made a mental note to read some more of that book. He needed to know if he should claim and construct his city before he started giving away parks and reducing his total resources.

Pulling Amanda in for a kiss, he let it linger for a good long while. When they parted, he said, "It sounded like you were a little jealous when you asked Helen if she was going to make herself a Princess. Does that mean you want the title for yourself? Cuz I know a guy…"

She playfully smacked his chest and gave him another kiss. "Maybe. I mean, I'd have to meet him first. Make sure that whole royalty thing hasn't gone to his head."

"I'll see what I can arrange." He gave her one more quick kiss, then the two of them headed for the door hand in hand, on their way down to join the celebration.

That night, before falling asleep, Allistor took time to assign his free points. His points had been accumulating since level fifteen, and he now had thirty-one of them available. He began by putting nine points each into *Intelligence* and *Will Power*, raising them both to a natural twenty. Then he added one to *Adaptability* and three to *Constitution*, smiling as he thought of Chloe and her advice to quit letting things bite him. Now he could take a few more bites. Next, he added one to *Strength*, three to *Stamina*, and two to *Agility*, in case he got into more melee fights. Lastly, he added one each to *Luck* and *Charisma*, because why not?

He hit the button to accept his choices, and felt the rush of all the increases changing his body and mind. And with that, he went to sleep.

Designation: Prince Allistor, Giant Killer	Level: 30	Experience: 186,000/3,250,000
Planet of Origin: UCP 382	Health: 21,900/21,900	Class: Battlemage
Attribute Pts Available: 1	Mana: 11,000/11,000	
Intelligence: 20 (22)	Strength: 6 (8)	Charisma: 7(9)
Adaptability: 7	Stamina: 8 (10)	Luck: 4 (5)
Constitution: 13 (16)	Agility: 5	Health Regen: 750/m
Will Power: 20 (27)	Dexterity: 3	Mana Regen: 410/m

485

Chapter 21

A Wing And A Prayer

Hel laughed and clapped her hands as she observed the human achieving the Title of Planetary Prince, even as her father shook his head, the mists around him relaying his frustration.

"Baldur's pet human is truly full of surprises!" She sent a feeling of joy and amusement through the mists toward her already annoyed father, knowing it would increase his ire.

"It's bad enough he defeated Xar' Dakra. Now the factions are all watching him. The amount of klax being wagered back and forth over this human is approaching obscene. Entire worlds are changing hands!" Loki pushed back the mists, refusing to share in his daughter's emotions. Among their people this would be an insult, normally. But Loki and Hel shared a bond that negated the requirement for normal niceties.

"Well, at least he has not tried to claim your island, father. What was it called?"

"Hawaii. The big green one with the volcanoes." The mist around Loki swirled less violently, his irritation fading as he thought of his newest conquest. Since the beginning, Loki had established a home on every planet that had been absorbed into the Collective. The only one of his people to do so.

"Yes, Hawaii. The new Prince is far from that place, and shows no inclination toward it at all. What harm in allowing him to continue? He has been amusing to watch so far."

"He has become a Prince, foolish child. Which means, at the very least, I shall have to deal with him during any planetary conclaves. Humans stink, daughter. I will not tolerate it!"

Hel simply sat still, absorbing the irritation and pettiness that her father exuded without comment. She dared give no hint of her emotions just then, as they might alert her father of her intentions. Loki need not worry about the human's stench, for he would not be claiming his precious island. There would be a Prince of UPC 382 in the family, but it would not be Loki.

*****

The remaining weeks before the end of the Stabilization period were hectic. Allistor and Chris spent more than a billion klax on equipment and loans to other Strongholds. The regeneration machines were purchased and delivered, as were spell scrolls and training manuals. The conversations and logistical planning continued on a daily basis with the other leaders across the continent. Military resources were distributed to Strongholds that needed them,

Allistor, Logan, Sam, and George had a particularly good time adding both defensive and offensive systems to all of Allistor's holdings. Each of the properties got a defensive dome, a liberal sprinkling of anti-personnel mines, and weapons. The Outposts each got a single plasma cannon, while the Strongholds each got at least four. The Stadium got six because of its size. The Citadel and Bastion each got a dozen of the cannons. And every one of the properties got at least one anti-aircraft gun.

After several long discussions, Allistor and his advisors agreed to award some of the parklands to the more cooperative and trustworthy leaders. Once the decision was made, he put his new Minister in charge of the distribution after the two of them spent an entire day going through her list and poring over the map. By the end of the next day, Helen had spoken to each of the selected leaders. She explained to them the potential benefit of having both the land and the titles that came with it, as well as the need for them to become vassals to Prince Allistor.

About half of the chosen leaders refused. Most of them were military leaders who felt that there would be a conflict to the oaths they'd already taken, or simply didn't want to give up their autonomy. The rest swore the oath and accepted the land.

And just like that, there were more than a score new Barons and Viscounts across the continent. Allistor made it a point to call each of them and congratulate them personally.

Allistor's citizens continued to push themselves. They crafted like crazy, gathering materials from hunting and foraging parties, or purchasing them through the market. Allistor had Chris set aside a million klax and three people to shop full time for his crafters, to make sure they had what they needed.

They also continued to seek out and clear dungeons or areas that were heavily populated by alien monsters. Nearly all of his people were at least level fifteen by then, and were among the best-geared in the world, as far as he could tell. Their throwaway gear was sold or donated to the less fortunate in other Strongholds so that no potentially helpful items would go to waste.

And with just over three days left on the countdown at the top of his interface, Allistor got a call he'd been waiting for. It was Andrea, letting him know that he had a visitor at the airfield.

The leader of one of the other Strongholds had agreed to send him a pilot in return for some plasma weapons. When Allistor arrived at the Cheyenne airport, he discovered that the pilot had brought along her family. Standing next to a twin engine prop plane with skids for landing on water was a family of four - the pilot, her husband, and two daughters. Allistor practically leapt out of the *Juggernaut*'s passenger seat before Helen had even pulled to a complete stop. He jogged over and greeted them, shaking each of their hands as he introduced himself.

"Welcome to Cheyenne! I'm Allistor. So glad you decided to join us!"

"Thank you, uhm, Prince Allistor?" the woman ventured, giving an awkward bow, which her husband and daughters quickly mimicked. "I'm Kira, this is my husband Gene, and my little ones Brooke and Hillary." Helen came walking up as the girls were introduced.

"Please, just Allistor. No formality here. And it's good to meet you all. This is Helen, my Minister of Parks and one of my best friends." They did another quick round of handshakes. "There are some airmen on the way to see to your plane. If you like, we can run you up to the Citadel and find you some quarters. Or if you would rather live in one of our other locations…"

"The Citadel would be just fine." Gene answered. "And I think it'll just be the three of us. Good luck getting Kira away from her baby before she gives it a complete post-flight inspection, fills the tank, and whispers sweet nothings to it for a while." The girls both rolled their eyes while nodding in agreement. "We'll go ahead and get our quarters in order while she does that. Just give us a minute to grab our bags."

He turned and popped open a door in the side of the fuselage and began pulling out heavy-looking duffel bags and dropping them onto the tarmac.

"Let me help you with those." Allistor easily hefted four of them by their straps and walked over to deposit them into the back of the *Juggernaut*. When he opened the rear door, Fuzzy sniffed at him and the bags.

"Oh, I uhh… I'd like you all to meet Fuzzy. Don't worry, he's my bonded companion. He won't hurt any of you." He motioned for Fuzzy to hop out, and the moment the bear rounded the back corner of the vehicle, carrying Fibble in his mouth, both girls squealed and charged him.

"He's *adorable!*" Brooke shouted as she wrapped her arms around Fuzzy's neck and buried her face in his fur.

Hillary was right behind her. "Can we ride him?"

Allistor saw momentary panic on Gene's face and a look of mild concern on Kira's, but they both held their ground while the girls cuddled Fuzzy. Eventually, they relaxed and smiled as they watched the girls and the three hundred pound bear get to know each other.

Fuzzy gently set the Fibble doll down and licked Hillary's face. The girl stepped back two steps and began wiping at her face. "Ew! His breath stinks! What do you feed him?"

Helen chuckled. "You don't want to know." she said, saving them from Allistor's standard, 'Some guy's face' response. But the image reminded her of their past battles with other humans, and that led to another topic. "Before we go anywhere, I'm going to need all of you to take the oath of loyalty. They filled you in before you came here, yes?" All of them nodded and repeated the oath after Helen. "Welcome to the family!" She hugged the little girls.

Gene resumed pulling bags from the cargo hold and Helen and Allistor loaded them into the vehicle. When it was all done, Allistor looked around. The folks from the Silo hadn't arrived yet, so he asked Helen, "Can you take them up and get them situated? I'll wait here for Andrea and her guys to arrive, make sure nothing sneaks up on Kira while she's distracted with whispering to her baby."

Gene grinned and moved around to get in the passenger seat. Fuzzy and the girls climbed in a side door, and Helen drove them up to the Citadel. She was a little quiet at first, remembering the last time she'd driven on this tarmac during the fight with the void titan. But the girls' enthusiasm eventually lightened her mood and she made a little game of listing all the horrible sounding things Fuzzy might have eaten. Like skunk butts, stinkbug nests, and octopoid feet.

Allistor waited and watched as Kira ran through a mental checklist while looking over her plane. Eventually, he asked, "Does the plane have a name?"

Kira tilted her head. "Not officially. Before this year she went by her tail number. Now I mostly just call her 'Baby'."

"She looks like a fine plane. How many people can you fly at once?" he asked as he peered in through a window. He could see six seats in the main compartment."

"That depends on how much cargo you carry with you. If it's just people, Baby maxes out at eight to ten. With cargo, that number goes down based on weight."

Allistor was slightly taken aback. It had been almost a year since he'd had to think about the weight of the items he carried around. Not since he'd gotten his inventory rings.

"Do you not have inventory rings?" he asked.

She shook her head. "Just found out about them the other day. My family and I were at an Outpost until yesterday, no access to the market kiosk. When the word came around that you were looking for a pilot, we hopped right in and flew Baby straight here."

Allistor produced one of the one hundred slot inventory rings and handed it to her. "Your cargo weight worries are over."

She put the ring on and her eyes unfocused as she looked at the description. "Uh, it says there's some food and water already in here. Something called 'murder chicken bbq'?

"Ha! I forgot I stored some of that in there. Just keep it. In case you ever find yourself short on supplies. The food will stay good in there indefinitely."

"Thank you for this. Let me know what I owe you, and-"

Allistor stopped her with a raised hand. "My gift to you. We'll get some for your family as well. All my people carry at least one." He changed the subject, anxious to get going on his planned mission. "Did they fill you in on where I want to go?"

"Nope, I didn't even ask. I saw the same message everyone else did a few weeks back, that you had managed to become a Prince. That means you've been doing well for yourself. My family and I have barely been getting by for the last year. My pilot skills weren't of much use, as nobody was flying anywhere. There are dragons in the skies now, and they don't like planes. My husband is a good hunter, though, and has managed to keep us fed. We spent a lot of time foraging for items to trade with the folks at the Stronghold when they came by. But, basically, we were glorified security guards, watching over the airfield Outpost."

"I'm sorry to hear that. I've learned from my discussions with some of the other leaders that not all of them are as interested in developing their people, or taking care of them. But we're going to work on that. You and your husband, and your girls, will be able to learn spells, crafting skills, and whatever other skills you want now that you're here. Everybody here contributes in some way, and I believe in making sure you have what you need to make those contributions meaningful."

Kira nodded. "Gene will be thrilled to hear that. He's an engineer by trade. That's how we met. I was flying for a flight school, training yuppies to be pilots. He was working for a small aeronautics company in the hangar next door. We started having lunch together, and a year later we were married. That's where we took shelter when the world ended. At the hangar, I mean. Eventually somebody came along and we agreed to let them put an Outpost at the airfield, and we agreed to maintain it. Since then he's tinkered with every plane on the field, modifying the engines or the hydraulics. He was pretty much out of things to fix, but he has leveled his *Mechanic, Engineering,* and *Manufacturing* skills quite a bit."

Allistor laughed. "Did you tell this to your Stronghold leader before you left?"

Kira grinned. "Nope. Screw that guy. He pretty much left us to rot. If he knew what Gene could do, he might not have let us come here."

"Well, at the very least he would have charged me a much higher price to let you come." Allistor mused. "But it would have been worth it. You saw the vehicle we brought? I call them *Juggernauts.* They run on hydrogen fuel engines, which means they literally run on water as fuel. You think Gene would like to start playing with those?"

Kira's eyes widened and she nodded slowly. "If you had told him that before they left, he'd have started taking it apart right here." She paused, and a small smile crept across her face. "Please, let me tell him? I'm gonna make him promise to replace Baby's engine with one of those. No more pumping fuel by hand!"

Allistor agreed, and she got back to work on her post-flight checklist. As she poked and peered at her plane, Allistor continued on the track they'd fallen away from earlier. "So, I want to go to the west coast to establish a Stronghold. Specifically, just off the coast of Santa Barbara. I now own a small group of islands there called Channel Islands National Park. There's a runway on Santa Cruz Island. If it's not long enough, there is a channel between the islands or a large cove that could be used for a water landing."

Kira paused in her checklist to grab a well-worn atlas from the cockpit. A little bit of quick measuring, and she nodded. "Santa Barbara is about a thousand miles as the crow flies. Baby's max range is about thirteen hundred miles. So, even if there's a headwind, we should be able to get there on a full tank. Do you know if there will be fuel on the island?"

"I assume so. But even if there's not, Santa Barbara has a large airport and it's just a few miles across the water. Plus, we can always have more fuel trucked in from here."

Kira looked at him, frowning. "Trucked in? How long is this trip? If it's going to be a week or more, I'll want to bring the family."

Now it was Allistor's turn to be confused for a moment, until he realized Kira didn't know some vital information. "Ah, shit. I should have told you. When I place the Stronghold out there, I'll also be setting up a teleport pad. The hub is here in Cheyenne. We can get from most of my Strongholds to any of the others in seconds. So, if there's no fuel on the island, we'll have a few airmen drive a fuel truck through."

Kira took a moment to absorb the new info, then finally nodded her head. "That actually answers the next question I was going to ask you. Which was how you planned to defend a Stronghold a thousand miles away. Instant troop transport. Guess it's good to be a prince!"

Just then, Andrea and two of her guys came driving up in a blue van marked USAF on the side. Allistor made introductions, and they quickly finished refueling and inspecting the plane. When they were done, Andrea offered, "You know, we have a few bigger planes you could use, if you want to bring more people."

Kira looked at Allistor. "How many people did you want to take on this trip?"

Allistor shrugged. "I figured you and myself, and four or five people with guns in case there are mobs or hostile humans when we land."

Kira nodded, turning back to Andrea. "Thanks, but for a small group, I'll stick with Baby here. She's small and fast, and not such a big target for the dragons. Those big fat C-130's waddle through the air shouting, 'come eat me!'"

Andrea laughed. "Good point. Well, they're here if you need them. We also have a couple fighter jets, if you're interested. Just been sitting there in the hangar all this time. We've got more than three dozen Air Force personnel here, and none of us can fly them." She smiled at Kira, who laughed.

"I'm not qualified to fly a fighter jet, I don't think. I've been leveling my *Pilot* and *Navigation* skills, but I think those are still out of my league. I *can* fly helicopters, if you've got any of those?"

"Sure do! Couple of old Hueys, and one of those big double-whirly Chinook cargo deals."

"Double-whirly cargo deals is a technical Air Force term." Allistor teased his friend.

Kira chuckled. "Those would be great for local use. Like for short trips to transport groups or cargo where I can stay close to the ground, hug the trees. Cuz, you know, dragons."

Allistor zoned out, picturing a big helicopter lifting his Howitzers up to be mounted atop Stronghold walls. When he began to pay attention again, Andrea was pushing him toward the van. He blinked a couple times, noting that Kira's plane had already been pushed into the nearest hangar and secured. He climbed into the back of the van and Andrea drove them up to the Citadel. Along the way the airmen complimented Kira on some of the upgrades to her plane.

Gene and the girls were waiting for them in the former food court area of the Citadel. Helen had procured ice cream cones for the girls, and Gene was drinking hot coffee. He handed Kira a cup without a word, and she sniffed it. "Mmmm… been a long time since we had real coffee."

Annoyed by the treatment Kira and her family had received, Allistor made a note to be less generous in his future dealings with her former boss. Then he looked at Kira, and made a suggestive eyebrow waggle before looking at Gene, then back again.

497

Kira laughed. "Okay, okay. So, honey? I'm going on a little trip tomorrow with Allistor and his people. But when I get back, I'm thinking you should replace Baby's engine for me. Would you mind?"

Gene took another sip, looking at his wife as if she were speaking gibberish. "What? I rebuilt that engine from scratch, with my best modifications. She'll outfly anything with a propeller. There's nothing wrong with her engine."

"Ah, but Allistor and his people, they have these new engines. Alien tech." She paused, taking a couple sips and savoring her own coffee as her husband began to shift from foot to foot, then his hands started to twitch.

Finally, he said, "Damn it, woman! Tell me."

She grinned, leaning forward to whisper in his ear. Allistor smiled as he watched Gene's eyes go wide. He immediately set down his mug and stepped toward Allistor. "Tell me about them! Do you have one here I can look at? Do they really run on water? What kind of conversion and consumption rates are you seeing?"

Kira grabbed the back of his shirt and pulled him away from Allistor. He resisted for a moment, then looked sheepish. "I'm sorry. It's just… a viable hydrogen fuel engine?"

Allistor patted the man on the shoulder. "The vehicle you rode up here in has one of those engines. Feel free to go take a look." He paused and looked at Kira. "As soon as Kira says it's okay. I don't want to piss off the woman who's about to fly me a thousand miles."

"Tomorrow." Kira said, her tone firm. "Today we meet people, eat some good food, and rest. You can play with all the new toys while I'm gone."

Gene nodded, though the hands wrapped around his coffee mug still twitched slightly. Kira took each of the girls by a hand and led them away, saying, "I'll see you first thing in the morning, Allistor? Say, 7:00am?"

"Sounds good. Enjoy your evening! And once again, welcome to the Citadel. I hope your rooms are comfortable enough. If you need more space or something, just let Nigel know. Oh! Uh, there's an AI that runs this place. Did you have one at your Outpost?"

Gene stopped in his tracks, forcing Kira and the girls to do the same. "An AI? No, we did not have one of those."

"Nigel, say hello to our newest citizens." Allistor looked up at the ceiling, causing the others to look up as well.

"Welcome, Kira, Gene, Brooke, and Hillary. I am Nigel. Should you need anything, simply call out my name and I shall assist you."

"Cool!" Brooke exclaimed. "Hi Nigel! Can I have more ice cream?" The little girl grinned mischievously as her mother shushed her.

"I believe it is customary for young humanlings to obtain permission from a parent before obtaining sugar-based food products, little one." Nigel answered, causing both girls to giggle and Kira to smile.

"Nice to meet you, Nigel. I have lots of questions." Gene spoke toward the ceiling.

"Tomorrow!" Kira insisted, resuming her march out of the dining area. "Show me where our quarters are." Gene jogged to catch up, still glancing repeatedly at the ceiling as he led his wife and daughters to their new home.

"Oh, I like them." Andrea smiled at the departing family.

"Me too! She seems tough enough. And he told me he's a hunter on the drive up." Helen added.

"He's much more than that. He's a trained engineer who's been leveling several related skills pretty much every day since the apocalypse."

"Well, how do you like that? He'll come in handy." Andrea mused. "Alright. Quick meal and back to the Silo. I'm due to check on Daniel and the dragon eggs. Have fun storming the island tomorrow." She walked off toward the kitchen.

"Are Fuzzy and I going with you in the morning?" Helen asked.

"You are, if you want to come along. I'm not sure how Fuzzy would handle a plane. And he's heavy. He'll have to wait until we set up the teleport before he can explore the island."

"Alright, see you here at 7:00am. I'm gonna go see about improving my gear."

*****

Allistor woke early and spent some time with Amanda before heading down to meet the others. Half an hour early, he was the last to arrive. Kira was there having breakfast with her family, sharing a table with Helen, Andrea, and four of her guys from the Silo. These weren't the usual security forces group that had accompanied Allistor to places like Matthew's Stronghold. Bjurstrom had taken them all out to investigate a dungeon not far from the Wilderness Stronghold two days before. Allistor knew these men's names, but not much about them. Fisher was one of the techs, and Allistor had heard rumors that he had a bit of a crush on Redd. Bagwell and Corvin had been among the group that helped him clear the Silo dungeon and claim it. The fourth was Monroe, about whom Allistor couldn't recall any details at all.

"Morning, everyone." he called out as he approached. The airmen all stood and were about to salute when he held up a hand. "Please, sit. None of that. Salute Andrea, she's your boss. In fact, as Prince, I hereby declare you, Andrea, my Minister of Defense. I confess I don't know how your Air Force ranks might mesh with that, but I'll let you figure it out." He grinned at her.

"Thank you, Allistor. I think." She stood and gave a slight bow before sitting and digging into the stack of pancakes in front of her.

"I made Amanda the Minister of Health this morning as well. So far, all of my ministry are ladies. I think I need to spend a little more time with the guys." he mumbled as he took a seat. There were plates in the center of the table with bacon, eggs, toast, pancakes, and fresh oranges. He helped himself to a little of each, pouring a liberal dose of maple syrup over everything but the orange.

Helen spoke around a mouthful of bacon. "You could make Chris your Minister of Finance. He's a dude."

"Good call! I'll tell him as soon as we get back. Speaking of which, everybody up to date on what we're doing?" He grabbed several slices of syrupy bacon and handed them over to Fuzzy. The bear took them, dropped them on the floor, and proceeded to carefully lick the syrup off before consuming the meat. A moment later, one of the kitchen staff brought him a platter stacked with roasted meat of some kind.

Kira answered for the others. "We fly to the island, land on the strip, and you throw up a Stronghold. Doesn't seem all that complicated."

Helen swallowed her bacon and said, "Might not be that easy. The park service books I read said there was a large number of feral pigs on the islands. The one we're landing on, and two of the other four. They might be hostile. And the location of the landing strip might not be the best location for the Stronghold. The island is over twenty miles long, and we might have to do some hiking to find the best spot."

Kira nodded. "We can take an aerial tour before we land, scope out the terrain and maybe pick the spot that way."

Allistor interjected, "I have been reading about the island as well. There's a cove with a bunch of sea caves on the north side of the island. I'm thinking that might be a good place to set up. The main point of this Stronghold is to set up a fishing fleet, and possibly a small navy. Having a protected dock or series of docks and a safe anchorage sounds good to me."

All of them nodded, nobody having anything to add. They finished their breakfast, and Kira said goodbye to her family. Andrea gave orders to her men that Allistor was to be protected, no matter what. And they were off. Fuzzy stayed with Andrea, who was feeding him another slice of bacon as Allistor turned away.

The seven of them piled into the plane and Kira performed a quick pre-flight. When she was done, she fired up the engines and said, "Buckle up, guys! We're gonna be cruising at about fifteen thousand feet until we clear the mountains. That's just a few hundred feet above the tallest peak. Then we'll drop down and hug the ground until we get to the coast."

A few minutes later, they were in the air. Allistor thrilled at the feeling of the earth dropping away below him. He loved to fly, but had only been on planes twice in his life. When he'd left for college, and when he'd returned for a visit right before the apocalypse. He sat in the copilot's chair, watching the city of Cheyenne drop away below them. He waved at the Citadel, though he knew no one could see him.

When they had leveled out and Kira had set them on a direct course for Santa Barbara, she chuckled a bit. Speaking into the microphone attached to her headset, she said, "Nice thing about flying these days is there's no air traffic control system. You don't have to zig and zag from one airport to another, and there aren't any no-fly zones. We can just point Baby here in the direction we want, and go."

Allistor looked at all of the controls in front of her. It looked incredibly complicated. "How long did it take you to learn to fly?" He was wearing a headset as well. The plane was a bit too loud for normal conversation.

"Not long. I learned as a kid, from my dad. Been teaching others for more than a decade now. Hey, you want to learn? We can start right now. We're going about two hundred miles per hour, so the flight will take about five hours. Plenty of time."

"Sure!" Allistor beamed at her. "I'd love to learn. How do I start?" He raised his hands and held them above the controls in front of him, waiting for instructions.

Kira shook her head. "Hands down, cowboy. First, we talk. This plane is a Cessna 414A Chancellor. It's what you might call an antique, built nearly a century ago. One of the most reliable small planes ever built. There are newer, faster planes, but this baby holds my heart."

For an hour she explained to him the basic specs of the plane and its workings. He learned that it had a max fuel capacity of 184 gallons, with its extended long-range tanks, giving it a range of about thirteen hundred miles. That it was manufactured in the late 1970's, and that this particular plane had been in Kira's family since it was purchased new by her great, great grandfather. He learned about aerodynamics and lift, and how changing the angles of the flaps or the tail rudder caused the plane to rise, fall, or turn. As she explained each action, she demonstrated, causing the plane to maneuver as she instructed. She taught him about thrust and friction, fuel pressure, hydraulic pressure, and air pressure. Finally, she let him take the controls and make a few tentative turns to the left and right. She had him point the nose down and go into a controlled dive, then pull up and climb back to fifteen thousand feet. At the end of the hour, he received a notification.

You have learned the skill: Aviator
By studying diligently under the direction of a Master Flight Instructor, you have sufficient understanding of the principles of atmospheric flight to pilot simple Level 1 aerial vehicles. Continue your studies and gain experience through more hours of piloting time to increase your skill level.

"Yesss!" Allistor held a fist out for Kira to bump. "I just got the *Aviator* skill. This is awesome! Thank you."

"Least I can do after you adopted me and my family. Gene is so happy he kept me up half the night talking about advanced engines and new alien tech to learn. And my girls ate bacon this morning for the first time in a year." She reached down to her left side and produced a thermos. "Hell, I'd have done it just for this coffee. God, I missed coffee."

Allistor spent the next hour flying the plane. Kira nudged him on which instruments he should be monitoring, how to study the clouds ahead to watch for turbulence, and how to handle it when it happened. "And here's the most important switch of all!" she said as she reached up and pointed to an overhead switch. "Autopilot!"

When they cleared the mountains, she took the controls back. "We're going to do some skimming for a while. Low to the ground where there's no room for error. Not that I don't trust you, boss."

Allistor removed his hands and leaned back, suddenly aware that he'd been leaning forward and tightly gripping the wheel for hours. He flexed his fingers a bit as he relaxed. "My skill is up to level 3 now."

"Good! If I understand this new system right, that means you can fly most prop planes, even the big cargo monsters that Andrea has. When we get back, we'll take one of the private jets up and you can boost your skill a bit more." as she spoke, she pushed the wheel forward and angled the plane so that it almost seemed to be sliding down the final mountain face. She leveled out at about a thousand feet, and the ground flashed by beneath them as she pushed their speed up to 250mph.

"Best to keep low and fast. Less likely to attract the attention of flying beasties." she explained. Allistor continued to watch what she was doing, making note of the small adjustments she made, watching the altimeter and the gyroscope that showed their relationship to the horizon. He was amazed at how steady she kept the aircraft without any apparent effort. When he'd been in control his heart raced, and he'd been sweating like a pig.

The rest of the flight was mostly uneventful, and they managed to avoid attracting any dragons. Allistor and Kira chatted about family, and life before the apocalypse. He outlined for her some of his plans for his people. When he mentioned that a yacht class spaceship would be delivered to him in a few days, she nearly crashed the plane. "You have GOT to let me fly that bad boy!" she shouted, forgetting her microphone. Allistor winced at the volume of the outburst in his ears, but smiled.

"Who else am I going to get to fly it? You're the only pilot I've got. Though, if you're able to fly it, I expect you to teach me, Helen, and maybe a few others. I intend to have more than one of them, eventually."

"Deal!" Kira grinned at him. "Wait till I tell Gene! He's going to be so jealous." Her eyes grew wide. "And don't you *dare* let him take that ship apart!"

Laughing, Allistor said, "He's welcome to inspect it. Along with some of my other techs and engineers. I want everyone to learn how to service and build alien tech as quickly as possible. But no, I'll purchase one of the smaller scout ships or fighter craft for them to actually take apart, so they don't accidentally kill the yacht."

"Damn right." Kira murmured, already taking mental possession of the spaceship. "We'll need to come up with a good name for her. Assuming she doesn't already have one."

A short time later they passed over Santa Barbara. It was clear the city had not fared well. Large sections of it were burned to the ground, or knocked down. Looking out one of the windows in the back, Fisher called out. "I've seen this kind of damage before, after an earthquake. Do you think that's what happened here?"

Allistor shook his head. "Don't know. My hometown looked a lot like this, and it was from a void titan stomping on everything. But this is a much bigger city." He looked at a couple of crumbled mid-rise hotels. "I think you might be right."

Kira took a moment to circle the airport when she spotted it. There were dozens of larger commercial

507

passenger planes, a few cargo planes, and at least a hundred private planes parked off to one side. Many of them were damaged, but most still looked intact, at least from the air.

"Sorry, just doing a little window shopping." Kira smiled at him. "Santa Barbara was full of rich people. Which means rich people toys. Like private jets." She pointed down at the private hangers. "If we have time, I'd like to take a look on the way back."

"You'd trade in your Baby?" Allistor gave her a mock shocked face."

"Nope. But I could bring Gene back here. Or you, once you've done a few take-offs and landings. One of you can fly Baby home while I adopt one of those fancy private jets."

A moment later, they were out over the water of the Pacific and approaching the Channel Islands. Santa Cruz island was easy to spot, being by far the largest of them. Kira expertly banked as they reached the eastern shoreline, and took them on a low circuit around the island. Allistor spotted the sea caves he was looking for on the north side. The cove, protected by high cliffs, looked deep and calm. There were several docks around the island, and, overall, he was pleased with all the options.

Kira then headed inland toward the western side. The airstrip was there, running along a high ridge. She circled it once, and nodded her head. "It looks a little rough. I think you guys were right about an earthquake. Not sure it's safe to land us on that. I'm thinking we make a water landing, and we can come up here later to check the strip. Maybe make some repairs if necessary."

Allistor shrugged. "You're the expert. I'm leaving this in your hands."

She banked the plane again, heading back toward the northern shore. "Water landings are always a little bit risky. But in this case-"

Allistor didn't hear the rest of her words as they were drowned out by a roar that shook the plane. Kira banked the plane hard to the right, and, when the roar ended, he could hear her cursing. If he wasn't so terrified, he might have been impressed.

"It's a damned dragon! Came up from below us. Must have been in one of those caves!" she shouted. The engine screamed as she pushed it to the max and banked away. "We can't fight it from up here. I'm going to try to land on that strip, and we can take cover."

"What about damaging the plane?" Allistor shouted, gripping his seat tightly and looking around, frantically trying to spot the dragon.

"We land, or we die!" Kira shouted back, then gritted her teeth and turned the wheel. The plane shot across the island about fifty feet above the surface. Looking down, Allistor saw their shadow skimming across the ridges. Then. all of a sudden. there was a second, much larger shadow.

"It's right above us!" he shouted, pointing at the dual shadows that were quickly merging into one. It was midday, and the sun was nearly directly overhead and slightly behind them.

"Shit!" Kira banked hard to the left, then immediately back to the right. There was a squeal of metal, and the aircraft shuddered. From behind them, Helen shouted, "It just ripped some pieces off the left wing!"

Alarms were buzzing in the cockpit, and Kira was scanning the various gauges as she leveled out the plane. The dragon's shadow was gone, but somehow that didn't make Allistor feel any better.

"We're still okay, I think. Baby took some damage, but I still have hydraulics. So we can land. I just need about one more minute…"

The roar sounded again, clearly behind them this time. Bagwell was shouting, "Can we open the door and shoot this thing?"

"No!" Kira screamed. "You open that door right now and we're all dead. At this speed, this close to the ground, the change in pressure and dynamics might drive us into the ground. And would definitely slow us down enough for that thing to catch us! Buckle up, this landing is gonna suck!"

Allistor could now see the landing strip in the distance. It was actually slightly above them as they skimmed a lower ridge line. He could hear Kira mumbling to herself over the headset, and saw that she had a white-knuckle grip on the wheel.

"Get ready to bail as soon as we land! Don't wait until we're stopped!" she shouted toward the back.

"Roger that!" Corvin answered.

"Twenty seconds!" Kira called out. Allistor spotted the dragon for the first time. It was coming up from their five o'clock and gaining quickly. The monster was easily three or four times the size of the plane, and its hide was a deep bluish-green that gleamed in the sunlight.

Water Drake
Level 15
Health: 19,500/19,500

"Ten seconds!" Kira practically screamed. Allistor glanced forward to see the plane was rising just high enough to clear the ridge and reach the landing strip. He turned back to see the dragon even closer. Its left wing was nearly touching their right wing. Its head was already forward of the plane's nose, and it gazed at Allistor with a deep, aquamarine shaded eye.

In a panic, Allistor cast *Mind Spike* at the monster. Its eye rolled up and it roared in pain, its wings folding inward. The left wingtip scratched a line in the surface of the plane's wing, causing it to tilt downward and Kira to start cursing again.

She fought to level the plane even as the nose crossed the threshold of the landing strip. Allistor barely noticed the dragon faltering, its head and body impacting the ground and rolling. It had been going even faster than the plane, and moving just a dozen or so feet above the ground. So, when the spell struck its brain, there was no room for error.

Allistor bit his tongue as the plane's landing gear struck the ground hard, and the plane bounced. His head hit the panel above him despite being strapped in. Blood began to run down over his eyes as the plane struck ground again, staying down this time. Kira slammed on the brakes, but, a few seconds later, one of the wheels hit a rough spot created by the earthquake. The landing gear was sheared off, and the plane spun to the right while tilting downward. The wing hitting the ground kept the plane from rolling over, but the force snapped off the end of the wing.

The plane slid across the uneven strip, metal screeching and pieces being knocked off as it impacted more rough spots. Kira was screaming as if in pain, but Allistor couldn't see well enough to know whether she was injured.

Finally, the plane came to a halt, the broken wing digging into something and stopping them abruptly. Allistor heard the folks in the back open the door as Bagwell began calling the roll to see if anyone was hurt. He fumbled with the clasp on his harness, pausing to wipe the blood from his eyes when he didn't immediately manage to unlock it. Finally, it snapped open, and he looked over to see Kira already out of her seat and reaching for him. She practically yanked him out of his seat and dragged him out of the cockpit.

The two of them were the last to exit the plane. Allistor used his shirt to clear more of the blood away and began scanning the sky. When he didn't see the dragon, he lowered his eyes to check behind them. He saw a cloud of dust back near the end of the runway, and, a moment later, the dragon emerged. His people raised weapons, all five of them holding plasma rifles. The dragon was much too far away for them to be useful, at least a thousand feet down the runway, but moving closer.

"Hunting rifles! He's too far out! Shoot him in the face!" Helen shouted.

Kira, who didn't yet own a plasma rifle, raised a flare gun and fired it at the dragon. The glowing projectile shot forward leaving a stream of smoke behind it. The dragon saw it coming and ducked its head, the flare passing above to bounce off its back.

Water Drake
Level 15
Health: 11,200/19,500

The high-speed crash had done considerable damage to the drake. Raising his own rifle, Allistor sighted through his scope and saw that one of its wings was badly broken, exposed bone shining white against its blue hide. The massive beast was limping toward them, suggesting that at least one leg was damaged as well. He took aim and fired at an eye, seeing the round strike a bony ridge just above the eye, doing little or no damage.

Handing his rifle to Kira, he asked, "You know how to use this?" In answer, she grabbed it, slid the bolt back to chamber a round, raised the weapon and fired. Allistor pulled his .50 cal sniper rifle from his inventory and dropped to the ground. While his people continued to send rounds downrange at the monster, he lay prone and quickly set up the bipod at the front of the weapon. Loading it, he situated himself and took careful aim. A thousand feet was a short shot for this weapon, and the scope let him zoom in on the creature's eye. Just as he was pulling the trigger, it shifted its head upward and roared. Allistor completed the pull, and the weapon recoiled, sending up a small cloud of dust. The heavy, penetrating round struck the roof of the dragon's mouth, drilling inward but missing the brain, and thick blood poured from the wound.

The massive drake whined like a wounded dog for a moment, lowering its head so it could scratch at the side with one of its foreclaws. After a moment the head shook violently, as if the drake were trying to shake loose the hot lead inside its snout. With a roar of frustration and rage it gave up and resumed its forward hobbling.

Still way too far away for him to use any magic, Allistor chambered another round and fired. This time he aimed for the neck just below the drake's head. As before, the devastating round drilled through flesh to disappear, and the dragon reacted. This time its roar was weaker, and blood sprayed from the neck wound until the roar ended in a cough.

Still the beast pushed closer.

Water Drake
Level 15
Health: 6,800/19,500

The conventional weapons were doing some damage, but not enough to kill it before it reached them. Allistor fired his sniper rifle twice more, both shots aimed at an eye and missing as the monster's head moved back and forth.

When it was within three hundred feet, Allistor shouted, "Plasma rifles!" and the four airmen switched out almost instantly. Hot plasma began to streak toward the dragon. Though it had shrugged off all but a few of the lead projectiles, the plasma strikes definitely got its attention. The closer it pushed toward them, the less energy was lost by the plasma projectiles, and the more damage they did.

At about a hundred feet, the dragon stopped and took a deep breath. When it exhaled, a cloud of vapor washed toward them. Allistor shouted, "Inside!" and grabbed hold of Kira, throwing both of them through the door of the plane. Rolling to one side, he made room for the others as Bagwell, Corvin, Helen, and Fisher stumbled through. Fisher screamed and clutched his leg as the door slammed shut behind him.

Monroe, still outside, had gone stiff and fallen against the door, pushing it closed. The majority of the vapor had remained outside, with just a small amount making contact with Fisher's leg. "I can't... my leg is... cramps!" Fisher practically screamed.

The others could hear a creaking noise as the muscles in his leg tightened and then snapped. Fisher screamed again.

Outside, the mist had blown past them, and Allistor kicked the door back open. Looking through the door's porthole window, he cast *Erupt* right in front of the dragon. The stone spike shot upward, penetrating the base of its neck and pushing all the way through.

A quick check on Monroe showed his body contorted and a vacant, dead look in his eyes. Allistor took a deep breath and channeled his *Storm* spell.

He did his best to hide behind the door as he channeled, not wanting to expose himself to the injured and enraged dragon. It tried to push closer, but the spike prevented it, shoving deeper into its flesh every time it moved. When it took a deep breath to exhale more of the mist, the spike seemed to block that too. The exhale was little more than a weak cough.

Finally, the storm above had formed, and lightning began to arc down onto the drake. Bolt after bolt struck its head, torso, and wings. The smell of cooking flesh permeated the air, but Allistor kept channeling, crouched behind the door and peering through the glass. At fifteen seconds, there were too many bolts to count, each one slamming into the target or the ground nearby. Finally, the massive head dropped to the ground, and experience points flashed across Allistor's interface.

He immediately turned to cast a heal on Fisher, but found Helen and the others had taken care of it. The man was sitting in one of the passenger chairs rubbing his calf and thanking his buddies. "Damn, that hurt. It was some kind of paralytic I think."

Allistor nodded. "Yeah, Monroe took a full dose. He's… twisted up pretty bad. He's gone." Allistor broke the news. The others just nodded, having assumed as much. A year after the apocalypse, they had all learned to accept death.

Allistor turned to Kira. "I'm sorry about the plane. We'll help you get a new one. And once this place is stable, I'm sure we can find people to help Gene repair this one."

Kira shook her head. "This baby is toast. Too much damage to the body. She'll never be structurally sound without replacing most of her, and then she just wouldn't be Baby." she paused, patting the seat next to her.

"But she saved our lives. Outran that dragon for almost a minute!"

"That she did." Allistor smiled. Turning his attention back to Monroe, he observed. "There's not much wood up here. Let's salvage what we can out of the plane, then give them both a funeral fire."

Kira nodded, and they went to work. She retrieved her maps, thermos, and other items from the cockpit and slid them into her inventory. The guys found some tools and removed the nice leather seats from the passenger area, as well as a couple of parachutes, extra gas cans, and other items that Kira pointed out. They stacked them all on the air strip, well away from the plane and the dragon. After moving Monroe's corpse inside and removing his inventory ring, Allistor cast *Flame Shot* into the plane.

None of them waited for the flames to die down. Instead Allistor directed them to loot the drake, then harvest as much of the meat, hide, and other useful parts as they could. The six of them worked until it was nearly dark and they were all coated in blood.

Not far from the strip was what was left of the airport structure. It looked like it had once been a short tower, before the earthquake. Regardless, Allistor stood among the ruins and opened his interface, creating an Outpost. Stone walls went up, and a single-story stone structure rose from the earth. Allistor added a basement level with sleeping quarters, kitchen, and baths. He'd heard that the west coast sometimes suffered powerful storms, and he wanted anyone stuck here in one of those storms to be safe. After adding the utilities and sensors, he called the others inside.

"It's too late to go exploring tonight. This place will keep us safe enough, assuming there are no more dragons here. In the morning, we'll explore the island and set up the Stronghold. Then we can teleport in more people and supplies. Maybe take one of those boats we saw across and get Kira her jet plane."

The others nodded, exhausted. They headed downstairs to get showers and try to clean their clothes. Allistor put a hand on Kira's arm. "The others already know this. But when you get to your room, just ask Nigel to connect you with Gene, so you can let him and your girls know you're okay."

Kira looked at him for a moment, then grabbed him and pulled him into a hug. "You're a good man, Allistor." She turned and headed down the stairs, leaving him alone on the ground floor.

Stepping outside, he began to fetch the plane seats two at a time, bringing them in and setting them outside the kitchen. When all six were in place, he went to an unclaimed room and stripped, standing in the shower for a solid five minutes, just letting the heat wash over him. Another of his people gone, just days before the aliens arrived. He needed to call Andrea and let her know. Out of the shower, he put on a clean pair of boxers, jeans, and a *GameLit Don't Quit* t-shirt featuring a honey badger wearing a Viking helmet. Sitting on the stone bench that would serve as his bed for the night, he placed the call to Andrea.

Apparently, one of the others had beat him to it. She already knew about Monroe, and exactly what had happened. Allistor felt guilty for not being the first to let her know. When he apologized, she scolded him.

"None of this is your fault, Allistor. The way I hear it, you managed to finish off the dragon by yourself before it could hurt more of you. If it wasn't for you, everyone there would be dragon snacks right now. Shake it off. Get some rest, and get that Stronghold built tomorrow. Time is short, and you've got a lot of shit to do."

The next thing he heard was Nigel's voice. *"I'm afraid she instructed me to terminate the connection, Prince Allistor. Quite emphatically."*

Allistor snorted at the ridiculousness of that. Leaving the room he'd chosen, he found the others already gathered near the kitchen. They were talking quietly, sitting in the plane's chairs. Allistor walked past them into the kitchen, finding some utensils in a drawer. He turned on the stovetop and grabbed a couple pans. "I've got dinner. There's this recipe for dragon steaks that I got from Meg…"

By the end of the evening everyone retired to their rooms with full bellies, a decent buff of +2 to both *Health* and *Stamina Regen*, and slightly tipsy from a bottle of rum that Bagwell had produced from his inventory. Kira had leveled up four times from the fight, and they'd all congratulated her with several toasts, as well as one each for Monroe and Baby.

Chapter 22

Bacon and Boat Rides

Allistor was awakened by the smell of breakfast. Sitting up on his stone bench, he quickly checked his armor. He'd cleaned it the night before, using the shower to wash the dragon blood off the leather, then hanging it up to dry.

Donning his armor, and sighing with relief as the buffs he was now so used to kicked back in, he left his room and joined the others. This time Bagwell was in the kitchen, frying up a large stack of bacon. There were some oranges sitting on the counter, and several packages of pre-apocalypse snack cakes.

"Breakfast of champions!" Bagwell greeted him, spotting him before the others. Allistor grinned at him, grabbing an orange and taking a seat while he awaited the bacon.

Corvin said, "Been outside already. First thing I saw was a bunch of pigs rooting around the plane. So, I shot one, and… bacon!" He grinned at Allistor, flourishing a hand toward the breakfast meat sizzling on the stove.

"Just regular pigs? Not like, mutant alien six-eyed spider pigs or something?"

"Regular old Earth wild hogs. The kind with tusks. One shot to the head with a plasma round, and it went down. This one was level 2, so it must have murdered some smaller creatures at some point."

"Just makes it that much more tasty!" Bagwell flipped some of the bacon out of the pan onto a growing stack. He quickly laid out some more strips in the pan and kept going.

"Well, it smells damn good." Kira added.

"Any thoughts on where we're going today?" Fisher asked. Allistor could tell the man wanted to say something by the way he fidgeted in his chair.

"Not sure yet. Got any suggestions?"

The man smiled, relieved at being asked. "That bluff above the cove we flew over. It was high enough that no waves short of a world-ending tsunami will reach it. The steep bluffs on two sides make it easier to defend. The slope up from the beach is gradual, and curves around. So anybody landing there planning to invade will have to walk under the ramparts twice in two different directions to reach the gates. Plenty of time to rain hell on 'em."

Corvin nodded. "And that is solid rock. Even earthquakes aren't going to break it. I was looking at this ridge while I was out there. On the other hand, the soil on either side of the runway is volcanic. They probably built it here because volcanic rock is softer and easier to break than granite. Which is also why it popped up and cracked in so many places."

Kira added, "I was thinking it would be a nice place to put a house as we flew over. Beautiful there. Plenty of room for a Stronghold. And the walk down to go fishing isn't bad. Five minutes, tops."

Allistor just nodded along as each of them spoke. He'd been thinking something similar himself. Though he had a surprise for Kira regarding the walk.

"Alright then, the bluff it is." He pulled out the map of the island he'd brought with him. Doing some quick measuring with his thumb, he guessed, "Looks like it's maybe eight miles from here to there. The good news is, about half of that is downhill. The bad news is, the other half is uphill." He grinned as Corvin and Fisher groaned. "There are several small ridgelines between here and there. How's the weather?" he asked Corvin.

"Beautiful. Sunny and maybe seventy with a strong breeze off the ocean. Good day for a long walk. Even uphill."

Bagwell came walking out with a heaping plate of bacon, and they all paused to consume the deliciousness. It didn't have the same buff as the dragon steaks, but it did provide a +1 to *Stamina* and a +1 to *Stamina Regen* that would last for three hours.

Not wanting to waste the bacon boost, they were soon on their way. Kira gave one of the chairs a last pat as they left. When he got topside, Allistor opened his Outpost interface and scrolled through until he found what he needed. He added the *landing strip* option, and the rough and broken tarmac at their feet smoothed itself out, widened, and sprouted lights running along each side. The charred remains of the plane simply sank into the earth. Kira whispered a soft goodbye to her plane, then turned and walked away.

Hearing that, and seeing tears forming in her eyes, Allistor fell into step beside her. "I really am sorry about the plane. I'll make it a priority to get you a new one as soon as we set up the Stronghold. We'll take one of the boats across to the airport and steal you one of those fancy jets you admired. And I'll buy you a compatible hydrogen fuel engine that Gene can install for you. Or if you prefer, I'll buy you a small alien craft."

She shook her head. "No need to spend all that on me. I'll miss Baby, but she was just an old Cessna. Worth less than one of those plasma rifles."

"Not to you. To you she was a family heirloom. And you sacrificed her to save all of us. That means something." He patted her shoulder, then added in a conspiratorial whisper, "Besides, I have more klax than I could spend. Don't worry about the cost."

As they walked, Allistor spotted and grabbed several plants he'd never seen before, hoping one of them might be useful for Nancy, either to plant or as ingredients. They saw several groups of feral pigs roaming up and down the various ridges, but none came close enough to be a threat. Kira pointed out a huge nest in a tree they passed, and a moment later an eagle landed on the edge with a fish in its beak. Several smaller eagle heads appeared, demanding their share. They stopped to watch as the majestic bird ripped pieces from the fish and fed it to the young ones. The hikers didn't push their paces, averaging between two and three miles per hour. They stopped a few times when they encountered streams to splash water on themselves and rest for a moment. Bagwell spotted fish in one of the streams, and amused everyone by splashing around trying to catch one with his hands.

Eventually the smell and sounds of the ocean grew more noticeable. They'd been going on dead reckoning based on the position of the sun as it rose in the sky. When they reached the northern shoreline, they found they were only about half a mile from the bluff they wanted.

"It's all downhill from here!" Fisher stretched his arms into the sky and then twisted himself left and right at the waist a few times. "Good thing, too. Haven't walked this far in one day since basic training."

They half jogged down the grassy slope to the base of the bluff's sloped side, where it began to rise back up again. "Damn. Mostly downhill." Fisher corrected himself, earning a chuckle from the others.

Allistor led the way up, all the way to the cliff face. They looked down at the ocean, the waves breaking gently against the rocks maybe a hundred feet below. Allistor turned to survey the area. From their vantage point, they could see miles and miles of ocean. To the east, he could see the coastline where what was left of Santa Barbara's skyline was waiting across the channel. It was hard to judge distance across the water, but based on his map, Allistor guessed it was thirty miles or so.

To the west, the island continued for several miles, though he couldn't see much of it, as it was at a higher elevation. To the south, a creek ran down from the ridge they'd just descended, feeding into the ocean at the bottom.

"This place is called Pelican Bay." Allistor said as he consulted his map. "Seems like a good name, yeah?" The others nodded, and he opened his interface. Pulling up the Stronghold tab, he confirmed that he wanted to construct a Stronghold at that location.

As always, the world became invisible and a grid appeared over the land around them. He positioned the structure about two hundred feet back from the cliff's edge, and placed the short wall much closer. On the landward side facing down the slope, he set the wall at thirty feet, with the gate facing due north. He made the structure four stories tall above ground, and added a couple towers for lookouts, leaving the top of one tower flat for landing alien craft. After adding the usual greenhouse, motor pool, power, water, and sensors, he grinned to himself. Now for the surprise.

He began adding subterranean levels. Access to each level was via a ramp that led down from the one above. He just made each level a wide, open space with twelve foot high ceilings, leaving it for later to customize. When he completed six levels, he added an elevator leading down at an angle, like a mine access elevator. The shaft stopped just inside the cliff face, about forty feet above the water. Then, he shifted the rock to create an opening that led out to a twenty-foot wide ledge that he'd spotted from above. The elevator exit was built sideways, so that spray from crashing waves wouldn't enter the shaft, and it couldn't be seen from the water below.

Lastly, he created a wide stone dock pushing out two hundred feet from the beach near the bottom of the slope.

Satisfied, he accepted the Stronghold and named it Pelican Bay. When the golden light faded, they stood in the middle of the main hall on the ground floor.

The others had all seen it before, but Kira was amazed. "That was *so cool!*" she cried as she spun around, taking in the newly built structure.

"You think so? Come on, I have something to show you." He led her out of the hall and over to the elevator that led downward. After they'd all piled in, he said, "Push six." She did so, and they began the descent. It felt strange, because the elevator didn't drop straight down. Instead, it slid downward at a forty-five degree angle until it reached the sixth level and slowed to a stop. When the doors opened, Allistor led the way. He stepped forward out of the niche he'd created, then around the short stone wall onto the ledge. The others reacted with gasps or laughter as they stepped out behind him and realized where they were.

"Your comment about walking down to fish got me thinking. Now, even in bad weather, you can get close enough to the water to cast out a line or a net without getting soaked walking back and forth."

"Very cool!" Kira gave him a high-five and stepped to the edge to look down. "It's still a long climb up for anybody looking to attack this place."

"Assuming they even know this is here. They shouldn't be able to see if from down there. And Nigel can always lock down the elevator and collapse the shaft if it comes to that." Allistor bragged.

Five minutes later they were all back topside. Allistor chose a spot near the gate and placed the teleport pad. As soon as it was up and active, he asked Nigel to open a channel to Andrea.

"Took you long enough." was how she answered his call.

"Hey, we walked like a million miles in the scorching heat to get here." he protested, the others nodding in sympathy. "But yes, we're here, and the Pelican Bay Stronghold is open for business. Send over some guards, crafters, and whoever wants to check the place out. Oh, and ask Gene to bring the girls. We're going to take a little boat trip while you guys do your thing. Ask Nancy and Chloe, and Sam and Meg, to come as well. There's a greenhouse to set up, and a kitchen, and I'd like them to watch over the girls while we're gone. They can learn some gardening skills or whatever." He looked at Kira, who nodded her agreement.

"Also, I need one of the *Juggernauts* brought through, and I'm giving you access to modify this place. Add some cannons, a shield dome, the usual. And bring through whatever I'm forgetting to tell you to bring through." He winked at Helen, who rolled her eyes.

While they waited for the reinforcements, Allistor led Helen and Kira up into the tower with the flat top. He'd set up the top level as a guard-slash-lookout post, intending to have people there in case a hostile ship landed up top. Below that he set aside a floor for the quarters he'd share with Amanda. The level below that he split in half into two quarters. A smaller one for Helen, with a master suite, an office, one guest suite, and a sitting room. The rest of the floor was for Kira and family. The same layout, except with a master and two guest suites, and a small kitchen-slash-dining area in addition to the sitting area and office.

"Kira, I'm putting you guys here so that you're close to the landing pad if you're needed quickly. And Helen's room is never far from my own. Fuzzy likes to be able to visit her and mooch snacks." He smiled at Kira as she explored her new quarters. "I don't mean this to be your permanent home or anything. This is just for when we're here, for whatever reason. You'll have similar quarters at the Citadel, and Wilderness."

"This is... so much." Kira's voice was filled with wonder. "Why?"

"You're our best pilot, and your husband is probably our most skilled engineer, in addition to being a pilot, apparently. I told you, I appreciate what my people contribute. The two of you might just lead us off this planet eventually, so that we can take the fight to the evil alien overlords that started this mess."

Nigel took the pause in the conversation as an opportunity to speak.

"Your citizens have begun to arrive, Prince Allistor. Lady Meg is quite loudly demanding your presence in the dining hall."

Rolling his eyes, Allistor walked them back to the elevator and down. "Kira, I think you're gonna like Meg." he said, as they approached the woman, who was standing with her fists on her hips and tapping a foot impatiently.

"'Bout time you showed up, Your Princelyness." she grumped at him. "Give me access to the damn facility so I can outfit this kitchen properly. And hand over the dragon meat. These fellas already gave me theirs." She motioned over her shoulder to the sheepish-looking airmen.

It was almost an hour before Allistor was able to free himself and join Kira, Gene, Helen, and the four airmen for a walk down to the cove. There were two boats moored there, tied to a rickety-looking wooden dock. Another, smaller boat sat high on the sand near the top of the dune. Its hull was caved in and it looked pretty beaten up.

"Looks like this one broke free and got washed up by a storm, maybe?" Gene observed. Passing it by, he went to the largest of the other two and began inspecting it. He fiddled with the controls for a moment, then said, "No key, I'm going to have to hotwire it."

Two minutes later, he had the boat started, but he quickly shut it off again when the engine sputtered and complained. "That doesn't sound good. Give me ten minutes." he said before disappearing into the bowels of the boat.

The others poked around and examined the other boat, which still had a key hanging from a cord on the rear-view mirror. This one started up as well, but didn't sound any better. Kira turned it back off. They split up and hopped into the water, carefully checking the hulls of both boats, looking for damage. The sides nearest the dock had some serious scrapes and scratches, but no holes that they could see.

True to his word, Gene appeared in just under ten minutes and restarted the boat. He sheepishly held up a key, saying, "I found it in the galley below. I'll fix the wiring later so the key works."

This time, the engine sounded much healthier. After they all piled in, Gene put it in reverse and backed it

529

away from the dock. Turning it to face the open ocean, he put it in gear and they were off. "It has enough gas to get us to the mainland, but I didn't see a pump around here. There may be one at another dock somewhere, but we should fill the tank wherever we dock in Santa Barbara."

Not wanting to push the engine that had lain dormant for at least a year, he kept to a reasonable speed, and it took them about an hour and a half to reach the mainland. After scanning the shoreline, he pulled them into a marina filled with expensive looking boats that sported a gas pump near the end of a stone pier. Kira hopped out and produced a pump from her inventory. The airmen assisted, and they managed to fill the boat's tank, and an extra couple five-gallon cans they found in the back.

Allistor looked at the airmen as he, Helen, Gene, and Kira prepared to leave.

"Can all of you guys drive a boat?"

"Doesn't look that hard." Bagwell shrugged his shoulders. The others nodded.

"Okay, it's going to take a good while for us to get to the airport, pick a plane, and get it flying. So, here's what I think. You guys fan out, pick some boats from here in the marina or close by. At least one of them needs to be a fishing boat. Preferably the commercial type, with nets and cranes 'n' stuff. Another can be a sport fisher if you want. And at least one should be a sailboat, in case we need to move quietly for some reason. If you find a rich family's yacht, great. So search around, find boats with keys. If you want to tie this boat and some other smaller boats to the sterns and tow them, that's good too. But make sure they have enough gas to get back. Any of you got a pump?"

Corvin raised his hand. "Had to pump some gas on the last foraging trip. Still have it in my inventory."

"Great! Fill up all the boats here before you go. Stick together, don't go anywhere alone. Be smart, be safe. I'm not sure if our radios will work that far away, so wait here until either we come back, or you see a plane fly overhead. If we fly by, take the boats and head back. You need to get there before dark. And again, stick together. If you have time after you round up the boats, feel free to do a little foraging. I'm sure lots of these boats have some good booze on them." He grinned and waved at the men as he turned to leave.

The smaller group moved up and out of the marina. Allistor had them wait as he walked into the large building at the west end of the main pier that included several restaurants, a maritime museum, and a marine works. "Can't hurt to have an Outpost here, right? Handy place to gas up the boats, or fix them if necessary?" The others shook their heads as he claimed the place, then put a wall around it. He added the usual features, then instructed Nigel to alert him if anybody approached. There was no way for him to reach the place quickly, but at least he'd know if somebody tried to claim the territory. He put three plasma cannons atop the walls and gave control to Nigel. If somebody wanted this harbor, they'd have to work for it. Lastly, he keyed his radio. "Uh, hey guys? New plan. If you don't think you can get the boats back to the island by dark, I just put an Outpost at the end of the pier. You can spend the night and head back in the morning."

531

"Roger that, boss. We saw. Not exactly stealthy when you build those things." Corvin replied.

Continuing on, they'd walked maybe a block when Gene spotted an old Ford pickup parked in a lot outside a surf shop. "Why walk when you can ride?" he asked. It took him less than a minute to hotwire the truck, and the engine came to life. Kira hopped in next to him up front, and Allistor and Helen climbed into the truck's bed.

Kira navigated for Gene as he drove them through the broken and debris-littered streets. Twice they had to stop and find another route because the earthquake had torn wide rents in the street that the pickup couldn't cross.

It took them an hour to go the ten miles from the harbor to the airport. And when they arrived, Kira blew out a breath and cursed. "These runways don't look a whole lot better than the strip on the island. This must have been one hell of a quake. Gene, drive us out there. No point in picking a plane if we can't take off."

Gene did as instructed, and they cruised up and down runways, Kira looking closely at the tarmac. The fourth one they inspected seemed acceptable to her. "This one's long enough, and if we stay to the left side, should be okay."

Gene turned around and drove back to the hangars. It took less than ten seconds for Kira to point to an open hangar with a long, sleek-looking plane parked inside. "That's our new Baby, right there."

Gene pointed to a different plane a couple hangars down. "I like that one. It looks, sturdier."

"No reason we can't take both." Kira grinned at him. Then she looked at Allistor. "You want to grab a prop plane and make it a whole air force?"

Allistor shook his head. "I don't know if I can handle the take-off and landing. Maybe next time."

"Might not be a next time." Kira pointed out. "The aliens come in a few days. I'm guessing this will be prime real estate when they do."

Allistor laughed. "You know what, you're right? Why shouldn't we have our own air force? I'm a damn Prince, after all. You guys go steal your planes, I'm gonna take Helen and steal an airport!"

Jogging toward the main building with Helen at his side, Allistor began to voice his thoughts. "This place is unstable. Another earthquake could flatten it completely. I'm not sure it's fair to ask anyone to come and protect this place. But I can't pass up the chance to deny it to the aliens when they come."

Helen wasn't as enthusiastic. "This is one of a thousand places we should try to deny them. But there's a limit to what you can accomplish, Allistor. Especially with just a few days left."

He didn't answer, though he agreed with her. He didn't need to. As they approached the nearest entry to the main airport terminals, Allistor saw that it was actually in pretty good shape. The place was reminiscent of an old Spanish mission, with arched doors and windows, sporting a tower made to look like a bell tower. The whole thing was built of white concrete and glass, and while the glass was all shattered, the structure itself had held up well.

Stepping through the side doors and past the rental car counters, with his shotgun at the ready, Allistor immediately opened his interface and tried to claim the structure. A message told him that other occupants had a previous claim.

"There's someone or something here, keeping me from claiming this place. We'll have to clear the building."

Helen snorted. "I have a better idea." She walked to the center of the building, where the ceiling arched high above and a second-floor mezzanine stood directly over her. Tilting her head up, she shouted at the top of her lungs. "Hey! Anybody home? Any monsters in here? We're in kind of a rush, so come on out! If you're human, we don't want to hurt you! If you're a monster... well, that's a different story!"

She grinned at Allistor as the acoustics of the domed ceiling sent her voice echoing through the building. There was a rustling up above, and a human face peered out through what had once been the mezzanine window. It immediately pulled back, and there was silence.

"It's alright." Allistor spoke just loud enough for them to hear. "My name is Allistor. Prince Allistor. You might have seen a system message about me? I've come to make this place safe. So no monsters will spawn here. You'll be able to sleep in safety."

The half face reappeared slowly, one eye peeking down at him. This time it withdrew more slowly.

"There aren't any monsters anymore. Not since the earthquake. I think it killed them all. Or the aliens decided this place was dead, or doomed, and moved on."

"Well, that's good to hear, I guess. But this place isn't dead, is it. You're here. Are you all alone?"

"No! There's hundreds of us here! You better leave, or I'll call them to come shoot you!" The voice was young, and female. Allistor thought she might be a teenager.

Helen spoke next. "We don't want any shooting. Every human life is precious. But you go ahead and call to your friends, sweetie. We'd like to meet them. I swear we mean you no harm."

The face reappeared, followed by a body. She was maybe sixteen or seventeen years old, and painfully thin. Allistor suspected it had been a while since she had a decent meal, or a good night's sleep. Looking around, he spotted a dining area with metal tables and chairs, all of which were overturned. Going to retrieve a table, he moved it out from underneath the mezzanine and set it where she could see it. Then he returned and grabbed three chairs. Setting them around the table, he sat, and motioned for Helen to do the same. Then he produced some bbq murder chicken. Helen disappeared for a minute, returning with plates and plastic utensils.

"Come on down. We've got plenty of food to share." Allistor spoke the invitation casually. "It's actually pretty good. The meat is from these giant chickens that tried to kill Helen and me. Oh, that's Helen, by the way. She's a former park ranger, and now my Minister of Parks? What exactly is your title again?" He looked at Helen and winked.

"Well, my official title is Minister of the Prince's Park Service. But my *job* is protector of his royal

535

fancypants' butt." She grinned up at the girl who was still hovering near the broken window. "Ask anybody. He's terrible at keeping things from biting him. I'm constantly having to shoot monsters that have clamped their teeth in his ass."

"Well, not *constantly,*" Allistor argued. "But it has happened. We've had to fight a lot of monsters this year. Just yesterday we killed a dragon out on Santa Cruz Island."

The girl leaned forward a bit. "A big blue one?"

"Yep, that's the one." Helen gave the girl a thumbs-up. "Its breath was some kind of paralyzing mist. Killed one of our guys before we got it. Allistor killed it with lightning."

"Yeah, I've seen it hunt. It would swoop down and breathe on cattle or people, and they just fell down. Couldn't move at all, then their bodies started to twist and bend. The dragon just landed and took its time eating them." The girl paused, tilting her head to one side. "Did you say lightning? He can control lightning?"

"Shoots it right out of his ass!" Helen giggled, and so did the girl.

"I do not!" Allistor protested. Then he grinned. "But that would be cool. What is your name, miss…?"

"I'm Maggie." she half smiled as she introduced herself.

"Well, Maggie, I feel bad sitting here eating while you stand up there watching. Please come down and join us. I swear we mean you no harm. And if you have friends up there, they are welcome, too." He looked over at the dining area. "There are lots of chairs."

Maggie nodded and disappeared. After a couple of minutes had passed, Allistor started to think she'd simply fled. But then he heard footsteps, and turned toward the sound. Coming down the stairs were Maggie and four children. The kids looked slightly healthier than Maggie did, and just as he was noticing this, Helen whispered.

"She's been feeding them instead of herself."

Allistor thought she was probably right. Helen got up to grab more plates, and Allistor fetched another table to put next to the first, then brought over more chairs with Helen's help. By the time the kids arrived, they were all set up.

"Well, hello there, little ones." Allistor smiled at the kids. The oldest was a boy that looked to be maybe ten, and the youngest a girl of four or five. The middle two were boys that might have been twins aged seven or eight. The ten-year-old was black, and the other three children looked Hispanic. Maggie was a blue-eyed blonde.

"Maggie, you can introduce us to your family as they eat. Looks like all of you could use a solid meal." He began cutting apart pieces of the murder chicken bbq and placing them on plates, which Helen passed around. She produced several water bottles from her inventory, and handed one to each child.

Nervous at first, the children sat with their hands in their laps, their eyes darting from the food to Maggie to the strangers. Maggie nodded her head, picking up a piece of the chicken and taking a bite. The little ones instantly dug in.

"Easy, easy." Helen chided them. "Chew the food before you swallow, or you'll get sick. We're in no rush. You're safe here with us. Take your time." she spoke softly, reaching out to stroke the hair of the little girl, who flinched away. "I'm sorry, darling. I didn't mean to scare you." She pulled back her hand and put it in her lap.

Maggie swallowed her food and said, "That's Lila. And this is Billy, Edgar, and Jose." She pointed to the eldest boy first, after nodding toward Lila.

"William." Billy corrected her. "My name is William Jefferson Johnson." He puffed out his chest.

"Nice to meet you, William. That's quite a name. Sounds presidential." Allistor held out a hand for the boy to shake. Then he shook hands with the two younger ones, ignoring the sticky bbq sauce. "Edgar and Jose. Are you brothers?"

They both nodded their heads, not pausing their meal to speak.

Allistor and Helen let them eat in peace for a while, cutting more pieces of chicken for them when they finished the first. Helen even produced some cookies for dessert, which the kids seemed oddly unenthused about.

Maggie saw her confusion and smiled. "We've been living off mostly vending machine food and stuff that's prepackaged. So a lot of granola bars, chips, cookies, and sugary foods."

Allistor chuckled. "I did the same for the first couple weeks. We lived off what we could scavenge from a convenience store. Until we learned we could cook and eat the monsters we killed."

Maggie nodded. "We were part of a larger group until a few weeks ago. We were living in one of the hotels near here. They did the same thing. There were always those canid things sniffing around, and we learned to cook them. But then the earthquake hit. The hotel collapsed and killed almost all of us. The monsters got some others. We're all that's left. And I don't have any weapons to kill the canids with. I don't dare leave these guys to go find one, so we just hide.

Helen put a hand on Maggie's. "You've done an amazing job keeping them alive." She reached into her inventory and pulled out a .45 pistol with a couple extra magazines, handing them to Maggie. "And now you have a weapon. Just in case."

"Speaking of hiding, if you want to come with us, you won't have to do that anymore. At least, not from the monsters. We can take you to a safe place. I plan to make this place a Stronghold, so no more monsters can spawn here. And we have other Strongholds up in the Rocky mountains. With thousands of people to help keep you safe."

"Are you really a prince?" Lila asked around a mouthful of murder chicken.

"I really am. Though I wasn't always. I was just a regular dude like William here, before the world changed. I got lucky, and met Helen. She did some special magic, and turned me into a Prince!"

Helen snorted. "He didn't just meet me. He saved my life. I was all alone and hiding from canids, just like you. I was starving in a dark basement. Allistor found me, and pulled me up into the light. He fed me, and protected me, and became my best friend. Now we watch out for each other."

Lila had already lost interest and gone back to focusing on her food. But Maggie and William hung on every word.

"Can you make me a prince, too?" William asked, hope written all over his face.

Helen smiled gently at him. "I'm afraid it was a one-time, special thing. I don't have that power anymore."

William looked disappointed, poking at his chicken with a fork and pushing it around his plate.

"But thanks to Helen, I have some power now." Allistor chimed in. "For instance, I have the power to make you a Squire. What do you think about that?"

"What's a squire?" William eyed him suspiciously.

Maggie answered for him. "In the old days, when there were kings and knights, every noble knight had a squire. Usually a boy or young man who helped him put on and take off his armor, took care of his horse, made sure his weapons were clean and sharp. And, in return, the knights would train them to become a knight themselves."

Allistor was impressed. "Exactly right, Maggie! Well done. Now, I'm only a Prince, not a king. And I don't have any knights yet. I do have cowboys, and hunters, and engineers, and crafters, and all kinds of other people. So, until I get myself some knights, you could be *my* squire if you like."

"And you'll teach me how to be a prince?" William wasn't ready to give up on princedom so easily.

"Ha! I don't have any idea how to be a prince. I'm just learning myself. But we can learn together."

William thought it over for a while, stuffing another forkful of chicken into his mouth and chewing slowly. Finally, he nodded his head. "Okay, but I need my own room. And a salary of like… a hundred dollars."

Maggie suppressed a grin as Allistor responded. "Oh ho! Quite the tough negotiator we have here. Maybe *you* can teach *me* how to be a good Prince!" Allistor winked at the boy. "You've got a deal!" He held out his hand for another sticky handshake.

William beamed at Maggie, his chest puffed out again. Then his face fell. "Shit, I should have asked for two hundred dollars."

Maggie smacked him on the back of his head, just hard enough to get his attention. "Language, Billy!"

Helen and Allistor suppressed their laughter. Helen said, "I can't wait for you to meet Chloe. I have a feeling you two are going to get along great."

Noticing the position of the sun through the windows, Allistor got back to business. "Listen, Maggie. I need your permission to turn this place into a Stronghold, since you were here first. The system works on sort of a 'finders keepers' basis right now. If you'll allow me to make the Stronghold here, and all of you swear the oath of

541

loyalty," he paused to look at William. "Just like the knights of old used to do." Looking back at Maggie, he finished, "We can take you guys with us and give you a new home."

Maggie didn't hesitate. "The airport is all yours." The little ones all nodded in agreement.

Allistor opened his interface and confirmed that he was now able to claim the airport. "Okay guys, there's going to be some bright light and noise, but nothing that will hurt you. It's actually pretty cool to watch. Are you ready? Watch this!"

He claimed the airport and created the Stronghold. Using the existing building structure, he added high walls around the entire airport property, excluding the runways. He added the same subterranean levels he'd just built on the island, and added a couple of towers. Next came the greenhouse and other ancillary structures, the utilities, sensors, et cetera. Then he addressed the concern he had about stationing people in this dangerous earthquake zone. While he worked, Helen had Maggie and the kids repeat the oath, making it a solemn event for the kids' sake.

Opening the Defense tab, he went crazy. First, he purchased a dozen of the plasma cannons and mounted them on the walls and the towers. Then he bought three anti-aircraft batteries and placed them behind the walls. He littered the ground outside with mines, except for the one runway Kira had chosen. Then he repaired that runway just as he did the island's strip.

Next, he pulled up one of the options that Logan had discovered, and purchased five battalions of battle droids, each a thousand strong. The army cost him a seven hundred fifty thousand klax, but he had money to burn, and big plans for the small army. With that done, he asked the kids, "What should we name this place?"

Distracted by the lights, and more than a little disturbed that their chairs now seemed to be sitting on empty space, the kids didn't answer right away. Eventually, Edgar spoke up. "How about 'the Mission'? My papa told us that this place was built to look like a mission that the priests built here a long time ago."

"Perfect!" Allistor patted the boy on the head, filled in the name, and completed the transaction.

He enjoyed watching the kids' faces as the Stronghold built itself. A few moments after the construction was complete, his own face adopted the same look of wonder as a side door of the market kiosk opened, and battle droids began to march out in a column ten-wide. They just kept coming and coming, marching directly toward him.

The droids were roughly humanoid in shape, walking upright smoothly on two legs. But their torsos sported four arms instead of two. Two of the arms held plasma rifles, and one carried a long staff weapon of some kind. Each of them sported a pack on their backs. Their bodies were made of a black metal composite that seemed to absorb light rather than reflect it. Atop their torsos, the droids' heads were angular, shaped in a wedge like a viper's skull. They had three eyes set in a triangle centered in their faces, two that glowed blue and one green.

The lead droid was nearly twice the size of the others, and had gold stripes across its chest. One out of every hundred of the droids in the column was larger than the rest, but smaller than the leader, and had red stripes.

The lead droid approached Allistor and bowed. Its motions were fluid and silent, none of the jerky movements Allistor would expect from a machine. "Brigade Commander Alpha, at your service, Prince Allistor." Its voice was deep and smooth, with no mechanical resonance at all. It was almost as if he were interacting with a human in battle mech armor.

Allistor was geeking out so hard he nearly forgot how to speak. He hoped the delay made him look impressive and royal instead of as doofy as he felt. Looking around at the shocked faces of Maggie and the kids, he felt a little better.

"Welcome to the Mission Stronghold, Brigade Commander. I have some questions about your capabilities."

"Of course, Prince Allistor."

"Please take a look at this Stronghold and its defenses. I'd like to know how many of your soldiers you think it would take to defend this place against an alien force that might try to take it."

The Alpha stood unmoving as its two blue eyes separated and moved around its head in opposite directions. A moment later they returned to the front, and it spoke.

"You have significant anti-aircraft capabilities, as well as more than the standard number of plasma cannon emplacements atop the walls. Proper estimation of force requirements is difficult without a specific threat assessment. However, a standard colonization ship would carry a force of approximately one hundred fighters in addition to the civilian contingent. Against such a force, with your current fixed capabilities, two hundred and fifty of my battle droids would be sufficient to successfully defend the Stronghold."

"Thank you, Commander. Do you have a name, by the way?"

"My current designation is Brigade Commander Alpha. You may choose to change this designation as you see fit."

"Good! Since you are my first commander, I think we'll call you Prime. You will command all of my current and future forces, should I need more. Giving you the effective rank of General. Is that acceptable?"

Prime bowed again. "Of course, Prince Allistor."

"Alright then! I have several Strongholds, a Citadel, and the Bastion to defend. Please assign… let's say five hundred of your troops to remain here and defend the Mission. Just to be sure. The rest we will distribute among the other facilities to support the human defenders."

"Very good, Prince Allistor." The droid saluted with a fist to its chest.

Immediately, the last five hundred droids in the column, including five of the mid-sized droids, separated from the rest and fanned out, taking up posts along the walls and up on the towers. Allistor was deeply impressed by their efficiency.

"Are there any specific parameters you wish to include with the standard defense protocol?"

Allistor looked at Helen, who was grinning like a kid on Christmas morning. She said, "Looting mobs?"

"Ah, yes. Any non-human attackers that your soldiers kill should be brought inside and looted. Can your soldiers loot?"

"Of course, Prince Allistor. Any items looted or resources gathered will be automatically deposited in the Stronghold's vault per standard operating procedure, unless you wish to designate otherwise."

"That's fine. Then have your troops loot their kills after the battle is over, and seize any resources left behind by the attackers. This includes vehicles. If you are unable to secure the vehicles inside the Stronghold, then protect them until we arrive to take possession of them."

"And for human attackers?"

"Give them a verbal warning to stay away. Use non-lethal force if possible, then detain them. Or if they retreat, let them go. But do not allow them to damage your troops or my property. Use lethal force if necessary. And in that case, treat them as any other attacker."

"Understood, Prince Allistor." Prime saluted again.

"No need to call me Prince Allistor each time. It seems clunky. How 'bout you just call me Sire?"

"As you wish, Sire."

"Alright. Last thing. And this goes for all of your troops in all our locations. I'm going to give you a list of my trusted advisors. You and your troops are to obey their orders as if they were my own. With the single exception that any order to attack me or my sworn citizens requires my direct approval."

"Understood, Sire."

"Good. Hold on for a moment while I arrange transport. Nigel, please update General Prime here on the size and defensive capabilities of our other facilities. I'd like a recommendation from the two of you on troop deployment at each."

"Of course, Sire." both droid and AI answered in unison. Allistor was impressed that Nigel had picked up his instructions regarding how to address him.

Walking over to the open market kiosk, he did a search for teleport pads. Not finding anything, he went back to his own *Stronghold* tab. He remembered reading that the pads were expensive, but didn't recall seeing where to purchase them. The answer came to him when he gave up after a long search of that tab and switched to one called *Transportation.* He found the pads there along with hubs for sale. The hubs were greyed out, Allistor assumed until the Stabilization period was over. But since he already had a hub, he was able to purchase another pad for five million klax. That price, which had seemed so unbelievably high to him when he'd first researched it, didn't even make him blink now. The value for the cost was tremendous.

He quickly installed the pad, then tried his radio. "Gene? Kira? How we doing?"

"Nice Stronghold, prince fancypants." Kira's amused reply came across.

"We've got keys for three jets. I'm looking them over, but really any one of them would be fine. We can

547

have the best two gassed up in about twenty minutes. You sure you don't want to try a plane of your own? There's a beautiful King Air turboprop just sitting here. I kind of want to hug it." Gene offered.

Allistor shook his head, though Gene couldn't see him. "Maybe another time? We're going to have some additional passengers. We found five survivors to bring home. Thought we might give them a little plane ride instead of just using the teleport."

"Roger that." Kira answered. "Hey, um, I'm looking at the gate. You need to make it bigger. These two jets have wide wings, and we won't be able to taxi out."

Allistor smacked himself in the forehead. He should have thought of that. Opening his Stronghold tab again, he made a quick adjustment to double the width of the gate. This required him to switch from swinging doors to a solid metal slab that rose up from the ground to fill in the gateway like a horizontal elevator door. Then, while he was thinking about it, he set some mines out along the other side of the runway, and under the other, still broken runways. Anybody trying to land here other than his people would have a bad day.

"Alright, the gate is fixed." he reported. Then, just to check, he called out. "Marina crew, can any of you hear me?"

"Loud 'n' clear, boss." Bagwell answered. "Congrats on the new Stronghold."

"Thanks, we're calling it the Mission. And boy, do I have a surprise for you guys. How you doing on the boats?"

"We found keys for two sport fishers and a friggin' yacht. I mean, a big one. The kind you can land a helicopter on. Right now, we're trying to figure out how to pilot the damned thing. It's all digital, and we need a security code. But we'll figure it out. We also found a real fishing boat with no keys, but Corvin was able to hotwire it. If we can get the yacht going, it can tow several other boats, so we're picking out some good ones."

"Alright, well, don't wait on us. We've got a teleport pad set up here, and you heard the update on the planes. If you have the boats arranged in time to get back before dark, do it. Otherwise, sleep at the Outpost and head back in the morning."

"Roger that, boss."

Mentioning the marina Outpost, Allistor turned to Prime, who was standing quietly, presumably communing with Nigel.

"Prime, can your soldiers walk about ten miles to our Marina Outpost and man that station?"

"Of course, Sire. Each unit now has the locations of all your facilities updated in their programming. My battle droids can march approximately one hundred of your miles before needing to recharge. I recommend sending twenty-five to the Marina Outpost. They can run there in approximately thirty minutes."

"How do your droids recharge?" Helen asked before Allistor could.

"We are capable of several charging options. The most efficient is to charge by connecting to charging stations using hydrogen fuel converters. A full charge can

549

be completed in twenty minutes. Next most efficient is connection to facilities like your own that have power provided by the system, taking one hour to fully charge. We can also use solar energy, though the charge time varies based on the intensity of the energy source. On this world, a solar charge would take eight of your hours. We can also convert certain materials to energy in emergency situations. This is an inefficient method, and not recommended for regular use."

Allistor thought about it for a moment. He'd certainly buy the hydrogen fuel charging stations for each facility. But he wanted to know about outside. Like field battles.

"We have the *Juggernaut* vehicles which run on hydrogen fuel. Can you connect to those and recharge?"

"I am not familiar with the *Juggernaut* designation. But most hydrogen fuel vehicles do allow for charging of droids and other systems."

"Good to know. Okay! Let's send a contingent to the Marina Outpost. They'll be okay without one of the uhh… officer droids?"

"Those are Centurions, Sire. Each operating unit of one hundred is assigned a Centurion. And yes, a simple Outpost defense is well within the operational capabilities of the standard droids without supervision. Assume the same parameters as given for this Stronghold?"

"Assume those parameters for all of my properties, please." Allistor nodded.

"Very good, Sire. It shall be done." Twenty-five more of the droids peeled off the back of the column and ran at a solid clip out the gate.

"Alright, General Prime, it looks like we're about finished here. I'll open the teleport pad to the Citadel and you can begin sending your troops to the various Strongholds. We'll arrange transportation to some of the outlying Outposts. Have you and Nigel worked out force disposition?"

"We have, Sire." Prime replied. "We estimate that it will require approximately three thousand eight hundred of my droids to effectively defend all of your facilities. I recommend placing reserve forces at the Cheyenne and Denver locations."

"Very good. I defer to your expertise. Both of you. Nigel, please use the pads to transport the troops as you and General Prime have planned. And uh, please put me on loudspeaker at all of our facilities."

"Whenever you are ready, Sire." Nigel replied.

"Hey everybody! It's me, Allistor. Your friendly neighborhood Prince. I have a little surprise for all of you. In the next few minutes, a small army of battle droids under the command of General Prime will be teleporting to all of the Strongholds. For those of you at Outposts, they will be arriving by more conventional means in the next day or so. These guys are going to assist us in the defense of our homes in the coming days. Please don't be frightened by them. They will not harm you, unless you somehow violate your oath and try to harm one of our own."

He paused to think for a few seconds, then added. "All of my advisors with access to the structures you're in, please order one of the hydrogen fuel chargers and install it at your location. Chris, please purchase enough for the Outposts as well, and send them with the troops we transport out there. If they're ridiculously expensive, let me know before you buy them. If they're cheap, buy two for each Outpost and ten for each of the bigger properties." He stopped again, feeling foolish.

"Oh! We have two new Strongholds, one called Pelican Bay on Santa Cruz Island just off the coast of Santa Barbara, and the other called the Mission at the Santa Barbara airport. We also have new Outposts at the island's airstrip, and the Santa Barbara Marina. We're in the process of commandeering ourselves a fishing fleet, a navy, and an air force! So, uhm, if any of you have an interest in becoming pilots, find Kira at the Citadel in a few days for training. And any of you who already have experience driving boats or working a fishing boat, we could use you on the island. Thanks for listening! Have a great day."

Allistor looked at General Prime. "Okay, my people have been warned, so nobody should try and shoot you when you step through the teleports. Please commence your deployment. I'd appreciate it if you would remain with me, wherever I am. And maybe an honor guard of two more of your troops? I have a habit of getting into trouble."

"Certainly, Sire. And may I say I appreciate your willingness to consider my advice." Prime saluted again. Two of the droids stepped forward to stand behind him, and the entire remaining column did a perfectly synchronized about-face. The first group stepped onto the teleport pad and disappeared, followed quickly and efficiently by a second group.

Allistor grinned, wishing he could see the faces of his friends when they got their first look at the droids.

Chapter 23

Potts Shot

By the time the battle droids had all gone through the teleporter, Kira and Gene were ready. Allistor, Helen, the kids, and the three droids walked over to the hangars to find the couple standing between two sleek-looking private jets.

Allistor introduced everyone quickly, then asked, "So, what do we have here?"

Gene pointed to his right at the larger of the two planes. "This is an old Gulfstream G650. It's much newer than the Cessna you guys killed yesterday, only about sixty years old. It has seating for eighteen people, and a range of seven thousand miles with its current systems. This will, of course, change greatly when we replace the engines with alien tech. But with this baby as it is, you could fly from here to Paris or Tokyo. The cabin is super-pressurized, so we can fly as high as forty-five thousand feet, hopefully higher than the dragons will go."

Kira pointed at her plane. "I went with a smaller one. The Learjet 70. About the same age as the Gulfstream, it'll hold eight passengers, plus two in the cockpit, and has a range of two thousand miles. This little darlin can fly low and small, and go over five hundred miles per hour. My little Baby almost outran that dragon at two fifty, so in this girl we should leave them in the dust!"

Gene pointed to a very cool looking prop plane parked in one of the hangars. "There's the King Air. You sure you don't want to try it?"

"Nope, but I was thinking I could ride with one of you, and maybe try the take-off and landing? You could take over if I mess up."

Gene bowed and waved a hand toward Kira with a flourish. "One master flight instructor, at your service." Kira rolled her eyes.

Helen said, "Gene, if it's okay with you, I'd like to ride as your copilot and see if I can pick up the skill?"

"You're welcome to try. Though, if I understand it correctly, Allistor picked up as many levels as he did because of a bonus for studying under Kira. I'm afraid I can't do the same."

"That's okay. I'd still like to try. No point in wasting the opportunity."

"Fair enough! And since Allistor's going to try his hand at landing on that short strip on the island, maybe the kids should ride with you and me?" He winked at Allistor to show he was teasing.

"Good idea, actually. Take the two battle droids with you as well, and I'll take General Prime with me."

They loaded themselves into the planes, and both pilots performed their pre-flights. When they were ready, Gene took the lead. Over the radio, he said, "I'll go first. That way if Allistor crashes and burns, blocking the runway, we won't be trapped."

"Speaking of the runway, I fixed the one Kira picked." Allistor replied, ignoring the jibe. He decided to write the bad jokes off as engineer humor.

Gene's take-off went smoothly, and Kira had Allistor taxi to the head of the runway, even as Gene was leaving the ground. She talked him through the process, had him run through it verbally three times, then told him to go for it. Gritting his teeth, his heart pounding in his ears, he increased the thrust, released the brakes, and began to roll down the runway. Picking up speed, he adjusted the flaps, pulled back on the wheel when Kira told him to... and all of a sudden, they were airborne!

"Well done, rookie!" She gave him a fist bump. "Pretty smooth for your first time. You must have had a great teacher!"

"She's a little gruff, but yeah." Allistor replied, keeping his eyes on the instruments. They weren't all that different from the Cessna, except these were all digital displays rather than analog gauges.

"You might as well keep the wheel." Kira leaned back in the pilot's seat. "The flight will take about three minutes. We'll circle a few times to let Gene land that big monster and get out of the way. Then you can try and land us."

Allistor steered the course she gave him, and, sure enough, it was just a moment before they passed over the marina. Allistor waggled the wings a bit to signal the guys below. "Heading back, guys. Join us as soon as you can."

"Nice plane, boss!" Corvin responded. "See you soon. Oh! And the robots are cool as hell!"

Grinning to himself, Allistor watched the island as it seemed to glide toward them from the horizon. When they got closer, and Kira had him circle, he could see that

Gene had already landed and moved the plane to a holding area next to the Outpost.

"Alright, let's do this." Kira brought him around and showed him how to line up with the runway. He reduced engine speed, lowered the landing gear, and adjusted the flaps. The plane dropped rapidly, and he thought his breakfast might come up, but Kira just laughed.

"Happens a lot on first landings. Takes a few tries to get the touch right. Just level her out a bit, good. Now adjust your speed… annnnnd… there!" She clapped her hands as he touched down, hitting the brakes and cutting the thrust. He started to panic as the plane rolled toward the rapidly approaching end of the runway, but the brakes did their job and the plane came to a halt.

Skill Level up! Your Aviation skill has increased by +1!

"Way to go, fancypants!" Kira bowed her head in mock respect. "Not bad at all. I've had students do much worse with more practice."

"Thank you, Kira. I don't think I can take credit, though. I think the system is somehow assisting me. Like, each skill level is giving me knowledge or skill that I haven't really earned like I would have had to before the apocalypse."

"Well, regardless, I'm proud of you. Now let's park this baby. Any chance you can build a big hangar up here so we can keep them out of the weather?"

Allistor thought about it. "I can. But I'm thinking maybe we should construct a strip closer to the Stronghold? It's a long walk from here to there."

557

Kira grinned and pointed out the window. "No walking for us. Our limo has arrived."

Sure enough, Andrea was approaching in one of the *Juggernauts*.

"But yes, Gene and I will check out the terrain closer to the Stronghold and see if there's space for a runway. In the meantime, the hangar?"

Allistor parked the plane and got out as Kira did her shutdown procedures. He opened his Outpost interface and located a few pre-designed hangar buildings. He chose one of the larger ones, made of a metal that looked a lot like the material Prime and his droids were constructed of. He pushed the button, and the hangar grew over top of the two parked planes.

When everyone was out of the planes and standing around the vehicle, Allistor said, "I don't think there's room for all of us inside. General, can your troops make the walk to the Stronghold?"

"Yes, sire. And I can ride atop the vehicle so as not to take up space in the interior." The two droids set off at a walk, heading directly toward Pelican Bay. The others piled in, and Andrea drove them back.

"This has been quite the day!" Andrea spoke to Allistor as they cruised up the side of a ridge. "Fisher called me from the Marina. He says they're bringing back like a dozen boats. Should be quite the sight to see. They'll be here before dark. And we have this shiny new robot army! And airplanes that look like rock stars should be stepping out of them. So, what new and amazing thing are you gonna do tomorrow?" she teased.

"I was thinking I might take a break and go fishing." Allistor replied. "If the boats are going to be here tonight, maybe in the morning we can catch a bunch of fish and send them out to everyone."

"Sounds more like work than a break, but if you don't mind, I think I'd like to come along. Might be fun. And I can work on my tan."

"Certainly! We can both try and boost our *Fishing* skill!" he said as they passed by the two walking droids. Andrea honked the horn at them and waved, and they waved back, much to the amusement of the children.

It wasn't long before they were back at Pelican Bay. The kids made 'ooh' and 'aah' noises as they saw the beach and the cove, with the shining white Stronghold on the cliff above. Allistor had to admit, it was beautiful. They passed by some hunters who were walking back, and offered them a ride. The three waved them off, saying they were enjoying the walk.

Once inside, Helen took charge of Maggie and the kids, bustling them off to find quarters and get them cleaned up before a visit to Meg for a proper meal.

Allistor took a moment to call the leaders of all the Strongholds, to make sure the troops arrived. Then he confirmed they were sending trucks or RVs pulling the big hover pads to deliver troops to the High School, Gun Shop, Ranger Station, Warehouse, and Gas Station Outposts. The ones at the Gas Station in north Denver and the Warehouse in Laramie were close enough to Strongholds that the troops could walk, and he sent someone along in a pickup to install the charger.

It turned out that hydrogen fuel chargers were considered very basic equipment on the worlds within the system. Like a microwave. They were ten thousand klax each, and Chris purchased a whole pile of them - - two hundred and fifty in all. They sent two to each Outpost, which only had twenty or twenty-five droids to charge. But the Strongholds got twenty each, and the Citadel and Bastion got fifty. There were nearly a thousand droids at each location, and having too few chargers would mean some of them would always be sitting idle waiting to charge. The droids themselves already had programming that allowed them to establish a rotating charging schedule that would keep them all at seventy five percent charge or higher at all times. Fifty chargers meant a hundred and fifty fully charged droids per hour. More if they were already partially charged. The extra chargers were kept in storage for distribution to future facilities or current properties that needed more.

Allistor received two messages that evening. One from Harmon, the weapon and vehicle merchant, asking which of his properties he wanted his shiny new space yacht delivered to. Allistor had assumed they'd just bring it to wherever he happened to be when the clock ran out, but the question made him think. He sent back a message asking about the size of the ship. The more he thought about it, the less he wanted others to see the thing land at one of his properties. They might make assumptions about him being in league with the aliens, or simply be jealous and want to try and take the ship.

When he received the reply with the ship's dimensions, he coughed and had to take a drink. As best as he could visualize, the thing was about the size of a navy battleship! He immediately replied that he'd like it delivered to the Wilderness Stronghold, where no prying eyes would see. He also had to quickly rethink his previous plans. None of the towers he'd built with landing pads on top were anywhere near structurally strong enough to support that ship.

The second message he received was from the military commander who'd sent him Kira and Gene. The man had apparently heard about Allistor seizing the depository in Denver, even though Allistor's people had strict instructions not to speak of it. There were things he wasn't ready for others to know about. The gold was one, the dragon eggs another, and his spaceship a third. He'd also told them not to mention their ability to teleport, but that secret had also gotten out.

The man's message asked for Allistor to contact him ASAP. Not sure what the man wanted, and with his opinion of the man pretty low after hearing how he treated Kira and family, Allistor decided to make it a group call. He gathered Andrea, Dean, Sam, Chris, and Ramon together in a conference room, then had Redd in the Silo radio room place the call.

The man, whose name was Colonel Potts, answered almost immediately. He was gruff and to the point.

Good evening, Allistor. I know you're busy, so I'll just get to business. After hearing about your successful clearing of the depository in Denver, I sent some of my people to Fort Knox to take that facility. I figured, better we have it than the aliens, right?"

Allistor made a face at his people. He was sure the man's greed was his main motivator. But he kept his voice neutral when he replied. "I agree with you there, Colonel. We don't want the aliens to get their hands on that gold. Can I assume that since you've reached out to me, you've hit a snag?"

"You could say that. My people can't take the place. We blasted past the security doors okay. And cleared the top floor. It was mostly low level monsters. But the minute my team went downstairs, something wiped out half of them. Six men gone in less than a minute. My guys who made it back upstairs and reported in said it was a level thirty elite monster. Something called an Occulant. They say the damn thing shoots lasers from its eyes or some shit."

Allistor looked around the table. "Anybody run into one of these before?" Every head shook to indicate a negative.

When Allistor didn't speak right away, the Colonel continued. "Anyhow, my highest level guy is twenty, and I've got half a dozen at fifteen. We're no match for that thing. My people tell me you reached level twenty, and some of your people have as well. And you have better weapons than we do."

Allistor bristled. Where was this man getting so much information about him and his people? "You seem very well informed about my business, Colonel. Can I ask where your intel is coming from?"

"Nah, I don't think so. I mean, you can ask, but I won't tell. I make it my business to know all I can about my enemies and my allies. People talk. It's human nature. Let's leave it at that."

"No, I don't think I will, Colonel. You seem to have been clued in on some bits of information that my people have explicitly been told to keep to themselves. If I have people I can't trust here, I need to know. And if you want my help, you need to tell me."

There was a long period of silence before the Colonel spoke again. "My information officer tells me it was a guy named Matthew. Got a real hard-on for you. Told us you killed his wife when you were seizing the depository from a dick named Paul. And his people saw you level up. There, you happy now?"

Allistor was relieved it hadn't been one of his people, but annoyed that Matthew had put that kind of information out into the world. Still, there was nothing he could do about it now.

"Thank you, Colonel. I'm not exactly happy, but I am relieved that none of my people have betrayed my trust. Now, about Fort Knox. What do you propose?"

"My people are holding the building's upper floor for now. And we established an Outpost in a nearby building. I've got a force of two hundred fighters there, patrolling the area for a quarter mile in every direction. We can hold the territory, but I need you and your people to clear the dungeon. In return we'll give you thirty percent of the gold that's down there."

Ramon snorted, rolling his eyes. Sam was less reserved. "Colonel, my name is Sam. Retired Marine sniper, and one of Allistor's advisors. I would like to say at this point that I am ashamed of you, boy. You call up here begging for us to break a bank you have no hope of breaking yourself, less than two days before the aliens land

563

and take it all, and offer him thirty percent? What kind of greedy asshole are you?"

The others suppressed their laughter, grinning at the angry old man.

The colonel's voice came back angry. "Me? I'm greedy? You assholes already got the Denver gold. You got more than you need! You need all of this gold, too? Why not let the rest of us have a share?"

Allistor spoke up. "So, your intention is to share the gold with the other Stronghold leaders? Not to keep it for yourself?"

"Why would I-" The man cut himself off, and Allistor could hear him breathing hard. "No, I do not friggin' plan to share with the others. They aren't here fighting for it. I'll give you forty percent."

Allistor shook his head. "Chris, how much gold is supposed to be in Fort Knox?"

Chris didn't hesitate. "About forty-six hundred tons. Not counting silver or other valuables that might be down there." They had researched this after taking Denver, but had discarded the idea of trying to take Fort Knox because it was too far away. But now that they could fly, Allistor was rethinking that position.

"And what is that worth, in klax?" Allistor led the man further.

Chris did some quick calculating with pen and paper. "At a price of twelve hundred klax per ounce, about one hundred and seventy-six billion."

"And what was the value of the gold we seized in Denver?"

"About fifty billion." Chris rounded down, and Allistor gave him a thumbs-up.

"So, you see, Colonel, there is much more gold in Fort Knox than there was in Denver. More than three times as much. I have a proposal for you. Let's put together a team to clear the facility. A couple of your guys, a few of my guys, the highest level people from some of the other Strongholds. Let's say nobody under level twenty. Strictly volunteers. And if we're successful, which is by no means guaranteed, then every Stronghold who participates gets an equal share."

"No way!" The colonel didn't even think about it. "I got there first! That gold is mine. I'll share it with you, fifty-fifty, if you clear it. But nobody else."

"Think about it, sir." Sam interjected. "And I only say 'sir' out of habit. Even if ten other Strongholds participate, that's still almost," He paused to look at Chris, who wrote a number for him. "Almost *fifteen billion* klax for you. More if there are fewer volunteers. We've tricked out a dozen facilities here with shields and weapons and spent less than five billion." Sam shrugged, pulling the number out of his ass. Chris grinned at him. They'd spent less than that.

The radio was silent for a while. When the Colonel spoke again, his voice was flat and icy cold. "Forget it. We'll take the place ourselves, even if I have to send a hundred people down there."

Allistor shot to his feet. "Colonel! Don't do that. You'd just be sending them to die. We're offering you a chance to give all your people a great start to their new lives here. And tens of thousands of others in the other Strongholds. Billions of klax will buy you everything you need! Your people can't take that monster down. Don't waste precious lives like that! We'll clear the dungeon, and you only have to risk one or two people! Think it through!"

"Screw you, you greedy bastards! I thought you might be reasonable. Seems like everything that Matthew guy said about you is true. You used your people to promote yourself to Prince, and now you want to keep everyone else down!"

"Listen to me! That's not how it happened! The money won't make you a Prince! The measuring stick seems to be territory. Land! The aliens value land! You don't have time to seize enough of it to become a Prince before they come. You might be able to purchase enough with a few billion klax. But if you don't work with us, you'll never see a single gold bar, Colonel!"

"And neither will you!"

"Colonel, if we don't take that gold reserve, it will be one of the first things the aliens go after. If we haven't claimed the land, it's free for them to take. You won't be able to hold them off for long. And it'll cost you lives. Please, I'm asking you. Cooperate with us. Share the wealth. Let the highest level people from our allied groups go in and clear the place. You can't do it alone, and I doubt I could either. But all of us together might pull it off."

"We're done talking. I'll be sure to let everyone know if the aliens get the gold, it was because *you* were too greedy to share." The sneer on the man's face was easy to hear in his voice.

"Me? I'm the greedy one? You've offered me fifty percent. I'm willing to help clear the place for ten percent and share the remaining ninety with you and the other Strongholds. You're the greedy bastard who won't take less than fifty percent." Allistor paused, taking a breath. "You know, I heard about how you treat your people from Kira and Gene. I wanted to believe that you were just incompetent, and not the self-centered, selfish asshole you seemed to be. But now it's clear. So here's what's going to happen, Colonel. I'm going to let the aliens wipe you out. Then I'm going to go there and kill them, and take the gold. I'll share it with whichever other Strongholds wish to help me. In fact, Redd if you can hear this, get the radio team busy contacting the others. If they have volunteers over level twenty, we'll stop by in a jet and pick them up." While he was talking, he was shaking his head and making a negative hand motion at Andrea. She nodded, getting up to leave the room and make a radio call to keep those calls from going out.

"Roger that, boss." Redd's voice came across the channel.

There was silence on the other end. Then some shouting, and the sound of something being smacked hard, followed by a single gunshot. A moment later, a new voice came across the radio.

"Prince Allistor, this is Captain Taylor. I'm one of the few survivors of the group the Colonel sent into that

567

hellhole. We've been listening to your conversation, and my men and I have just relieved the Colonel of his command. Permanently. We would appreciate it if you could gather the volunteers you mentioned and help us clear this facility. When it's clear, it's all yours. We'll take ten percent of the gold, and you're welcome to the rest. I lost good people down there, and, frankly, I never want to see this place again."

Allistor was thrilled at this news. He found smiles all around the table at the change in circumstance. He found he didn't even regret the man's death. He was directly responsible for who knew how many of his own people dying. Still, he needed to be diplomatic.

"I'm sorry for your losses, Captain Taylor. Though not for this most recent one. That man's greed could have cost a lot more lives. For what it's worth, I think you did the right thing."

"Thank you, sir. Uh, your highness?"

"Just Allistor, please. And I will begin rounding up volunteers immediately." Andrea, who had just walked back in, rolled her eyes and stepped back out to countermand her previous orders. "I'm going to need a few things from you, Captain."

"Tell me what you need, and we'll make it happen, sir."

"First, we'll need to be able to land a couple planes. I need to make sure there's a clear airstrip at the nearest airport, and transportation for... let's say up to fifty people."

"There's an airfield here at the Fort, sir. Allistor. It's already clear, and a few hundred yards from the depository. I don't think transpo' will be a problem."

"Great! Now, is there going to be an issue among your men? Is there a faction loyal to the Colonel that might make trouble while we're there?"

"No, that won't be a problem. I was among his most loyal. The men will follow me." The confidence in his voice was reassuring.

"Alright then, Captain. We'll be there in the morning. If you have any volunteers willing to go back in, get them the best gear you can scrounge up. I'll bring some weapons."

"I'm going in with you, Allistor. Just me. And thank you for the weapons. We lost our plasma weapons down there. I'm ashamed to say I ran before I could recover one."

"No shame in retreating to stay alive when faced with an unbeatable enemy, Captain. You did the right thing. If you hadn't, I'd be on my way to try and kill the Colonel right now, and probably a lot of your men in the process. Don't worry, I'll bring you a plasma rifle. See you tomorrow."

Nigel terminated the call, and there was silence around the table. Allistor was the first to speak.

"Well, shit."

*****

Baldur strode into the great hall, where Odin was striding back and forth in front of his throne, cursing loudly. The mist in the room swirled madly with the force of the curses. When he noticed his son's approach, he halted his pacing and sat down. "A level thirty elite occulant?"

"Yes, father. I have no explanation for it. A creature that formidable should not have been sent to UPC 382 at this time. And, as usual, I suspect Loki's hand in it, but have no proof."

"It may not have been Loki, my son. After all, there is a significant amount of gold there. Enough to tempt any number of potential colonists to break the rules. I will find out who is responsible, and punish them myself. In the meantime, we must deal with the problem. One of us must go and retrieve the beast immediately."

"That would be violating our own rules, father. The system rules clearly prevent any interference on a world during its Stabilization period. Even good intentions cannot change that."

"You wish to simply leave the beast there to slaughter the humans? It has already taken the lives of many who, by all rights, should have survived the Stabilization and been able to claim land. Already our creatures have culled a larger than expected percentage of the humans. Rather than ninety one percent, the casualties have reached closer to ninety six percent. Yet I have not acted to prevent this. And don't remind me of the rules, impudent boy. I helped create the system *and* its rules!"

"You have clearly been following the events on this planet, father. So, you are aware of Allistor, the human who has attained the rank of Prince?"

"Of course. Most of the Collective is aware of him. He's smart, for a human, and has a good heart. But his position was gained largely through luck. The award of so much land by his companion…"

"Yes, luck. But his actions helped create that luck. He took the time to explore, to save the life of that companion, and thus put himself in position for that stroke of good fortune. He inspires loyalty among his people because he truly cares for them. They fight, and train, and increase their skills at his urging. He displays a sense of honor. I can think of few Princes of other planets who deserve the title more."

Odin sat there, the mists swirling more calmly around him as he contemplated his son's words. Finally, he nodded his bulbous head. "Agreed. I assume you wish to allow Prince Allistor to deal with the occulant?"

"With a small measure of assistance. As you said, this is an unusual situation created by a clear violation of the rules. While direct action by either of us is forbidden, we are not prevented from assisting a local in correcting the infraction."

"Ha!" Odin was on his feet again, his tentacles wide as he stepped forward to embrace his favored son. "I will leave the details to you. I trust you will be… discreet?"

"Of course, my lord Odin." Baldur stepped back from the embrace and bowed to his father. "If you'll excuse me? Time is limited, and I have much to do."

"Go. And I shall find the one who is responsible for this mess." The force of Odin's fury pushed the mist completely away from him for several seconds before it slowly drifted back to soothe his skin.

From the shadows in the back of the great hall, Hel watched and listened. When the mists transferred the fury of Odin's intent throughout the room, her whole body shuddered. She had not planned for others to learn of the occulant's emplacement for several more days, at least. It was just supposed to have prevented any humans from claiming the gold before the end of Stabilization, when she could be first to claim it. Now that it had come to Odin's attention, she needed to be sure the trail led away from her. And the most obvious choice for Odin's wrath?

Her father.

Chapter 24

It's A Hard Knox Life

The next morning, Allistor was prepared for war. His Strongholds were all as well protected as he could expect them to be. His people were trained, leveled up, and wearing the best gear his crafters could make them.

His fishing trip was cancelled, and he was busy loading his own volunteers onto the planes to begin a long day's journey.

The previous afternoon, Redd and her team had reached out to the other friendly Strongholds scattered across the continent. Eight of them had volunteers who wanted to try and clear the dungeon at Fort Knox. Only a few others had fighters over level twenty, and those either weren't willing to join, or were prevented from joining by their leaders.

Allistor had stayed at Pelican Bay long enough to enjoy the sight of the seafaring 'convoy' that the airmen brought from the marina. The lead ship was a yacht that did indeed have a helipad on the aft deck. The thing was at least two hundred and fifty feet long and looked like a small floating luxury hotel. Behind it on tow ropes were three smaller boats, including a cigarette boat built for speed. Next came a commercial fishing boat with small cranes both port and starboard amidships, and a larger one at the stern. The deck was covered in furled netting. It too towed a couple smaller boats through the calm waters just outside the cove.

The other two lead boats were sport fishers, but very fancy ones. And each of them towed a sailboat as well as a smaller fishing vessel. The one in the rear also towed the boat they'd taken from the island to the marina earlier.

Most of the crowd at Pelican Bay turned out to cheer the incoming fishing-slash-naval fleet. The airmen pulled the lead ships into the wide cove and dropped anchor before climbing into one of the smaller boats and bringing them in to shore. They were greeted at the pier with cheers, claps on the back, and cold beers.

Bagwell took his beer, opened it with shaky hands, and downed it one go. Noticing this, Andrea ordered, "Bagwell. You're shaking. Report."

The man nodded his head, accepting another beer and taking one more swig before he answered. "There's a damn sea monster out there, boss."

The others nodded their heads, but left the talking to him. "I was driving that last boat." He pointed to the sport fishers that had come in last. "There's two boats behind it now, but I left with three. Since I was on a fishing boat, I dropped a couple lines in the water in case I got lucky. And I did! Pulled in a big tuna. Like a three hundred pounder. We stopped the boats long enough for me to bring it in. I didn't want to stink up my boat, so we ran a line through its gill and were towing it. We were about half an hour out from the island and just about to get underway again when something bumped my boat. A second later, the water exploded behind the boat, and this monster cleared the surface, my tuna already gone and the rope sticking out of its mouth. The cleat that the tuna was tied to just ripped right off the rail. When the monster landed, it took one of the small boats with it."

"I got a good look at it." Corvin added. "It wasn't like any fish I've ever seen. It looked more like a damn dinosaur, or maybe a dragon. Long jaws kind of like a gator, but with a rounded head, long flippers, and a tail like a whale's. It was nearly as big as the damned yacht, boss."

Allistor sighed. One more thing to deal with on a long list of things he didn't have time for. "Alright, guys. I'm glad you're back safe. For now, let's restrict fishing to here in the cove. Hopefully the thing's too big to come in here. And let's avoid dragging bloody fish around in the water for a while?"

Bagwell nodded his head, looking sheepish.

When the boats were secured and everybody was back in the Stronghold, Allistor asked Gene and Kira to fly the planes back to Cheyenne. With the speed of the jets, they could be there in three hours, and he wanted the planes ready to go from there first thing in the morning. He, Helen, and the General joined them, because both humans wanted to work on their piloting skills.

The rest of the volunteers among Allistor's people used the teleports to make their way to the Citadel that evening. By 6:00am they were geared up and ready to go.

The volunteers that would be joining them were in Texas, Oklahoma, Tennessee, Michigan, Pennsylvania, and Virginia. They were splitting up the planes, Kira taking the faster, smaller jet to pick up the three northern states' volunteers, while Gene hit the southern states. The Texas Stronghold was sending three people, and Tennessee was sending two. Michigan was also sending two, but with just Kira, Allistor, Amanda, Nancy, and Prime from Allistor's group, there was room enough on her plane for the others.

Gene's plane was going to be full. But, besides its eighteen passenger capacity, it could carry significant cargo weight. So, a few folks might have to sit on the floor, but the plane could handle it. Gene and Helen were in the cockpit, with Sam, Meg, Lars, Logan, Ramon, Bjurstrom, Campbell, McCoy, Goodrich, Dawn, Virginia, Richard, Andrea, and two volunteers from Denver named Pete and Norm in the main cabin. Fuzzy was there as well, curled up on the floor in the back, because Gene wasn't about to let him scratch up or dirty the custom leather seats.

The cargo holds of both planes held cans of extra gas, though neither expected to need it. Gene's plane also carried one of the regeneration machines. And everyone's inventory rings were packed with weapons, rations, potions, everything they could think of. Allistor even had three five-hundred-foot lengths of rope. Cuz one should never go adventuring without a friggin' rope.

Allistor had purchased another teleport pad, intending to install it the moment they claimed Fort Knox so that reinforcements could be brought to bear quickly if needed. It meant exposing his secret to the others, but the Stabilization period was ending anyway, and they'd be able to use their billions to buy a hub for themselves, so they presented no real danger to Allistor at that point. And if they failed to clear the dungeon… well, his secret would still be safe.

He also purchased more battle droids. Two more battalions. His intent was to have them help defend Fort

Knox after he claimed it, and possibly to lend some troops to others in the coming days.

Allistor purchased something else on the market that evening, selecting inventory belts with five hundred slots' capacity for every volunteer that was going to fight, including those from the other groups. He also bought an extra twenty for his advisors. They weren't expensive, at least not for him, at ten thousand klax each.

> **PPD Belt**
> **Quality: Exceptional**
> **Capacity: 500**
> *This personal pocket dimension belt will store up to five hundred individual items in a secure private dimensional space. Items stored within will be preserved in a dimensional lock, unaffected by time. The physical weight of each object stored will be reduced to .01% of normal. Identical items such as currency or mass-produced items will stack within a single storage slot. Items within the storage inventory may not be removed by anyone other than the user. The item itself cannot be bound to the user, and thus may be stolen.*

While he had the market interface open, he received a message like no other he'd seen before. It flashed red and gold to get his attention, and when he looked at the sender name, it was just a series of question marks.

Curious, he opened it. The message was short, and to the point.

> *To: Prince Allistor of Earth*
>
> *From: ????*
>
> *Examine your Prince's Seal carefully. And don't forget the scroll.*

He waited until he reached his room, then pulled out the Prince's Seal and Examined it. He had assumed it was simply a symbol of office like the Baron's Seal, used for official functions or to certify documents and such. What he saw sent him ass over teakettle.

Prince's Seal
Item Quality: Legendary
Attributes: +2 to all Attributes when equipped.
This Seal symbolizes the power of a Planetary Prince. In addition to granting two points to each of the Prince's attributes when worn, it awards a morale boost of 10% to each of the Prince's citizens. All of those invited into a combat or raid party with the Prince receive a buff of +1 to all Attributes until the party is disbanded.

That buff was simply amazing! With a total of ten attributes, this buff gave him the equivalent of ten levels' worth of points. And the additional boost to morale and the party buff were nearly as exciting!

After petting the Seal for a while, he put it back in his bag. He'd make a show of putting it on before they entered the dungeon and give his people a boost.

The second part of the message had him digging through his inventory. "What scroll are they… oh, shit!" He grinned as he realized what the message meant. With his new levels and the points that went with them, he was more than capable of using it now. Opening the scroll, he learned the magic, the grin never disappearing from his face.

*****

He passed out the belts before they boarded the planes, saying, "These are for the gold! We're going down there to kill this elite creature and hopefully clear the dungeon, but if we can't do so, I expect each of you will want to grab as much gold as you can carry. These belts reduce the weight of a twenty-five pound gold bar to less than an ounce. So, if we have to stop, I'll give the command to load up and retreat. But, let me be clear. Anyone caught looting gold before then will be dealt with harshly." He looked around, and none of the faces seemed to object.

"If we manage to clear the place, you can fill those belts with monster loot. For those of you representing other Strongholds, we'll work out a number of gold bars each of you can take home to get things started. Each bar is worth about half a million klax, less if we flood the market. So maybe each of you goes home with a half billion worth of gold, and we can work out the transport of the rest."

579

With everyone boarded, they took off without incident. Allistor piloted Kira's plane for the take-off, and Helen tried her hand with Gene watching over her. With no flight plans required they were able to fly directly to each location, pick up their volunteer, and take off again without delay. Kira stopped long enough to refuel the plane in Pennsylvania because the pump was right there.

By noon, both planes had landed in Kentucky. Allistor had picked up two more points in *Aviation* by flying the jet under Kira's supervision. Helen had picked up the skill plus two levels as well.

Captain Taylor met them at the airstrip and escorted them as they walked toward the depository. Allistor gathered together the new volunteers and handed out belts, giving them the same speech regarding loot. They all agreed without hesitation. Half a billion sounded like a lot of klax, after all.

It was a warm fifteen minute walk to the depository, and when they entered the Outpost next door, Taylor offered them all cold bottles of water. There was a short discussion during which he related the details of what they'd found down below.

"The monster is basically a huge head with tentacles that it uses to move around. The thing is fast, it crossed the room in just a few seconds. It has more eyes than I could count. Different colors. The red ones shot laser beams at us. The blue ones fired plasma. I saw green and black eyes as well, but we didn't last long enough to see those in action."

"Were you able to damage it at all?" Allistor asked.

"The plasma rifles did a little damage. But the thing was still at about ninety percent health when we bailed." Taylor's voice was hoarse as he pictured the disastrous battle. Andrea began handing out plasma rifles to each of the volunteers who didn't have one. She also handed them each two reload battery packs, in case they depleted the rifle's charge.

"Alright, before we go down, how many of you volunteers have healing spells?" He watched as just three of them raised their hands. "Attack spells or stuns?" This time four of them raised hands.

Ramon didn't even wait to be asked. He pulled them all off to one side and began handing out scrolls for *Restore,* and *Flame Shot.* He asked each of them about their stats, then handed a few of them *Restraint, Erupt,* and *Mind Spike* scrolls as well. While they did that, Allistor sent out party invites to everyone, including Gene and Kira, who would be staying behind. When the group returned, one of the volunteers from Michigan hugged Allistor.

Letting him go, she said, "This is incredibly generous of you."

"I'm sorry, I didn't catch your name?" Allistor asked awkwardly.

"Anneliese. And this is Frank." She motioned toward her partner.

"Anneliese, I'm counting on you, all of you, to help keep us alive. If we beat this thing, that's awesome. But my priority is to preserve our lives above all else. And I need each one of you to be as prepared as possible. So these spells are basically my way of protecting my own ass." He grinned at her as the others chuckled.

The woman from Tennessee, whose name was Lisa, spoke up. "I have a spell that I got from a scroll, too. Not sure if you guys have it, but I thought I should let you know it's available. It's a simple freeze spell that I can either cast as a bolt that coats the target in ice and slows it down. I can channel it until the target freezes solid, or I run out of juice."

"Good to know. Anybody else?" Allistor asked.

The man from Virginia said, "My name's Charlie. And I can go invisible. For up to one minute."

Andrea spoke up as well. "I can use that *Dissolve* spell now."

"Alright, cool. We'll keep those in mind. We haven't fought together yet as a group, but I've fought with most of my people. We'll figure out how to coordinate as we go. I'd prefer to run another dungeon somewhere else first, but we don't have the time. Also, I've got one more little surprise for all of you."

Pulling his Seal from inventory, he held it in his hand so the others could *Examine* it while he opened his interface. Pulling up his status sheet, which had his likeness as an avatar to one side, he equipped the Seal. It appeared on his left breast, opposite the Vindicator's Seal on his right. It depicted an image of Earth's western hemisphere drawn in fine gold lines, with a star over the Rockies to identify his territory.

A thrill ran through him as all of his stats boosted by +2. He heard gasps and mutterings from the others as

582

they all got +1 across the board, and their morale got a little boost as well. He noticed that everyone in the party was now sporting a simpler version of his Seal drawn in silver over their hearts as well.

"Alright, we're set. Let's go kill this thing." They left the Outpost and walked to the main entry on the ground floor of the depository. It was a simple, square two-story stone building positioned in an open space for security purposes. Once inside, they found several dozen of Taylor's men armed with automatic rifles. They were clustered mainly around the stairways at each corner of the building.

Taylor pointed to the right. "We went down this way." He led them to the stairwell, and his men parted to make room. One of them put an ear to the door for several seconds, then nodded and opened it for them.

Allistor put a hand on Taylor's shoulder to stop him from advancing. "Let me lead the way. I have three or four times as much health as you. And a magic shield." He cast *Barrier* in front of himself, and began to descend. The others followed silently, except for Fuzzy, who was sniffing everything. In all, twenty-eight humans, a bear cub, and a battle droid passed through the door into what Taylor had described as hell.

When they reached the next level, Allistor paused and put an ear to the door. He probably needn't have bothered, as there were several holes burned through it. He could see from the holes that the door was three inches thick and almost solid steel. There were burn marks on the concrete wall opposite the door as well.

He whispered to Taylor, who was right behind him. "These holes from the monster? Or plasma weapons?"

"Monster. Half the guys I brought down are dead in that hallway." Taylor looked grim.

"Any smaller mobs?"

"There were, we cleared them before that thing found us. It was down the hall, around the corner to the left."

Taking a deep breath, Allistor nodded to the group bunched up on the stairs behind him, and yanked the door open. It squeaked slightly, mainly because of a partially melted hinge. He motioned for Taylor to hold the door, and he passed through. The first thing he saw was a pile of corpses just inside the door. Four men with so many holes in them Allistor found it hard to look. All of them had plasma rifles still in hand, but Allistor left them there. They could retrieve the weapons and check them for damage later. One thing he remembered his father saying was "Never go into combat with a weapon you're not 100% sure of."

Moving slowly and crouched low, Allistor kept his plasma rifle aimed toward the corner Taylor had mentioned. He glanced into each open doorway that he passed, finding all the rooms empty. Three quarters of the way down the hall, he heard the stairwell door close gently behind him. They were in it now. The whole group had joined him in the hall. Turning to glance back, he saw that General Prime had taken the position directly behind him.

Allistor nodded, and continued forward, motioned to the rooms on either side. He heard footsteps shuffling as his people checked and cleared the rooms he'd only glanced at. While they did so, he proceeded to the end of the hall, pausing and hugging the wall just before the corner. He listened carefully for any sound other than his own people, and could detect none.

Curiosity was killing him, and he was dying to peek around the corner. But if the thing had even decent hearing, it knew they were there. And he didn't think he'd survive a laser to the face.

Turning back, he pointed to Charles and crooked a finger at him. The man crept forward with admirable stealth, his boots making no noise on the concrete floor. Allistor leaned in and whispered directly into the man's ear. "Think you can do a little invisible man recon?"

Charles gave him a thumbs-up, and, a moment later, faded from view. Allistor knew where he was, but couldn't detect him at all. He felt a tap on the shoulder as the man passed him by, rounding the corner. Allistor held his breath, fighting the urge to peek again.

Half a minute later, Charles reappeared in exactly the same spot. He leaned in close to Allistor, keyed his throat mic and whispered, "It's in the room at the end of the hall. Big ugly thing. 'Bout the size of an elephant, but round. Squiggly legs. About a million eyes. Level 30 elite with sixty thousand health. Scary as hell."

Allistor looked back along the hall to see if everyone had heard. "Everyone copy that?" Every head, including Prime's, nodded once. Fuzzy just sat there looking at him.

Allistor motioned for everyone to move back a bit from the corner, then whispered into his own mic. Bjurstrom had brought radios for everyone, and Allistor sincerely hoped that the earbuds were quiet enough that the monster couldn't hear them.

"Alright, here's the plan. I'm going in first, alone." He paused as Prime tapped him on the shoulder and shook his head. "Correction, Prime and I are going in first. I'm going to try to distract it. When I say go, I want everybody but Fuzzy firing at that thing. Meg, hand out three of your grenades. If you can get close enough, tag it with those. We'll see if we can't burn some of those eyes. Then pour on the plasma. I'll try to stun it. Healers, you do the same if you're not healing right away. *Restraint* or *Mind Spike*, I don't care. Anything that might interrupt it. Andrea, *Dissolve* that bad boy. Lisa, freeze it. Our best bet is to pour on as much damage as possible. Fuzzy, you stay back behind cover, buddy. Questions?"

"I have one." Prime looked at Charles. "Did you see anything in the room that might be used as cover?"

Charles looked at the ceiling, thinking back. "Some crates, but nothing I'd trust to stop lasers that could burn through that door."

Prime nodded at Allistor, and they were ready to go.

Allistor decided his best bet was surprise, so he burst into a run as he rounded the corner, rifle held in front of him. Prime was somehow right next to him, and taking the lead. Allistor didn't see the monster as they approached the door at the end of the hall, so he plunged on through.

That was about the time all hell broke loose.

He spotted the monster off to his right, just emerging from behind a pallet of crates that stood eight feet high. As he was moving his rifle to bear on the monster, one of its red eyes flashed, and he felt a sting on his leg even as he was shoved aside by Prime. As he fell, he managed to cast *Mind Spike* on the creature.

With his new levels and the sheer number of times he'd cast the spell, it was rewardingly effective. The creature screamed and thumped to the floor as it used all of its tentacles to grab and flail at its head. Allistor heard a dual discharge of plasma rifles from Prime, and saw several of the thing's eyes dissolve as the rounds struck. He fired his own weapon from the ground as he struggled to get up.

Occulant Sentry
Level 30
Elite
Health: 58,100/60,000

There was a sharp pain in his left ankle, then suddenly he was scooting across the floor, pulled by the droid at a rapid pace. He fired once more before the monster disappeared and the crates filled his vision. Prime let go of his ankle and used both free hands to lift Allistor to his feet. The motion was so effortless, Allistor felt like a rag doll.

"That spell seemed effective, whatever it was." Prime observed, pushing Allistor around the next stack of crates as his eyes moved to the back of his head. Allistor cast a heal on himself as he answered, "Mind Spike. Does a little damage, causes a lot of pain. Good stun spell."

The creature roared in anger when the spell faded, and Allistor could hear tentacles slithering on the floor. He and Prime exchanged a look, and he nodded. He shouted into his radio this time. "Hold! We're gonna tank this bad boy and turn his back to you. When I say go, pour it on!"

Prime moved first, dashing out from behind the crate and instantly firing a deluge of plasma bolts at the monster. He moved incredibly fast, then stopped abruptly in the middle of the room. Allistor was right behind him, casting *Mind Spike* again. The creature screamed once more, And Allistor paused to cast *Barrier* in front of himself. "Go!"

Prime's weapons appeared to be in automatic mode, as both rifles spat rapid-fire plasma bursts toward the occulant. More and more of the eyes were being burned into oblivion, but the thing seemed to have a thousand of them. Every few inches of the surface was covered in eyes, big and small. As Prime continued to fire, a devastating volley blasted into the thing from behind. Tentacles melted off as they waved about. Black goo dripped to the floor under the monster.

Allistor saw Lisa's freeze spell take effect, and she must have been channeling it. The frost fought to cover the beast as plasma impacts thawed it back out. And the top of its head began to melt as if acid had been poured on it. Andrea's *Dissolve* spell.

The occulant roared again as the *Mind Spike* wore off. Blasts of red lasers exploded from the beast's eyes in every direction. Allistor heard human screams, and shouted into his radio. "Take cover! Fire from cover! Move the wounded!"

He saw two of his party icons go grey out of the corner of his eye as he cast *Erupt* underneath the occulant's body. This spell, too, had increased in power with his new levels and buffs. A spike the size of a tall parking cone shot up into the beast's belly. It screamed and fired, one of the lasers penetrating Allistor's side and burning straight through. Now it was his turn to scream, and he half dove, half fell behind the crates he'd been moving toward earlier. Prime grabbed him with a free arm while firing with two others, and hurling his staff weapon forward with the fourth. The droid gave him enough momentum to get behind cover.

Just after Allistor lost sight of the monster, the screams began again. And the floor just past the edge of the crate, where they'd been standing a moment before, began to sizzle and bubble under a pool of acid. Amanda shouted, "The green eyes! The green eyes are acid!"

"Healers! Keep them up! Everybody, use your heal spells on yourselves and each other! And keep out of sight! I'll call for another volley."

As soon as he was done speaking, there were blue flashes and plasma bolts flew past their crates, some going over the top to splash off the high ceiling.

"Shit! This thing switches weapons so fast." Allistor said to himself.

"Indeed. They are quite formidable. Which is why they are often used as sentries." Prime held up one of his upper arms and examined a scorched section. The arm moved slowly, but appeared to still be operational. On a whim, Allistor tried casting a heal on the droid, but it had no effect that he could see.

"I will draw its fire again. My frame is somewhat more resistant to its lasers. I suggest you stun it again, and have your people fire more volleys.

Allistor nodded. "Ten seconds." Then he spoke into his radio, "Okay, Meg, grenade time. The rest of you, fire in ten seconds. Mark!"

Prime dashed out, firing with both hands. Allistor stuck his head out and cast *Erupt* again, followed by another *Mind Spike*. A couple seconds later he saw Meg's crystal ball grenades shatter against the beast and flames engulf it. Someone else must have cast the *Flame Shot* before he could get to it. Then, plasma poured into the monster from seemingly everywhere.

Occulant Sentry
Level 30
Elite
Health: 31,700/60,000

Andrea shouted through the radio this time. "It's about to hit fifty percent health! Everyone move back and take cover! Get out of the room if you can!"

Allistor decided to try *Vortex*, channeling the spell at the monster. To his horror, once the wind had reached a speed that caused the monster to begin to spin on the axis of the spike in its belly, it also lifted the body of one of the dead. The corpse, belonging to a Texan whose name he didn't know, was pulled into the vortex, his body crashing into the beast over and over again. Allistor could hear bones breaking, and was nearly sick. He stopped channeling, and the body fell.

He heard someone over the radio whisper, "Damn. That was hardcore."

The monster reached and surpassed the fifty percent mark during the vortex without activating anything other than its usual attacks. Though now they were less frequent, as more than half of the occulant's eyes had been destroyed. Prime had taken several hits, and was now limping back toward him. Allistor got an idea, and cast *Levitate* on the droid. He motioned with his hand and moved him up atop the nearest stack of crates. The general nodded at him, then lay down.

As the last winds from the *Vortex* spell died down and faded away, Allistor tried *Mind Spike* again. Whether it was a bad roll from the RNG, or the fact that the creature was already in great pain, the spell failed. He tried *Restraint*, and it froze mid-scream.

"Fire! Three seconds!" Allistor shouted, and immediately his people each took another shot or two at the thing. He could hear Prime firing with both barrels above him.

Occulant Sentry
Level 30
Elite
Health: 18,600/60,000

Allistor reached into his inventory and pulled out the epic Titan Bow he'd received after killing the void titan. A quiver appeared at his waist, and he immediately seized an arrow. Nocking it and pulling the string with all the strength he had – his physical attributes boosted by the bow – he loosed the titan-bone arrow. It whistled as it flew, impacting the monster and driving it backward. The arrow completely disappeared inside its body. Allistor fired another, then dashed out from behind the crate. The creature spun to focus on him, and he cast *Restraint* on it again. It froze, and Allistor paused to fire one more arrow before ducking down behind the other crates.

A part of his brain recognized that the crate in front of his face was stamped 'Gold Bullion' before he ignored it and shouted, "Fire! Three seconds!"

Prime, whom he could now see clearly atop the other crates, had never stopped firing. His head and shoulders showed several burns, and one of his eyes was damaged. But the determined droid general kept firing and held the thing's attention.

Another burst of red laser fire erupted in every direction. There were fewer beams this time, but still Allistor heard screams. A quick check showed him there were still only two dead, but several others were very low on health.

All of a sudden, he heard a familiar roar. His bear cub had disobeyed him and decided to join the fight. Horrified, Allistor dashed back out in the open and cast *Mind Spike* again. He saw his bear cub dash up underneath the monster, grabbing one of the thicker remaining tentacles and biting down. Black blood erupted as Fuzzy continued forward, dragging the tentacle with him. The monster was unbalanced by the bear's weight, and fell backward to slam into the floor. Fuzzy continued forward, dragging the thing with him even as the humans on either side fired into its body.

Fuzzy put his front feet on the tentacle, pinning it to the floor before giving his head a violent shake. The tentacle ripped free and the creature let out a high-pitched wail. Fuzzy was instantly covered in a torrent of the black blood, having apparently severed a vital artery. The poor bear snorted in disgust and ran toward Allistor.

The occulant tried to right itself using the remaining tentacles, but the movements were weak. Allistor seized the opportunity his bear had created. "Finish it! Everyone fire!"

There was another volley of plasma, and Andrea hit the thing with *Dissolve* again. A second volley finished the monster off, and everyone in the room except Allistor and Prime leveled up.

Everyone living had their health bars shoot up to a hundred percent, though most were still short a good deal of blood. As everyone emerged from behind cover, he didn't see anyone without at least a few burn holes in their gear.

Allistor made a quick check of his party roster. The other fatality was Richard from the Stadium Stronghold in Laramie. Searching the room, Allistor spotted Virginia sitting against a wall, holding the man's body. She was crying and shaking her head, as if denying the man's death. Allistor went to sit with her, tears forming in his own eyes.

"I'm so sorry." his voice cracked as he spoke. He'd liked Richard a lot. The man had been instrumental in running things at the Stadium, and been a good guy.

"He pushed me out of the way. I was too slow, and he saved me." Virginia sobbed. "I'm too old for this, I shouldn't have been here."

Amanda knelt in front her and took hold of Richard, pulling him out of Virginia's grasp and laying him gently on the floor before taking both of her hands. "Lots of us were too slow. You can't outrun a laser, hun. And thanks to you, eight or nine of these people are still alive. You did an amazing job healing. Better than Nancy, better than me. You and Richard did that. Saved us all."

Virginia leaned forward and hugged Amanda as the others tried to give them some privacy. The Texan's shattered body was gathered up as gently as possible and set down next to Richard. Allistor sought out the other Texan, who was leaning against a crate and checking out the battery pack on his rifle.

Approaching the man, he shook his head. "I'm so sorry. I didn't intend for the vortex to pull him up like that. I couldn't see his body, and didn't know he was that close."

The Texan nodded once. "Fool got hisself killed in the first few seconds of the fight. Charged right at the damn thing. As for the vortex, I think he woulda laughed at that. Been happy that his dead body did some damage to the thing, and did a pretty good job interruptin' it too." The man winked at him, and Allistor felt a weight lift off of him.

"You guys were from the same Stronghold, right? We can arrange for you to take his body home."

"Nah. I mean, yes, we was from the same place. But he wouldn't want me to tote him all the way back.

We'll burn him here with your fella, and I'll take his hat and boots home. He had a girl back there that might want 'em."

"He was married?" Allistor was surprised.

"Nope. Just met her a few months back. Since the world ended, relationships seem to move a mite faster, ya know? Dunno how serious they were."

"Well, you've both earned your Stronghold a great deal of money. The weapons and other resources you can buy…" Allistor didn't finish the thought as the man shook his head.

"Not yet we ain't. There's more stairs goin' down, and my bet is there's more critters to kill before we're done."

Allistor's mouth dropped open and he immediately opened his interface and tried to claim the building. He got the dreaded message about previous occupants.

"Well, shit. You're right." He put a hand on the man's shoulder, then turned to face the others. "Seems we're not done here, folks. There are more monsters to kill. Sam, Lars, Logan, take Fuzzy and check out every inch of this floor. They're probably downstairs, but let's make sure. And let's hope it's something easy like a rat nesting under a desk or something." He waited while they corralled Fuzzy, who was rubbing his nose on the floor trying to get rid of the creature's blood.

"Loot the monster before you go. That goes for the rest of you, too. And those who aren't with Fuzzy, break open these crates. I want each of you to take a hundred gold bars and put them in your belt storage. If this thing

595

was just the mini-boss, I'm afraid to think what might be downstairs. Let's load up in case this is all we can get. If there's still gold left after each of you takes a hundred, we'll see about the rest.

Allistor looted the occulant, then went back to join Amanda and Virginia as the sound of splintering wood echoed through the room. Amanda was sitting next to the older woman, holding her hand and speaking quietly to her. Allistor took a seat next to Amanda and quickly reviewed his loot notifications.

He'd received ten thousand klax, a nondescript scroll that didn't glow purple or orange, some occulant meat, which he quickly dumped on the floor, and an item that *did* glow, this time with a golden light.

Occulant Sentry Elite Power Core

There was no description beyond that. Allistor assumed it was some kind of crafting ingredient or something, and ignored it.

A moment later Prime approached and stood in front of Allistor. "My condolences on your losses, Sire. Are you in need of medical attention?"

Allistor saw the multiple burn scars on his own gear. "No, thank you General Prime. I'm fully healed. And thank you as well for saving me. At least three times during that fight that I can recall. Probably a couple more I didn't notice. Are you in need of attention?"

The general's body was scorched in dozens of places, and his one arm hung at an improper angle compared to the others. "I am in need of repairs, yes. But I am still at eighty percent operational capability. If there is more fighting to be done, I am ready."

"How do we repair you?" Amanda asked, and Virginia looked up with some curiosity as well.

"I am capable of self-repair, Lady Amanda. There are parts in the pack on my back. I would need approximately ten minutes to effect proper repairs to most of my damaged systems."

"Go right ahead, General. We can wait ten minutes if it means you'll be back at full fighting strength."

"Thank you, Sire. I shall begin immediately." Prime turned and walked a few paces away, then sat down and used three of his arms to remove his pack. Allistor intended to watch the repairs, but he was distracted by the sound of plasma rifle fire, and a roar from Fuzzy, outside the room somewhere.

He'd just gotten to his feet and was running for the door when Sam's voice came across the radio. "Found one of them octopoid things in the stairwell. It's dead. Maybe that was the last one?"

Allistor quickly checked his interface again, and tried to claim the Stronghold. This time, the button was green.

"YYYESSS!" he shouted, surprising everyone in his party. He clicked on the button, and the world around them went golden. He didn't waste time with frills, just leaving the building the way it was. He added the usual utilities, greenhouse, walls, and gate. Then he selected a shield dome, several plasma cannons and anti-aircraft guns, and placed the teleport pad he'd purchased just to one side of the gate. When all of that was done, he named it Fort Knox and finished the process.

When the light faded, there were cheers from the group. Allistor quieted them down after a minute, and then said, "Nigel, can you get me Redd in the radio room? And put us on loudspeaker? In every one of our facilities, please."

"Of course, Sire. One moment."

Almost immediately Redd's voice came across, echoing from everywhere in the room. "I'm here boss. Everything okay?"

"Everything's great, Redd. We killed the monster. I need you to get the other Stronghold leaders on the line. The ones whose volunteers are here with us."

"Already on, boss. We've been talking a while, waiting to hear from you. Hold on, I'll patch you in." There was silence, then some clicking and static as she patched him in. "Go ahead, Sire." Allistor smiled at the change in title from boss.

"This is Allistor. I am pleased to announce that we have defeated the elite occulant and taken control of Fort Knox. Though we lost a couple of heroes in the fight, their sacrifice helped ensure our victory, and a more secure future for everyone who can hear this message."

He paused while the cheers and congratulations echoed through the room. When they had died down, he continued.

"As promised, each of the nine groups, plus my own, will receive an equal share of the gold. For all the

Strongholds in Texas, Tennessee, Oklahoma, Michigan, Virginia, and Pennsylvania that participated, and our two allies in Denver, that means about seventeen and a half *billion* klax worth of gold. Maybe a little less, as I'm guessing the market is about to be flooded and the price per ounce will go down." Again, he waited as those on the radio and those in the room reacted.

"Since we were successful, I'm going to share some information with all of you. First, I suggest you spend some gold immediately on a teleport hub, once Stabilization ends, and a few extra pads if you have more than one Stronghold. This will allow you to move your people from place to place instantly, and make it much easier for me to transport your gold to you. Second, my people can walk you through how to purchase shield domes, cannons, and other defensive weapons to protect your properties before the aliens come tomorrow night.

I'm going to send each of your people home this afternoon with a half billion in gold. That is enough to buy the items I just listed. The moment you have your teleport pads set up, we can quickly ship you the rest, though I'm going to need you to send people to retrieve it. I suggest you also purchase a couple of the industrial sized hover pads for moving that much weight. It'll take several days to move this much gold, even with the teleporters."

Pausing to think for a moment, he decided to go all in. "I will be stationing two thousand battle droids here at Fort Knox, both to defend this place from invaders and to *assist* your people in moving the gold. I suggest you all look into purchasing some as well. Yesterday, I established a new Stronghold out on the west coast. Starting tomorrow, we'll be operating a small fishing fleet. For

599

those of you who have teleport capability, in a few days there will be fresh fish on the menu. Assuming we're not at all-out war with the aliens."

Unable to think of anything else to say, he brought things to a close. "I want to thank all of you for your support in this endeavor, and for your determination to survive the last year. We'll be dropping off your people as quickly as possible. I'll remain here to coordinate further distribution of your gold. Have a great day."

He made a cutting motion to Nigel, who disconnected the call. Looking at the Texan, he said, "If you'd like to make a private call home to tell them about your loss, feel free to use one of the rooms in the hall."

The man nodded. "Thank you. I'll do that."

"Before you go, there's something else I want to say. I meant it when I said you're all heroes. And you deserve to be rewarded. So everyone here, including the two we lost, will received twenty-one gold bars from our share. That's about ten million klax for each of you, along with my sincere thanks and admiration." he announced loud enough for everyone to hear.

There was another round of cheers, and the Texan shook Allistor's hand before leaving the room. Virginia, back on her feet, hugged Allistor. "I know Richard's family will appreciate that. I'd like to be the one to give them the news, if you don't mind?" she said before turning away and wiping at her eyes. She left the room as well, not waiting for him to agree.

Sam, Lars, Logan, and a few of the others helped load up the volunteers with their half billion in gold. First, they all turned over their belts to Sam, who verified how much they'd already gathered. Then, one of Allistor's people filled the belts with five hundred and ten million worth of gold, which Ramon helpfully calculated to be one thousand and sixty-four bars. That was actually almost a million extra, but Allistor wasn't going to quibble. These people had earned it.

When the gold for the volunteers was loaded, and all of his people had gotten their share, Allistor sent them upstairs to be flown back home. He gave the dead Texan's share to his comrade, and Richard's share to Virginia. And had Sam load up a pair of the extra belts for Gene and Kira.

When they were on their way, Taylor approached Allistor.

"We've already decided to purchase a teleport hub with the gold you gave me. How do we connect our hub with your pad?"

"That is a very good question, my friend." Allistor clapped him on the back. "Nigel, how do we connect teleport pads with different owners?"

"Permission must be given by both parties. Restrictions are normally set for direction, number of parties allowed, and duration of authorization, down to as little as a single teleport basis."

"Okay, how about this. I give permission to connect this pad to Captain Taylor's hub as soon as he has one. For the sake of experimentation, we will make it for one day only. And only one direction, from here to his Stronghold." He turned to Taylor. "You've got plenty of men here, and you can use the kiosk upstairs to purchase a couple of those industrial hover pads. Then you can use the teleport to take your men, and the gold, home with you. We can work out future connections for trade or support later. Sound okay with you?"

Taylor nodded. "Nigel, I authorize the connection between your pad and mine under the conditions Allistor just set. Is that sufficient?"

"It is. As you do not have an active AI at your Stronghold, I will establish the connections on your behalf."

"Nigel, how many gold bars are in this facility?"

"When you claimed the depository, there were three hundred sixty-eight thousand, three hundred and seventy-nine bars. Since then, nine thousand six hundred and eighteen bars have been removed by the volunteers from other Strongholds."

Alright, thank you Nigel. Some of those were from my own share that I gave as rewards. So, please use the total number of bars at the time I claimed the depository, and divide it by ten. That would give us each group's total share. What would that be?"

"Each of the ten Strongholds are entitled to thirty-six thousand, eight hundred thirty-seven bars in total, Sire."

"Thank you, Nigel." Allistor turned to Taylor. "As I'm sure you can guess, it will take quite a while to move even one group's share through the teleports on hover pads. Several days, I'm sure. So, we'll need to set up some kind of rotating schedule to keep from tripping over each other."

Taylor was nodding his head and about to speak when Nigel spoke first.

"Sire, General Prime wishes me to inform you that your two battalions have arrived here at Fort Knox. Also, if I might offer a suggestion, Sire?"

"Certainly, Nigel. Hit me!"

"I understand the need for efficiency and the short time frame available to you before this facility might be put at risk. I have the ability to transfer funds directly from your vault to another Stronghold or Citadel with an upgraded AI. Much the same as with the teleport connections, it requires authorization for each transaction. If the other groups were to upgrade their AIs today, the transactions could be completed within a matter of minutes. The system charges the receiver a set fee for such transactions of one half of one percent of the total transferred amount."

"That's a huge fee." Allistor grimaced, and Taylor mumbled an agreement. But the man was thinking it over.

"But it eliminates the risk of this place falling to aliens and all the gold being lost." Taylor mused.

"Well, it's up to you and the others. I'm certainly willing, as it costs me nothing. I'll be defending this place either way, because my share will still be here."

"I would also add, Sire, that having an upgraded AI offers many benefits to your allies, including improved communication between you. You would be able to call each other directly through your AIs from anywhere in your respective facilities. Much as you called Airman Redd earlier. This would allow you to instantly coordinate

603

common defense and troop transportation if needed. Not to mention all the day to day facility management a properly upgraded AI offers."

Taylor smiled up at the ceiling. "Oh, you've sold me already on the AI, Nigel. I'm just debating whether to pay the fee to have you do our transfer."

Allistor looked up at the ceiling too, though he knew Nigel wasn't in any single location. It just felt right somehow. "Nigel, would you please contact Redd, have her dial up the other leaders, and share this information with them?"

"I would be honored, Sire."

Chapter 25

Every Girl's Crazy 'Bout A Well-Dressed Orc

Allistor remained at Fort Knox through the evening. After Nigel's explanation of the benefits and fees, and with the hours speeding past before the end of Stabilization, all of the other leaders chose to upgrade their AIs and execute the transfers. By the time the sun set the next day, only Allistor's gold would remain in the facility. He made sure his people all received their ten million bonus, and retired back to the Citadel with Amanda. Andrea arranged for a couple hundred of Allistor's people to move to Fort Knox to guard it along with the battle droids. Dean and his wife actually decided to relocate to the Stronghold, saying they preferred the milder winters in Kentucky anyway. Most of his original group from Cheyenne went with them.

The morning of their last day alone on Earth dawned, and Allistor awoke with a feeling of dread. Not fear of the aliens so much as a feeling he'd forgotten something. He spent an hour talking to his advisors over breakfast in the conference room, going over all the defenses and details that they could think of. Still, something was bothering him.

Finally, after he'd paced back and forth across the room about fifty times, Amanda grabbed him and pulled him into a hug. "It's just your mind playing tricks on you. You've covered all the bases you can. Everyone agrees. Now we just have to sit back and wait. If the aliens who land near us turn out to be hostile, we'll deal with it. We even have a plan to abandon the outlying Strongholds and

605

consolidate everyone at the Citadel, Silo, and Bastion if things go horribly wrong."

"I know. I just can't shake this feeling. I need a distraction. Maybe if I stop thinking about it, it'll come to me."

"Then let's go fishing. Knowing you, you'll catch that big honking sea monster that almost ate Bagwell, and we'll hold the biggest ever monster fish fry!"

Smiling at her enthusiasm, he squeezed her tightly and kissed her forehead. "Sounds perfect. Let's go."

They teleported to Pelican Bay, bringing Sam, Meg, Nancy, Ramon, Helen, and Fuzzy with them. The group walked together down to the cove and out onto the dock. The fishing boats were all out and working already, but there was a small motorboat in the sand. They loaded everyone up and cruised out to the yacht, which was anchored near the center of the protected cove.

Tying off on the stern platform, they all climbed aboard the yacht. Unsurprisingly, they found Bjurstrom and Goodrich lounging on the deck drinking beers and working on their tans.

"Oh, heya boss. We didn't know you wanted to use the yacht today." Bjurstrom got to his feet, followed quickly by Goodrich.

"Neither did we until about an hour ago. Relax boys. We're just here to do a little fishing. Any idea where the gear might be?"

Both men hustled toward the stern. "We found a bunch in a locker near the launch bay. We'll grab a pole for everyone and meet you guys on the aft deck where you tied up. You'll find some folding chairs behind the door marked 'storage'. It's where we got these ones." Goodrich called to them as he slid down the first ladder.

Twenty minutes later, everyone was relaxing, lines in the water and poles set, drinks in hand. Amanda had decided she would rather work on her tan than fish, and Helen had joined her, saying, "Every time Allistor and I fish together, I embarrass him. Don't want to make him look bad in front of his people."

They fished for a good four hours as the sun rose in the sky. Occasionally one of them would get a bite and reel in a fish. It seemed the rules of the wilderness applied in the sea as well. Fish that killed and ate others got bigger and stronger. So the fish that they landed were obscenely oversized, and correspondingly more challenging to bring in. Meg hooked a tuna that was so large they had to strap her into a chair mounted to the deck and then take turns helping her reel it in. Sam, Allistor, and Ramon all took turns lending their strength to the battle. An hour later they used a winch to haul in a six hundred pound, hundred and twelve inch long tuna. Combined with the other fish they'd caught, they had more than two thousand pounds of fresh fish for the day.

Deciding to call it quits, they stored the fish in their inventories, wished Bjurstrom and Goodrich a good day, and told them there would be a fish fry back at the Citadel if they were interested.

Hopping back in their motorboat, they returned to the beach, walked up to the Stronghold, and teleported back. Meg and Sam immediately took charge of the meal prep, and Amanda and Helen volunteered to round up folks and get tables and benches set up.

By five o'clock they were all enjoying a feast with their people. Most of the Silo had emptied out to join them, everyone being aware that in a few short hours they might be in a fight for their lives. The celebration lasted until after dark, then everyone helped clean up before retiring to grab a few hours' sleep.

The countdown timer was just under eight hours when Allistor, Amanda, Helen, and Fuzzy teleported to the Wilderness. Harmon had promised to deliver their space yacht the very hour that Stabilization ended. Which would be just before sunrise.

Too keyed up to sleep, Allistor climbed to the top of the wall that overlooked the lake and sat with his feet hanging over the edge. He could hear the others chatting in the courtyard below, their voices echoing up to him. Helen was pondering what the aliens might look like, and how many different species there might be. Amanda was suggesting wild combinations of known species, like aliens with human bodies, fish heads, and beaver tails.

Smiling to himself, Allistor watched the reflection of the stars ripple in the water below. Several times, something large broke the surface, then disappeared again. He thought back to the massive sturgeon that he'd encountered at the lake right before he met Fuzzy. Looking down into the courtyard, he saw Amanda staring up at him, one hand scratching the bear's ears as he lay next to her.

"All in all, it has been a good year." he said to himself. "I found Fuzzy, fell in love with Amanda, and Helen has turned out to be the best friend I've ever had. I lost my family, but I've gained a much larger one. If we all still have a roof over our heads and food to eat by this time tomorrow, I will count myself a very lucky man, indeed."

Eventually Amanda came up to join him, pulling two sleeping bags out of her ring. "Seems like a nice place to gaze up at the stars." she said, laying them out on the wide rampart. Allistor looked left and right down the wall, seeing only the battle droid sentries, who were focused outward.

He helped Amanda arrange the sleeping bags, then settled in next to her. She put her head on his shoulder and sighed. "It's beautiful up here. You know in this entire year since we found out that aliens are real, I've never once taken the time to just sit like this and look up at the stars. There are so many more of them here than we had before."

Allistor mumbled his agreement, choosing instead to focus on the clean smell of her hair and the warmth of her next to him.

"Are you listening to me?"

"Mmmhmm… many stars. Pretty. But not as pretty as you."

She snorted, poking him in the belly. "Dork."

They sat in silence for a while, and Allistor eventually drifted off to sleep. He was awakened by the same foghorn sound that had awakened him on the day the Earth was moved. A system alert popped up on his interface, and he heard a voice read the words aloud in his head.

Attention humans and other residents of UCP 382!

Your planet's designated Stabilization period will expire in one hour. Each human still surviving will be granted a parcel of land of their choice, up to ten acres. Land already claimed by other humans is not eligible for selection. Your chosen parcel can be sold or traded, but your rights to the land can not be taken from you so long as you live. Further, to prevent hostile land acquisitions, even in death your rights will be protected, and the land will go into probate. If no heir is designated, the System will place the property into probate for a period of one hundred years.

To claim your territory, simply occupy your chosen ground and select the Awarded Property tab that will appear on your interface. Follow the directions and claim your land.

Congratulations on surviving the Stabilization period. Initial estimates for necessary human population reduction were exceeded. Total reduction percentage as of now is ninety-five point nine eight percent. For this reason, excess resources allocated for expected survivor population awards based on initial estimates will be evenly distributed among the smaller survivor population. You have the option of claiming an additional acre of land, or receiving a monetary reward of one million one hundred thousand klax.

Welcome to the Collective, citizens of UCP 382

Allistor and Amanda sat in silence for a minute. Amanda broke the silence with a question. "Did I hear that right? Did it say humans and other residents? What other sentient species are they referring to? The dolphins, maybe?"

"Or pigs. Or whales. Maybe dogs? Who knows, maybe Bigfoot is real, and sentient." Allistor smiled at her as her eyes widened.

"How cool would THAT be?"

They were joined by Helen and Fuzzy, who both plopped down on the stone next to them. "So, less than an hour. And did you catch that part about hostile land grabs? Sounds like they try to discourage it." Helen sounded hopeful.

Allistor decided to boost her spirits. "Yeah, that hundred year probate thing sounds like a good deterrent."

"So maybe we won't have to fight for our lives an hour from now?"

"I sincerely hope not. With all my heart and soul. I'd love for the aliens to be a bunch of huggable teddy bear types who only want to grow crops, drink beer, and shake their booty with us. In fact, maybe you'll find yourself an alien boyfriend. A big minotaur-lookin' dude with rippling muscles and horns you can-"

"Allistor!" Amanda cut him off, elbowing him in the side. He was suddenly reminded of Nathan, and Helen's recent loss, and was worried he'd just hurt his friend's feelings. But one look at the grin on her face, and he relaxed.

"I was thinking more along the lines of a centaur. You know, human upper body attached to a horse's lower half..." She waggled her eyebrows, and they all laughed. It felt good. In the face of what was about to happen, it was good to laugh.

They spent the remainder of the hour making small talk, taking comfort in each other's company. There were many glances up at the stars above as the sky began to lighten at the approach of the dual suns. Fuzzy, typical for him, wanted no part of the conversation and plopped himself down between Allistor and Helen. In just a few minutes he was snoring.

"Must be nice." Helen nodded at him. "Nothing to worry about except his next meal and where to poop."

Allistor shook his head. "He might have saved a bunch of us when he attacked the occulant. I was terrified it would kill him. He just took it in stride, like that's just what bears do. But you're right, I do envy him sometimes. He got lucky when he met me. Just like you two!"

Both women rolled their eyes. "Okay, Prince Fancypants. Just remember who put you where you are now. And if I hadn't met you, I might be a Princess myself right now!" Helen nudged him with a foot.

"And I'd be free to hook up with one of those sexy minotaur fellas." Amanda leaned into him, giving him a sidelong glance and a smile.

"Better not! It might anger your Prince, and I hear he's got a short temper. Kills monsters by the hundreds. A mighty warrior, that one. And handsome, too." Even as he teased her, he saw the timer on his interface reach zero.

The wall beneath them vibrated as a series of sonic booms echoed through the surrounding mountains. Looking up, Allistor saw hundreds, maybe thousands of points of light descending from the dawn sky.

A moment later, almost directly above him, two of the points resolved into the solid forms of spaceships. They moved toward him, their noses looking like projectiles aimed at his Stronghold. But when they came within a mile or so, both ships slowed to a halt, hovering. The larger of the two hovered over the forest, just beyond the lake. It was a monstrous beast nearly as large as the Stronghold itself. Up close it looked less like a weapon and more like a transport or cargo ship. Though there were several guns visible in various locations on its hull.

The second ship was smaller, and Allistor immediately guessed it was his yacht. Its exterior was all curves and domes with graceful angles that just seemed to scream luxury. As it settled toward the ground on the sloped area outside the gate, Allistor said, "Nigel, give me loudspeaker, everywhere please."

"Go ahead, Sire."

"Hey everybody. Welcome to the new world! This is it, the aliens have arrived. I'm about to go and make first contact here at the Wilderness. If any of you have ships landing in your immediate area, please alert Nigel at once, and he will let me know. Before I go out, anybody having any problems already?"

When no one spoke up, Allistor changed his request. "Okay, let's do it this way. I need the leader of each facility to call out your status, please."

"All clear at the Citadel. No sign of aliens landing, though we did see some ships fly over." Andrea reported.

"Same here at Fort Knox." Dean checked in.

"Saw a whole bunch of ships pass over, and one circled for a minute, then moved on." Lars reported from Denver.

"Bastion's all clear, same situation." Chris called in.

Allistor and company walked down the ramp from the wall and across the courtyard toward the gate as his people were checking in. Each Stronghold and Outpost gave the all-clear, though General Prime reported that his droids had seen a *Dauntless* class colony ship land north of Santa Barbara.

As Allistor approached the gate, he asked Helen to bring the *Juggernaut*, so that Nigel could alert them. She hopped in and started it up as the others walked out and down the slope toward the waiting ship. Its engines, which had surprisingly been almost silent, had shut down and the ship rested quietly. When he was nearly there, an opening appeared in what had seemed to be a smooth section of the hull, and a ramp extended to the ground.

Standing in the doorway was an enormous humanoid with mottled grey skin. It stood eight feet tall, with wide shoulders and bulging muscles. Its jaw was slightly elongated and sported sharp tusks protruding upward from the lower jaw.

Allistor whispered, "That's an orc. Just like in the VR games. Gotta be an orc."

Contrary to its savage-looking physical build, it was dressed quite smartly. It wore soft, black leather boots on its oversized feet, shined to perfection. Its pants were neatly pressed with a perfect crease on the front leading down to where they tucked into the boots just below the knee. An equally pristine white shirt that looked to be made of silk was partially covered by a vest of some dark, shiny material that seemed to reflect and absorb light at the same time. The shirt sleeves were rolled up to reveal impressive forearms.

Allistor *Examined* the creature, then smiled when he saw the name.

"Harmon! My favorite weapon and vehicle merchant! Welcome to Earth."

The orc bowed gracefully at the waist before advancing down the ramp. "Prince Allistor! My favorite customer on Earth!" The two approached each other and Allistor offered a hand to shake. "Ah, yes. Greeting custom. I have been studying this." Harmon reached out his own hand, which engulfed Allistor's as if he were a small child. The orc shook once, firmly but gently, clearly worried about harming the fragile human. Allistor gave the orc's hand a good squeeze, to salvage a little of his pride.

"Ah, you have increased your *Strength* attribute above what I am told is the human norm. Then you are a warrior!"

Allistor grinned, releasing his hold. "When I need to be. Killed my first void titan with a spear."

"Oh ho! You must tell me this story! I confess to having been monitoring your progress, and watching some

615

of your battles since our first transaction. But I'm afraid I missed that fight."

Helen had parked the *Juggernaut* nearby and joined them. Amanda whispered, "How 'bout this one?" And got a shoulder bump in response. Allistor was reminded of his manners.

"I'm sorry, may I present Lady Amanda, Minister Helen, and Fuzzy, my bonded companion."

Harmon gently and gallantly kissed the hands of each of the ladies, then squatted down so that he was face to face with Fuzzy. "This one will grow to be a mighty beast!" he said approvingly, holding a hand-out for Fuzzy, who placed a paw in it. "Smart, too!"

Standing, he looked past the group at the second ship that was still hovering. "I'm afraid I failed to mention that I would be bringing my own ship as well. One must have a ride home after delivering such a prize to a customer, yes. I'm afraid there isn't a landing zone large enough for my ship."

Allistor looked across the lake. "If it can land where it is without being damaged, feel free. We can use the broken trees for firewood or construction materials later."

Harmon spoke quietly into a bracelet on his wrist, and a moment later a blue beam extended downward from under the ship. Two large mechanical objects were lowered down to disappear into the trees. Within seconds, Allistor heard splintering, and trees began to fall.

"You are most gracious, Prince Allistor. I have dropped a few construction bots, and they will have an area

616

sufficiently cleared in moments. They will stack the lumber for you to retrieve later." The orc smiled. "I plan to establish a base here on Earth myself. So, I'm afraid I must not tarry too long, or all the best spots will be claimed. My scout ships are exploring several possibilities as we speak."

"Of course! I thank you for delivering this ship, though I'm curious how it became your responsibility?"

"Ah, yes. I shall explain while I show you around inside, yes? Follow me." He led the way up the ramp, the humans and grizzly following close behind.

"The system awarded you this fine craft for your World First achievements. When something like that happens, the reward - in this case, a yacht - is pulled from a dimensional warehouse created by the founders and maintained by the system. No one knows how long ago, or who exactly the founders were. At least no one that I'm aware of. In any case, the system then designates a proxy to deliver the reward if it is too large to simply send through the market kiosk. In this case, I requested the honor of delivering your ship. You have quickly become one of my valued customers, and I confess to being excited at the prospect of meeting one who achieved the Title of Prince so quickly. That has rarely been done on a world still in Stabilization. And, even then, it was only accomplished by existing rulers who started with extensive holdings. You began with literally just the clothes you were wearing. Impressive." The orc bowed his head again.

"It was mostly luck." Allistor mumbled, distracted by the ship's features. They were in a long central corridor that appeared to run the length of the ship. It was ten feet wide with a fifteen-foot ceiling, and all of it seemed to be made of the same composite material as General Prime, though in a lighter, marbled coloring. Metal rails ran at waist height along both walls, and the grey floors resembled polished granite, but seemed softer. Their footsteps made no noise as they proceeded.

"Ah, but I know better. As I have said, I have observed your more recent actions. You will be a good Prince, I think. You care about your people, and work hard to provide for them. To protect them. You have a good heart, yet you do not hesitate to kill when it is necessary. A warrior's heart!" Harmon grinned at him, revealing two rows of sharp teeth behind the tusks.

"To your left is the main galley and dining hall. You'll find it has room for about one hundred guests to eat in comfort. There is another galley, a dining area for the crew, one deck below us, which is the service deck. Down there you will find engineering, maintenance, and storage, mostly. The actual engine room is another level down and to the rear. In front of that, on the same level, is the main cargo hold. The ship can carry approximately two thousand tons of standard cargo. It also features three interdimensional storage vaults, each with a capacity of five thousand slots."

Allistor stopped walking, his mind spinning as he tried to comprehend that amount of storage. "That's... I could move a whole Stronghold, furniture and all. Maybe two."

Harmon nodded. "You mentioned luck before. You have been most fortunate with this choice of vehicle. The system chose one that was constructed to dimensions that would be comfortable to your race. This particular vessel is one of the most impressive I have seen, and I have been a merchant for more than a century. It was built for comfort, utility, and action! You'll find it has an impressive weapons array and a defensive shield that should withstand attacks from most other vessels. Barring, of course, large military vessels."

They progressed down the hall toward the front of the ship, Harmon pointing out a lounge, then a room for playing something called *Dar Jot* that looked a lot like a racquetball court to Allistor. Nearer the front, Harmon stopped and indicated rooms on opposite sides of the corridor. "Here are the captain's quarters, and the captain's mess." He opened the door to the quarters, and the humans stepped in.

The suite was tastefully decorated, part luxury finishes, part naval spartan motif. The room they entered was an office, with a large desk in front of a wall full of monitors and controls, and a comfortable looking swivel chair in between. There was also a small sitting area, and a bar. Beyond that was a meeting room with a long table and ten chairs. And through another door they found the captain's bunk, which featured a king-sized bed, sofa and chairs, large walk-in closet as well as a full wall of drawers built right into the structure, and a well-appointed bath with double sinks, a large soaking tub, and a shower.

"This is nicer than any hotel room I've ever stayed in." Amanda said as she spun around, taking it all in. "I could be comfortable here, if I had to, I suppose." She grinned at Allistor.

"Oh, no Lady Amanda. This is merely the captain's quarters. The owner's suite and the guest suites on the level above are much more spacious and luxurious." Harmon sounded almost offended that she would consider such accommodations.

He led them back out to the corridor and up to the bridge. Despite all that they'd already seen on board the yacht, Allistor was stupefied by what greeted him there. The space was maybe fifty feet across, from left to right, and about the same front to back. From a wide viewscreen in front that stretched the width of the room, it curved around in a gentle arc toward the back wall where they stood. There were two levels, the upper one on which they stood that featured what had to be the captain's chair as well as four smaller chairs positioned in front of work stations. The lower level featured six more stations in two arcs that radiated out from the captain's chair above.

And, off to one side, Allistor spotted what looked like a gnome. The bald little fellow wore a grey robe and sat in an oversized recliner with his feet sticking straight out, holding a large mug of ale.

"Oh! Hello!" Allistor started toward the gnome. He tried to *Examine* the creature, but all the system would show him was the name. The rest appeared as question marks.

Bob
Level: ???
Health: ???

"Oops! Sorry, wrong ship! Too much of Dave's strong ale." the grey-clad gnome said. He waved and smiled, then simply disappeared.

"Who?... What?" Allistor turned to Harmon.

The orc shrugged. "I do not know. He wasn't here when I landed."

Shaking it off and looking around at the multitude of seats, Allistor asked, "How... how many people does it take to fly this thing?"

"Well, to be honest, much of this is for show. One pilot can operate the flight systems in concert with the AI. Do you have an AI? If not, the ship has one of its own."

"Nigel, are you here, buddy?" Allistor looked to the ceiling.

"*I am indeed, Sire. And please allow me to congratulate you on obtaining this magnificent vehicle. With your permission I shall communicate with the ship's AI directly and coordinate operations.*"

"Thank you, Nigel, please do. And, uhm... ship AI, can you hear me as well?"

"*I can, Prince Allistor.*" the voice was vaguely female, as befitted a ship.

"Do you have a name, ship?"

"*My current designation is simply Galleon Class Yacht Interface Alpha.*"

"Well, we can't call you that all the time. We'll have to think of a name for you. In the meantime, it is a

621

pleasure to meet you, Alpha. Nigel is my trusted advisor and friend, and I hope the two of you get along."

"Thank you, Prince Allistor. It is my pleasure to serve."

Harmon's face registered surprise when Allistor referred to his AI as a friend, but quickly recovered. "As I was saying, the ship can fly with minimal assistance. The stations you see here are for communications, weapons, engineering, defense systems, logistics and cargo management, and so on. A full crew complement would be thirty specialized individuals to man each of the stations you see here, the galleys, the engine room, valets and wait staff."

"Wow. I wouldn't even begin to know where to find folks to fill those positions." Allistor mumbled as he stepped closer to the captain's chair. He went to sit down, then hesitated. Harmon laughed.

"Sit! Sit! It is your ship, after all. And as a Prince, even were there a captain sitting in the chair, they would offer it up to you out of courtesy."

Allistor sat in the chair, which molded itself to fit him perfectly. It even pushed slightly against his lower back to provide lumbar support. "Ahhh, now THIS is a chair! I need one of these at home. And maybe in the conference rooms. Can I make one of these into my throne?" He winked at Amanda. "Or two of these, so that Lady Amanda can sit in comfort."

"Hey, what am I? Chopped liver? Your hard-working minister doesn't get a comfy seat? Move over."

Helen all but pulled him out of the chair before sitting herself down. "Ohhh, you're right. That feels gooood."

Again, Harmon was shocked by the lack of reverence shown toward the Prince, but kept it to himself. "If you'd like, Prince Allistor, I can assist you in hiring a proper crew. It is one of the many services I offer to my favored clients. In fact, I can obtain most anything you need."

"Thank you, Harmon. I just might take you up on that. I... need to absorb all of this for a bit. And I'm not entirely sure I won't be fighting to protect my people and property before the day is out."

Harmon shook his head. "Unlikely, Prince Allistor."

"Please, just call me Allistor? And why do you think it unlikely?

"You are a Planetary Prince. With the backing of several powerful factions. And based on your purchases, your property is reasonably well defended. Even were someone willing to risk offending the factions who support you, taking your property by force would be costly. Not a good business decision, especially with most of the planet available to purchase without a fight."

"Oh! You need to claim your own territory. And here I've been delaying you. I'm sorry, Harmon. Please don't let me keep you any longer. We can explore the rest of the ship on our own. And when you get yourself settled, I would like you to be my guest for dinner."

"Very gracious of you, Allistor. I shall indeed take my leave. Though I would ask your advice. My scouts have given me several options, in places called Paris, Los Angeles, New York, and Tokyo. Could you advise me on these?

"We were just on the west coast, where Los Angeles is. The area suffered at least one major earthquake in recent weeks, and sits near a major tectonic fault line. I would not recommend it. Tokyo is across the Pacific Ocean on a large island. It too is subject to earthquakes as well as tidal waves. Though, I've not heard of any recent damage. Tokyo was one of the most heavily populated cities in the world before the world ended. A city of high rises and small apartments." Allistor paused to take a breath.

"Paris is across the Atlantic Ocean on the European continent. It is, or was, a major city and cultural center. I'm afraid I don't know much more about it, or how well it fared after the apocalypse. Europe was densely populated, with several capitals and major cities within a few hundred miles of each other. And Paris is one of the oldest cities in the civilized world."

Amanda interrupted him. "I spent some time in New York City. Hundreds of tall high rises, something like twelve million people living in the city. Several rivers and bridges, and very little green space. Huge tunnels and an extensive subway network run underneath. It was our nation's main financial center. I was going to suggest that Allistor establish a Stronghold there, as well. But, until the last few days, we didn't have the means to travel that far."

Allistor nodded at Amanda. "I think I'd like to have a place in New York. We just established our west coast presence, it would be good to have a Stronghold on the east coast as well." The two of them looked at each other, both clearly thinking of the New York gold depository.

Harmon nodded. "My scouts tell me the city was badly damaged in the early days of Stabilization. Many of the tall buildings have fallen, and fires ravaged the island called Manhattan. But there still seems to be a large number of survivors present. If you'd like to accompany me, we can both check out the area and see if we can find suitable accommodations. We can go in your yacht, if it is alright for me to leave my ship here for a bit."

Allistor looked at Helen and Amanda.

"What do you think? Road trip?"

End Book Two

Acknowledgements

As always, I want to thank my alpha readers, my family, who spend endless hours reading and re-reading my nonsense, seeking out plot holes and typos. And who occasionally provide original monsters to play with. And a big thank you to my beta readers, who offer up more rude comments than anything else, but still manage to find some typos and such.

A big thanks to Anders Hemlin for the wonderful cover art.

For semi-regular updates on books, art, and just stuff going on, check out my Greystone Guild fb https://www.facebook.com/greystone.guild.7 or my website www.davewillmarth.com where you can subscribe for an eventual newsletter.

And don't forget to follow my author page on Amazon! That way you'll get a nice friendly email when new books are released. You can also find links to my Greystone Chronicles and Dark Elf books there! https://www.amazon.com/Dave-Willmarth/e/B076G12KCL

PLEASE TAKE A MOMENT TO LEAVE A REVIEW!

Reviews on Amazon and Goodreads are vitally important to indie authors like me. Amazon won't help market the books until they reach a certain level of reviews. So please, take a few seconds, click on that (fifth!) star and type a few words about how much you liked the book! I would appreciate it very much. I do read the reviews, and a few of my favorites have led to friendships and even character cameos!

You can find information on lots of LitRPG/GameLit books on Ramon Mejia's LitRPG Podcast here https://www.facebook.com/litrpgpodcast/. Also thank you to Ramon for early feedback on this book when I was thinking about discarding it, and some good advice. You can find his books here. https://www.amazon.com/R.A.-Mejia/e/B01MRTVW3O

There are a few more places where you can find me, and several other genre authors, hanging out. Here are my favorite LitRPG/GameLit community facebook groups. (If you have cookies, keep them away from Daniel Schinhofen).

https://www.facebook.com/groups/LitRPGsociety/

https://www.facebook.com/groups/LitRPG.books/

https://www.facebook.com/groups/GameLitSociety/

https://www.facebook.com/groups/litrpgforum/

https://www.facebook.com/groups/541733016223492/

Printed in Great Britain
by Amazon

67325137R00356